THE GIRL BEHIND THE WALL

Mandy Robotham saw herself as an aspiring author since the age of nine, but was waylaid by journalism and later enticed by birth. She's now a former midwife, who writes about birth, death, love and anything else in between. She graduated with an MA in Creative Writing from Oxford Brookes University. This is her fourth novel – her first three, *The German Midwife*, *The Secret Messenger* and *The Berlin Girl*, have all been *Globe and Mail*, *USA Today* and Kindle Top 100 bestsellers.

The Girl Behind the Wall

Mandy Robotham

avon.

Published by AVON
A division of HarperCollins*Publishers* Ltd
1 London Bridge Street
London SE1 9GF

www.harpercollins.co.uk

This paperback edition 2021

First published in Great Britain by HarperCollins*Publishers* 2021

Copyright © Mandy Robotham 2021

Mandy Robotham asserts the moral right to be identified as the author of this work.

A catalogue copy of this book is available from the British Library.

ISBN: 978-0-00-846291-8

21 22 23 24 25 LSC 10 9 8 7 6 5 4 3 2 1

Typeset in Bembo by Palimpsest Book Production Limited, Falkirk, Stirlingshire
Printed and bound in the United States of America by LSC Communications

To those that lived with, endured, survived and lost their lives alongside the Berlin Wall.

Author's note

Walls are part and parcel of our history, from the ancient Great Wall of China and Hadrian's Wall to the newest cordon in Donald Trump's controversial Mexican barricade. Some are purely protective, though almost all are divisive in some way – and more than just physically. Though it was never the biggest, longest or the most grandiose of these partitions, the Berlin Wall captured the world's imagination – and the contempt of the West – for what it represented in the chilly war between political ideas. Rough, jagged and ugly, it became a symbol against democracy in the twenty-eight years that it stood.

I remember distinctly being in a motorway service station on a freezing night in November 1989 when the Berlin Wall fell, watching those television scenes of people clambering to the top and hacking at the graffitied concrete, their joy radiating from every feature. I'd grown up with the Wall as part of Europe's fabric, with the Olympic Games and the World Cup always having two distinct German teams, and yet when the barriers fell, it seemed the most natural thing in the world; everyone in that service station was silent and smiling as we watched it crumble.

The dismantling was a result of months of protest and political negotiations, and its end seemed inevitable. Yet the erection of the Wall, once I looked into it, came as a shock to me – the secrecy and duplicity; the deceit of an entire nation, both east and west, and the speed with which it went up overnight. I began to wonder at the impact on families, the potential of having your entire life severed, simply by being in the wrong place at the wrong time: visiting a friend, for instance, and staying over because you missed the last tram, or being out of town on a weekend and returning to find yourself on the wrong side. It led me then to ponder: what was the wrong side? Who were the real prisoners? And the biggest question: how do you simply slice an entire city in two, physically and emotionally?

These questions form the basis of *The Girl Behind the Wall*, and much like my previous works on World War Two, I tried to imagine how those living under such oppressive skies functioned day to day – went to work, fed their children, lived life and found happiness – when such an unjust spectre sought to regulate every aspect of it. The current unprecedented shadow of a pandemic has given us all a taste of restraint, but it is only an inkling in comparison: imagine that control multiplied ten-fold, with troops and guns and the tangible prospect of losing a life should you push at the boundary. Karin and Jutta are fictional examples of those real families forcefully segregated for years, by an edifice that sought not only to divide, but to punish those who opposed its strength. Inert as it was, the Wall killed many.

Researching this book was an eye-opener, but also a joy, thanks to the concise histories on offer – Frederick Taylor's *The Berlin Wall* and Christopher Hilton's *The Wall* among them – alongside the excellent documentaries and films of history taking place; I spent many an hour peering at black and white films of the era and gathering clues. A huge credit goes to the city of Berlin for preserving not only parts of that painful history, but the museums detailing every aspect of life under the Wall: the quirky GDR museum and its mock-ups of East German living, the Stasi Museum – in which everything seemingly *is* brown – and the Hohenschönhausen prison, where I stood in the cells of former prisoners and tried hard to imagine the helplessness of being in the Stasi's clutches.

The numbers that are quoted tell a story, too: the Wall spanned more than 43 kilometres through Berlin, and almost 113 kilometres around the city outskirts, using over 68 kilometres of wire mesh as the initial barrier, with almost 114 kilometres of alarmed fencing, 186 watch-towers and 484 guard dogs, as quoted in Hans-Hermann Hertle's *The Berlin Wall Story*. It was a huge engineering undertaking.

The human cost, though, was markedly higher. West German police state there were at least 5,075 successful escapes through the Wall and the death strip, including 574 desertions of East German military and the police. They included 1,709 cases where border guards used firearms, and at least 119 injured escapees. There were 37 bomb attacks, and, the most chilling statistic, 138 people died on the Berlin Wall or as a direct result of trying to escape. The youngest was little over a year and the oldest aged eighty, although most were young people in their twenties. An unknown number died as a result of worry or of the desperate impact on their lives and that of their families. Everyone lost something.

I hope I have done justice to a city that has survived so much in the twentieth century to become the Berlin of today: a vibrant city of culture and art with an emphasis

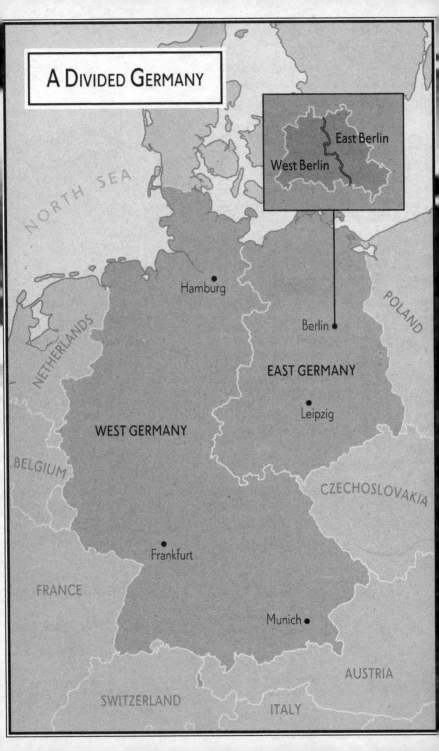

'No one has the intention of building a wall.'
Walter Ulbricht, leader, German Democratic
Republic, East Berlin, 15 June 1961

'Freedom has many difficulties and democracy is not perfect, but we have never had to put a wall up to keep our people in.'
John F. Kennedy, United States president,
West Berlin, 26 June 1963

PROLOGUE

The Unveiling

13th August 1961, West Berlin

Looking on at the scene of quiet chaos in front of him, his mind goes oddly to the mapmakers – colleagues in his own government offices – who will need to redraw their lines dramatically after this day. For now, they remain blissfully unaware, safely tucked up in their beds. But on waking, Hans Fleisch knows they will be called on to sharpen their darkest pencils and bring out the black, permanent markers to take account of the phenomenon occurring before his very eyes, having been plucked out of his bed at a moment's notice to be an official 'observer' on the West side. He palms at his face, eager to rub fatigue and disbelief away. Hoping, but not expecting, that this nightmare might just disappear.

Those junior government workers like himself have sensed rumblings for months now, alongside the Allies – the British, French and Americans who control the Western half of Berlin. They've seen evidence of troop movements and diplomatic scraps over borders controls, and it was

1

obvious the East German government and their Soviet mentors were up to something. Except nobody knew what – least of all the East German people. Yet, even the best of fortune-tellers could not have predicted this.

Later, he learns of the East's furtive preparations: by eight p.m. on Saturday 12th – a cool evening in Berlin by summer standards – a few select officials had been apprised of Europe's best-kept secret. Sealed orders for 'Operation Rose' were opened; only senior officers from the East German police, border patrols and army are given details, with thousands of border guards, police and Factory Fighting Groups made to stand by for an unknown task. They might well have muttered among themselves, standing and smoking in groups: 'On standby for what?' Even those on the front line couldn't envisage the scale of what was about to happen.

At midnight, the calendar rolled into another day – in mid-August, in a decade that already promises great change – though this particular sunrise is one that historians will later mark in red. Soon after, the order to 'march' was given by a senior politician in the East German government. By one a.m., Operation Rose was underway. And now, as Berlin sleeps, Hans Fleisch looks on in horror at his own city, while the world faces a fresh, bleak dawn in the Cold War. And a new life, as all Germans are then forced to live it.

PART ONE

1

Separation

The pushing and pulling invades Jutta's dream, like a poker into hot fire, as she stirs from under a cloak of sleep.

'Jutta, Jutta!' A hushed urgency from Hugo as her eyes adjust to the velvet black of her bedroom. His hands nudge at her, but her cousin remains a ghostly outline in the dark.

'What's wrong? Is it Karin? Is she worse?' Jutta's first thoughts go to disaster, and possibly death, such is the anxiety that has been a constant in her shifting nightmare – thoughts of Karin swimming in dreams. Nothing but her.

'No, it's not Karin – at least there's no word.' Hugo's whispers weave through the air, his desperation rousing her.

'What's wrong then?' She sits up, rubbing irritant sleep from her lids.

'There's something happening in the streets. I'm going to investigate. Come with me?'

It's barely a question, or a choice. For whatever reason,

5

Hugo hopes she will come. On one or two occasions previously, Jutta has accompanied him on a story for the Berlin radio station where he's a junior reporter, one up from a trainee and the teaboy. The last was a skirmish six months before, near the border on Invalidenstrasse, where kids on the West side were lobbing missiles at the East German guards and scurrying for shelter as if racing back to retie their mother's apron strings. The brief episode was shut down swiftly by police on East and West sides, neither enjoying a full-scale conflict over pieces of rubble, and Jutta hadn't particularly relished the experience.

'Do I have to?' she says lazily.

'I think you'll want to. The station says this is big. They think there's a wall going up.'

Despite the heat of past weeks, West Berlin at three a.m. is chilly; Jutta shivers under her light jacket, her arms clinging to Hugo's waist as his small, two-stroke motorcycle drones through the darkened streets, east towards the tenuous border line that divides their city, her hastily tied hair flying like a black pennant behind them. The closer Hugo weaves towards the main thoroughfares, the more people they see; not hordes but more than would normally be returning home from the club land of Kurfürstendamm on a Saturday night in August, especially as the city has been partially emptied by Berliners headed for their rural summer houses for the weekend. Still, the pair can see no discord, not yet, nor hear any protest. So far, only bodies trickling towards their own destination of the Brandenburg Gate.

When they arrive, there are people collected at the monument – the vast, stone symbol of Berlin's hard-fought freedom. Around a hundred or so, Jutta guesses, though it's eerily quiet. All, without exception, are looking in one direction: towards the Gate. Except it is no longer a gate, because gates generally open and shut. This one is now firmly closed, barricaded by a lengthy coil of barbed wire on the Western side, and by the close-knit line of East German People's Police – Vopos – on the East. In the eerie blue glare of portable searchlights, Jutta squints at the string of military men, mixed with oddly clad Factory Fighter soldiers in their peaked caps, whose shambolic dress makes it seem as if they've been plucked from their beds at only a minute's notice – though she notes they've had time enough to supply each with a short, stubby machine gun.

Hugo parks the bike and leaves Jutta's side; he's on a serious mission now for the radio station, pulling out his recording equipment and hoisting it over his shoulder. Jutta moves as if in a dream towards the Gate, eyeing the West German police, who are shuffling in their own makeshift line in front of the ugly wire – unsure whether they are meant to prevent people from crossing, or simply keeping the peace that might be broken. Because they've had no warning. No one has.

Some sense of division is no stranger to Jutta and her fellow Berliners; since 1945, Germany's capital has been split by a border junction between the Eastern Soviet side and the Western Allies. Except it's been drawn in chalk almost, moving on occasion as the four powers busy themselves fighting over control of this service or that – transport, water, electricity. Meantime, Berliners simply step over the divide – albeit through the eighty or so checkpoints dotted across the city – and get on with their lives, some living in the West and working in the East and vice versa. Berlin as a city floats in the sea that is the new East German

Republic – or GDR – but everyone mingles. They are Berliners, first and foremost.

But this . . . Jutta has never seen such a tangible barrier through her city: one not designed to move out of the way, that's metallic and sharp and would surely pluck and score at her skin if she dare breach it, a physical restraint that means she cannot cross – or else.

As Jutta gapes, it scares her to her core. The idea that this obstacle will stretch the length and breadth of her home city is petrifying, because of what's on the other side. Not the Soviet troops and tanks that hover in the hinterland of East Germany, ready to help out the newest of their communist allied states; nor even the universally feared East German Secret Police – the Stasi – who pervade every inch of Berlin, East and West, with eyes and ears everywhere. Not them. Karin. Her sister is on the other side, in East Germany, by pure misfortune. Not just a sister: her only sister, her only sibling. Her twin. Her entire other half.

Panic surges through her: how long will this last? What if they won't let Jutta in, or Karin out? What then?

Jutta peers past the Gate and through the bodies, past the guards that are rolling out yet more spirals of wire and the armoured troop carriers flooding the area. Beyond them are people hovering, fellow Berliners now trapped on the other side. Jutta wonders if they look and feel equally bewildered. On her side, people sidle past as she stares, muttering to themselves and anyone within earshot: 'What's happening? They said there would be no wall. He said it plainly, didn't he? No plans for a wall.'

People in the crowd nod that yes, they'd heard and read it too: Walter Ulbricht, East Germany's communist leader on a lectern in front of press and witnesses just a few months prior, announcing that there would be 'no wall' to divide the city. The two countries, well, that's been another matter. The Iron Curtain has existed between the countries of East and West Germany since soon after World War Two, leaving Berlin as the only permeable membrane between the two. It's hard to picture an entire metropolis as floating in the land-sea of East Germany, 160 kilometres adrift from the remainder of West Germany, but that's how it is in the post-war world. For the Allies, West Berlin is an expensive but symbolic presence behind the Iron Curtain that they strive to keep buoyant with funds and troops. For East Germans, however, the city border acts as a portal to the West, a porous escape route for those desperate to flee communism, with hundreds of thousands using the gateway in recent years, draining the GDR of its most valuable workers.

But not now, it seems. Not here, and not today. Not anymore.

Jutta's reverie is broken by Hugo, who appears at her side, tugging her sleeve.

'Come on, we should go,' he says. His long, lean face is flushed with excitement in chasing this, the biggest of stories, but also fear at what might lie ahead, for him and every other Berliner. His wiry body runs towards his bike, clearly impatient for Jutta to clamber on.

'Where?' she says. It's virtually her first word since glimpsing the barbed wire and it feels odd rolling off her tongue.

'Need to check if it reaches all the way down – circling.' Hugo is talking in excited shorthand, but Jutta catches his meaning, and it chills her even more. Will there be more wire, at every checkpoint? If it engulfs the entire Western side, as she fears, reaching Karin will be near impossible.

9

She pictures herself fighting her way across the sharp metal spikes, clawing at her clothes, catching on her skin until the pain forces her to stop and wrench the barbs from her torn flesh. And then what? Arriving bloodied and injured at the hospital where Karin already lies, incapable of engineering an escape for either of them.

'I need to find a way across, to Karin,' she shouts at Hugo as they speed north along West Berlin's streets, filling up now as word spreads even among the sleeping. Bewildered, some are still in their nightclothes, pyjamas poking above hastily donned trousers and shirts. Quiet confusion reigns.

'We'll have to find an open checkpoint first,' Hugo calls behind him.

It's less calm, though equally disordered, when they stop briefly at the interchange on Bornholmer Strasse, one of only eight crossings now open, where crowds are beginning to find their voice.

'This isn't right,' one man cries weakly. 'This isn't democracy!'

He's right – because beyond the thin wire is communism, but perhaps he feels better for saying it. Another voice: 'They've stopped the S-Bahn at Friedrichstrasse station, sending the trains back to the East.' Someone else shouts that the underground U-Bahn is also blocked, signalling that the link – the rail loop circling the city – is broken. Breaking one chain, erecting another.

Hugo disappears into the crowd again, his microphone pitched awkwardly in front of him, like some medieval jouster. Jutta looks hard beyond the line of protesters and pinpoints a young East German border guard standing alongside the guard post. With one eye on the machine gun they all seem to be sporting, she weaves her way up

10

to the wire, and his face shows surprise; no one else has dared venture so close, instead protesting from a distance and inching backwards as angry words are tossed and left to float in the air. Despite the wild look in his eye, he has the decency to dip his weapon as Jutta approaches.

'Can I . . . can I get through?' she asks.

His look of alarm intensifies. Why on earth would she want to cross? She's on the free side, the enclave of Western symbolism. Why would she want to go into the East?

'No,' he says through his incredulity. 'No one gets through. Not today. Not without a permit.' Then, seeing her despair multiply, adds: 'I'm sorry, Fräulein.'

'But my sister, she's in hospital on your side,' Jutta pleads. 'She's a West Berliner' – and for the first time she feels the full force of the distinction – 'she'll be allowed to come back, surely?'

'I don't know, Fräulein,' he says. He resumes a detached air, eyes focused on the distance. Jutta thinks he looks fearful of any potential emotion; perhaps as long as old women or children don't crumble, or weep on him, he can keep it together. Maybe he has a mother who is intensely proud of his place in the East German military, boasts to the women in their apartment block of his prowess as a guard. All the same, he looks to be praying: *Please don't cry, Fräulein. You can shout at me, berate me, and I will show you the butt of my gun, just please don't cry.*

But if she lingers, Jutta feels she might. She peels away, her face beginning to crack with distress as she turns. Hugo is nowhere to be found, though she needs him now, her tall slip of a cousin, to bury her head on his bony chest, on his clean white T-shirt, and share her despair. *Karin, oh Karin, why on earth did you go there?*

No one could have known, of course – about the wire

11

that would become the Wall, or the unfortunate sequence of events leaving Karin in the East Berlin Charité hospital, with the red welt of a scar hovering where her angry, swollen appendix so recently was.

'Karin, can't you wait until tomorrow, then I'll happily come with you?' Jutta had said only the day before. It was a sunny Saturday afternoon, and both were keen to escape the heat of the family's second-floor apartment: meet friends, sit outside in the park, or a café.

'But I promised I'd meet these people – they're big on the fashion scene,' Karin protested. 'If I can just get one of my designs noticed by them, then I might have a chance, break out of that dead-end job I'm in.' They both knew Karin's quiet, steely determination would win through in the end, but she was already impatient.

So Karin, an aspiring fashion designer, had scooped up her portfolio of drawings and gone to the art college bar in East Berlin alone, despite their mother's insistence that she didn't look well, and Karin's secret confession to Jutta that she wasn't 'feeling that great either'. Jutta had heard her in the night, groaning in the lavatory with stomach pains. In the morning, she'd looked pale, though not in pain.

Jutta, meanwhile, spent the afternoon watching a French film in West Berlin with her best friend, Irma, returning home to find her mother in tears. 'We've just had a call from the Charité,' Ruth said. 'Karin's just out of theatre.'

'Theatre? What on earth . . .?'

Having collapsed in the college bar, Karin had been taken by ambulance to the nearest hospital and operated on immediately – a previously grumbling, now perforated, appendix swiftly removed. As she slept in recovery, the nurses had searched through Karin's belongings and found the number for the family home.

'Let's leave now,' Jutta had told her mother. 'We can be there in no time on the U-Bahn.'

'There's no point,' Ruth replied. 'They say she's sleeping off the anaesthetic and will be drowsy all night. The doctor feels it will be more helpful tomorrow, when she's awake.'

And now it is tomorrow. And Lord knows how wretched that doctor must be feeling, Jutta thinks. Because if it's remained the world's best-kept secret, if the politicians in West Berlin and beyond didn't have an inkling of how kilometres upon kilometres of barbed wire were hidden and distributed across a vast city, then how would an average doctor know? But all that doesn't change the simple fact that Jutta is on one side of the Berlin divide and her sister on the other. For now, imprisoned.

When Hugo finds her in the crowd, spiralling emotions have given way to practicality, and Jutta's brain is split between determined routes to reach Karin and ways of telling their mother. The latter she dreads the most. Then Aunt Gerda – Hugo's mother and Ruth's older sister. Though not twins, their bond as sisters is almost as tight as Jutta's with Karin.

'Hugo, I need to get back home,' she says. 'Mama will be getting up, if she's not already awake. We didn't leave a note.'

'I left one,' Hugo assures. 'Just a brief scribble, but they'll know we're safe.' *Are we?* Jutta thinks. With machine guns and barriers, unrest beginning to bubble like the innards of a peevish volcano.

He carries on, awash with adrenalin. 'Besides, I've bumped into some *contacts*' – he says the word with pride – 'they're British journalists with an office on the East side. It seems they can come and go across the border, and they'll take a note to the Charité, to Karin.' He looks both pleased and relieved. Living with the twins almost since they were born means the trio are more like siblings than cousins.

They skirt the crowd and push through to where a man and a woman are standing.

'Jutta, this is Douglas and Sandra – they're journalists with Reuters.'

She smiles out of politeness at a youngish, well-dressed couple who may live in the East but shop for clothes in the West, clearly.

'Thank you for your offer,' Jutta says. 'We don't know how else to reach Karin yet. A note will put her mind at rest for now.'

Jutta rifles in the small shoulder bag across her body and pulls out a notebook, turns Hugo's body to lean on his back as she puts pen to paper. What to write? '*Hello Karin, you might be imprisoned in the East, but we will get you out.*' No, of course not. Jutta scribbles a simple: '*Darling K, I hope you are feeling better – Mama and I will visit as soon as we can. Be good and rest up or else! Ja-Ja.*' She swallows hard as she signs the name her sister has called her since they were tiny, Karin unable to pronounce 'Jutta' then. She rips the sheet from her notebook, folds it and addresses it to 'Karin Voigt – patient' in the hope it will reach her intact – and soon. Hugo darts away again, having spotted something newsworthy.

'What do you think is happening?' Jutta asks the reporters then. 'What's on the other side?'

'Bewilderment, much like here,' the woman says in German, her British accent clipping the words. 'We've seen Soviet tanks, but thankfully they're stationed well back from the border line.'

'And will it become a Wall?' Jutta voices the question

that's been on her, and everyone's, mind since she first glimpsed the barricade, a mere hour ago.

The man and the woman look at each other, their lips thinned in unison. 'Officially, the GDR isn't calling it a Wall,' the man says eventually. 'To them it's an "anti-fascist protection barrier". But yes, all my sources so far tell me it's here to stay.' He sighs heavily, already lamenting a life gone. 'It's very likely to function as what we all know to be a Wall. And soon.'

His words send arrows through Jutta, enough to jolt her body from the exhaustion she's beginning to feel. It's just gone four a.m., still dark, and her body is signalling in no uncertain terms she should be in bed. Yet her mind won't stop racing. Sleep is a long way off.

Hugo arrives back into their little fold, having broadcast into his station for a few minutes, via his portable radio.

'Let's see if we can find any more checkpoints – you never know, some might be open,' Jutta urges her cousin. *One is all we need to let us through*, she thinks.

'Good luck,' the woman says, clutching the note for Karin. 'We've not found one that's fully open to anyone except press and diplomats, but you might try further south.'

Hugo pushes the tiny engine of his motorbike to capacity as they weave through the streets, harder to navigate now as more and more Berliners have woken to the noise outside and taken to the streets on foot, looking uniformly bemused – a hangover for the whole city. Jutta scans their faces as she and Hugo whizz by, the people hopelessly drawn towards the border points, not by any one person but by an invisible light almost, an irresistible beacon to their confusion.

The two journalists are right: every crossing is closed,

and the border guards are unbending, despite Jutta's pleas, even when she's finally moved to tears. They stare resolutely ahead as she sobs. Wiping her tears, she can see the fear in some – mere boys on military service and not hard-and-fast devotees – but it is what they've been trained to do: to look as if they don't care.

The sun begins to rise just before five as they reach the vast open scrub of Potsdamer Platz, where it meets Leipziger Strasse. There, the full force of the East's meticulous organisation hits Hugo and Jutta squarely; they watch as civilian workmen wield jackhammers in a deafening dawn chorus, breaking the concrete and sinking heavy posts into the uneven ground, on which the thorny wire is then strung like fairy lights across the space.

'They can't do this, can they?' one old woman asks of them. 'We're Berliners – we have a right to cross.'

'Looks like we're purely West Berliners now,' the man next to her replies gravely. Pointing to a cluster of onlookers on the other side of the wire, he adds: 'And they are East Berliners.' The identity of East and West residents is years old, though the lines to date have been drawn in the sand between nations and never enforced. Now they are being pressed, with guns and hardware, into accepting it.

'One of those is my daughter,' the woman murmurs, and waves a white handkerchief into the rising light of the day. On the other side, a bright green scarf flutters in response. Hugo nods sympathetically while the old woman weeps her despair into his microphone. 'Will I be able to see her, visit her?'

Jutta turns away then, because all she can see in her mind is a tiny, shrunken version of Karin, furiously waving, her voice getting smaller and smaller as the layers of wire thicken.

There's plenty of conjecture, but no one seems to know anything for certain, least of all the smattering of West German guards who are now trying to keep the confusion from cultivating into outright dissent; if the West Berliners cannot reach the East's guards to protest, they will surely turn on any authority. Though, still the guards seem conflicted: why are they protecting it when it isn't even their barrier? It's the opposing line of East German guards, with fixed expressions and fingers tight on their machine guns, which acts as the best motivation to keep order.

Hugo patches into his station again, while Jutta tunes into the crowd. She hears that no checkpoints are open to the south, and then mutterings that 'things' are happening on Bernauer Strasse. She's desperate to turn tail for home, to seek comfort in her mother and aunt, but she is also hopelessly drawn to the gash that has been created across her city, pulled by the magnet that is Karin towards the divide. She knows too that Hugo needs to continue reporting: tragic though it is for Berlin, this is an important day for him and his work.

They head north again on the bike, through the large Tiergarten park but skirting the Brandenburg Gate, parking up a few streets away from Bernauer Strasse and following the sounds of unease. People are concentrated in the wide V-shape of the street, made by the tall terraced buildings of dark red brick, some seven storeys high, and which forms a boundary in itself; the border across Berlin has never been entirely straight, but meanders and zig-zags almost randomly from north to south, sometimes slicing through cemeteries and parks and even houses. Bernauer Strasse is one such place: the pavement in front of the terraces falls on the West side, in the Wedding district, while the fabric of the building and rear entrances are in the

East's Mitte district. The residents are East Berliners, though judging by the steady trickle of people appearing on the pavement in front, hauling their life's belongings in hastily packed shopping bags, they plan on switching allegiance rapidly.

Hugo is soon swallowed by the wealth of human feeling to be captured by his tape recorder, and Jutta wanders towards where the buildings end and the wire begins, the cold metal spirals piled on one another. She looks intently at the mesh of barbs and thinks of the stories already circulating, of people hurdling the wire with bravado and dashing to freedom, their blood and flesh left on the barrier. Over the past hours, she's heard more talk of its permanence, concrete blocks being amassed to be piled like children's bricks and produce an ugly and uneven grey sore, in a city that's already seen more than its fair share of wartime rubble.

Again, Jutta is thinking intently of Karin, of how she herself might possibly scale these blocks in reaching her sister, when a woman walks up beside her and calls out to someone on the other side of the grey mesh. Two older women turn sharply and run towards the obstacle, both faces a pained grimace. 'Greta!' one keens.

The younger woman promptly hoists a small child, no more than six months, forward into the air, so that its wriggling torso is just above the wire tangle. The baby's legs cycle with delight as those on the other side coo at the child: 'Hello Franz, hello gorgeous boy. Remember your grandmama; we'll see you soon, my darling. We'll see you soon . . .' until an East German Vopo approaches and pulls them away, their voices tailing off in sobs, in the true knowledge that 'soon' won't be any time near; bewilderment is slowly giving way to a feeling of misery at how enduring this is likely to be. Jutta's eyes catch the young mother's sideways glance and they trade looks of despair, and perhaps a vision of Berlin's future.

The mother cradles baby Franz close, pushing her head into his chubby body and sobbing loudly, his round face peering over her shoulder, smiling his toothless grin at Jutta as if nothing in his tiny world has changed.

Unable to look, Jutta turns her gaze up to the bluest of August skies raining down on Berlin's streets, and sees only grey.

Hugo is swamped with material and needs to go back to his office to refresh his equipment and make contact with his news desk. He knows he won't get to bed any time soon, needing to feed off coffee and the city's angst for hours yet. He'll drop Jutta back home, he says, and check in by phone for news of Karin.

They stop first for coffee, drinking it quickly on the side of the street. With each mouthful, Jutta fights her rising nausea, thankful there's something propping up the insides of her stomach before she has to face Mama and Aunt Gerda. That will be bad enough, stemming their joint distress, but then what?

How and when will she reach Karin, with what's rapidly becoming a massive fault line between them?

2

Captured

Her eyes are heavy as she attempts to open them, faintly aware of a sickly disinfectant smell in her nostrils and the echoey clip-clopping of shoes in one ear, her remaining senses clouded.

'Karin . . . Karin . . .?' A flat voice and the sour taint of coffee floats into the black space above her, then into the air beyond: 'Get Dr Simms, will you?'

She prises open her sticky lids and is blinking against the light when a blur of white floats into view.

'Karin?' A different voice. Deep and masculine, though gentle. 'Karin, I'm Dr Simms. Can you hear me?'

She nods, feels her hair scratching against a pillow, and it hits her then where she isn't – she's lying down, but it's not home. And although the voice is male, it's not Hugo's or Uncle Oskar's. The realisation ambles slowly towards her brain: she's somewhere without the slightly musty, comforting smell of her ancient eiderdown, somewhere Mama and Jutta and Aunt Gerda are not.

'What happened?' she manages. Her tongue is bone-dry, the inside of her mouth chalky and rank.

'You collapsed,' the man's voice says – his name has floated away already. 'You're at the Charité hospital. You had an emergency operation on your appendix. We had to remove it.'

She holds onto 'hospital' but the complicated words don't penetrate, and it's only when she moves her leg and a searing pain takes hold somewhere in her belly, ripping through the whole of her middle, that things start to fall into place. The sensation marries sharply with what he's said: operation goes with pain, doesn't it? Thoughts reach out to each other behind her eyes, grasping for links, sidling against each other for a split second of clarity before they slip away again.

'Where's Mama? Does Jutta know?' she croaks from arid lips. 'Where are they?'

'We've called your family,' he says. 'They know you're all right, and where you are.' Then he's walking away, voice floating in a little bubble inked at the corner of her vision – since childhood, she often thinks and dreams in black and white doodles. What he says is enough for now, enough to dampen the brief sense of alarm. Jutta knows where she is. *She'll find me*, Karin is reassured, before the blanket of anaesthesia draws over her again, lids drooping into sleep.

3

Clipping the Wings

13th August 1961, West Berlin

The house is awake, of course it is, and Jutta senses the angst the moment she opens the door. Mama's frisson of worry reaches her first, followed quickly from the kitchen by Gerda's concerned expression.

'What's happening? Where have you been?' they cry in unison, both still in their dressing gowns, hair pressed to their heads with pins.

'With Hugo, out there.' She extends an arm towards the window in taking off her jacket. Despite the coffee, she's exhausted, her energy and patience flagging.

'On the radio, it says there's a barrier – they're calling it a Wall.' Mama's whole body is trembling. 'They say the borders are closed to the East. Is it true, Jutta?'

What can she say but yes? *There's an ugly canker growing in our city which, for the time being at least, will prevent you seeing your sick daughter, and me my beloved sister?*

'It seems so,' is all she can say, allowing herself to be pumped for answers to their questions while they ply her with dense bread and jam, food that unusually tastes of nothing today. Uncle Oskar is in the corner armchair, half dressed in his trousers and his grey, sleeveless vest, a cigarette hanging from his lips, twiddling the dial of the radio to switch between RIAS, the American Allied station, and Hugo's own Radio Free Berlin.

'Hey, listen up,' he says suddenly, and the women stop mid-sentence, to hear Hugo's familiar voice push out of the little red box, a taped recording from his and Jutta's stop at Bernauer Strasse. Beyond Hugo's slightly tremulous tone, she recognises the background babble of despair. Gerda's face is torn in two: one half the pride at her boy on the radio broadcasting to all of Berlin, the other drawn at the news coming from him.

Jutta looks at Oskar, trying to read the twitching behind his moustache – her uncle, more than once described as a 'dark horse' and oft berated by Gerda for his unreliable qualities, but good fun to the children. Now, he looks only troubled. Deeply so.

The talk is largely of Karin and how they will reach her. They've already tried ringing the Charité but the lines are blocked, and Jutta listens as the two older women speculate among each other for comfort:

'Surely, once the panic is over, West Berliners will be allowed to come home?' Ruth says. 'It's their right, isn't it? They aren't East Germans, and Karin can't be the only one trapped across the border? There must be some concessions.'

They are somewhat appeased by the written note that will hopefully reach Karin, then bubble with fresh anxiety over her condition; as a midwife and former nurse, Gerda can give some reassurance, but she'll be all too aware of what a perforated appendix could lead to – infection and sepsis. Jutta is relieved that her aunt doesn't openly voice such concerns, though she does catch her aunt's eye and her intense unease alongside. Since childhood, it's plain Gerda has always regarded Jutta as the one with unusual insight, with a tendency to think long and deep. Though she treats both her nieces with adoration and clearly views them as daughters, there's no denying Karin — as the quieter one — has always been a slight favourite. Jutta has never minded, and she's aware that Karin is the more tactile of the twins, ready to throw her arms around her aunt, drawing her beautiful cards and sewing small gifts simply for the pleasure they bring. While Karin is tenacious in her creativity, she would be satisfied to stay all her life in Berlin, with a little studio to design and stitch her clothes in. Jutta, by contrast, wants to spread her wings beyond the city eventually, and it's obvious that Gerda sees it. Worse, Jutta senses her mother knows it too and dreads her daughter's flight. But not today — today, wings are being clipped.

4

Waking up to Reality

13th August 1961, East Berlin

Karin wakes more easily, no longer having to fight off a morphine-wielding mermaid intent on dragging her back to the depths. Propped up on pillows, she sips at water, balancing a swill of nausea with a desperate thirst. More than ever, she's desperate to brush her teeth, though the prospect of sitting up and the pain involved means she will put up with the sour taste for now.

The ward is wide and white; pale blue curtains are drawn around her, save for the space in front, so she can see doctors and nurses pass by – nurses clip at a pace, she notices, and doctors glide on silent footwear.

A nurse marches smartly up to her and plumps the pillows, as if by rote, and Karin is disappointed neither Jutta or Mama are behind, being led to the bed. Instead, from under her apron, the nurse pulls out a folded note. 'This was left at reception,' she says, and smiles. It's disconcerting to Karin in that it's so obviously a forced expression, and she senses a trace of pity behind it. There's something the nurse is not saying.

With one glance, Karin sees it's Jutta's handwriting. But why isn't her sister here? Her confusion has cleared enough to know it's Sunday, when most of the household won't be at work, Jutta certainly. So why isn't she sweeping through the door with a smile and a bunch of grapes, chiding her sister for going into the East when she was clearly so ill? Being on the ward means she's not in isolation, and Karin has watched a handful of other visitors go in and out. So why is there only a slip of paper in her hand?

She unfolds it eagerly and sees immediately it's been hastily written – Karin's keen eye for detail tells her that much. And it's brief, wishing her well, and saying they'll visit her as soon as they can. So what's stopping them? She's faintly annoyed, feeling a little sorry for herself, and wondering if Jutta and her mother are cross at her reck-lessness, going into the East while she felt unwell. In hindsight, even she can see it wasn't a good decision. Still, the Charité isn't that far over the border, and easy to travel to.

In the midst of her disappointment, a doctor arrives at the bedside.

'Dr Simms,' he reminds her, and she recognises his voice as the one previously floating above her bed. He tells her the operation was a success, but any longer and it might have been more serious.

'Is there a reason why my mother and sister can't visit?' she asks.

His face washes with that look, the one the nurse tried to hide.

'What is it?' she says. Her abdomen pricks with pain, her head beginning to throb.

'Things have . . . happened overnight,' he tells her.

'What *things*?'

26

'The border is closed to the West.' He says it quickly, as if delivering a death sentence, in a practised way he must have had to use many times.

'For how long? All day?' she quizzes. Like every Berliner, Karin is used to impromptu border closures on the whim of the guards or the GDR command – sometimes for no reason at all except to cause disruption. They've all learnt to be scathingly tolerant of the childish scraps between the Soviet and Allied commands. But the closures have almost always been short-lived, and only one or two checkpoints at a time.

'In how many places?' Karin asks.

Dr Simms looks increasingly grave. 'All of them.'

Karin's own face drains of what little colour it has. 'Why?'

'No one's quite sure, but it looks as if it's not temporary, not this time,' he adds. 'It's surrounding half the city – wire and concrete.' Then quickly, no doubt fearing for his patient sinking further into the pillows, he's more upbeat: 'But once you're recovered, I don't see why they wouldn't let you back across the border. You're a West Berliner by birth.'

The pain and the panic bubbling inside Karin subsides a little. 'But my family can't come to visit?'

'No, not today, though perhaps soon. I'm sorry. But we'll look after you, I promise. It'll be a few days, probably. Then you can go home.'

She nods, trying to absorb the new scenario, picturing the potential panic on both sides. 'And you?' she asks with interest. 'Aren't you worried about access to West Berlin, its freedom?'

Dr Simms startles a little, as if people rarely see beyond his white coat. His reply is automatic, honed by years on this side of the border. 'I'm an East German,' he says, as if it's the only explanation needed. With a faint, apologetic smile, he turns and moves away.

As she lies there, Karin can't help but feel imprisoned — first by her body, and now by this barricade that's described as being solid. Immovable. But the doctor is right; she is a West Berliner, and should still be able to show her identity card to pass through the checkpoint, hobble back to her bed and under her eiderdown to recover. They can't simply hold her captive, can they?

Exhausted, she lies back on her pillow and hears murmurings through the thin bedside curtains, imagines a man whispering to his sickly wife. She catches some of his words: 'Brandt . . . furious . . . tear it down . . . violation . . .' Karin can guess who he's talking of – West Berlin's colourful, larger-than-life mayor Willy Brandt. Judging by his forthright politics, it's not a leap for anyone to picture Brandt apoplectic with rage at being caught out by the East, calling on the Allies to do something immediate and concrete. But will they? All Berliners know the military might of the young GDR is not a danger to the West, only what's behind it: the insidious Soviet threat, their swathes of tanks, and now the nuclear shadow. Her fellow West Berliners are acutely aware too that their citadel is an expensive enclave propped up by the West, as a necessary symbol; 'an irritant inside the belly of the Red Beast,' Karin once heard it called. But will it become too costly now, and impossible to maintain? And where will that leave her?

But that's too big to think of now. All she can do is close her eyes and draw the simple lines of her sister in her mind, a picture of her closest soul in this world.

'Jutta,' she murmurs. 'I know you'll come and get me. Just don't leave it too long. Please Ja–Ja.'

5

LOSS

13th August 1961, West Berlin

Jutta wakes in her bed for the second time on August 13th, though fully clothed and caught in a shaft of sunlight streaming through her bedroom window. She's hot and disorientated, and it takes her a moment to remember what day it is, what she's already seen and heard with her own eyes. She turns from the sun and finds herself faced with Karin's side of the room they've shared for years: empty. The shadow of loss sits heavy already, anchoring her to the bed for a while.

When she gets up, the apartment is unusually silent, and Jutta bathes in the luxury for a few minutes, torn between her hunger for news and her reluctance to pad out the air by turning on the radio. Hugo is clearly still at work, Uncle Oskar 'out and about' as he so often is these days, and she guesses her mother and Gerda have ventured into the streets, unable to simply sit and wait for news of Karin. The neighbourhood gossip may well heighten their anxiety, but how much worse can it get?

Whatever they learn, it won't change the fact that Karin isn't here, to wander out for pastries with her, as they do early every Sunday.

Jutta's brain is fuzzy and the pot of coffee she brews doesn't have the desired effect. She wants to lie back down but the sofa – one of Oskar's 'acquisitions' – is notoriously lumpy and she can't face the bedroom again or stomach staring at the empty bed and that old, musty eiderdown her sister refuses to give up. Jutta cannot understand why this feels so much like a bereavement, when common sense tells her it should soon be sorted: Karin is only twenty-four, young and healthy. She will get better. Jutta will make her sister's case to some officious person in a faceless GDR building, and Karin will return home to their portion of the divided city. And if everything happening out there today is to be permanent, they will adjust to a new normality, because that's what Berliners have done for centuries. So why doesn't it feel straightforward?

Ruth and Gerda bustle through the door at just gone three, laden with gossip from street corners and the few local shops that open on Sundays, women milling about their own news points for tittle-tattle, and whose sensors are on high alert today.

'One man from behind the bakery says he saw a whole stream of lorries driving into the city in the last week – he works on the East side,' Ruth reports, busying herself with the kettle. 'He doesn't know what he's going to do if he can't cross over to work. How will he manage?'

'Apparently, the U-Bahn and the S-Bahn are running, but they stop at Friedrichstrasse station and won't go any further,' Gerda tells Jutta. 'Hugo was on the phone earlier. He's circled almost the entire border and it's the same everywhere. No one's allowed across, except foreign press and the military, and a lucky few with passes.'

'And did our police and the army really not know?' Jutta questions. Much like the rest of the Western world, she sees what is happening but cannot believe it went undetected, that an entire city has been corralled so suddenly. So secretly, and with so much bulky, heavy hardware.

'Seems not,' Gerda says. 'What police there are don't seem to know what to do. And as for the Allied armies . . . pah!' – she throws up her arms in disgust – 'Nowhere to be seen. There are Soviet tanks hovering at the city limits and the Americans do nothing. No British or French either. Neither sight nor sound.'

It's then they both hear Ruth's distress above the hiss of the kettle. Jutta knows, because she feels it too, that when her mother is busy and animated, she can almost forget for a few moments that her daughter isn't here to share everyone's disbelief at the news. But when Ruth stops, even for a second, the tears start. Jutta watches as Gerda pilots her sister into the living room and lowers her onto the armchair, couching her sibling's distress with her big, muscular arms, those that have skilfully caught a thousand and one babies over the years. She looks up at her niece and, though she is silent, Jutta hears Gerda's stout voice loud and clear: *Your mother shouldn't have to go through this. Not again.*

It's true that Ruth has lost more than most. And in the post-war rubble-scape of Berlin that Jutta remembers all too well, it amounts to a lot. Living under the thumb of Hitler's increasingly draconian Germany was tempered for a young Ruth only by meeting the dark and handsome Rolf Voigt at a dance in early 1935. It was an instant attraction, with true love hot on its heels. After a whirlwind romance: they were married later that year, and by early 1936 Ruth was happily pregnant. With Rolf a skilled carpenter, he had enough work to provide for his family, and Gerda – then a nurse and midwife – was able to support her sister through a heavy, tiring pregnancy, their bond as children even tighter in the face of a rapidly changing nation. In the event, Gerda needed to physically hold her sister through the labour itself.

If Gerda had ever suspected there was not one but two heads fighting for space and sustenance, eight limbs instead of four, she never said. As per the story she's told countless times since, she was not in the least surprised when Ruth pushed out one beautiful baby girl with a cap of dark hair on her living room floor, after an intense, rapid labour at thirty-seven weeks, the thick December snow on the streets preventing a dash to the hospital. The baby was a little smaller than average and Gerda's radar as a midwife began to twitch then, since the baby's neat proportions did not account for the sizeable girth of her sister over the previous six months, especially as Ruth had always been the slighter of the two sisters. And nothing, bar one conclusion, could explain away the continued rippling of her sister's only half-flaccid belly. In all her years caring for mothers, Gerda had never seen a placenta fidget.

'What's happening, Gerda? It's coming again!' Ruth had panted. With such a quick labour and no other midwife to hand, Gerda was forced to place the newly born Jutta, at just ten minutes old, into the nearest clean receptacle, a wooden box that Rolf had recently crafted. She lay wrapped and silent as her womb companion slid feet first from the confines of its mother, a second girl and identical in almost every way, though smaller, feet a little daintier.

battlefield, along with two of his fingers lost to frostbite. Considering he still had use of two legs and two arms, however, he remained valuable to the increasingly desperate Reich, and was set to work in the defence of Berlin as the Allies marched towards Germany's capital. It was here that he finally succumbed in April 1945, during the ferocious and bloody Fall of Berlin, defending a city he loved, alongside a cause he'd always hated. Rumour had it that he perished just a mile or so from the family home, having survived the brutality of war thousands of miles to the east, only to die in chaotic crossfire from one of his own battalion – though Ruth still chooses not to believe that precise detail. In her heart, Rolf was simply valiant in the protection of her and the girls, who had decamped from under the kitchen table with Gerda to the basement of their building. This was where the 'liberating' Soviet soldiers found them: filthy and afraid, the children wide-eyed and silent.

It was the twins, subsequently, who proved to be the family's saviours. Even now, women in Berlin can hardly speak of the atrocities that followed Germany's surrender, many of them victims at the hands of a hungry and bitter Soviet army, starved of female company. Survival was in one of two ways: capitulating to the Red Army marauders or befriending them. By pure chance they came under the gaze of a somewhat kindly Russian colonel, who'd left his own identical twin girls back in Moscow, around the same age. The sight of nine-year-old Jutta and Karin – tall, dark and willowy, with their sea-green eyes – brought big, burly Yuri Kalinov to tears. In exchange for the simple company of a family, he brought them food and the security of his rank. Whether it was fate or just good luck in meeting Yuri, it nonetheless kept them alive, especially since Oskar had been forced into hiding on the city's outskirts.

Yuri left Berlin in 1946 and the Red Peril diluted in time, but money still needed to be made. With Oskar gone, it was down to Ruth, as the youngest and fittest, to take to the streets as a *trummerfrauen*, a 'rubble woman', part of the army of wives and mothers hauling mounds of debris from bombed-out buildings strewn across the city. She arrived home each night exhausted and plastered in the grime of defeat, the girls ritually washing and oiling the ribbons of flesh on her battered hands. It was clear that Ruth left part of her soul among the broken bricks and dust, though she rarely spoke of the bodies they found: some long decayed, some kept fresh by being packed in concrete, others entwined in a last embrace before the certainty of death.

The long winter of the Berlin Blockade of 1948 proved another draw on the women's already spent resources, reminding them all of empty bellies and hunger pangs. In a currency war with the West, the Russians closed off road supply routes to West Berlin, leaving the 'island city' marooned. The Allies were forced to keep their political stronghold afloat for almost eleven months, with plane upon plane loaded with food and fuel, only a little of which made its way into the Voigt household; even now, Jutta painfully recalls the sight of her mother hovering outside a local café for any leftovers in those weeks when Oskar and his black-market supplies were conspicuously absent.

Cold and hungry as they were, it also marked the beginning of a very Cold War. That same war that has just become a good deal chillier.

So yes, Gerda is right, as she pours her concerned gaze

into Jutta: Ruth cannot live through the trauma again. Not after Rolf and, with it, a third of her life. One more third in Karin is unthinkable.

'Try to ring the hospital again, will you, Jutta, my love?' Gerda says.

Jutta does as she is asked, though she holds out little hope. Yet, the constant ringing on the other end is finally answered, and the doctor summoned to the phone.

'What's wrong?' she murmurs into the receiver. 'How ill? But I thought you said that the operation had gone well?'

She listens intently and with horror, and Jutta feels the older women close behind her, straining to catch each word.

'How long until you know?' Jutta questions again, panic rising as her heart deflates. 'She will be all right, won't she?'

6

Relapse

13th August 1961, East Berlin

Karin floats above herself, half in and half out of something like life, she thinks with a strange clarity. It's less the shroud of anaesthetic and more as if she's actually perching on a cloud over her own body – like those pictures of cherubs reclining in a puffy haze that she remembers from Sunday school, when she wondered why they didn't just fall through the cotton mist. Karin feels she might easily fall now. But to where? Is it just her own shell below her, or something like hell?

'I've no doubt it's an infection, but it's come on swiftly,' someone is saying below the cloud, Dr Simms possibly. There's a male grunt alongside and mutterings about 'antibiotics'. She senses the sheet being pulled back, releasing the roaring furnace of her body.

'Ice!' she wants to shout, but can't. 'Please, just bury me in ice!' Instead, she watches intently as the two heads bend over her own body and peer at the red gash on her belly, and perhaps even hears them sniff at it, muttering some more.

'Prepare the theatre, Nurse,' one voice says, and Karin wonders if they will transport her there on her little cloud, or whether her fiery body will soon burn through its candy-floss fibres and then she'll simply drop to the floor with a great thud.

'Where are her family?' someone asks. 'We should let them know. Just in case.'

'They're in the West. She's a West Berliner.'

'Oh, Christ.'

And then the white veil closes over, sucks in against her flesh and she's back below, in her body again, she imagines. All she hears is the rattling wheels of a gurney beneath her, and she opens her eyes briefly to see the faint, white haze of Dr Simms above.

'Don't worry,' he says.

7

The Scar

13th August 1961, West Berlin

Jutta needs to get out. The nerves of her mother are knitting into a tangled mess; she understands Ruth's level of angst after that phone call with the hospital, and she wants desperately to comfort her, but fretting within four walls will not help Karin. Jutta has her own anxiety to work through, and the apartment is fogged with fear.

'Where are you going?' Ruth says with surprise as Jutta pulls on her sandals.

'Just to see what's going on out there,' she says.

'But we've got the radio,' her mother protests. 'And Hugo will bring back news.' She says it like he's been sent out to fetch a loaf of bread.

'I know, but I want to see for myself,' Jutta replies. 'I need some air.'

Ruth looks disappointed, but Gerda gives her niece a look from the kitchen that says: *You go on, I'll look after her*, and Jutta loves her aunt all the more.

★

It feels strange on the street, with clusters of people still moving about, though with little direction. And now that she's outside, Jutta isn't sure where to go, feeling there's only so long you can stare at barbed wire and concrete. There's an undercurrent of unease, a hum of disquiet, though no loud voices. But then, she wouldn't hear them all the way over in Schöneberg, in the west side of the West. Jutta sees a neighbour from the same block across the street, the one her mother calls 'the hippy', and she holds up a hand in greeting. You couldn't call it a wave, because it's anything but cheery.

'Are you going to the Gate?' he cries. 'There are crowds gathering, though it's okay.'

By 'okay' Jutta thinks he must mean there's no violence. Not yet anyway. Hugo has already reported across the airwaves that crowds have gathered on the East side, moving around the city's main thoroughfare of Unter den Linden and Friedrichstrasse in shoals. But still, no one knows what to do. Continued bewilderment is the GDR's biggest advantage, more effective than a cosh at this moment.

The evening sun is still strong as Jutta heads through the leafy and eerily quiet Tiergarten and up towards the Gate, not knowing if it's her own will or curiosity driving her limbs. If Karin were here now, she would be right by my side, she thinks, urging us to go, always keen to hear people's opinions, though never loud herself. 'A subtle revolutionary,' she remembers labelling her sister once during her art school days, and Karin had laughed, with her wide, enticing smile.

She has to close her eyes and work hard on imagining Karin's face. It's not as if she can simply look in the mirror and remind herself, because Jutta cannot for the life of her see the resemblance. She knows it's there – in pictures she recognises two babies with the same features: girls dressed in identical outfits, two women who sport the same long, black hair, green eyes and distinct aquiline nose that Karin has always hated and Jutta doesn't mind so much. But in the mirror, it doesn't translate. She and Karin are so different and yet complementary; truly two halves of one soul. Yes, they've thought of separation, talking in the dark of their bedroom after the lights go out. They each want something different from life, keen to find partners, even husbands, and that means their lives will fork. Inevitably divide. But not yet. They hadn't planned for it so soon. And not in this way. Not with an ugly scar forcing them apart.

As Jutta reaches the Gate, a smaller portion of the not very substantial crowd makes a surging motion in response to water cannons being used across the wire against the throngs of people on each side. Each is whistling a high-pitched, tuneless complaint, but it's not clear who the targets are: the military, other Berliners, or the Gate itself, just for representing a barrier in the first place. There are shouts on the West side of 'Away with the goatee beard!' – a direct dig at the GDR's leader Walter Ulbricht and his distinctive facial hair. Jutta hovers on the edge of the gathering, next to a man with a small transistor clamped to his ear who acts as a conduit in shouting to the crowd: 'Two have escaped at Treptower and one swam across the Spree,' to a small cheer, then: 'There are more crowds at Wollankstrasse.'

On the other side of the wire – Jutta reflects at how quickly it becomes 'the other side' in the collective mind – a sudden orange glow appears as someone tosses a Molotov cocktail at the East German line, only to hear the sinister hiss of a water jet dampen its radiance and the dissent of the one who threw it. They can hear the muffled protests as he's bundled away by men in uniform and some who aren't – Stasi disguised as protesters. Overhead, the rotors of an Allied helicopter drone as it circles near to the West side. Jutta squints upwards, and imagines the pilot's bird's-eye view, wondering if they can clearly see the zig-zag line from north to south: a grey, jagged incision fully laid out across an entire city.

In the groups surrounding Jutta on the West side, disquiet and unrest bubbles, simmers, bubbles again, but flashes of true anger are drowned by sadness and steeped in help-lessness, and there's no one person brave enough to lead the opposition. The man with the radio reports that Mayor Willy Brandt is not at the Wall because he's making an impassioned speech at the West Berlin parliament, labelling the growing insult as 'the barrier fence of a concentration camp', and calling on the Allies to send reinforcements to match the Soviets. At the same time, he's asking West Berliners to exercise restraint on the streets, to not give the East Germans any reason to retaliate.

'So, what should we do?' the man with the radio asks. 'Protest in whispers?'

'He's good with his words, that Brandt fella,' someone else moans, 'but he doesn't have any power, does he? He can ask the Allies all he likes, but what are they going to do?' He spreads his hands outwards and twists his head side to side. 'They're not here now, are they?'

Where does that leave ordinary Berliners, Jutta thinks, the ones with half their lives on the other side? She's suddenly exhausted – by the day, by the loss and emotion, and by the futility of standing in the street doing virtually nothing, realising now that being nearer to the Wall makes her no closer to Karin. They remain poles apart.

Oskar is still absent when Jutta gets home, though Ruth and Gerda hardly seem to notice, still so wrapped in their own distress. Hugo is working but has dropped in for some food, warning his mother he may need to sleep at the station overnight to monitor the news feeds.

'I know he's keen but it can't be good to miss out on so much sleep,' Gerda says to Jutta, though there is continued pride in her voice that her son is out there, helping to weave the city's history into something palpable, doing a service of sorts. She says they've tried to ring the hospital for news, but with no luck, and her voice tries to relay optimism. 'I've told your mother we'll try again first thing tomorrow. The Charité's a good hospital, the oldest in Berlin, and the best. I know they'll look after her,' Gerda says, though it sounds to Jutta more as though she's trying to reassure herself.

Ruth is just drifting to sleep, Gerda having administered one of her small supply of sleeping tablets she keeps back for 'special needs', and Jutta feels guilty at her own relief; her mother has always been a source of strength, and Jutta knows that she owes her the same now, but she can't bear to rake over the same embers of anxiety repeatedly tonight. She needs silence and a quiet corner of her mind to contemplate – and her own bed so that she might bury her face within its pillows and expel her sadness into its fibres.

In their bedroom, shafts of moonlight lie across Karin's bed, and Jutta has to close her eyes to the void. The radio chatter that Gerda finds so comforting drifts down the hallway: the voice reports around sixty Berliners have made

43

their way across since the 'birth' of the Wall around twenty hours before – rushing the wire, swimming the Teltow canal and creeping their way across small areas not yet permanently patrolled, often patches of allotments backing onto the border, places where it's sliced indiscriminately through public places. She muses over the strange description: the 'birth' of something so ugly and divisive. Babies are born, and they are beautiful. Birth *is* beautiful; it's an unspoken fact in the Voigt–Zelle household. What happened today amounts to a growth, a weed of the type that drives upwards through dirt, extracting oxygen from the air, just as the wire today sucked hope from an entire city and its people.

She turns her head – such thoughts take her mind from the real weight, for a few seconds. But it's still there, because Karin isn't. Jutta pushes her ear into the pillow, hard enough to hear the whooshing of her own blood pounding, the pulse of her own life that she might, just might, imprint onto Karin – to keep her alive.

Please Karin, fight hard – for Mama. For me. Please.

8

Surfacing

14th August 1961, East Berlin

Karin rises again to the surface, sucking in bubbles of air she's convinced are out there somewhere.

'Fräulein Voigt . . .' A touch on her arm, one part of her that mercifully doesn't hurt. 'Karin, can you hear me?'

It's a woman's voice, older, matronly. Karin twitches a response, and then feels the sheets being rearranged. Do they always have to fuss so? Gerda doesn't do that, even when we're ill, she thinks. Her lucidity rises and falls again – she remembers being in the hospital, though little after that. It's easy to suppose that's where she is, still, and the disinfectant smell confirms it. Eyes closed, she senses more bodies moving into the space around her, a presence around her toes; someone coughs.

'So everyone, this is Fräulein Voigt, twenty-four years of age, presented with acute appendicitis . . .' Dr Simms' voice, though more formal, drifts in and out. '. . . Initial operation to remove ruptured appendix . . . secondary infection, returned to theatre and abraded operatively. Antibiotics are ongoing. Any questions?'

'How long for recovery?' a young male voice asks.

'Possibly a week or so now, with the added complication of infection,' Simms replies with authority. Someone else asks about 'prognosis' and Simms answers swiftly: 'Good.' It's what Karin grasps onto as the space twists around her, fading in and out. She crawls her hand to the edge of the bed, searching for Jutta. Why isn't she here?

Where clarity fails, Karin falls back to meandering in the comfort of her memory, unable to remember a time when Jutta wasn't there. Some at school called them 'twinny', as if they were like those Siamese twins physically joined at the hip. Karin never minded the association of closeness, since she's always loved being a twin, but she hated the presumption that they were each half a person. In her mind, she and Jutta simply created a bigger whole, radiating strength from one to the other. It's something she could do with now.

So where is Jutta, when she needs the touch of her sister's hand the most? Didn't she hear something about the border – a Wall? Or was that just in her dreams? She looks into the blackness of her lids, trying to imagine Jutta across the tiny divide between their beds at home, conjuring the smell of their room, her sister's fresh soap smell and her eiderdown as the best medicine.

9

A New Dawn on the Divide

14th August 1961, West Berlin

When Jutta wakes to a blue sky and the early promise of summer sun, it takes several seconds for reality to dawn. Whatever happened overnight, Berlin is certain to be changed; older, maybe wiser, but still cruelly dissected. In her clear and colourful dreams, wildly painted bulldozers came and tore down the grey wire, but since the marauding group was led by GDR leader Ulbricht, she can easily separate fact from fantasy. The wire will still be there: steely and ugly, heavy and unyielding.

'Where is everyone?' She stifles a yawn as Gerda sets down coffee in front of her in the kitchen.

'Your mother's still sleeping, Oskar was up and out early and Hugo slept at the station.'

'Have you tried ringing the Charité?' Jutta asks.

'Several times since six a.m., but they're not picking up. How can a hospital not answer the phone?' Gerda is irritated, despite her heartfelt allegiance to nurses and midwives everywhere. Jutta feels a new anxiety dawning; something doesn't feel right.

'We'll just keep trying,' she says to her aunt.

'Will you go to work?' Gerda pitches.

'I have to – no reason not to. When I'm there, I'll ring Mama's office and tell them she's sick. And Karin's place too.' She looks at Gerda, who nods in agreement. Ruth *is* sick – sick of distress and loss, and ever weary of her dull desk job.

She passes Hugo on the outer stairs as she heads out, noting he looks grey and beyond tired. 'Long night?' she asks.

'You could say that.' But his eyes sparkle with the knowledge of what he's seen – real news being made, a witness to history. He can't help it. 'Any news on Karin?' he asks, a portion of the glimmer receding when Jutta tells him the latest. 'She'll be all right, though, won't she?'

'I hope so.' What else can she say? That deep, dense tugging in her heart, the one signalling that her other half will pull through, well, that's just a feeling. It's not science. It's not reliable. She can't pledge assurances to her mother, in case nature and its cruel streak wins out. It's only that fragile thread of hope coupling her and Karin that allows Jutta to step through the door and put one steadfast foot in front of the other.

The streets are quieter than normal, and yet still industrious. Much like her mother's descriptions of the war, and her own memories of the '48 blockade, life has to go on. Even torn in half, Berlin needs to function. Jutta's short journey towards the university library where she works doesn't take her towards the border, but she can picture a scene where confusion still reigns, not least among the ten thousand or so *grenzgängers* – Berliners who traverse the border every day for work. Some will have turned up on the East side, lunch in their bags, hopeful of getting through to a workplace and the wage it brings. If they aren't allowed across today, will they be allowed permits once the dust has settled?

It seems unlikely, since everyone now knows the true motivation for the Wall. It's not – as the Eastern politicians claim publicly – to stop the insidious evil of capitalism infecting the GDR state, but quite the opposite: to halt the haemorrhage of East Germans bleeding out through the border, using West Berlin as the passage to a life on the other side of the Iron Curtain. Once the escapees reach West Berlin, they are fed through the refugee centre at Marienfelde, processed and flown out to a new life in West Germany 160 or more kilometres away.

The seepage has steadily increased since the GDR came into being in 1949 – three and a half million so far and reaching a record flow of late. In recent months, thousands of families have crowded the small refugee centre, clutching their lives in a single suitcase. Everyone in Berlin knows of East Germany's 'brain drain', with doctors, teachers and engineers fleeing to the West, leaving some towns in East Germany without a solitary teacher for their schools. GDR leaders see that for communism to have any chance of succeeding, it must have workers. And yet those workers are quitting the country in droves, escaping what they view as a lifetime of austerity, hemmed in by the Party and all it represents. So the Wall is not a 'protection barrier', but a steely way of stitching up a heavily bleeding wound. For good. It's merely a bonus if they succeed in barring the wicked capitalists of West Berlin.

This is what frightens Jutta the most: the GDR's determination to plug the tiniest of holes, to seal every last crack. It means she will be forced to rely on the goodwill and the mercy of the state in allowing her sister to slip back through. And that's a dependence which makes her very, very uneasy.

The university campus and its library is relatively quiet, as is usual in the summer break, but it has that buzz afflicting all of Berlin right now, with a constant whispering conjecture in corners of a building that ordinarily encourages a near silence. Jutta rings her mother's office and relays her white lie; despite their sympathy, she can imagine the irritation among Ruth's fellow office workers, with every business suddenly in uproar. Calling Karin's boutique is easier, since she is genuinely sick, and, when they naturally assume she is in a Western hospital, Jutta feels too weary to explain fully. Once Karin is back, they won't need to know.

Next, she rings the Charité while mentally calculating her 'to-do' list for the day, anticipating a lengthy ringing before someone answers. As a result, Jutta is not prepared for the cavernous, dull and endless tone – worse than the unanswered ring – and it sends a thunderbolt to her heart. It constitutes nothing. And everything. She can feel her lungs emptying in a second, still consciously scooping in breath as her colleague, Heidi, comes into the office.

'Have you tried ringing anyone on the East side?' Jutta says nervously.

'No point,' Heidi comes back, voice clipped, face grave. 'Didn't you know? They cut the phone lines this morning. Telex as well. And the post – no mail back and forth.'

'Until when?' Jutta manages, and Heidi simply shrugs.

Jutta replaces the receiver. They have nothing now; no strands of communication left. Only the invisible thread that she and Karin have, cultivated to be strong and unyielding over the years, remains. And with no word, no touch, no way to extend a message that they will get her back, she wonders how long the thread will endure before it frays towards a breaking point.

Jutta's manager is sympathetic, since his own mother lives in the East, and grants her leave for the day. She thinks of calling in on Hugo for access to his press couple, to relay another note, but he's getting much-needed sleep. Instead, she heads to the town hall in Schöneberg for . . . she doesn't know what. Guidance? Advice? This is in no handbook, there's no contingency for half a city being detached, out on a limb. Maybe she'll find someone with an idea, or a modicum of common sense, because the world appears rapidly to be running out of it.

The town hall corridors are running with anxiety and people harbouring papers and worried expressions. Through the confusion, Jutta squeezes, talks and pushes her way through a small throng and into an upstairs office and towards the desk of one Hans Fleisch, 'senior administrator'. He snaps his head up at her with uncontrolled irritation and she recognises the drowning-in-paperwork expression, coupled with a *please leave me alone or I might scream* feeling that she sometimes experiences.

'Yes?' He's gone back to scratching at a pile of forms.

'Are you dealing with requests for travel permits?' Jutta ventures. 'Only downstairs they said it was y—'

'Yes, it's me.' Hans is not enjoying his job today, clearly. 'But there are very few permits being issued. Don't get your hopes up.'

She deflates, visibly and audibly, a small moan escaping from somewhere inside, enough to cause Hans to look up and gesture her to sit in the chair opposite his desk. He lays down his pen, too.

'Sorry,' he sighs. 'It's just that I've had to say it countless times today. I'm sick of the sound of my own voice.'

Jutta has never set eyes on Hans before, but she imagines that he has aged today, his skin taking on the arid look of the paper pile beside him. Her own features sag. She should have expected it – her first port of call was never going to be a success, not in this new chaos. He clearly reads her distress, tries to offer what he can, which isn't much.

'Why do you need to go into the East?' he says. There can be no *want* about it, since all human traffic is heading the other way.

'It's my sister, she's over there in . . .' Jutta can no longer save her tears for solitude, and Hans offers her a tissue from the box on his desk.

'Thank you . . . sorry,' she sniffs, and goes on to explain about Karin. 'Surely, she can't be the only one caught on the other side?' Jutta avoids using the words 'stuck' or 'trapped', because they have too much finality.

'No, she isn't, and some West Berliners with papers have been able to talk themselves across the border,' he says. 'But it's hit and miss at the moment. They should be allowed back eventually' – there's heavy emphasis on the 'should' – 'within a certain time frame, but I have no route to query anything, with all the communications down.' He reaches for a pack of cigarettes, then hesitates.

'You can fill in a form to request a permit for yourself to visit your sister' – he lays a hand instead on a large pile of forms already completed – 'but it might be several days, or even weeks. The GDR are already sensitive about visitors helping to plan escape attempts. Did you know that sixty-six came across yesterday, in just one day?' Hans can't disguise a certain admiration in his voice for those who jumped, swam or simply hurtled through with their courage and cunning, while Jutta focuses on 'sensitive' and wonders if building a Wall can ever go hand in hand with such an attribute.

'But what if my sister is recovered before I get a permit and she's ready to come home?' Jutta asks.

'Then it's up to the hospital to appeal on her behalf. I suspect she'll be vetted by the security services and then taken to a checkpoint where you can meet her.' He offers a weak smile as encouragement, fingers the cigarette packet again.

To Jutta, however, this does sound more promising – something routine and relying less on the humanity of one individual, though it doesn't stem her yearning to see Karin immediately. She fills out the form and leaves it with Hans Fleisch, turning her back on his heavy sigh as he goes back to his scratching.

Outside, Jutta sits on a bench in front of the town hall, knowing she should go home and relay even her small amount of news to Mama and Gerda, and yet not wanting her heart to be further deadened by the heavy mood of the house. Equally, she can't face returning to work, sitting on her anticipation within the hush of the library for all those hours. Jutta feels empty and baseless, the void sitting alongside a sensation that is entirely new in her lifetime – loneliness.

She gets up from the bench and walks towards the western end of the Tiergarten, to Berlin's zoo, not consciously, though she knows where her feet are taking her – where Karin is piloting her. It's early afternoon when she arrives at the busy interchange on Kurf'damm and sees its two most prominent landmarks: the partially bombed-out Kaiser Wilhelm Memorial Church, craggy and grey in its old age, and almost opposite – in total contrast – the modern, circus-like red and white striped awning of Kranzler's café.

There are tables outside on the wide pavement, but Jutta climbs to the circular balcony and sits at their table, hers and Karin's. Mama insists this new Kranzler's can't hold a flame to the ornate original on Unter den Linden, bombed out during the war, but it's the place where Karin most loved – *loves* – to people-watch with her sketchbook, spying on the well-dressed women parading up and down the busy thoroughfare. She sometimes makes a lightning sketch, adapting and tweaking the image, holing herself up in their bedroom in the next days, her heavy electric sewing machine whirring at pace until she emerges with the new creation draped over her body and fitting to perfection. Jutta, who can barely sew on a button, is endlessly aghast, envious, and hungry for her own version of the design, though Karin is careful to alter it so that they look less like 'twinny' and more like well-dressed West Berliners.

The street is busy, as always, and Jutta lingers over her coffee, trying to read the atmosphere of this new Berlin in throwing off her melancholy. There are clusters of people collected on the street, some with hands gesticulating wildly and their necks at full stretch with impassioned speech. It's not hard to imagine the topic of conversation. She wonders how much each person has invested in the Wall – a mother, a close friend, or a cousin twice removed on the other side. Everyone will know someone behind the barbed wire; no one is untouched.

But there is one question more than any on everyone's lips, familiar to Germans both East and West: after two world wars lost and a city in ruins, how was this ever allowed to happen?

10

Recovery

14th August 1961, East Berlin

The eventual smile on Dr Simms' face is everything to Karin – he gives nothing away while looking at the chart hooked on the end of her bed, nor when he draws the curtains around and scrutinises her wound, though she watches carefully for any twitch to his nostrils.

'You've reacted very well to the treatment, Fräulein Voigt,' he says at last. 'I imagine that's what it is to be young and fit.'

'Does that mean I can go home soon?'

The smile drops a little. 'Perhaps in two or three days,' he assures her. 'Your body is weak, and it's taken quite a beating from the infection. We need to get you up and about first, or we risk a relapse. And we have to apply for a travel permit so you can go back to your family.'

Somehow, the way he makes no mention of the Wall is jarring, as if she is about to embark on a holiday or a pleasure trip.

'Do my family know how I am?' she goes on. 'Has anyone spoken to them?'

'Only the day you were brought in, after the operation, and again when your condition worsened,' Dr Simms replies, 'but not since. There are no telephone lines open, or ways to post them a letter.'

In reaction to Karin's crestfallen expression, he moves closer and lowers his voice. 'But I think I might be able to help. I have one favour I can use until we get the order for you to go.'

Karin's mood lightens in one minute, darkens the next, seesawing as she weighs up the news trickling in. Nurse Selig has already filled in the details since her brain threw off the anaesthetic and its foggy shroud. Perhaps her gratitude for waking, for being alive, dampened the shock at first and she hasn't the energy to feel worried. She's horrified, of course, at the Wall itself, feeling the betrayal of every Berliner, but it explains why Jutta, Mama and Gerda are not by her side. They are not cross with her, as she'd imagined in her drugged-up state. Still, she feels hopeful that in a few days an ambulance will take her to the border, where she may have to hobble across the threshold, but she doesn't care because they will be waiting, in Oskar's old truck, to throw their arms around her and envelop her in their soft, caring folds, like the old eiderdown. Soon, Karin thinks, soon I will be home. I will be safe. Then, when I'm well, I can help fight the injustice.

'So, can I try now, to get out of bed?'

11

Beads of Hope

14th August 1961, West Berlin

Hugo is awake and looking less like an apparition when Jutta arrives home around four o'clock, though for a young man he appears to have aged. He raises his eyebrows and gestures with his head that they should meet outside once the maternal grilling is over.

She offers the news of a potential permit to her mother and Gerda with an upbeat tone designed to relay confidence, leaving out Herr Fleisch's cynicism. The two women have garnered promises of help from the local parish priest and are collecting beads of hope like charms on a bracelet. Jutta goes along with it, though she's inclined to question how much power a man of the cloth has against the might of Soviet communism, and what increasingly looks to be a long and large concrete dam.

Hours later, and several floors up, on the building's roof, the pair are sitting in two of the three deckchairs previously arranged in a circle. Hugo has collapsed the third, mindful that it can only remind Jutta of the missing member of their trio, and he's blowing cigarette smoke towards a molten sun.

'No, thanks,' Jutta says as he offers her the cigarette; she rarely smokes and feels it won't help the sediment of nausea lodged in her stomach. 'Do you feel human again?'

'Well, I slept, if that's what you mean,' Hugo replies. 'I'm not sure about the human element.' He smiles weakly, takes another puff.

'So, what is the word out there? About what it means for the future?' Despite that initial tour with Hugo, Jutta feels as if she's been in a glass bubble over the past thirty-six hours, solely focused on Karin. With Hugo's position as a reporter and his degree in politics, she trusts his scrutiny of the facts.

Her cousin blows out his cheeks this time, no smoke necessary for the impact. 'It's bad – our contacts say the Allies are running about like headless chickens, forming some sort of verbal protest, which pretends they mean business when they've got no intention of fighting it. They won't give up West Berlin, but equally they won't insist on the Wall coming down. It's here to stay, Jutta.'

They both regret losing a portion of the city for varying reasons – the theatres that offer communist-subsidised tickets, and the bars with cheap beer and good vodka, sometimes with atrocious bands but vibrant company. More, though, it's the loss of freedom for others – friends and good people in the East who don't deserve to be confined – and the sheer barbarity of herding one half of a city into a space and barring the other from entering.

Jutta shifts uncomfortably. 'What do you think it means for Karin?'

Hugo shrugs, seems genuinely perplexed. 'I think that it's likely to change day by day,' he sighs. 'And whether or not she's fit enough to come across on a good day.' In truth, neither knows for sure whether she is alive, critically ill or recovering, but they need to imagine her crossing – to picture the reality of it – for everyone's sakes.

'Can we get another note to her via your press friends, that couple we spoke to?' she asks.

'I can try,' Hugo says, but there's scant hope in his voice. 'They live just over the border in the East, but right now, with the phones and the telex down, they might as well be in Timbuktu. The West Berlin journos are banned from crossing so I have to rely on bumping into them if they come over the border. But I've asked all my colleagues to keep an eye out.'

Jutta sinks into her chair and lays her head back against the old, striped fabric. The sun is dropping low over one side of the city, casting a golden glow across the now smaller island of West Berlin and its mixture of old and grey and vibrant, new architecture, as if it's some sort of utopia blessed by good fortune. Which, of course, it is to some. By stark contrast, the East appears cast in a gloomy shadow, the light sucked free from its very fabric; anyone looking at the image on such a day would need reminding the sight is simply the result of the sun and earth's daily cycle, and not Mother Nature's disdainful comment on global politics.

Jutta peers hard across the landscape in the direction of the Charité, beyond the blanket green of the park and the crowning statues of the Brandenburg Gate that she can't quite see, but imagines in her mind. Beneath it, the Wall gets higher and more solid by the hour. Beyond that, there's Karin.

She closes her eyes against the glare, sees orange burning the inside of her lids. *Hang on, Karin. Hang on.* She can only sense that their unique thread has neither snapped nor unravelled, but it's all she has.

Life in Berlin grinds on in the next days, like some mythical two-headed monster hauled in opposite directions, each head pushing and pulling against the other, the machinery of politics grating behind the sorrow of families still reeling from their lifelines being severed. Jutta stands on a street corner, watching on dejectedly as the wire is replaced by the true Wall: labourers on the East side piling concrete blocks higher and higher, the cement between oozing out like icing on a cake and forming a crooked, undulating line of ugly grey. As it rises, the faces of the people on either side, their distressed expressions set like the stone of the Wall, disappear.

In the Voigt–Zelle household, Ruth has gone from distressed to almost numb, and even Gerda can barely persuade her out of a silent melancholy as she thumbs for hours through photograph albums of the twins together. Jutta feels desperate to comfort her mother, yet she's acutely aware the mere sight of her prompts Mama's sorrow to heighten further, in repeated waves. She spends as much time away from the apartment as possible, stalking checkpoints up and down the Wall, trying her luck at access to the East wherever she hears a good number of West Berliners have been allocated passes. She doesn't imagine how she might get back if she manages to cross – the only goal is to reach Karin and see that her sister is alive.

Each time it's the same: if she does make it to the checkpoint windows, the border guards narrow their eyes and scrutinise her identity card, then her, before moving languidly to a list beside them. She sees their eyes crawl up and down the paper. Always her lungs hold both air and fear. Repeatedly, the guard comes back to the window with a shake of the head and occasionally a sympathetic expression. 'No, Fräulein – you cannot gain access.'

Her pleas for an explanation are never answered. Why would her name be on a list? She's never been in trouble, or part of any demonstration that would mark her out as a dangerous dissident: a threat to the GDR. She's in the East far less than Karin, as most of her friends live in West Berlin. So why? Jutta can only walk wearily away and hope to try again, chance upon a slapdash guard who might not check so thoroughly. But does such a person exist in the GDR, where it seems unlikely anyone would dare to be either careless or sloppy?

On Wall day plus three, Jutta is at work in the library office when she's called to the front desk of her department. She imagines the young man facing her to be a student until he asks who she is and promptly hands over a small envelope, then turns tail and disappears before she has a chance to question him.

The address is very specific and typed on a brown envelope; it looks official, although there's no stamp. Inside, Jutta unfolds a small sheet of notepaper, and her heart plummets on seeing the Charité heading – is this THE letter? The notification that her beloved sister is dead? *Oh God no. Please no.*

Fingers shaking, she scans the typed words at lightning speed for tell-tale phrases: 'I'm sorry . . .', 'I regret to inform . . .'. Instead, there's a polite tone and brief message to say Karin is recovering well, and may be ready to leave the hospital in two days. 'We will endeavour to make sure she reaches home using the appropriate channels', the short note ends. There's no signature, or name, but Jutta knows

61

in an instant that it's genuine; at the bottom right-hand corner is a tiny doodle of two stick figures, each with a crude triangle to denote a simple dress. It's Karin's own sign-off, a signature for her sister. It's them as a pair, little stick hands entwined. Their thread in ink.

Inevitably, relief mixes with confusion. Who sent it? And why not an official letter to Karin's home address? Despite the official notepaper, the anonymity and the delivery must mean someone is helping Karin. Jutta is flooded with gratitude, anxiety chasing at its rear: if the letter has to be so covert, does it follow that her sister's release will need to be equally underhand?

Jutta leaves work in the early afternoon, clutching the letter. She's torn about showing it to her mother, giving her a rush of hope that may never be realised. Hugo needs to see it first, and one other still before him.

At Schöneberg town hall, Hans Fleisch remains fraught and besieged, the pile of papers on his desk now a good deal higher. Still, he recognises Jutta, manages a smile for her and examines the letter.

'Your sister may well have a guardian angel in the East,' he says at last.

'So, do we just wait – until they contact us, or me?' she says.

'I think so,' Herr Fleisch says, rummaging in a smaller pile of correspondence to his side. 'I was just about to contact you myself. This came back.'

She recognises the well-handled form he tenders, her written request for passage across the border under the heading of 'Family emergency'. What's new are the large letters stamped in red, skewed at an angle: 'REFUSED'.

Jutta's eyes are wide, her mouth paralysed, leaving Herr

Fleisch to fill the void. 'It came back today – much more swiftly than I would have imagined,' he says.

'But . . . but why? Is there any explanation?' she stutters. 'Does this mean just now, or forever?' Even saying the word sticks in her throat.

The look of genuine pity from Herr Fleisch alarms Jutta the most. It tells her nothing can be done, that fighting is futile. And it can mean only one thing.

'Is this the Stasi's doing?' she dares to suggest.

'I'm not entirely sure, but maybe,' he ventures. 'Everything about it suggests so. I'm sorry.'

Jutta imagines the possible reasons behind a stark refusal from the Stasi. Ruth and Gerda could never be a fly in the communist ointment, or Karin, aside from her arty friends. And she herself works as a simple library assistant. It's possible Hugo is a target for surveillance, as a Western journalist. Or could it be Oskar? Despite living with him almost all her life, her uncle's occupation remains a mystery to Jutta, although she knows that he often crosses the border for 'business'. Correction: he *did* cross the border.

There's little sense in analysing; if Herr Fleisch is right, there's nothing they can do, with no pathway to appeal on 'humanitarian' grounds. The word is simply not in the Stasi vocabulary.

Wandering home with a heavy despondency, Jutta passes newsstands that relay the hysteria, the daily *Bild* and *Morgenpost* papers shouting the Allies' betrayal in bold headlines: 'The West is doing nothing!' The global press has woken up too; the well-timed snap of an East German border guard vaulting the wire instantly becomes a worldwide image of freedom, with numerous black and white images of weeping women reaching across the wire to their loved ones. The citadel of West Berlin, with its two million residents, has become a symbol for liberty, as statesmen scrap over the definition of democracy.

Except Jutta doesn't care what the world thinks, least of all politicians, unless it helps Karin: the GDR may refuse her family access, but what could possibly be the point of preventing her sister from returning? Surely, it's in the communists' best interests to expel Westerners? Karin is the last person in the world to ever infect another human being with her personality, except in a positive way. But the world isn't thinking straight right now, is it? As the Wall climbs higher, life as they know it comes crashing down.

Jutta is two streets away from home and in a world of her own when she's startled by Hugo's voice above the popping of his motorcycle engine, drawing to the side of the kerb.

'I've been looking everywhere for you,' he cries over the hum. 'Hop on – I've tracked down a contact to help us.'

They drive to a café just off Motzstrasse, where it's not the British couple waiting for them but a young man in his twenties, with neat, dark hair and a well-fitted brown suit, who wouldn't look out of place on either side of the Wall.

'This is Lucien,' Hugo introduces. 'He's a French journalist – and as such, with his magical passport, he's got the run of the city.'

Lucien nods and smiles, draws hard on his fragrant French cigarette and gestures for them to sit down. 'I can take a message to your sister, but I won't be able to wait for a reply,' he tells them in a low voice. 'I'm fairly sure all journalists have a Stasi tail the moment they go through the checkpoint.'

Jutta doesn't doubt what he says, not after today. 'We appreciate anything you can do,' she says to Lucien, though it burns inside that a foreign citizen has more right to enter parts of her city than her. Hugo talks work and politics while Jutta scribbles another note. She's normally so articulate with a pen, always had the words while Karin commands the pictures, but now she can't assemble anything worthy of her emotions. They're stuck somewhere between her heart, her brain and the fingers of her writing hand.

Karin - make no mistake, we're here waiting for you. We would come at a moment's notice if we could, Mama and me, Gerda too. Please get yourself well and come back soon. We all miss you madly and love you so much. Your home is waiting, Your Ja-Ja.

She mimics Karin's stick figure couple as best she can; it's not a patch on the original, but Karin will recognise her pathetic attempt as genuine.

Lucien leaves and she and Hugo stay on for a beer, her cousin feeding the jukebox while Jutta calls home with news of the letter, that Karin is alive and recovering. She hears the prayers and tears of her mother in the background, glad that Gerda is there to share in the relief.

'What if she simply isn't allowed back?' Jutta voices her fears to Hugo, above the familiar backdrop of Elvis.

'There will be ways and means,' he says, though not with any relish. 'But it might take some time.' Already, he's heard of groups mobilising, students mostly, to help people to traverse the Wall in every way possible, over, under or around. The true rate of early escape attempts, successful or not, isn't known outside the GDR, but the Western press is keen to highlight those who have made it, including the nine border guards who've chosen to defect rather than enforce the Wall. Hugo tells her that a good number of escapees have also made it through the forest and greenery on the western border line between West Berlin and the East German countryside – it has a line of wire and is patrolled, but the sheer length makes it harder to police. For now.

'Do you think it might come to that?' Jutta says. Her eyes, neatly rimmed with black kohl, reflect horror. 'I mean, a real escape for Karin?' She's not let herself think that far ahead yet.

Hugo shrugs. He won't admit as much to his mother or hers, but it seems that nothing would surprise him about the determination of the GDR to tighten the noose around its people, or anyone else in its reach.

Jutta and Hugo linger a while longer before they ride back to Schöneberg and the town hall, not to see Herr Fleisch this time but West Berlin's self-styled protector, Willy Brandt, high up on a podium, addressing the people, who stand like sardines in the sun-baked square. Taking a defiant stance behind a bank of microphones, his thick hair swept back, the city's charismatic mayor addresses a huge crowd in the West, and those on the other side of the Wall 'who can no longer speak out or come to us'. Fist aloft, he talks of peace without capitulation, of a firm stance with no weakness, but in the end the speech smacks of his disappointment with the Allies, in doing virtually nothing to reverse the situation. He reveals the content of his forthright letter to President Kennedy, in a rallying cry: 'Berlin expects more than words. Berlin expects political action!'

The crowd of more than two hundred thousand explodes,

cheering and whistling, caught in a wave of solidarity for all Berliners, chanting their defiance and a determination to fight this affront to freedom. And Jutta, pushed and jostled in the clammy sway of bodies, feels entirely alone again.

12

Trapped

17th August 1961, East Berlin

Propped up on pillows, Karin reads the note over and over, so close as to see the grain of the paper, smiling to herself. From the brief message, she determines that her family must have received her own note, and now know both where she is and that she's no longer at 'death's door'. They will come and get her, that's the main thing. Jutta promises it. And her sister won't let her down, because she never has and never will.

She knows a little of what's happening beyond her curtains, thanks to the staff who ghost in and out. 'People are having to bring stepladders out onto Potsdamer Platz so they can see over the Wall, it's gotten so high now,' one student nurse says, eyes wide with the transfer of news.

The white, unsoiled hospital walls act like the soft-spun silk of a cocoon, though it's not entirely immune to outside events; at intervals the overhead lights flicker and fizz, until the hospital generator coughs into life. On one such occasion, a porter trudges by and quips: 'Watch out, they must be working late again tonight.' When Karin asks what he means, she's alarmed to hear it's the power of the Wall searchlights sucking the nation's electricity supply. 'The picture on my television goes small,' he grumbles. 'I can't see a bloody thing.' Day by day, it's clear the Wall is going nowhere but up.

Karin hears extra snippets from the loudspeakers attached to street poles and vans roaming the streets, pushing out the official GDR line: no travel permits for East Berliners to be issued until the conclusion of a peace treaty that absorbs West Berlin into the GDR, something everybody knows will never happen. Karin is reassured that as a West Berliner she is fortunately exempt, and needs only the permit that Dr Simms has promised to apply for.

She slides a hand under the thin blanket and palms at her belly, fingering the rough, crinkled skin surrounding her scar now the dressing has been removed. It hurts, more so when she walks up and down the ward to the bathroom, not letting any of the nurses see her wince with the persistent jab of hot pokers inside. The more she walks, she reasons, the sooner they will let her home. The pain she will deal with later.

She sees Dr Simms as he enters the ward and he seems to be making a beeline for her bed. She readies a smile – she likes Dr Simms especially for taking extra efforts to reassure her, when she has no family on hand.

But he doesn't match her smile, as he often does. Is it bad news? More test results? *Oh please, no.*

'I've heard from my family,' she says quickly, in the hope that good news might override any bad. 'They're waiting for me to come home.'

He pulls up the chair next to her bed. He's never done it before, always stood, straight as an arrow. Maybe he's just tired, Karin thinks, though a sense of dread is beginning to settle like a layer of fog over the Spree.

'Well, that's good,' he says flatly. He leans over to look at her chart, clearly delaying, but Karin's earnest look prompts him to reach into the pocket of his pristine medical coat and pull out a piece of paper.

'Karin, we've had this back from the administration department,' he starts, offering up the slip. It feels like no time for manners and Karin snatches it from him, her long, lean fingers shaking as she unfolds what is effectively a permit request from the hospital. The plain, black type swims in front of her eyes, only the stamped capital letters, huge in their redness, almost pulsing at her: 'REFUSED'.

'But . . . but, you said . . . I thought it was just a formality?'

His sigh oozes regret, perhaps for his easy promise. Perhaps it's for the system he lives in and – possibly until now – wholeheartedly believed in. 'I'm sorry Karin. I really thought so too. We've appealed, questioned it, but . . .'

'Why won't they let me go home? Why?' She's furious and frightened in equal measure. 'I'm no threat to anyone, I don't even know any . . .' As her face creases with distress, the tears roll and flow and Karin clutches at her belly to prevent the pain from her convulsed sobbing. She doesn't consider herself worldly – while she's no less intelligent than Jutta, she does admit to being less curious about life beyond Berlin than her sister. But Karin is not ignorant. She listened intently at art college, absorbing the late-night political discussions in candlelit student rooms. She knows what the GDR is capable of, in protecting its borders and what they view as 'their' workforce. She's heard of the Stasi stories, the tales of people plucked from the streets of East and West Berlin by men in dark cars and taken across the

70

border, sometimes never to be seen again. She's often viewed as a wallflower, a quiet presence, but Karin Voigt is not stupid. She can predict all too well what this might mean.

Through the warp of her tears, she sees the bright, clean ward suddenly as the dankest of dungeons, feels locked in its confines. What will she do? What *can* she do? How will Jutta, Mama and Gerda reach her now?

Head bowed, Dr Simms stands and places a hand on Karin's shoulder, then seems to sense the futility of such a gesture as she rocks with distress beside him. He walks wearily towards the nurses' station and the exit.

'Watch her carefully, please,' she hears him say to the ward nurse. 'I'll be back to check on her soon.'

13

The Wall Closes In

'Quick, there's another one!' someone shouts and Jutta's eyes snap up to the windows above the throng of people lining Bernauer Strasse – firemen, reporters, television crews and ordinary, bemused Berliners like herself. The cameras swing towards the building while firemen hover under the windows, one at each corner of a large blanket, as an old woman climbs into the window space on the third floor and sits teetering on the ledge, her thin legs swaying. Even from a distance, Jutta recognises the fear etched in her features, her mind clearly wavering between one fate or another. The fate below is possible freedom mixed with potential death or injury if she misses the blanket; the one behind is a permanent life in the East, since the windows left and right have already been bricked up by Vopo police, all two thousand block residents facing eviction and forced to hand over their keys. Jutta's heart aches at the split-second choice this poor, petrified woman faces: leaving a life, and possibly a family, behind.

The crowd gasps again. The decision is made more urgent by the sudden appearance of a Vopo from behind, clawing forcibly at her limbs as she wrestles to make her leap of faith. It's a bizarre human tug-of-war, the Vopo wildly grasping the arm of her coat as she flails and tries to squirm free, one terrified eye on the ground below. Eventually, gravity wins out and the horde holds a combined breath as the woman slips from the confines of her coat and into the air. Her terrified squeal is muffled by the blanket, but still Jutta doesn't dare breathe until a hand rises to signal the woman is all right – alive at least – and then a cheer of relief goes up through the crowd. Until the next one.

Exhausted by the angst of watching, and yet compelled to witness it, Jutta peels away with a heavy sigh. It's six days since Karin's operation, and five days since the GDR's 'barrier' went up. As it gets higher, a lengthy hotchpotch of rubble and concrete slabs, the will to pull it down seems to lessen. They hear on the radio that the Allies have moved thousands of troops into West Berlin to showcase their defence of Western democracy, but with little action. Hugo comes home with news of panic-buying as West Berliners fear their walled city could be entirely cut off if the GDR restricts road access again, prompting Ruth and Gerda to patrol the streets and shop for whatever they can find, the memories of the '48 blockade and the threat of hunger still fresh in their minds.

Jutta observes it all, with her own eyes, or via the radio and newspapers, but she is consumed by waiting anxiously for news of Karin. She hovers impatiently at work in the hopes of receiving another visitor, and checks the post box at home at every opportunity, but nothing. Frantic, she tries her luck at more checkpoints, sometimes waiting to piggyback on a long line of visitors – those with foreign

14

Hope and Kindness

Karin's progress is better than expected and it soon becomes clear that she's well enough not to occupy a precious hospital bed any longer. It's perhaps a testament to her youth and fitness that she's outdone even Dr Simms' estimation of her recovery, and he arrives to tell Karin of her imminent release.

'Will there be a further appeal for my permit?' she asks.

'I'm afraid we've already tried again,' he replies gravely. 'And it's the same answer.'

'So what will I do? Where will I go . . .?' She feels the panic spiral again, the same dread that has kept her awake the past two nights, swimming in visions of herself on the street, dirty, hungry and begging, even though the propaganda tells her there is no such thing as homelessness in the people's state of the GDR.

But Dr Simms is prepared for her distress and is ready to offer some respite.

'You can come and stay with us, my wife and me,' he

says quietly. 'Our daughter is away at university and, well, we have the space. We'd welcome the company if I'm honest.'

'But won't that put you . . .' – her eyes skitter left and right – 'under the spotlight?'

He nods his understanding, but there's a smile on his lips and his normally intent, grey eyes are bright. 'Luckily, I'm too useful as a doctor for anyone to think about getting rid of me,' he says. 'Not just yet anyway.'

Karin stares through the beads of tears collecting on her lower lids, swallows and thinks she may now cry not with distress, but with gratitude for his kindness, that there are people like the Simms in the world.

'Yes, I would like that. Just until I manage to get ho . . .' Her voice cracks.

'Just until then,' he finishes for her. 'So, it's settled. I'll take you to my house tomorrow. Though I'm guessing that my nursing skills aren't anywhere as good as your Aunt Gerda's. But, luckily, my wife used to be a nurse.'

The dread in Karin subsides and she manages a laugh. The grim tableau of an itinerant life on East Berlin's streets recedes. For now, she will be all right. But what then? Will a breach in the East German will – or the Wall – ever let her through? More, perilous visions rear up in Karin's mind: of being forced to hunt for her own chink in the brick-work, scrabble in darkness over or under the wire, or risk drowning to see her family again. In the end, will it really come to that?

15

An American Comes to Town

19th August 1961, West Berlin

In her cocoon of the Charité's white walls, Karin can't be aware of the tumult happening across the city, near to where she has always called home. Jutta, though, is there to see it, balancing on the back of Hugo's bike again as he points his microphone in the direction of the crowds, capturing the excitement of those that have come to see, cheer and applaud the visiting US representative: President Kennedy has sent his second-in-command, Vice-President Lyndon B. Johnson, to pacify West Berliners with reassurances that they are supported by the might of the United States. It's a Saturday of hot sunshine between brief showers and, looking at the streams of people on the streets, Jutta tries to imagine her city only a week previously, as she had headed to the cinema and Karin in the opposite direction, with her identity card and her portfolio of designs tucked under her arm, full of hope. The colourful summer had been in full swing then. As sisters, they'd had few cares, both having decent jobs and feeling secure in the household they loved, though they had talked in private of breaking free and renting an apartment together, not daring to tell Mama or Gerda until they were sure. That ideal seems a long way off to Jutta now.

Today, the city is awash with good feeling, old women leaning over their balconies and waving white handkerchiefs at the motorcade winding its way slowly through West Berlin. Its first stop is Potsdamer Platz, where 'LBJ' and Willy Brandt walk ten metres from the patchwork grey of the Wall, young East German soldiers clambering up and taking pictures of the pair. Back on the road, the big American stands tall in the open-topped car next to Mayor Brandt and dodges the bouquets of flowers raining down upon him; if Berliners have been irritated by the Allies' muted reaction to the Wall's sudden arrival, they aren't showing it. LBJ works the crowd almost as if it's an election rally, hopping out and kissing available babies, shaking the hands of excited Berliners, who stretch to touch him as if he's bringing the city some material hope. Better that he'd brought a sledgehammer in his suitcase, Jutta muses.

Her cynicism has grown within the last seven days and her expectations of tangible Allied action are low. But, amid the rubble, the continuing barricades, the expanding, emergent carbuncle of a concrete divide, Berliners need something to hold onto, and their near hysteria at a visiting American reflects it.

She and Hugo park the bike some way from Schöneberg town hall and immerse themselves in the swaying crowd of three hundred thousand or so in the square; the early evening sun bathes one side with an orange canopy, the other half in shadow. Another divide.

Settling the masses by dipping his head and putting on his glasses, LBJ sets his voice to a sombre growl up on the plinth. 'The president wants you to know that the pledge we have given to the freedom of West Berlin and of Western access is firm.' He pauses for the roar that goes up in the heated crowd, then with a firm defiance: 'This island does not stand alone.'

When the cheering subsides, Hugo points his microphone towards the people's chatter nearby. 'So, does it mean they'll actually *do* something now?' a woman says, bobbing her baby high on her hip.

'I doubt it,' someone else responds. 'They talk well enough. They bring in more troops, more armoury. But did he say one thing about getting rid of the damn monstrosity that's killing our city? I'd rather Kennedy had sent a bulldozer.'

Hugo gestures for the two of them to leave as the numbers begin to disperse and again Jutta feels at a loss. Now is the time on a Saturday night when she and Karin would be thinking of getting dressed to go out and meet friends, for drinks and sometimes on to a party. They weren't keen club-goers, but often just sitting at the pavement cafés around Kurf'damm, surrounded by the lights and the buzz of life, was enough to amuse them for an entire evening. Jutta would tune into the different languages and accents in the air, picking up some English and French, and a little Russian, mostly idle chit-chat. She loved also to watch Karin's fingers twitching, desperate to record what she saw, as fashionable men and women paraded up and down the boulevard, small nuances that she would squirrel away and absorb into designs of her own. The boutique she worked in had sold a few of Karin's handmade dresses, with enquiries for more, and she was considering employing a sewing shop to stitch up her little collection.

'I'll start small,' she told Jutta with real conviction. 'That's the way all of the big designers progress. I will make it, Ja-Ja. I will.'

Back then, Jutta had never doubted it. Does she now? Seven days already seems like so far into the past, the longest they've ever been parted. It feels like an age. Her sister, her soulmate, is barely a few kilometres away, and yet it might as well be a million miles, at the end of a rainbow. With each day, her hope of clutching at Karin again dwindles. The city has been bisected and segregated, made smaller and turned upside down, and still it feels as if she's floating in a vast sea of nothingness, with no horizon to focus on.

Jutta looks towards the east and wonders how the residents of East Berlin and the GDR are feeling on this Saturday night. They are beyond the Iron Curtain, effectively restrained, while West Berlin becomes an unreachable and solid fortress, behind a monstrous, jagged fence.

Jutta wonders inside her head: *just which side is the prison, and who are the prisoners?*

16

A New Existence

10th November 1961, East Berlin

The noise startles her, heavy footsteps running towards her with urgency, echoing off the hospital corridors. Instantly, Karin flattens herself against the wall, trying to make herself small as she had two days before when men in long, dark coats had marched into the building and swept past her. They had stopped abruptly only a few yards on, surrounding a fellow cleaner and her newest friend, a diminutive young woman called Dora. Karin heard her protestations: 'No, I don't know anything, really I . . .' before she was swallowed in the folds of the Stasi wings and dragged away, sobbing. Karin's last vision of Dora is etched in her mind: eyes wild with sheer and utter terror.

Trembling with shock, and some relief at not being the target, it had taken a half hour for Karin's heart to stop racing. *They're not after me, they're not after me*, she chanted to herself, curled up like an animal in the dark confines of the cleaning cupboard.

Now, the footsteps are equally swift and a tall man careers

around the corner, almost skidding on the tiles she's just mopped. His features are stricken, eyes blazing, and Karin freezes as he stops abruptly.

'Which way is the men's medical ward?' he pants, and Karin points tentatively to her left.

'Along the end of the corridor, last set of doors on your left.' She can't control the tremor in her voice, but he doesn't seem to notice.

'Thank you,' and despite his hurry, he nods.

Karin is hauling her floor polisher into the storage room almost an hour later when she becomes aware of a presence behind. On turning, it's the same man, though he's much less anxious she notes. He's young and lean, handsome. More importantly, he appears friendly.

'Oh hello, can I . . . Are you lost again?' Karin ventures.

'No, no,' he says. 'I just wanted to apologise for surprising you before – you seemed quite alarmed.'

His face breaks into a warm smile and Karin wonders how his world could have improved in so short a time.

'I'm fine,' she says. 'Actually, I thought it was you who looked worried. Is everything . . . Sorry, I don't want to pry . . .' She's suddenly flushed with embarrassment, oddly conscious of her coarse nylon overall and hair held back with grips.

'It's my father,' the man nods. 'A suspected heart attack – gave us a bit of a shock. But thankfully, it's not too serious. He's just resting now.'

'That's good. I'm glad.' The pause sits between them, though the man doesn't seem inclined to move.

'Well, I'm pleased you're all right,' he says at last. 'Have a good day.'

And then he's gone, though only until the next day, when Karin is working the same corridor. The man arrives at visiting time with a small bag of fruit, making a point of saying 'Hello' on his way past and holding up the bag. 'I've eaten several pieces on the way over,' he says with an air of mischief.

'I won't tell if you don't,' Karin calls after him.

The next day she finds herself lingering a little in looking out for him, pleased when he arrives with a greeting. She's even more delighted when he stops the day after and asks if she's free to join him in a cup of coffee sometime after work. Should she? After only a few months, Karin knows that Stasi officers come in all shapes and sizes – Walter Simms and his wife, Christel, are solid East Berliners, but even they've taught her to be naturally guarded. They've been so kind in making her feel wanted, at home – if the East ever can be – taking her out to functions and introducing her to friends of their daughter. Even so, she's made only a few friends of her own – and one had been dragged away from her as quickly as they'd met.

So, Karin is all too aware of the risk, of going out with someone who seems nice, if only on the surface. But what more can the GDR wring out of her? Their Wall has already stolen her family, and any hope of the career she loved so much. What possible harm can it do?

'Yes,' she says. 'I'd love to.'

17

Happy Birthday to Me

11th December 1961, West Berlin

Jutta squats on the stool between the tall library shelves, cocooned by stacks of books and the white blanket of snow outside, quietly sobbing. Alongside the books she's filing sit several birthday cards: one from Mama, another from Gerda, Oskar and Hugo. But not Karin.

Normally, she wouldn't work on their birthday – she and Karin always take a day's holiday, either shopping or skating on the frozen ponds in the Tiergarten, followed by lunch and cocktails at the chic Hotel am Zoo. Not this year. Mama had tried her hardest, splashing out on a dress she thought her eldest daughter would like (though without Karin's eye for her taste), but the forced jollity at breakfast only bruised Jutta's heart more, and she spied her mother squirrelling away Karin's present in the hall cupboard 'for when she comes home'. Jutta imagines Ruth at her desk now, quietly weeping behind her office typewriter, keen to shed her distress before the evening birthday meal at home, with Karin's place at the table conspicuously empty.

A student approaches and begins scanning the shelves, and Jutta hastily rubs away her tears. He hovers, looks furtively around and bends towards her, whispering: 'She says happy birthday. She's well, being looked after. Don't worry.' And then he's gone, sidling between walls of books before Jutta can rouse herself from the shock and pursue him for more information. Anything. The words are fleeting, and Jutta has to repeat them over and over to remind herself the encounter was real, before they disappear like snowflakes in a flurry. *She's well*. What does that mean?

The family chews it over repeatedly that evening.

'But it's good, isn't it?' Ruth says. 'She wouldn't have sent a message if she wasn't all right, would she?' Those few words have breathed a tiny amount of colour in her cheeks. Today of all days, it's a less crippling reminder of her loss.

'It is good,' Gerda encourages. 'If someone says she's being looked after, it means she's not alone, and that's all we can hope for. Someone to help her.' Ruth nods enthusiastically and, between them, they wring every ounce of consequence from eleven simple words.

Jutta and Hugo leave the older women to their weaving of hope and retire to the roof again, despite the intense cold. It's stopped snowing at least.

'It does mean she's free and not in custody,' Hugo says, breaking their own bubble of silence above the muffled hum of street traffic below. He pinches the cigarette butt between his frozen fingers and tosses it into the small pile that's collected by his chair.

Jutta looks at him sideways. 'What does free mean? Come on, Hugo, you know as well as I do how the GDR treats Westerners, Berliners especially.'

They treat them as traitors – as East Germans who had

previously chosen to opt out and hide in a pocket of the capitalist West. Hugo will know this because he hears and reads everything across the wire at the radio station, gleans information from foreign journalists who can traverse the border with their press cards – though the press talking to ordinary East Berliners in the street is frowned on by the Stasi informants, who are never too far away. Jutta has made herself aware, dipping back into the student body of the university where she studied and now works, hanging out in the campus café and listening to the *fluchthelfers*, the radical Wall-breakers who help to plot and plan escapes. They are tenacious and have no worries, it seems, beyond not being caught themselves. More importantly, they have little fear. But Jutta has little interest in their tall tales of adventure: instead she listens intently for any titbit about real life in East Berlin. And what she hears about those like Karin isn't reassuring.

'My girlfriend is still over there,' one of a new group of tunnellers reveals one lunchtime. 'She works part-time in a state shop. One of her colleagues used to work in the West, has a degree in engineering, but they refuse to let her study anymore or work as an engineer. They're apparently paranoid about sabotage. So, instead, this woman is left stacking shelves, as punishment for choosing to favour the West.'

Jutta's heart had creased. Her sister has never been afraid of toil, had worked in a café all the way through her time at art college, but the idea that Karin's creativity, her hankering to design, is being thwarted cuts her to the core.

Getting her out, though, carries its own risks – not least the East's determined 'shoot-to-kill' policy. Only that morning, Jutta had stared at the *Morgenpost* headline of yet more loss on the Wall: Dieter Wohlfahrt, just twenty, shot while helping others escape. She read the details of his death with true sadness, partly because such news is now all too frequent; this poor boy not the first but the tenth to lose his life, thanks to the Wall.

The East German defence of their 'protection barrier' is zealous but sometimes haphazard, while the people's will is determined and creative; in the first month alone after the Wall goes up, the successful escapes totalled four hundred and seventeen, though the attempts are likely to number many more. Some throw themselves at the Wall like a bull in a china shop, crashing through the jumble of breeze-blocks in heavy trucks, with mixed success. Others swim the River Spree cutting through Berlin, or the Teltow canal to the south, and a clutch have made an odorous journey through the sewers. Only the week before, one desperate train worker drove his scheduled passenger train full pelt towards the barriers of a border station, with twenty-four making the escape, including some family members. The first of many tunnels is already up and running. Berliners are nothing if not determined.

But the consequence of failure is painfully clear to Jutta. In the East, they hear that hundreds − possibly thousands − are being imprisoned by the Stasi for long periods, since *Republikflucht*, or fleeing the Republic, is now officially a state crime in the GDR.

Each senseless death and separation makes her think of Karin, of every family's loss and bereavement, but the world doesn't seem to share her pain. And yet Berlin does remain a political focus: over six days in October 1961, the walled enclave saw the world teetering on the edge of nuclear disaster, the consequence of another diplomatic spat over border access. Soviet tanks were deployed, met in equal numbers by American military hardware at Checkpoint

Charlie, only feet apart, with their engines snorting fumes on one another. Each side inched towards the border – and all-out conflict. With bated breath, nations around the globe watched a high-risk game of poker being played out, neither government willing to give an inch. At stake was a full-scale war, possibly nuclear.

Finally, and when the world could hold its breath no longer, John F. Kennedy and Soviet leader Nikita Khrushchev decided a small checkpoint was not worthy of a global catastrophe and resolved their differences over the phone, sending the tanks into reverse and trundling away. Alongside the rest of the world, Jutta sighed huge relief.

That's why Karin's escape – if they get anywhere near planning it – needs to be foolproof.

'Hey, let's go in – it's freezing out here,' Hugo says, plunging into Jutta's deep and dour thoughts. He holds out a hand to pull her up. 'And cheer up for goodness sake – it's your birthday.'

'Yes,' she murmurs. 'Happy bloody birthday to me.'

18

'Happy Birthday to You'

11th December 1961, East Berlin

The alcohol makes her happy at first, slightly giggly and glad to be alive. Karin has never drunk champagne, and although Otto admits it isn't the best, it's still streets ahead of the cheap, fizzy Rotkäppchen wine East Germans seem to swallow heartily. But as they head towards her tiny flat after an evening out, the bubbles fall suddenly flat, causing clouds to mass above Karin. Dark clouds.

Inside, Otto examines a card from Walter and Christel and their generous present of a sewing machine, albeit one that's second-hand and a little rusty. Walter's other gift – begging a last favour to deliver a message to Jutta – is not so visible.

'They think a lot of you, don't they?' Otto says. 'I bet they're nice people.'

'They are,' Karin says, and it's then she can't help the choke in her throat – with the day, the void of Jutta's card, which she knows would have been sent if at all possible – but also the Simms' unending generosity, and the fact that now she has someone to celebrate with. Otto Kruger. The man who had careered across the hospital corridor and whose loyal, heartfelt character is proving a big attraction. It's taken only two or three dates, of coffee, dinner and then cinema, for her to realise he's something special. And she thinks – hopes – he feels it too.

Still, there's a great hole in her heart, and the tears push forth for what she's missing today: Mama, Gerda, Hugo and Oskar. And, most of all, Jutta. Otto knows she has a sister, but for some strange reason she can't admit to him that Jutta is her twin. The other half, the reflection of her. It's something Karin feels compelled to contain, from Walter and Christel too. Jutta's mirror image she keeps safe. For her eyes only.

Otto hears her sadness, sees the twist of her mouth. 'Hey, come here,' he comforts, pulling her into his torso, where her head only just reaches his chin. 'I'm sure you'll see them soon.'

He can't be sure, of course, and neither does he make excuses for the regime, but she's glad of the words, that he's trying. And she has plenty to be grateful for: her role at the Charité, a job Walter managed to secure after her convalescence; her own flat, albeit damp and tiny, plus the friendship of the Simms. And now Otto. The frustration is ever present, of writing endlessly to the apartment at Schöneberg and hoping that just one of her letters will reach them, then the crushing sight of an empty post hole every day. The fear of being plucked from the street and the crime of being a West Berliner have become things she might just learn to live with. And against Otto's solid chest, she has never felt safer.

He reaches into his pocket, pulls out something small and wrapped and offers it to her. 'This seems all the more appropriate now I've seen your other present.'

When Karin unwraps it, the tears spring again. It's a simple, hand-stitched pin cushion in the shape of a ladybird, bright and beautiful, and she imagines he could have picked it out only with her in mind.

'Oh it's perfect,' she breathes, palming at her wet cheeks.

'Cheer up,' he says, stroking her hair, his fingers reaching down to wipe away her sadness. 'Not every day is your birthday, is it?'

'No, it isn't,' Karin breathes into the rough wool of his jumper. *Thank goodness.*

19

In Between

1961–1963, Berlin

Inevitably, as it did in the first world war and again in the second, life goes on in Berlin. There is worldwide opposition but no sledgehammer, no physical pawing at the rough concrete blocks. In time, even the East Germans cannot pretend that their 'anti-fascist protection barrier' is anything other than 'the Wall', although they continue to defend it to the world both politically as well as physically.

The initial fury from the West German side flares and fizzles to small pockets of opposition, consisting of underground operations rather than all-out defiance.

Jutta watches her fellow Berliners with pride in the way they carry on. They've seen off Nazism, war, firestorms, invasion and famine, their city reduced to rubble rebuilt time and again. The increasingly fortified Wall divides but does not flatten the spirit of the people, though the international language slowly morphs: the 'East' comes to mean the grim austerity across the grey partition, and the 'West' represents freedom and democracy in a cosmopolitan ghetto

– access to the latest clothes and Western music, the liberty to stroll into a hotel bar and order whatever you want, dance the night away to the latest hits from America or England. Like most Berliners, Jutta hopes this simplified description does not apply to the people, or the Berlin spirit, but inevitably it creeps into the general psyche.

For the Voigts and the Zelles, there is life – there has to be – but loss too. For a few months, Jutta makes regular trips to the town hall and Herr Fleisch for advice, a little comfort and to fill in her requisite form for access across the border. Sometimes she goes just to talk, or to pluck at the box of tissues he keeps on his desk. He's always kind and endlessly forbearing, never falsely encouraging, although his hair recedes a little more with each visit. The form always comes back with the same red stamp of refusal, until Herr Fleisch reveals he can no longer submit any forms. All West Berliners are henceforth to apply for a permit or visa at one of the 'travel agencies' the GDR proposes to set up in West Berlin, except the Western authorities won't allow such agencies on their soil since it means recognising the communist state as legitimate. It's a classic chicken-and-egg situation, with people – real people like Karin – stuck in the middle.

It makes Jutta both sad and awash with fury in equal measure, and she spends many hours either crying or shouting her frustrations to Hugo up on their rooftop. Downstairs, in the apartment, she does her best to keep it under wraps, though when she does confide in Gerda about yet another refusal, she can't help noticing that Oskar shrinks further into the armchair, turning away and busying himself with the radio dial. Over time, his face slowly becomes as grey as his undershirt, and Jutta is driven to ask Hugo: 'Is your father ill?'

'Depressed rather than ill,' he mumbles, between puffs of his cigarette into the chill rooftop air, as they sit wrapped in jackets against the harsh winter. Hugo has grown professionally since the Wall, gained respect for his daring and guile in his reports to the radio station. Strangely, it's been good for him, but these days he's out more than he was before. 'I suspect Papa had quite a bit of business over in the East, and that means he's lost a lot of contacts.'

Night after night, as she lies in her bed, staring at the smooth empty covers opposite, Jutta hears the whispered quarrels between Oskar and Gerda over money, Gerda berating her husband and his whinnying defences of 'But what can I do, Gerd? Do you want me to dig a tunnel for business?' Having virtually retired, Gerda is forced to pick up more work as a midwife to keep the apartment functioning. Deflated and in her own deep depression, Ruth tolerates the dull office job she hates, with too much time to sit and dwell over Karin's fate.

Of course, they contact the Charité frequently, but all enquiries are met with a resolute 'We can't discuss former patients.' The British couple, fellow journalists in Hugo's circle, have been ejected from East Berlin for 'anti-communist actions', and quit the city entirely when their reporting rights are curbed. Lucien and his valued foreign passport has gone elsewhere too. All avenues are at a dead end, it seems, leaving them with no clue as to where Karin is or what she's doing.

Jutta dreams of finding just one contact, a glimmer of Karin's whereabouts, which would allow her to act. The university group she's ingratiated herself into has passport holders who can apply for a permit and cross over to deliver messages: if only she knew where Karin was, she might begin to sow the seeds of an escape.

The tunnelling and sewer routes Jutta discounts immediately, since Karin suffers from crippling claustrophobia, but there are alternatives. Some groups move fake Western passports over the border, with the escapees taking a circuitous path out of East Berlin, crossing the border into Denmark and then into West Germany. It's successful for a while, until the GDR tightens up entry and exit visas and that method of escape is swiftly capped off.

The extremes are to be applauded – one couple successfully swims the Havel River near Potsdam, towing their eighteen-month-old baby in a bathtub. The runners and jumpers continue, but those reckless attempts are dragged sharply into focus by eighteen-year-old Peter Fechter in 1962, who chances his luck with a friend in making a run for it. He loses. Shot several times by border guards, he lies limp and dying in the channel of land between the two barriers known as the 'death strip', the Wall having multiplied, grown thicker and higher with each passing month. His cries for help echo off the brickwork, with desperate West Berliners only yards away on the other side of the divide. For an agonising hour Fechter lies bleeding, until East German police scoop up his flaccid body and take him away. The hour is enough for worldwide press and television to record the tragedy and, once again, Berlin's ugly scar is under the world's spotlight. Fechter becomes an icon, an unwitting martyr, and there are violent protests and a series of small explosions on the Western side to mark the anger.

For Jutta, the sad demise of Peter Fechter, along with the other escapees, serves as further proof that any attempt to free Karin has to be watertight. Nothing is ever risk-free, but as much as they want her back, it has to be in one piece.

Depression is not in Jutta's nature, but she finds herself existing in a kind of half-life, even when Irma, being a good friend, does her utmost to keep her included in their circle. Still, Jutta avoids the Kurf'damm when she can, although sometimes it's hard to resist. One day in late September of '62, she is sitting with Irma under the red and white pavement canopy of Kranzler's and glimpses a woman walk by, in a simple but distinctive shift dress, edged in a deep purple. It's unmistakable. Jutta has seen it hundreds of times, hanging in their wardrobe. From the back, she sees the woman has short, bobbed dark hair, and the same build and gait as Karin. Could it be? She might have cut her hair. To Irma's surprise, Jutta leaps up and bounds forward, grasps desperately at the woman's shoulders, causing her to spin.

'Hey, what are you doing?' she cries with alarm, instinctively jerking away from Jutta.

Same build, same walk, but it's not Karin.

'I'm so sorry, I thought you were . . .' Jutta stammers.

The woman stands aghast, affronted, but still doesn't move. She sees the distress of her would-be attacker and is either curious or blindsided.

'. . . someone I knew,' Jutta goes on, feeling tears butting up against her frustration. 'I recognised my sister's dress.'

The woman looks more confused than anything, until Jutta explains it's an outfit her sister made by hand: her own design, a one-off.

'I got it in that boutique near Wertheim's,' she pouts with irritation. 'It is mine. I bought it.'

Of course, it's the boutique where Karin worked, one of those designs she proudly placed on the peg to sell, with her own label hand-sewn into the collar: '*Ka-Ja*'. If it ever took off, they were going to be partners, with Jutta handling the business side of things, using her gift for languages in dealing with the 'huge' exports they would inevitably have. Karin always emphasised the 'huge' part, beaming widely at the dream. The sudden, startling memory shifts the tears to just under Jutta's lids, barely contained, and the woman moves awkwardly away. Jutta stands in the busy thorough-fare of colourful Berlin, solitary in a sea of bodies, with only the faint tweak of the bond between the sisters as twins for comfort. As days blur into months and months into years, the thread appears thinner, sometimes a mere filament as their time apart goes on. But it's still there. She won't let that go. And she's certain Karin won't either.

As for the Wall, while families continue to fracture, it only gains strength, fortified by metal and materials, driven by the GDR's determination to corral their precious work-force and repel the contagion of capitalism, punctuated with watchtowers and armed guards, whose view is improved by powerful searchlights, ready to set loose the highly trained dogs on any escapees. And like so many incursions on Berlin in the past – swastikas, Stormtroopers and bombs – it becomes strangely normal after a time. Jutta often stands and watches her fellow Berliners walk by without a second glance, skirting the barrier as if it's always been there. The tourists come and go, they look and peer over the Wall to another land, at people who squint their eyes back at the West. They comment on the atrocity and they go away again. But still there are no bulldozers, no widespread will to tear it down. The Wall endures.

PART TWO

20

The President Comes to Town

26th June 1963, West Berlin

Another day, another year. Another president. If Berlin had managed a show of adulation for the vice-president of the USA, they go all out for the head man himself. John isn't the first Kennedy to visit Berlin; the year before brothers Robert and Edward had stood on a platform and stared over the divide, with 'Teddy' Kennedy venturing into the East and marvelling at a line of shoppers and the shortage of apples to buy. But John F. is the darling – the one whose presence matters – lending far more kudos than the British Prime Minister Macmillan or French leader De Gaulle, both of whom have made a point of staying away. Berlin isn't forgotten if JFK comes to town.

Jutta is here again on the square facing Schöneberg town hall, compressed within an even bigger crowd than for the last American dignitary, losing Hugo to the swell of bodies almost as soon as they arrive. For a few moments, she tracks his microphone, taped to a broom handle pilfered from the apartment and which now bobs above the crowd. But it's soon swallowed and she's alone again in the sea of expectant, upturned faces.

Early news reports suggest almost three-quarters of West Berlin's two million residents have turned out to welcome America's golden boy on his whistle-stop tour – at the airport, on the tickertape motorcade that inched down the main avenues, at Checkpoint Charlie and the Brandenburg Gate, its columns still resolutely behind the Wall. But judging by the crush, Jutta thinks most of them are here on Rudolph Wilde Platz. There are people squashed into every surrounding window and balcony, the flat, grey apartment blocks dripping colourful flags, so that if you pivot full circle the sight is that of an overdressed Christmas tree. Only it's eighty degrees in what little shade there is.

She catches traces of body sweat in her nostrils, the dedication of some who camped overnight to gain the best spot. For almost an hour the excitement ebbs – Chinese whispers of his arrival making heads crane upwards towards the large platform where he will speak in front of a bank of microphones – and recedes, settling and simmering with an occasional waft of breeze. By the time the platform begins to fill with dignitaries, Mayor Willy Brandt among them, the atmosphere is electric. Deafening chants of 'J-F-K, J-F-K . . .' fill the air, loud enough that the echoes are carried across the city and over the concrete – the GDR not yet able to build a Wall dense enough to deflect the noise of determined adulation.

Then the riotous cheer to signal his actual presence. Standing on tiptoe, Jutta can just about see the man they have invested so much faith in. Has she that belief? In quieter moments, no, though she feels herself swept along by the day's zeitgeist and his undeniable charisma; he's all hair, looking down with his big, white smile. Berliners need this. They need him.

Finally, finally, the crowd quietens enough for him to speak. His words are all about freedom, of course, and divisions between the free and communist world; there are those who say we can work with communism, he suggests, making eye contact with the huge assembly and pausing briefly as only a statesman and speechmaker can. 'Let them come to Berlin,' he asserts firmly. The people go wild, whistling and waving furiously, and some of the elders in the audience can't help but notice an uncomfortable quiver zip through them; they recall the last man to attract such frenzied worship on these streets. It didn't turn out so well for Berlin, Germany or the world then.

But for Jutta, who has only scant memories of the Führer and war, there's something else that inflates a large ball in her throat, pushing her tears up and out onto her hot cheeks as JFK reminds everyone of what the Wall has done to the people in its shadow, in 'dividing husbands and wives and brothers and sisters'. Not that she – or anyone – needs reminding, but when it's said by arguably the most influential president of the free world to date, it hits home. And hard. She feels winded, could easily sag towards the floor if it weren't for the tight knit of bodies she's sandwiched between. Her sniffs and sobs are swallowed back by the noise.

Buoyed by his own wave of fervour, JFK saves the best until last. Leaning hard on the lectern, full hair blowing in a timely breeze, he unleashes his master stroke: 'Today, in the world of freedom, the proudest boast is *Ich bin ein Berliner*,' he pronounces.

The entire square erupts, a thousand flashbulbs popping and press men frantically scribbling JFK's gift of a quote, as if they already know it will go straight from their note-books into the annals of history. Amid the deafening chant of 'Ken-Ne-Dy! Ken-Ne-Dy!', grown men are weeping next to Jutta, so entranced that they instantly forgive his awkward pronunciation. And all she can think is: *Karin would love this*. She would be the one cheering, waving a banner, pulling her sister through the crowds towards the front and swaying with the applauding acolytes. Can Karin hear this? Doubtless even the East German politicians are unable to close their ears to this tidal wave of sound. Earlier, Jutta had heard rumours of the East Germans erecting hoardings near the place where Kennedy went to observe the Wall, so that the GDR's citizens could not see the man they may or may not glimpse on television. But surely, Karin knows it, hears it, senses it; no barrier can corral enthusiasm, passion and the sheer tumult of liberty. Not forever. Can it?

21

The Noise of Freedom

26th June 1963, East Berlin

Karin pushes her head down, engaged in her task, but the noise bleeds into her brain. You can't help hearing it — there's nothing distinctive, and no words to hook onto, only a resonant beat to the hum of noise from the direction of the Wall, almost a thumping. A rhythmic incantation of adoration.

She knows all too well what it is, although they aren't supposed to, as state television refuses to acknowledge the visit of a serving United States president only a few miles away. But anyone brave enough to have a radio tuned into the West Berlin RIAS station hears the detail. Through the window one floor below, workers are clustered at the back entrance of the boiler room — she can just glimpse them shielded by the huge, metal refuse bins, muffling the noise of a tiny transistor held in someone's hand. No one has sparked up a cigarette, as they usually do in their breaks, so as not to send smoke signals and be caught by one of the managers. Not today, of all days, and not with a radio in their midst. Part of Karin wants to go and join the group, but for the other part – the bigger portion – it's too painful. She knows for certain two of the people she most loves in the world will be there; in days of old Jutta, Hugo and she would have gone together, as they did to any major gathering or rally. She would have been the one to urge them to go, spinning wildly in the sunshine, almost drunk on the atmosphere, on the prospect of people making change. In her world. Her Berlin.

She's certain too, that while Jutta is there in the square heaving with people, she will be thinking of the two of them together, as sisters and best friends. And Jutta will be sad. For her part, Karin has harboured an odd sensation throughout the day, something tweaking inside her, pulling, but she can't explain what or how it makes her feel, only that it unnerves her. And makes her sad, too.

In that moment, the sunshine and the day's heat combine to cause irritation too. She's especially fretful. She pushes back the fringe of her hair with annoyance, her skin prickly with sweat underneath, and sets to her task again.

Why can't they make contact? After the initial lock-down, every avenue was closed, every method the hospital tried capped off. It was the same for everyone then – hundreds of families prised apart in one night by that rapidly growing beanstalk of the Wall. Now, almost two years on, there is a stuttering passage of post from East to West. She understands that Jutta and Mama may not know where she is, but why is there no reply to the scores of letters she's sent home? Everyone knows each envelope is steamed open and screened in the bowels of some government building, but there's nothing in what she writes that the Stasi could possibly object to – they are merely 'How are you? I'm fine, don't worry' messages.

Once a flow of letters is established, Karin is sure they can branch out with some form of code, confident Jutta would catch on very quickly. Because she has so much to tell them.

Karin hears it again as she works, that thrum from the side of the city where the day always seems to set in an amber glow, as if the entire land over the Wall is bathed in a magical radiance. She sometimes watches the fervent Easterners, the true communists and believers, scoffing at the golden hue, as if nature itself is conspiring to create capitalist propaganda, that the streets are paved with gold. 'They'll see one day,' she heard one old man mutter in the shopping queue. 'It might look like a honeybee haven, but really it's a wasps' nest waiting to turn. Better here – at least we don't have to fight for our bread.'

'I like not having to fight,' the woman next to him had countered, 'but do we really have to queue so long for it?'

And that glow from across the Wall, to Karin it's still alluring, despite everything that's happened, her survival since the operation, her life now with Otto. She's grateful, maybe even happy at times, but to her the West holds its halo aloft and she remains hopelessly enticed. It's where her heart – or at least a portion of it – rests: in Mama, Gerda, Hugo and, of course, Jutta. The other portion? Well, that's more complicated.

22

A Chip in the Concrete

26th June 1963, West Berlin

The square takes an age to empty; clusters of people linger long after the star has left the podium, not wanting to allow their joy and enthusiasm to dissipate, needing to hold on tight to that feeling of being centre stage and not forgotten.

Jutta feels the opposite: she wants to be alone with her thoughts. Besides, there's no hope of finding Hugo now, even as the crowds seep away. She finds herself walking east, pulled by something inexplicable, yet which feels strangely like a magnet, encouraged on her way by an occasional warm wind that blusters along the street, sending flecks of abandoned rice, flour and tickertape flurrying like a summer snowstorm.

Oddly, Jutta finds herself being reeled in, having avoided the Wall for the past year or more. In the first six months after Karin was . . . she wants to say 'captured', but it feels more like 'incarcerated', she was there all the time, hating the sight of its presence yet hopelessly drawn. She spent hours staring through the wire in segments not yet fortified, or hovering on a nearby balcony of a friend, in the hopes of catching just a glimpse of Karin, their strand surely strong enough that her sister would know to come. Each time, disappointment. Was Karin even looking towards the Wall? Jutta realised it was becoming something of an obsession when the same border guards recognised her pleading face, shaking their heads with pity and a little humour: 'Here again, Fräulein? We'll have to give you a special spot in the queue.'

She shared the gnawing hunger with no one and it came, eventually, to eat away at her. Even Herr Fleisch moved on to a different department. Postal services between the two sides of the Wall were slowly and haphazardly reinstated, but there was never any reply to the hopeful letters she addressed to Karin via the Charité, alongside the mystery of why Karin didn't send any letters of her own to the apartment. Even now, a black and seemingly infinite void remains. Jutta determines their sibling strand will endure, that the fibres cannot snap, but equally it's been weakened with too much pushing and pulling.

Once or twice, she almost gained enough courage to approach the *fluchthelfers* at the university for help in finding Karin, but she knows that help doesn't come free. The group's unappointed leader, Axel, had been holding court at the table with growing confidence and Jutta found hers shrinking. For her own sake, she decided to let go a little. And so, her trips to the Wall ceased, and she concentrated instead on keeping hope alive.

Now, the occasion and the swell of human faith – perhaps even JFK himself – is propelling Jutta once again towards the rough breeze-block divide, though to what purpose she doesn't know. To stare at its ugliness? As she walks amid a city still settling from the day's events, she convinces herself this will be one last time. She has to get on with life; she has to live. Karin would want that. *Does* want that.

It takes her some time to effectively cross the city on foot, skirting the top end of Tempelhof airport, but she's always loved walking and it doesn't seem tiring.

There it is: the spiky crest of the barricade comes into view at the top of Harzer Strasse, one of those residential streets almost bisected like the ill-fated Bernauer Strasse, but not quite. Here, the square apartment blocks hug rather than sit on directly on the Wall, with only a pavement between the front doors and the grey, pitted concrete, so that windows above the first floor look out directly onto the wire and the vista of the death strip. They could even wave at the border guards at a nearby watchtower if they so wished. Only they don't, of course; the Wall is an unwelcome intruder and the stares over the space remain sombre.

Jutta stands, walks a few yards and stops again, unsure of what she feels. Not the same magnetism as in those early months, to be near it, as if it meant she was closer to Karin. It's more of an overwhelming sadness that she can't share this day with her sister. That they're not allowed. And all because of this stupid war between halves of the same country, in what the wider public see not as deep differences in political ethos, but as a petty quarrel between infantile men. It makes her think back to the rows she and Karin had as children. They shared everything, but sisters inevitably fight, giving rise to ridiculous squabbles, name-calling, vicious words being traded and even, on one occasion, clumps of Jutta's hair being pulled out, to their mother's utter horror. But their rancour never lasted (even after the hair episode) and it wasn't long before they were apologising and snuggling up in one bed, arms curled around each other. That's the life of a twin. Just occasionally you can't live with them, but mostly it's the opposite.

What they never, ever did – even during the fiercest of battles – was build a wall between themselves. That would have been going too far.

Drawn ever closer to the Wall, Jutta turns the corner towards an area of abandoned buildings, their windows bricked up. Like many of the dwellings where the Wall simply ploughed through indiscriminately, they are waiting to be demolished, to make way for more transparency across the space and better vision for the Wall guards. A small clump of what look to be garages attached to a solitary, two-storey house sits in the turn of the Wall, no doubt destined for the same fate as the terraces of Bernauer Strasse – a date with the bulldozer. But for now, the red bricks adorned in razor wire form the west side of the barricade.

A few yards on from the scatter of buildings, Jutta inches towards a peephole that's been gouged into the crumbly mortar between bricks. Glancing up to the tip of the watchtower to make sure the guards can't see her, she bends down and puts her eye to the tiny hole, which has been bored into the concrete at child height, small enough not to be detected from the other side. There's nothing but grey in her sights, a small slit next to a ground-level building, a sliver of East Berlin that perhaps relatives might stand in and be seen. But that's all they can do – be seen. No contact, nothing worthwhile.

Jutta turns tail, intent now on taking her unsatisfied curiosity back home, though her steps are heavy and slow. It's a part of the city she's been to only once or twice in her life, and so she can't make the comparison of how it was before. She tries to imagine who lived in the red-brick house pierced by the Wall – the garage owners perhaps? Maybe once it was a thriving business, until it simply got in the way of GDR progress. She stops alongside the wire, which closely wraps the brickwork like a Christmas parcel, just thinking – daydreaming almost – when she hears a sound: a faint but high-pitched mewling. She casts about for a cat, her heart lurching with the horror of it being caught on the wire and having to disentangle the animal, painfully, and tend to its bloody fur. But it seems to be coming from inside, and the only 'inside' in this mini-wasteland are these buildings.

There it is again. Not in pain as such, but constant. Hungry. She pushes her ear as close to the brickwork as she can without catching her hair on the barbs. Yes, it's inside the building. Trapped perhaps? Cats are known to manoeuvre themselves into the smallest of holes without a thought as to how to get out. Especially if the building is shored up firmly on the other side.

Jutta scans the brickwork high and low and her eye settles on a small breach near to the ground, ample for a dog to squeeze through, or maybe an urban fox. A large enough animal could have displaced the crumbling bricks, bit by bit, and slipped between the wire. There's something dark behind, perhaps wood, helping to camouflage the existence of a hole unless you're up close.

The mewling continues: needy and desperate. Unlike Karin, Jutta has never been soppy over animals, but she can't ignore suffering of any kind. And that's what it sounds like to her. She scrabbles in her bag for an elastic band and scrapes back her hair into a rough ponytail. Checking there's no one in sight, and that the Wall guards can't see, she crouches down, bends up the razor wire firmly and care-fully, hooking several strands together over a nail, and eases her head and slight shoulders through the hole, pushing against the wood. It gives way with some force, though Jutta feels the coarse brick scraping at her bare arms and chafing against her thin dress material; she imagines soon having the battered kneecaps of a child, but the constant mewling keeps her going.

The brickwork is double thickness and has a layer of plaster behind, but it's not a tunnel as such – Jutta gives a forceful shove and the wood yields, enough for her to crawl through and into the room, where she discovers it's actually a small cabinet butting up against the inside wall. The mewling stops instantly as she replaces the cabinet again, and there's a shuffling to her left. She's in the kitchen of the old house, with signs of habitation, though not recent. Scouting around in the dimming light, Jutta finds the source of the squeaking: a cat, along with three kittens – a family of mini grey and black-striped tigers. Wide-eyed, wary and staring, the mother looks up with alarm, but firmly refuses to leave her babies.

'Hey there, how are you doing?' Jutta bends and holds out a hand for the mama to investigate, rummaging in her bag for the ham roll left over from lunch. It's squashed in the paper bag but the mother leaps on the meat, pushing it towards her babies, purring loudly. Jutta has no idea if cats eat bread, but she places it in the makeshift nest anyway.

Leaving the cats with their spoils, she picks her way around the bottom of the house. The furnished rooms are frozen in time, the family clearly having packed their personal possessions in a frenzy, and there's still evidence of their lives – cupboards half-filled with tinned food, a single, lost shoe in one corner and a small toy car on the shelf, which surely must be missed.

Jutta is nervy and on edge, being in the cavity of the

113

Wall itself, but her curiosity is too heightened to leave immediately. For some inexplicable reason she thinks of *The Lion, the Witch and the Wardrobe*, and the suspense of reading as Lucy pushes through the back of the wardrobe for the first time. If she's thinking in fables, any door in this house might open onto an entirely different universe. Except, in this world, each one is likely barred, bricked or plastered up against any breach. The front door is – bricks just visible through the opaque glass panel – but there's a side door from the kitchen, and she's surprised to find the handle turns and it opens with a small nudge. The doorway leads to a sizeable garage, more than a domestic car space but big enough for a small business, hinted at by a pungent odour of grease and engine oil. Again, she thinks of the family and the livelihood they've had to leave behind, the throb and rev of Volkswagen Beetles with their rear engines exposed, the mechanic father washing his hands after a day's work and joining his family for dinner. Another family torn, and she wonders if they retreated to the West or were propelled Eastwards on that fateful day. There's what looks like a small office leading off the garage, and although it's almost dark with the boarded windows, Jutta can see enough to feel her way in, half with her eyes, the rest with the pads of her fingers, all on alert.

In the darkness, her eye is caught by something. Beyond the office, at the end of what looks like a dingy tunnel, and in the direction of the German Democratic Republic, she sees it: small, circular and not in the least bright, given the natural dimming of the day. But it's there.

A chink of light.

Jutta leaves the partially satisfied cat family and goes to squeeze back through the hole, recoiling swiftly on seeing the wheels of a bicycle whizz past, gasping as air is stolen from her lungs. Listening intently for any more traffic, she propels herself, heart racing as the top of her head hits the air on the West side, praying no one happens to be looking in the direction of the garage complex and witnessing the near-comical sight of a woman being birthed from a hole in the brickwork. She replaces the wire, dusts herself off and finds the nearest grocery store, knowing that a return into the Wall is foolhardy, and yet unable to bear the thought of starving animals. Under cover of near darkness, and taking advantage of a broken street light, she hurries back in through the hole, to fresh surprise from the mother cat, who laps up the extra food and milk.

Back out in the quiet of Harzer Strasse, Jutta finally breathes. She strides towards the nearest tram stop, wiping the plaster dust from her eyelashes while smiling to herself. She's eager to reach home and the solitude of her bedroom. She needs to think, alone and without interruption. Her mind is racing, alive with possibilities. She's on fire.

23

A Glitch

27th June 1963, West Berlin

Jutta's night is restless and filled with dreamlike fantasies. Tiny circles of light feature in every scenario – on waking, one episode she's able to recall distinctly is a tiny flaw in a children's cardigan Gerda once knitted, identical to Karin's. As much as she'd tried to resist, Jutta had picked at the wool on the sleeve, scratching at it like an itch until it grew larger and more obvious. She marvelled in how it opened up like a sunburst, the solid weave simply falling away to nothing. It was Karin who'd saved her from Gerda's hurt and wrath, finding scraps of the wool and expertly darning the hole, deft with a needle even then.

Now, it's that process of the opening getting larger – being *made* bigger – that she thinks about intently. The light at the end of the corridor clearly came from outside. However dim, it had that quality of daylight, and not an artificial bulb. But from where? Her curiosity is at full stretch, though she tries to temper it with common sense.

It might simply lead to the no-man's land of the Wall and the dreaded death strip.

But what if it doesn't?

Hugo is cutting slices of dark brown bread as she hurries into the kitchen.

'Hey, what happened to you yesterday? I looked for you after the rally.'

She tests the heat of the coffee pot with her hand, and pours herself a cup. 'I thought you needed to work, so I went for a walk and a coffee.'

'Hmm, yeah I suppose I was busy,' he says. 'It was amazing, wasn't it? I got some great audio from the crowd.' He slants his head to one side. 'Do you think what he said will make a difference? Shift the GDR's thinking?'

Jutta is surprised he's asking, and with such naivety. 'Honestly? No, Hugo, I don't. I think it was great to watch, great for Berlin and our profile in not being forgotten. But no. Look at the Wall: every day they build it higher. They've no intention of taking it down. If anything, after JFK's words they'll be slapping on a bit more cement and concrete today.'

She realises her tone is petulant, and it shouldn't be directed at Hugo. She gets up, scraping her chair, and heads towards the bathroom. She has no idea where her cynicism or the thinly veiled anger comes from but it silences her cousin, who simply munches on his bread in deep thought.

All Jutta can think about is that hole, an aperture that might, if pushed, get bigger. And she's already proven to be adept at squeezing through holes.

Jutta and Ruth walk half the way to work together, Ruth mildly interested in hearing of JFK's showmanship and the feeling among Berliners on the streets, even though she'd

117

heard his entire speech on the radio. But there's no hope in her voice that it will change anything, enough to see Karin. That's all the politics any of them are able to focus on.

'So, I'll see you at dinner later,' Ruth says, kissing Jutta on the cheek as they go their respective ways.

'Oh, um . . . I said I'd meet Irma after work, and I'll probably grab something to eat with her,' Jutta says. It's a split-second excuse, her subconscious taking the reins.

'Oh well, don't be too late,' Ruth says. 'I've hardly seen you lately.'

'I won't. Love you, Mama.'

The day at work drags, inevitably. She can think of nothing else but that blasted ring of light. One minute she tells herself it's fool's gold; in another second, the prized pot at the end of the rainbow. One thing Jutta knows for certain: she is unable to keep away from Harzer Strasse. *It's the only chance we have.*

She lingers in a café after work before taking a tram south-east towards Treptower, where she buys a small torch and some tins of cat food. Then, she walks to Harzer Strasse, arriving after the work crowds have cleared, and likely while plenty of residents in the area are holed up eating their supper. It is quiet again, although this time Jutta is naturally more guarded in approaching her destination; she wants to look directionless rather than suspicious, to stop anyone wondering why a well-dressed woman is loitering in a near wasteland.

The portal looks unchanged and she hovers for a minute, her back tight into the concrete of a half-fallen wall opposite, its cool, porous texture a relief against the heat of her anxiety. In an instant, she launches towards the disguised opening, levering up the wire and then bending down onto her knees, pushing her bag through like a snowplough and the cabinet with it, her body slipping in more easily this time.

Inside, it's unchanged, thankfully, and the mother cat seems pleased to see her, looking up from tending her babies and purring. Jutta rifles in the kitchen drawers for a tin-opener, wondering how many mouths it had helped to feed before 1961 and abandonment. But she can't be distracted by sentiment, and the mama cat is soon feasting away.

Jutta steps into the darkened corridor beyond the garage's office, switching on the torch but keeping the beam directed towards the floor, wary of any eagle-eyed border guards within sight of the house. It's just enough light to allow her to dodge the debris underfoot where some of the plaster has peeled away. She inches forward, wincing at the sound of her footsteps, terrified that a line of Vopos or Stasi could be just feet away, hearing every crack or crunch.

The pinprick brightness ahead grows larger with each step, and she stops, listening out for any reaction. There's none. Suddenly, she's in front of it – up close the light isn't rounded, but a two-inch square pushing through wooden boards, which cover the glazed top half of a door. Warily, Jutta puts an eye to the white light, seeing more glare beyond: not the grey concrete of the death strip or even the street, but what looks to be another room or corridor with a larger beam flooding into it.

Surely that opens directly onto the Wall's inner strip? It must do. She braces herself for inevitable disappointment. Still, it's human nature and innate curiosity that makes Jutta try the door handle, which gives with a firm push. There's no breath of open air, though she looks left and right before bobbing her head swiftly into the void. It's another abandoned room, perhaps once a small warehouse built onto the garage, this time empty save for a pile of pallets and the sweepings of a once used but neglected space. All but one of the windows are above head height and boarded up – that precious light source is oozing from one just above her head, smeared and cracked.

Despite the unease quivering through her entire body, Jutta cannot stop now. She gathers several pallets and stacks them under the window, teetering as they bring her eyes to the bottom of the ledge. It's not what she expects. Beyond is not gravel or even the jumble of breeze-block indicative of the Wall, but a corrugated building opposite – perhaps another garage – and below it a rutted and neglected path. If she's not mistaken, it's an alleyway, strewn with assorted debris, bricks and planks of wood. Can she have come far enough across the divide to reach the East? Has this warehouse attached to the back of the garage acted like an extended limb, nestled into the turn of the Wall? The realisation almost causes Jutta to wobble from her wood pile, and she has to grip onto the window fitting to steady herself. Unbelievably, it gives too, affording a swift rush of air. East Berlin air, if she's right.

For a second or so, Jutta pushes her ear against the gap, hearing only a faint sound of car exhausts in the background, no shouting or military-style barking. Could she have stumbled across a glitch in the GDR's mighty edifice? A back-door anomaly? And why hasn't anyone, aside from the maternal cat, found it before?

The window is big enough for Jutta to climb through, and, as much as she hankers to test it out, to satisfy her growing curiosity, she knows now is not the time. She is not prepared, either for success or capture, and she needs

120

to think, plan and gather every ounce of courage. It's all very well her landing in the East, but what does she do then? And how will she find Karin?

The cat family are sleeping as Jutta returns to the kitchen, and for a second she envies their simple comforts. But then the mama cat has her family close by, doesn't she? It's the sheer empty space left by Karin that drives Jutta to even contemplate something both so daring and possibly stupid, the same void that, no doubt, has fuelled many a dangerous quest in history.

Emerging back out onto the West side feels like coming out of a fog, as if she's been on a lengthy voyage. But everything is the same – the Wall is just as ugly, with people skirting around it just as they were half an hour previously. Only Jutta is significantly changed. She's dipped a toe into the other side and she wants – no, she *needs* – to dive in. It could be dangerous, with shark-infested waters on the other side, but, as she strides towards home, she knows she has no choice but to plunge in head first. Knowing there is a way in, how can she possibly hold back?

24

Light at the End of the Tunnel

1st July 1963, East Berlin

Karin wakes to a dull ache in her stomach, which twists to pain when she moves. She palms her lower belly and groans inwardly – it's not like the hot, searing pain of her appendix in revolt, simply that time of the month. She's not ill, just a woman. Still, she would love nothing more than to call in sick for work; it's what she would have done back in West Berlin, where most of the boutique girls had at least one day off per month. But here, it's not the done thing. Workers of all ages haul themselves in to their shifts day after day, healthy and pink or weak and ashen; it's what you do for the good of all, for the glory of the GDR. And she owes it to them, the other workers, because didn't they save her life?

From across the room, Karin eyes the half-sewn garment lying on her table, her fingers itching to get back to her needles and thread and her rusty sewing machine. This month's copy of *Sybille* magazine is open on the page offering the inspiration for her latest creation, her own paper pattern cut from old newspapers. She could spend the entire day finishing the dress, blissfully in her own world. Easy then, to imagine she is back home in Schöneberg, at the window of her and Jutta's room, the treadle of her more modern machine ticking away to a steady rhythm, her mother or Gerda clanking dishes in the kitchen down the corridor.

Karin shakes the memories away. Sometimes they lift her, but equally they can have the opposite effect of pitching her into a darkened cave of despair. She rolls herself from her bed and her feet hit the cool, bare boards of her room. In the echoey bathroom, she reaches for an aspirin to get her through the day; at least she has something to look forward to, something to pull her through eight hours of her shift. A date, a bar, some music. Bad beer, but at least it has that liquefying effect after several glasses. It's time away from work and the tiny room where the walls often close in, but where, if she closes her eyes, the privacy allows infinite space to dream. That – and Otto – are the only elements keeping her going. A light at the end of what is often a deep, dark tunnel.

25

Looking to the East

1st July 1963, West Berlin

Jutta wakes to a dull ache in her stomach that she recognises as anticipation, wrapped around a solid nugget of fear. Today is the day.

The weekend seemed endless, even though she'd been flushed out of the apartment by Irma to a bar in Charlottenburg, where they listened to a band trying their best to emulate any four-piece ensembles from England. The latest single from The Beatles echoed through the tinny speakers; 'From Me to You', the band sang jovially, and it took on a whole new significance for Jutta. Nothing could take her mind off that corridor and the window, her own gateway through the back of the wardrobe, into a different land entirely.

After some thought, Jutta decided not to chance going into the East at the weekend – too many people milling about on Harzer Strasse, curious children playing out on their bicycles. And she has no idea what a weekend looks like in the East anymore. Are people holed up in their homes, or out enjoying the sunshine? It might as well be the moon, for all she can predict. Monday seemed to her the best option: a day when people are at work, cafés and shops open, with hopefully enough bodies to blend in, not stand out as the woman who asks odd questions.

Jutta knows she will start at the Charité – it's a tenuous link as it's now nearly two years since Karin was a patient, but the only one she has. The hope is to find a sympathetic receptionist who will take pity on her embellished sob story and not question the holes in its truth. She's thought again of approaching the Wall-jumpers on the university campus, as they have ways of faking Eastern ID cards. But that means revealing at least a portion of her plan, and prompting some suspicion about her access. And for now, the hole in the Wall is hers, and hers alone.

At various points, just the thought of setting foot in the East makes Jutta's heart pound. Equally, there are some things you have to leave to chance, she thinks. And luck. God knows the family is due some good fortune. *Please let it be soon.*

Jutta sets off as if she's heading for work, but lingers in a small café a street away from Harzer Strasse, gauging the flow of people in the area. She's dressed down for the occasion, not because she presumes East Berliners exist in a uniform of grey, but to avoid standing out as a visitor from the West. She doesn't want to be noticed at all. So, it's a plain jersey T-shirt, and a skirt that she hopes doesn't show up the grazing on her knees – no stockings as they will certainly snag as she crawls through holes and out of windows. Most importantly, shoes low enough that she can run.

She checks her bag in the café for the small amount of

East German Ostmarks that she'd found in pots and drawers in the apartment. Any visit to the East before the Wall had meant changing up the required amount of the virtually worthless currency in order to cross the border, but since no one in the family has needed it for two years, it's lain discarded in varying pots, jam jars and drawers. Only Uncle Oskar had eyed Jutta curiously as she scrabbled in the sideboard for coins, muttering that she was looking for hairpins. Amid the pens and paperclips, she also found an old map of the complete city, which she pulled out and held close to her body, her back turned away from Oskar.

At ten a.m. and in bright sunshine, Jutta saunters towards the Wall at Harzer Strasse and the secret opening. It's relatively quiet, no children about and few shoppers on the streets. She smiles at one or two gossiping women as they pass, though her insides are roiling, flipping and grinding, and she swallows down the sour taste of angst in her mouth. She flattens herself against the bricks opposite again, sensing any human traffic nearby, and then – before she has time to think it over too deeply – leaps for the hole. The cabinet that she'd hastily replaced pushes away more easily, but she can't be sure if anyone has glimpsed her rear disappearing into what must appear to be a mysterious rabbit hole.

Inside, the cats are ravenous. It's been three days since her last appearance and the mother looks thinner, no doubt being stripped of her own milk by the squeaking, demanding kittens. There's the tiny carcass of a mouse nearby, but the mother goes at the cat food like a gannet.

Jutta hurries through the corridors, noting the piece of string she'd hooked loosely over the door handle hasn't been moved, and arrives at the window, pulling up another pallet to hoist herself higher. She waits two or three minutes and sees no one walking in the alleyway, then leaps so her waist balances on the ledge. She hooks one leg through, followed by the other, before turning and easing herself out backwards and feet first, dragging her bag behind her. Her chest scrapes over the rough window frame and she feels her heart bound out of its cavity and pummel against the splintering wood, fast and fierce. Hanging there, exposed across the divide, it's the first time that real doubt hits her squarely: *what the hell are you doing, Jutta?*

But it's too late. She has no leverage to scrabble back up, and she can only drop the foot or so to the ground, luckily with no resounding thud. She spins instantly and scans the area quickly with ears and eyes. Nothing but background city traffic. Brushing herself off, she loosens the grip on her hair and shakes it out, reining in her heaving breath. Tentatively, she steps beyond the workshop opposite, bracing herself for border guards to shout and approach at any second.

'Fräulein, what are you doing here?'

Jutta recoils instantly, hand to her mouth, her eyes – no doubt wild – settling on a man not in Vopo grey-green, but a grubby, oily overall. He puffs resolutely on a thin cigarette, runs his eyes up and down her clothes. Leering, mixed with suspicion.

'Um, I'm . . .' Jutta spies a garage sign above his head and grasps for an excuse '. . . looking for a mechanic called Rainer.'

'Are you sure?' The man puffs some more. 'We've no Rainer working here. Can I help?'

'No, it's Rainer I need. I've obviously got the wrong place. No problem, I'll find him.'

'Perhaps you better had. Good day then, Fräulein.'

Jutta smiles, perhaps too hard, and begins walking, seeking

breath from somewhere inside and pushing out beyond the alleyways. It wasn't even close and yet she is trembling from head to foot. *If it wasn't for Karin . . .*

Rounding the corrugated building, there is nothing unremarkable about the scene in front: a war-torn, half-built everyday street in Berlin, buildings pocked with bullet holes and memories of conflict. An old East German Trabant – much mocked in the West as a 'sparkplug with a roof' – drives by, its tiny engine whining, and she almost laughs at the timing. There's no doubt. Jutta is in East Berlin. She is a Wall-jumper.

She steadies herself, pushes back her shoulders and strides out north, guided by the memorised map. It feels an age since she was in East Berlin, not having crossed the border to see friends as frequently as Karin, and she tries to remember what it was like. Now, Jutta emerges from the cluster of workshops to a street where there are still sporadic gaps in a strip of once grand structures – either fallen or demolished from war wounding. It seems not so much grey, as the Western news reports often paint life here, but washed out and bleached. Like an old black and white image that has been given a watery coating of colour and is struggling to retain the pigment. She walks away from the sight line of the guards' watchtower and towards residential blocks, where there are men with newspapers and women pushing baby carriages and people hovering outside shops. Momentarily, she wonders why they don't just go in, and then remembers it's the queues that are talked of: scoffed at by Westerners, tolerated by the East.

With each step away from the Wall, the tremors within begin to settle. The sight of a yellow, wide-snout bus is familiar and comforting, and the traffic distinctly thinner, with Trabants – or 'Trabis' – and the heavier Wartburgs chugging out dense exhaust fumes, dominating the traffic in the same way that VW Beetles do in picture-postcard West Berlin. It's her Berlin – and yet not. With each step, Jutta gains confidence, easing rather than throwing off her paranoia entirely, but when no one looks at her too hard or scrutinises her mode of dress, she begins to move with purpose.

Reluctant to use her map and appear lost, Jutta uses the Wall as her guide, following the signs for checkpoints off to her left, but staying clear enough not to glimpse the harsh sight of its hardware. She's walking so briskly that her calves begin to ache and she yearns to dip down into one of the U-Bahn stations, but she has no idea which lines go where now, and it strikes her that one half of her home city – the place that has been so open all of Jutta's life – is alien to her.

When plotting her path in the days prior, Jutta felt determined to avoid Berlin's main thoroughfare of the Unter den Linden, fearing it would draw her to the Brandenburg Gate, the site of raw memories that still sting like an open sore. But the Charité is directly north of the square on which the Gate stands, and she is struggling to get her bearings in this strange new city. There's no choice but to hug closer to the Wall.

In Jutta's lifetime, the grand avenue has been transformed dramatically time and again; she and Karin would have been only four or five when Mama brought them down in the early years of the war, heading towards Alexanderplatz. Then, the whole boulevard seemed awash with the crimson flags of the Reich, draped from the grand buildings or fluttering from white, gothic columns. Her memories are patchy, but she recalls vividly the deep red and the squeeze of Mama's hand as she pulled the twins along swiftly, as if the grandeur was overwhelming. Only later did Jutta realise that her mother found the scene unpalatable, alongside a good deal of Berliners.

Then, just after the war, the complete lack of life and colour; the Unter den Linden as a moonscape of bombed-out buildings, the sad sight of the grand but ruined Adlon Hotel, its sign coated in brick dust and doors firmly closed. But as the red carpet road to Berlin's beloved gate to freedom, the avenue was pledged to be rebuilt and restored after the war. It would be grand again, so everyone said. That was before the divide. Now, the avenue is sharply nondescript and almost empty, but she is pulled again towards the Wall by some inexplicable force.

This is the first time Jutta has seen the Gate since the days after the barricades went up; she viewed it then as if in a fantastical dream, the confused, milling crowds peering through the barbed wire to a cut-off world. Now, the twisted metal is an embellishment to the cemented breeze-blocks, in perhaps the neatest part of the barrier. There are the inevitable border guards, peering from watchtowers, but nothing much is in evidence in front of the Wall itself, and Jutta cannot see through to her part of Berlin, towards home. Even the towering columns of the Gate on the East side seem smaller, their grounded stumps hidden by hoardings. Jutta crosses quickly from the Adlon across the Pariser Platz, forcing herself to look at the stark breeze-blocks against the elegant stone of the Gate, and it gives her the courage to keep moving; if she takes Karin out of the equation, it's the saddest sight she has seen since that day in 1961.

Right now, though, she can't change it, and so Jutta wills herself to push on, ignoring the ache in her feet until she reaches the edge of the Charité's complex. When the grand old red-brick hospital comes into view, she braces herself for confrontation and disappointment. If this doesn't bear fruit, then what? Where is there left to search?

The reception area is a clinical white, contrasted with age-old darkened wood of a sweeping stair bannister, its history as Berlin's oldest hospital unable to be wiped out even by socialism. Muted voices are swallowed by the lofty ceiling, and the area is as calm and hushed as you'd want a hospital to be. Jutta pulls in her courage, like a woman of old gathering her skirts, and strides up to the reception desk, manned by a stern-faced woman in a shapeless tweed suit.

Jutta manufactures an instant smile. 'Good morning, Fräulein,' she begins.

The woman stares, heavy jowls squatting on her face like another blockade. 'Yes?'

'This is a strange request, but I'm looking for an old school friend – I've just arrived in East Berlin, and I don't have her address. All I know is that she was a patient here almost two years ago. In fact, it was the same weekend . . . well, when the barrier was erected.' Jutta is careful to gird her language. It's not a Wall here.

Nothing. The scowling fräulein is in no mood, and needs gentle manipulation.

'I'm aware it's not the done thing to reveal anything of former patients,' Jutta forges on, 'but I've heard everyone at the Charité is very kind, and I know my friend would be so grateful to you for helping me to reach her.'

The woman harrumphs. 'Not such a good friend if she doesn't write and tell you where she lives, is she?'

The gentle massage of the woman's ego is not working, and Jutta's panic begins to climb, lungs wheezing inside her chest and breath catching in her throat. Any minute and it could overwhelm her into tears.

131

Do not cry. Sadness will not soften this fräulein.

'I can see you're very busy. Is there an administration office I can try?' Jutta tries again, the pitch of her voice beginning to surge towards the ornate ceiling.

Not even a dismissive grunt this time, just a determined glare.

'Her name is Karin Voigt – you don't recognise it, do you?' Jutta prods one last time, in growing desperation.

The fräulein folds her arms, donning her full suit of armour.

'Is there a problem here, Fräulein Bruner?' A man's voice comes from behind Jutta and she spins at the words – his tone is conciliatory, not challenging. What's more, he doesn't look as if he's about to show her out, or call in the Stasi. Judging by his white coat, he's a medic, and he looks nice. Kind, as doctors should be but aren't always.

She gulps back air and relief. 'I'm looking for a good friend, someone who was treated here,' she repeats.

He puts a hand on her upper arm, and leads her away from the ogre Bruner, with persuasion rather than force, and Jutta relents. She's too weary for anything else.

'I heard,' he says, gesturing his head. 'And the name?' This doctor, with grey eyes and short, thinning brown hair, is looking at Jutta intently, as if he somehow recognises her.

'Karin Voigt. Do you know her?' Jutta says, her anguish too obvious.

He seems startled by hearing Jutta's voice again and pulls back a little, as if reassuring himself that it's not her exactly. But someone very like her.

'Come with me,' he says, and ushers Jutta two flights up the commanding stairway and down a long corridor, where the building becomes distinctly less ornate, the walls a tired tobacco yellow. The doctor says nothing, just guiding her along. He might be leading her to the hospital's security office, with a phone hotline to the Stasi, but Jutta has no choice but to follow. With only intuition to rely on, she senses that this man knows of Karin and is taking her somewhere quiet to reveal good information. It's the only thing she can hope for.

At the end of the corridor, he opens the door to a large room, thick with cigarette smoke, overpowered by a pungent smell of grease. People in uniforms of varying colours – nurses and porters – sit in lines of tables, forking food into their mouths and talking, largely in a hushed whisper.

'Have a seat in the corner over there,' the doctor gestures to an empty table. 'I'll be back in a minute.'

'So, do you know my . . .?' Jutta begins, but he's gone, the flap of his white coat already at the door.

Despite her angst, Jutta is glad of the seat, with her feet starting to throb. She's thirsty too, and even though the coffee smells bitter, the thought of a mouthful preoccupies her. Then, a sudden presence, a shadow to the side, and it's not the build of the doctor. Instantly, there's a certain familiarity, a sensation of that thread being tweaked. She almost doesn't want to look, in case her mind is playing tricks and only servicing her most intense desire. Eventually, she does, flicking up her eyes in disbelief.

'Hello Ja-Ja,' Karin says.

26

Together

They don't throw their arms around each other, hugging and kissing in making up the lost months. The magnetism between the both of them is like a life force that would thrust nature's elements together, but the shared understanding of a need for restraint is stronger. No joy on show, not yet.

'Hello Karin, you look well.' She doesn't – Jutta is spinning a minor lie for her sister's sake; in reality, she thinks Karin looks pale and wan, bled of the particular zest that always made her sister so lively, vibrant and determined. But why would Karin want to hear such truth, today of all days? Her glorious long, black hair is now cut into a blunt bob, one side hooked behind her ear, and she has lost weight: her face more angular now, even bordering on gaunt. For someone of twenty-six, she looks simply tired.

Karin slides in beside Jutta and finally they're allowed the connection, a fizz as their bodies meet, two elements of a lightbulb touching to produce light; their hands lock under the table and grip firmly. For a second, almost two years of their lives slips away.

'So good to see you,' Jutta begins, but she's not entirely sure how to go on, having imagined the words would come tumbling out, but they don't. They're stuck in a halfway house of disbelief and hope.

The white coat of Dr Simms returns and he half-smiles at Jutta and leans in close to Karin. 'I've cleared it with your supervisor,' he says in a low voice. 'Why don't you both go to a café, have a talk? You've an hour at least.'

Karin nods and smiles, looks as if she might reach out to clasp at his hand in thanks, but doesn't. 'Yes, we will. Thank you, Walter.'

He turns and strides up to the food counter, while Karin inches out of her seat.

'I'll just get my cardigan from the locker,' she says.

Inside, Jutta oozes relief – it's good that Karin keeps up the pretence of merely leaving for the allotted hour. Still, she feels for her sister then, in having to leave everything of her new life behind; she can picture that Karin will have made even the starkest of rooms warm and welcoming, spread with her sewing paraphernalia. But they can't chance a return to Karin's home, risk a neighbour even suspecting she is packing the smallest bag to leave, that much Jutta has gleaned from her eavesdropping on the escape helpers and their conversations. The advice is always to drop everything and go, taking only the clothes you stand up in.

It's warm enough outside that Karin doesn't need a cardigan, but Jutta can see why she would want to shroud the washed-out blue of her shapeless dress, covering the indelible stain on one pocket. It's the same uniform that Jutta saw a hospital worker wearing as she piloted a weighty electronic polisher over the corridor floor, and it strikes Jutta for the first time that her sister is not a nursing employee, but a domestic one. She has every respect for the cleaners in the university, keeping the library spotless despite the slovenly students, but for Karin, with so much creative ambition running through every sinew within her? Jutta feels a rollercoaster of intense sadness squaring up inside her. But that's about to change. From today, they can go back to some sort of normality.

They hardly speak as they head out into the early afternoon sunshine. Instead, their fingertips glide towards each other as they descend the hospital steps, brushing and sparking with the familiarity they might have felt in the womb, if only they could remember that far back.

Karin walks assuredly beyond the gates and strides forward. They cross a bridge over the Spree and still she keeps going, silently. Jutta longs to hug her tightly, or to link arms at the very least, but each time she moves closer or begins a sentence, Karin caps her off: 'Not here, not yet.'

It's a good while before they reach a busy interchange near to Friedrichstrasse station and Karin pilots them between two grand, old columns and under the sign that says *Presse Café*. Jutta is itching to simply head south and towards the portal, wary of the passing looks, which might be registering two very similar women side by side. Or maybe they look different enough now? She wants to get going, but is also desperate to sit down and drink something, thinking of the lengthy walk back to the workshops.

Inside the café, they head into the corner, amid the jumble of old wooden tables. It's only a quarter full, and clearly a hang-out for students, the clientele largely in their twenties.

'I've got a few Marks,' Jutta says. 'Do you need . . .?'

'No, it's okay,' Karin answers and goes to order, chatting to the bartender as if she's a regular. She returns with two coffees, heavy on the milk as Jutta likes, and two bland but bulky bread rolls, a few slices of wurst slotted in.

'Sorry, this is all they have,' Karin apologises.

'It's fine,' says Jutta, who's starting to feel light-headed and would eat virtually anything at that moment. The strong coffee goes straight to her head at the first sip and she coughs, eyes wide.

Karin's mood switches and she laughs, her familiar tinkle of cut glass. 'I always think of you when I come here,' she says. 'I imagined you'd like the coffee – the taste isn't great but at least it's strong.' She pauses. 'And here you are.'

There's so much to say, and Karin seems conscious of the time, but Jutta is keen to impress one thing. 'I've got a way out, Karin,' she blurts in a whisper. 'I've found access – I didn't come across the border. I found my own way. If we were to head there now, we'll be back at home for supper.' It comes in a tidal wave, breathless as she's conscious of keeping her voice and enthusiasm in check. 'Mama's going to be so delight—'

'I can't, Ja-Ja.'

Time, even on the ancient and dusty wall clock, seems to stand still.

'What do you mean, you can't? It's not a tunnel, Karin, I promise, or the sewers – I know you couldn't do that. It's tucked away but above groun—'

Karin cuts in again, clutching at her sister's hands across the table, her own red and raw, doubtless from the harsh cleaning fluids she works with. Her voice is heavy with guilt. 'I mean I can't leave here. East Berlin.'

After the Wall, Jutta imagined there was nothing much

left to shock her. Yet here it is, from her sister, of all people. 'But why not? Surely, you miss home, *want* to come home?'

'Of course I do,' Karin urges, low in to the table. 'Oh Ja-Ja, you can't imagine how many times I've thought about it — returning to you and Mama, Gerda and Hugo. Even Uncle Oskar. Every day. But here there is real fear. As much as any intelligent person knows it's propaganda, they instil fear' — as if to prove a point her eyes sweep across the room, watching for those watching them — 'and that fear grinds into you. Not just the prospect of being shot, but the consequences if you're not. Those that have survived an East German prison say they almost wished they'd died on the Wall.' Her expression is grave, and Jutta sees the deep-seated terror within. 'I can't chance being caught. I'm sorry. It frightens me to the core.'

For a second, Jutta runs with dread at the thought that *she* has to make it back across — and today. In reaching her sister, she hasn't dismissed the journey back through the portal, but imagines it will be easier in reverse. Her entire focus so far has been on finding Karin, and returning together. For the last time.

'Well, okay — now that we know how to contact you, I could get a fake passport, a good one. I know people,' Jutta pushes, masking her intense disappointment.

'There's something else,' Karin says quietly. 'Another reason. Some*one* else.'

For one crazy second Jutta thinks it's the doctor who brought them together at the Charité, although he's easily old enough to be their father. Even within minutes, she glimpsed an unspoken bond between them, the looks they exchanged.

'The doctor?' she quizzes.

'Walter?' Karin half-laughs. 'No, Ja-Ja, though I do love

him – he saved me, at the beginning.' She takes in a breath. 'No, it's Otto. He's the reason I can't leave. I'm in love, Ja-Ja. In love with Otto.'

Karin pulls a bent and dog-eared snapshot from her uniform pocket, a square, colour portrait of a young man. It's a formal pose, so he's not smiling, but Jutta thinks it could be nice when he does. His blond hair shines out, blue eyes intent on looking to the left of the camera. There's an embossed stamp in one corner and Jutta just makes out 'Department of . . .'.

'He's in the *Party*?' Jutta's voice rises, incredulous.

'No! No,' Karin assures. 'But he does work for a government ministry. He's an architect.' Here, her face softens, at the mere thought of him, and Jutta can't help but detect a real tenderness in her sister's voice. She's never seen it before in Karin, for any man or boy, though she recognises the frisson, the way her tired eyes sparkle in just saying his name.

'So, he can come too,' Jutta urges. 'West Berlin – the whole of West Germany, in fact – is crying out for architects. He'll find a job easily.'

Karin lets out a second sigh, hard enough that her breath hits their hands still clasped over the scratched wood and coffee stains of the table. 'He wouldn't – he won't leave,' she says. 'I know Otto. His father has been sick recently, and still is. Plus . . .'

'Plus what?' Jutta's voice has a sudden edge.

Karin takes a breath, looks into the grain of the table. 'He's passionate about the rebuilding of Berlin, of East Germany. He believes in equality – a good life for all, somewhere safe to live. For everyone.'

Jutta can't help that her brow flattens with doubt, and

sees that Karin catches it instantly. 'I know you find that hard to believe, and I did at first,' she goes on. 'But the more I know Otto, the more I see what he envisages.'

'So you believe in this way of life, Karin? *You're converted?*' Jutta pulls her hand away sharply, her irritation threatening to bubble over. This day has already been incredible enough, without what she's hearing now.

'No, of course not, not all of it,' Karin replies. 'There's bits I hate . . .'

'Not least the way a woman of your talent is made to swab floors!' Jutta spits. But what she's thinking inside is more personal – Karin's decision is an affront. Her sister is not choosing the family, or Schöneberg, or their old life. Or her.

Karin looks momentarily hurt, but her resolve has clearly grown since August 1961, and she merely blinks it back. 'But I love Otto. He's already sacrificed for me, had to be scrutinised for even being seen with a West Berliner. Maybe he won't be promoted because of it. But he's done it for me. Because he loves me. I can't leave him, don't you see?'

Jutta is silenced by her sister's passion, the deep-seated emotion she has when talking of the man she loves. But the leaden weight in her own chest is like a solid ship being dragged to the bottom of the ocean. It crushes her. When she set eyes on Karin less than an hour before in that grease-laden canteen, she thought the nightmare of the past two years would be over by the day's end. That they would slip back through the secret opening, not to set foot in the East for years to come, all of it a horrible chapter in the past. She's thought all day of Mama's face as Karin walks back through the apartment door, of Gerda's shriek of delight and Hugo's hugs.

140

Karin looks at the clock. 'I have to go,' she says. 'It's best you don't walk back with me.'

They go one by one into the toilet instead, standing outside the clean but worn stall doors, daubed with graffiti, until the room is empty.

'Are you sure, Karin, that there isn't a way to persuade him, given time?' Jutta stands opposite her sister, perhaps not such a mirror image as they were in the past.

'Yes. No. Oh, Ja-Ja, I don't know!' Karin peels away and turns her back, shoulders quaking as she can't hold back her distress any longer. Jutta nestles up against her from behind, her arms circling her sister's undoubtedly thinner frame, and holds her fast, head bowed into Karin's neck and choking back her own sorrow.

'I just know I can't leave, Ja-Ja,' Karin sobs. 'I love him. I could come back but without him I would be miserable.'

'I know,' Jutta comforts her. 'I know.'

But she doesn't, can't understand why Karin won't turn tail with her at that very minute and hurry towards their only chance of freedom together. Possibly because Jutta has never known such love, except for her family, and her sister especially. What is one man against an entire life to be lived?

But it's clear that Karin does know those depths now. And it's for someone else. It had to happen, eventually. But Jutta never imagined it would hit on this day. In this way.

Despite her bewilderment, she can see Karin's distress is multiplied; the separation by the Wall was forced and unequivocal. It's been agony, but easier than the divide she's faced with now, one of her own choosing. Jutta yearns for some way to make it right, for everyone.

'What if you had time, to talk Otto round gradually?' she suggests. 'Do you think he might see what type of life you could have?'

Karin looks up and turns to her sister, the side of her mouth moving upwards a little. 'Maybe,' she says. 'I could try. I mean, there's his parents, but yes, if I had some time. Is that possible?'

'Yes, for a while, I think,' Jutta finds herself saying, though she has no idea how it might work in reality. 'We can sort it out, I'm sure.'

'Oh, Ja-Ja, if only it were simple,' Karin says.

Jutta half-laughs. 'And if only we didn't have a bloody great Wall carving up our city!'

27

Divided Again

1st July 1963, East Berlin

Karin walks back towards the Charité alone, her cheap shoes dragging on the pavement, mind in complete turmoil. The tender, tearful goodbye with Jutta had been up against the sour urine smell of the toilets, hugging so hard her bones felt they might break, but neither of them willing to let go. Why is the Wall severing their lives like this, forcing her to yank on her loyalties and decide? She folds her arms while walking, as if to wedge together the two sides of her heart.

At least there is progress, since Jutta now knows where she lives, although she would be wary of having any visitors aside from Otto to her shabby, two-roomed apartment. At night, he often lies in her bed, staring at the damp patch on her ceiling with frustration, and she likes to think it forms part of his motivation to make better homes for all in East Berlin, in the entire GDR. It's true what she told Jutta, that she's never met anyone like him. Not a devout communist, but simply passionate about improving the lives of those around him.

Whenever he talks about his work, his eyes are so alight and his fervour so intense that she can't question his vision of a more equal future. Her upbringing, not to mention her current internment inside the GDR regime, made her initially cynical of his zeal. And she still is to some extent, since Otto's version of utopia neatly sidesteps the menacing presence of the Stasi, as if putting everything right means the need for surveillance will simply melt away. But it's also the hope that he possesses – his intellect alongside his naivety – that she loves so much. And the truth is, she's afraid to tell him everything about herself, to offer him a chance of a different kind of freedom. He would never betray her to the authorities, she's certain of that, but their love might not survive such a monumental shift. Not yet anyway. Otto has lived in a divided Germany almost all his adult life. If she forces him too quickly, she's scared of which he would choose. His family or hers, his ethos or a freedom that he's never truly known.

So now she has a quandary of her own: how to convince Otto to defect to the West, to leave his beloved job, and his ailing father and doting mother? And in just six months. That's what she promised Jutta, hoping her own sister will see the value of breaching the Wall again. That there is something worth waiting for. Even with the pledge, she wonders if Jutta will risk another journey into the East – if she does make it back safely today. They may both lose the precious contact before they can relish it, perhaps forever, and with it her own vital gateway to letters for Mama too.

Though Karin hates the idea of Jutta in repeated jeopardy, the mere notion of crossing the Wall herself, either over – or worse – contained in a suffocating tunnel or in the cramped boot of a car, makes her whole being shiver.

That's before even a thought of capture and the Stasi. She yearns to be braver, to share the risk with her sister as they've shared everything in their lives so far. Yet now she's seen her cherished Ja-Ja and sparked the fuse they have, she simply can't bear to let it fizzle again.

It's past Karin's allotted hour, but she'll face a rebuke from her supervisor, she decides, and sits on a bench outside the hospital's imposing entrance. It's not just Jutta's disappointed face that pushes up in front of her, but Mama's and Gerda's. Their hurt, at her choosing Otto over them, even for now. How can she justify it? She can't, that's the truth. There are no winners when it comes to this Wall; boundaries never unify, despite the GDR's insistence that it benefits their country.

Karin pulls herself up, wipes at the river of salt crust running into her neck and takes a breath. Her dreams of seeing Jutta have been satisfied, a wish come true. So why does she feel as if a large part of her has died inside?

28

Ghosting Back

1st July 1963, East Berlin

Jutta's hurried steps are driven by a melting pot of hurt and disappointment, and the anger that she refuses to recognise just yet; a cauldron of simmering emotion that bubbles into hot tears as she walks, head down, allowing her hair to fall like a curtain and hide her deep sorrow. All weekend, she had dreamed of making this return journey with Karin by her side, leading the way back to the window and into a world they would resume. But Jutta is returning alone, and the sense of loneliness is tenfold. Though she has Karin's pledge to coax Otto round, neither broached what they would do if faced with his refusal, and now Jutta tussles with that prospect. But however wounded she feels, she's determined not to see Karin's choice as disloyalty. More that her sister has the capacity for a steadfast fidelity towards another. It's admirable, and so very Karin. It's what she – everyone – loves about her. And yet, if she's entirely honest with herself, Jutta can't help a new sensation festering inside – bilious and ugly, a toxic green hue: jealousy.

Despite the enduring ache in her feet, she walks on, fuelled by the trepidation that may well turn to terror before she reaches the portal if she's not careful, cultivated by Karin's obvious fear of capture. She glances sideways at the vehicles driving past, wary of any slowing up, even slightly; Karin had warned her of the small grey Barkas vans common to East Berlin, which are made up to look like grocery or laundry delivery trucks – sign-painted with names and wares – but are more often Stasi 'collection' vehicles, kitted out with cramped holding cells inside. Several greyish vans pass by as Jutta moves south, retracing her earlier route because she's too afraid to get out her map and work out a new trail towards the garage work-shops, but none stop. Women with children eye her as they pass, but it could be out of sympathy for her reddened eyes and the pinched expression of someone about to shed more tears. Even a young Vopo smiles at her weakly, and she manages to turn her mouth upwards accordingly; he's barely twenty and looks out of place shouldering his gun, let alone using it. As Karin had insisted back at the café, the Stasi have made spies out of many, but not all; East Berliners, she'd insisted, are stoic and solid, 'loyal to humanity mostly'. For a minute, Jutta had imagined Karin was on the brink of saying 'us East Berliners', which might have struck the day's final blow. Thankfully, she didn't.

There's a rush of alarm when Jutta's memory doesn't register the street she's on, or the buildings alongside as familiar. With the well of tears blurring her view, has she missed a crucial turning? It's not about to get dark any time soon, but any light in this side of Berlin remains shadowy, unfamiliar and definitely uncomfortable. Why hadn't she committed the name of the street next to the workshop firmly to memory, instead of looking only towards finding Karin? *How can you be so stupid, Jutta?* She's almost on the point of sidling into an alleyway and pulling out the map when she recognises a corner shop with a distinctive window display – an impending two-for-one price offer on bread that is sure to see the queues double – and her heart begins pumping again. She pushes all thoughts of her sister aside. It's about survival now. That's clearly what Karin has done for almost two years now: just focused on getting by.

The edge of the industrial area comes into view and Jutta makes a sweep of the street by pretending to fiddle in her bag near a bench, noting it's nearing three p.m. and an hour before some homeward workers begin to populate the streets. With no one obviously loitering, and no sign of the all-too-curious mechanic still lurking, she slips into the lane between the workshops, ears on alert for any footsteps behind – that's if the noise can make it past the pounding of blood in her ears. On the way to the window, she scouts for pallets or boxes to use as a makeshift ladder, cursing herself for her own lack of planning and prompting a wave of shame. Once again, her only outward focus had been on finding Karin.

But she's in luck; the alleyway provides one pallet and two pieces of roughly squared-off stone that she hauls towards the window without causing too much noise, aside from her own huffing and puffing. The window is as she left it, seemingly closed but popping ajar as she prises her fingernails under it. Jutta has always been the more agile and sporty of the twins, and here it serves her well as she pulls herself up to full height and levers one leg inside the window, balancing precariously for a second before pushing herself over to part-fall and part-manoeuvre herself onto the pallets on the other side. Grazed and

148

bruised, Jutta holds herself low on the dusty floor, motion-less for several seconds. When there's no clattering of military footsteps, no repercussions, she stands and drives her body forward through the corridor and into the kitchen, where the mama cat leaves her babies' nest and greets Jutta with a friendly purring, inching over to offer fur and solace, gratefully received by a woman shaking visibly at her day's endeavour.

29

The Knowing

'But what do I tell Mama? Or should I keep it back for now, until I'm more certain of Karin?' Jutta says, fingers twisting at strands of her hair, something she does only when she's either extremely excited or impossibly anxious.

Hugo cocks his head and swirls the ice in his brandy – Jutta had insisted meeting in a bar when she'd called him at work, her need for alcohol being unusually great.

'Oh Christ, Jutta, how am I supposed to know? It's not my mama.' Except he's clearly aware it's no defence, as the decision to tell or not will affect his mother almost as much; Gerda's love for Jutta and Karin is entirely maternal and equally intense. 'Do you think she will be able to persuade this boyfriend of hers to defect?'

Jutta shakes her head slowly. 'I don't know, and I don't think she does either.' In all truth, she's not sure who she met on the other side of the Wall this afternoon, and whether it was her sister at all.

Hugo tries another tack. 'Well, at least you know she's

150

safe, and not at the mercy of any dodgy individuals,' he says.

She looks at him with concern, knows that he's hinting at the stories circulating of East Berlin women – some of them Westerners – forced into prostitution as a way of earning their fake passports over the Wall to freedom. She's heard the stories, too, and always tried to banish the image of Karin in the same scenario.

'And you have plans to link up again, don't you?' Hugo prods.

Jutta swallows back her brandy. 'In a week, though I don't know how often I can do that, go through the Wall. I was terrified on the way back.' She scoffs and swirls the remaining ice in her glass. 'I may well become an alcoholic if I do it too frequently.'

The brandy with Hugo is her second since leaving the garage-house. After scrambling through the rabbit hole, she'd leapt into the nearest bar beyond Harzer Strasse that didn't seem like a dive and ordered a brandy just that bit too enthusiastically, enough for a man alongside to turn and smile.

'That bad, eh?' His accent was American, his look entirely clean-cut, and although he was wearing jeans and a shirt, she pictured him instantly in uniform – a sergeant perhaps. Despite the endless talk of democracy, West Berlin's foundations remain firmly military.

After one large mouthful, Jutta had re-engaged her power of speech. 'Something like that,' she'd said and smiled weakly. *If only you knew, soldier.* She felt his eyes follow her to a table and settle for a second or two, but he was soon joined by friends and they moved to a cluster of seats across the bar.

Hugo's practicality brings her back from her reverie.

'Well, why don't you wait until you see her again before revealing all at home?' he suggests. 'I mean, today was weird for all sorts of reasons. Getting our mothers' hopes up is pointless and cruel, especially as nothing is certain with . . . what's his name?'

'Otto.'

'Yeah, well – Otto. I think you wait.'

'Yes, you're right,' Jutta agrees, and she's relieved to adopt Hugo's common sense. She's physically and emotionally exhausted, and the thought of letting Mama and Gerda down gently while facing their inevitable inquisition makes her crave sleep. Still, she's surprised that Hugo hasn't warned her off going again, or that he's not more shocked – and impressed – by her bravery in going at all. On the one hand, she thinks he has the sagacity of an old man puffing on a pipe and, on the other, he's a man-boy who floats on a wave of excitement, hooked on the city's dynamism.

'Let's get home,' Hugo says. 'But I'd smarten yourself up in the toilet first. I hate to say it, Jut, but you do look like you've been dragged through a hedge backwards.'

'And you don't know how right you are.'

30

Admissions

3rd July 1963, East Berlin

The days drag for Karin. The vast stretches of boredom at the hospital, where she has always delved inside her head for inspiration, now become a mental battleground and a tug-of-war with her own reasoning. Has she made the right decision to stay for now? Thanks to his work, it's two days before she can see Otto again. They watch a play, a thinly veiled portrayal of East German strength and tenacity dressed as a love story, where loyalty for the nation overrides all. Karin has to excuse herself at the interval and retch drily into the toilet, while Otto quizzes her if she's ill. Can he do anything? Does she want to leave early? But she knows it's an enduring sickness that will be unresolved for a long time.

'You're pale,' Otto says, palming her forehead in the lobby before he walks her home. 'Are you really all right?'

Karin so wants to tell him – to begin gently sounding him out, planting the idea of a better life elsewhere. To explain about Jutta. But it's too soon. He knows she has a sister, but not a life's soulmate. It's a portion of her she can't seem to let go, as if that particular Karin doesn't belong to the East, reserved for another life. In the small hours, she ponders whether – subconsciously – she's clutching at her secret for a more practical reason, perhaps to aid her escape? How or why remains a mystery, but she's learnt not to question it.

Walter Simms, though, he's seen the evidence now with his own eyes and Karin can no longer hide it.

'So, your twin sister . . .' he says a day or so later. It's a statement of fact rather than a question.

'Hmm.' Karin grasps her fork and picks through the beef stew that his wife, Christel, has left them for dinner, having gone out to her weekly, Party-approved women's group. Normally, Karin visits for supper on a day when Christel is in, but Walter had sought her out in the hospital corridor and asked her for an impromptu meal. Given the state of her own larder, it's always a welcome invitation, and she guesses at the topic for discussion. At the very least, she owes him an explanation.

'Does that make it harder? Missing them, I mean?' Walter's voice is softer in his own home, less of the commanding voice of experience he uses at the hospital.

Karin looks up, in time for a lone tear to drop and fall into the thick gravy below. He's at her side in an instant, enveloping her in his arms as any parent might. The stew goes cold as Karin weeps out her frustration and guilt, and then, while the food is rewarming, she tells him of Jutta, of her sister's risk and sacrifice, and her own refusal to return home instantly.

'Have I done the wrong thing? Will I live to regret it, Walter?'

Dr Simms – a man of enviable reason and genuine

kindness – shakes his head. 'Not if it was your gut feeling,' he assures. 'Have you put yourself back there, on the other side, and imagined how you would be feeling – without Otto? If it would seem right?'

She has, hundreds of times since Jutta disappeared from the Presse Café. She knows exactly how it would be: basking in Mama's love, brimming with Gerda's comforting food, endlessly delighted to be sleeping again at Jutta's side. Those thoughts make her smile into the floor as she's mopping the hospital corridors. Then, a sour sensation follows the joy: wretchedness that Otto is not breathing beside her, that she can't nuzzle into the fresh smell of his neck, or run her outstretched hand through his thick, blond hair. Yes, there are the freedoms of West Berlin to consider too – the bars and clubs on Kurf'damm, enticing boutiques and access to fabrics and opportunities she can only dream of now. But they are merely things, and it's people Karin has come to rely on – the likes of Walter and Christel, who took her in without question when she was cast afloat in the GDR sea, and Otto who refuses to bow to the pressure over his relationship with a West Berliner, a born capitalist and a traitor to communism.

So it's people, and not places or trinkets, which nudge Karin this way or that. They swing in her head like a pendulum that may never, ever settle. But now she must *make* it swing – in the right direction.

'Have you told Otto yet?' Walter spoons out the piping hot stew a second time.

Karin is alarmed. 'No! And you mustn't either. Please, Walter. I can't tell him yet. Just knowing would put him and his family at too much risk, and his father is still recovering.' Otto's parents, hard-working communists and firm believers, have never quite warmed to Karin, likely because of her origins. Yet again, she's certain Otto has defended her fiercely in private. But for all their coldness, she wouldn't wish the spotlight of the Stasi anywhere near the Krugers.

'Just be careful,' Walter says quietly. 'Very, very careful.' He doesn't ask the details, though it's clear that he suspects Jutta's visit will not be a one-off. Like all Easterners, he'll recognise that what he doesn't know can't be wrung out of him. And he'll want to leave it that way. Though they've known each other such a short time, Karin senses that Walter thinks of her as family, a second daughter, but in reality he has another daughter to protect, one born from his blood, and a wife too. A job, and a good life helping people. Of all the people Karin knows, Walter Simms is not naive. He sees through the system, in the same way she's sometimes watched him peer deep into X-rays up against the light box. He once told her: 'In each one the heart is there, in its right place. It just needs fixing sometimes.'

If only there was an easy remedy for her own heart.

31

A Welcome Distraction

5th July 1963, West Berlin

In the Presse Café toilet, Jutta had agreed hastily to revisit the next week, on a Monday again, knowing that if she was left to ponder over the prospect too long, she might well renege at the last minute. But if she's promised Karin, if her sister is there waiting for her, she won't let her down. Not now they have renewed and restrung the thread.

At work, the time drags, and the sidelong glances from Gerda, who's far too intuitive to hide much from, make it hard for Jutta to spend time at home. She joins the *fluchthelfers* again in the university refectory – though keeping herself on the sidelines – and is keen to glean any up-to-date information on successful attempts over the Wall. But there's little news, and her own secret is in danger of worming its way out as a confession if she sits too long. She clutches at her coffee cup and presses her mouth firmly closed.

It's both a welcome distraction and an irritation when Irma pleads with Jutta to make up a foursome on a Friday night.

'Come on, we haven't seen each other for ages,' Irma entreats. 'I really like this guy, but he's quite shy. He wants to bring a friend, assures me that he's very nice. Please, Jutta?'

Drinks at the Hilton are a rare event on Jutta's budget, and seem somehow frivolous when there are more critical elements to her life. She knows also that she'll be thinking of Karin as she sips cocktails in the relative opulence. Equally, it will make the clock hands turn and preoccupy her mind with more than thoughts of having to weave her way through the Wall again. And saying yes pleases Irma too.

They meet in Charlottenburg, just south of the Tiergarten. The Hilton is one of Berlin's more distinctive new builds; it's an impressive chequerboard black and white structure that screams fashion and places West Berlin firmly in the Western world. The interior is equally vogueish, and Jutta hates herself for smiling inside at the gleam of the chrome and the clean lines of the furnishings, for even liking the luxury. *Karin always wanted to come here.*

Seating themselves in a booth, Irma pulls down her too-short dress and arranges her legs at their best angle before the men arrive. Jutta's only concession to a date is her hair, washed and backcombed, plus a light tinge of pale pink lipstick and some understated earrings. And, of course, she's wearing a dress of Karin's design.

'Where did you meet this guy?' Jutta says, eyes sweeping the busy bar and its clientele – chic, moneyed and not worried about the price of the cocktails, clearly.

'The Hotel am Zoo,' Irma says. 'I was waiting in the lobby for a friend, and he came up and asked me for a light. His German accent is terrible and I knew straightaway he was from the US.'

'He's *American*?' Jutta's eyes are wide with alarm. 'Am I to presume his friend is too?'

'Didn't I tell you?' Irma says with mock innocence. 'Anyway, what have you got against the Yanks?'

'I've nothing against them. I just wish you'd told me, that's all.' It simply means there's less chance for Jutta to escape thoughts of her subterfuge, the cloud of risk hanging over her. The Allies are not entirely against Wall-breakers, in fact they often applaud them privately after the act. Equally, they have to be seen to be upholding some form of law, and not rubbing shoulders with those who flout the rules. Those like her.

It turns out they are not only Americans, but servicemen too. Smart, well pressed and good-looking, but military all the same, causing an extra reminder of Jutta's recent incursion. Irma's date, Tom, is not in the least bit shy and makes a beeline for her, leaving his friend to make his own introductions. Not that he's unfamiliar; Jutta recognises him instantly.

'Hello again,' he says, sitting beside her and holding out a hand. He's smiling while gesturing at her half-drunk cocktail. 'I see you're not knocking back the brandy tonight?'

'No, not today,' she smiles. He inhabits the tan-khaki uniform as if he was born in it – the same all-American look she remembers from that convenient bar near the Harzer Strasse, the one where she was enthusiastically sinking alcohol to steady her frayed nerves after ghosting through the Wall. Illegally.

'Forgive me, but I just have to say it,' he adds. There's a real glint in his blue eyes and, with his neat dark hair, he looks every inch the army boy. And yet, she detects something else too.

159

'And what would that be?'

'*Of all the bars in all the world . . .*' He laughs. 'A true movie moment, don't you think? It must mean we're destined to be together.'

Except he says it with enough mockery, in his faux-Bogart accent, that it's saved from being a dreadful flirtation. Jutta can't help laughing, and a large portion of her week's stress drops away in an instant.

Irma and Tom are head to head in one half of the booth, and so she and the formally introduced Danny Strachan inhabit their own portion of the bar bubble. And Jutta finds, for once, that it's not awkward, or embarrassing, or that she's the spare part to Irma's consistent search for a husband who might whisk her out of Berlin and Germany.

'Do you make a habit of being "the other guy"?' she asks Danny, tongue firmly in cheek, loosened by a second cocktail that he ordered with a well-practised flick of his fingers. They've morphed into talking English – Danny's German is passable, though slightly wooden, and Jutta's English easily more accomplished.

'I try not to,' he replies, 'but Tom's a good friend. He'd do the same for me. And really, this is not hard work.'

He says it while sipping at his own drink, hiding a wry smile. Jutta hadn't wanted to like her blind date, had been almost determined not to, but she finds she can't help it. He's undeniably attractive, mid-height and solid rather than stocky, but, more than anything, his easy demeanour is a welcome respite.

To Jutta, Lieutenant Strachan seems as if he was born into a uniform, and he admits his presence in Berlin is a fait accompli. 'The military is in my family,' he explains. 'My dad was in the Air Force, some hot-shot in the war, and my uncle is on the Allied staff here.'

'Really?' His assertion causes that tweak of discomfort to surface in Jutta again.

He nods. 'I don't mind admitting that I rather traded on my uncle's name to get my place over here. Not that we see much of each other. But I was intrigued.'

'By Berlin?'

'By everything – the city, the people, the Wall . . .'

'We're not exhibits in a zoo, you know,' she flashes instantly, her brow furrowed with irritation, enough that he pulls back slightly.

'No, I didn't mean it like that,' he counters. 'Really, I didn't – only that I couldn't imagine how it would be, surrounded by something most people hate, being cut off . . .'

The words hack into her, a spasm in her stomach so piercing that Jutta pulls her hand to her abdomen and gulps back a cry, Danny's words firing a memory of that first day and night without Karin by her side. *Cut off.* Now the incision feels like it's stabbing with fresh purpose from the inside.

'I'm sorry, I have to go,' she says, picking up her bag and scrambling from the booth.

'Was it something I said?' Danny is blindsided. 'I'm sorry if I offended you.' He's following her from the bar at a pace. 'Really, it wasn't my intention to . . .'

Jutta keeps on walking, knows that her manners are wanting, but she needs to get home, to sink her face into her pillow and block out the memory. Or sob it out.

Danny Strachan, however, is insistent, and he follows her out of the bar. 'Jutta, please. Hold on.'

She stops, if only out of politeness, turns and fiddles with the handle of her bag.

'Look, I don't know what I said to offend you but, whatever it was, I apologise,' he urges.

'It's not you. It's me,' she replies flatly. 'I'm . . . I don't know what I am, but I need to leave. Now. I'm sorry.'

His eyes are even bluer out of the darkened bar: vibrant and friendly. Too intent to ignore. 'Can I least see you again, start off fresh? C'mon, give a Yank a chance, eh?'

She can't help but consider. Just his bright, open face is easing the twist inside. 'Yes, of course. Let's do that,' she nods.

He walks her through the lobby to the front entrance, hails a taxi from under the awning and slips the driver several notes. 'Here's looking at you, kid,' he says through the taxi window.

She angles her head.

'*Casablanca*? Rick and Ilsa? Remember – we're destined.'

What was that? Jutta stares out of the taxi window as it draws away from the Hilton. The agonising torque of her gut has left a soreness beneath the dress that Karin stitched for her, a cool jersey cotton she remembers her sister battling to control under the machine's needle. She holds her hand firmly there. *Oh, Karin, why didn't you come back, to drink cocktails at the Hilton? Just a taste of the luxury that you deserve. To laugh with me again. To feel normal. Whole. Why, Karin?*

'You're home early,' Mama says from her armchair in front of the small television. 'Was your evening good?'

'Fine,' Jutta lies, and plants herself on the chair opposite. 'Where is everyone?'

'Oh, Hugo is with his friends, and I've persuaded Gerda and Oskar to go out for dinner. It's about time.'

'Are they all right, those two?' Aside from their occasional walks to work, Jutta and her mother rarely seem to have time alone to talk, especially in the apartment. Once Jutta retreats to her bedroom and shuts the door, her mother respects her need for space.

'You know Gerda, she's always fine,' Ruth says. 'But Oskar – no, he isn't himself. Not since . . . well, that time.' She can't bring herself to say 'since the Wall, since Karin', but Jutta nods an understanding.

'Is he ill? He looks it sometimes,' she presses.

'Well, if he is, he hasn't told Gerda, and she tells me everything. I suspect it's something to do with his business, which he *does not* tell Gerda about, that's for sure.' Ruth wraps her cardigan around her body in a gesture of disdain, even though the evening is still warm.

The television voice twitters into the silence between the chairs.

'Are you all right, my love?' Ruth says eventually.

Jutta looks up, disguising alarm. 'Yes. Why?'

'Oh, I don't know, you seem a little distracted recently.'

Unease takes flight again inside Jutta's gut. 'Do I? Sorry, I don't mean to be. Stuff at work, that's all. I'm fine, Mama. Really.'

They chat about almost nothing for half an hour – a new member of staff at Ruth's work, someone who's leaving to have a baby – each aware they are skirting the issue of the anniversary fast approaching: the date that has a dual signif-icance, for the city and the family in unison. Soon, it will be two years since the Wall, and Karin. *How can I not tell Mama? And yet, how would she begin to understand Karin's delay?*

Jutta pushes back the urge to confess, saved also by Gerda coming through the door alone, weary but resigned to the fact that Oskar has sloped off to the local *kneipe* after being forced to have dinner with his wife. She and Ruth settle in for a lengthy moan about the limitations of the male race and Jutta takes the opportunity to sidle away.

Lying in her room, she reflects on the week; not in the least taxing at work, but elsewhere it feels as if she's living in either a novel or a parallel universe. She has become – officially – a Wall-jumper, a 'border violator', a rule-breaker and a risk to the family. She saw, touched and held Karin, and yet she has to reach deep down inside herself to recall the intimacy. Her sister's choice delivered a crippling disappointment, though it's been alleviated slightly by something nice in meeting Danny. She cringes with embarrassment at her own behaviour and the abrupt end to the evening, which was not his fault, and came entirely from within her. Hopefully, she'll be able to make it up to him, especially as his face, and those eyes, insist on nudging unexpectedly into her vision.

The next morning, the weekend continues to wax and wane, the hands on the clock seemingly stuck and then circling impossibly fast. On one of his rare weekends off, Hugo senses Jutta's agitation and pulls her out of the city centre. They borrow some bikes and cycle out to the lakes at Havel, ending up exhausted and starving on the grassy banks.

'So, what's the plan?' her cousin asks, as he bites into a chunk of his mother's apple cake. 'For Monday?'

With the effort of pedalling and the ache in her legs, Jutta has forgotten for a second and is jerked back to her dilemma, though she can't be irritated with Hugo for his concern.

'I honestly don't know,' she says, lying back on the grass and squinting at the drift of snowy clouds. 'I mean, I want to see her, of course I do. But can I go back and forth for six months?'

'It's risky, Jut,' he murmurs.

'I know it is. And I'll be careful. But how can I keep away, when we have this window?'

Silence signals his agreement. Thank God she has Hugo to confide in; the crossing is bad enough, but if she had to suppress her secret from everyone, it might be her undoing.

Still, Jutta is surprised that Hugo hasn't posed the obvious request, either to go with her, or for the exact whereabouts of her gateway. His curiosity as a reporter is keen enough, and it occurs to her for a second that his restraint is down to fear. He's afraid of being caught, of being a young man in the Stasi's grasp. And that's good. He should be. Gerda should not go through the loss of her only child. And Jutta has to make doubly sure her mother does not lose another.

The respite over, she wakes in the early hours of a new week with a familiar twist in her stomach and massages it away with reason. She will not be caught, it's as simple as that. At the same time, there is no avoiding the Wall; she has to see Karin. There is only one way forward, and that is to ghost through again.

32

Twins Entwined

Karin wakes suddenly, her eyes snapping open suddenly like a porcelain doll's, and she stares in the half-light at the patchy ceiling, Otto's breathing deep and steady beside her. He stays over almost every Saturday and Sunday night, and perhaps once in the week now, Karin having long since soothed her own conscience over sex before marriage – she's been deprived of too much to believe in the higher morals of the church anymore. Besides, she loves him, and he tells her he loves her often enough, and they allude to a future together. She can picture herself at the altar, though perhaps not in ostentatious white, even if she could get the material to make it herself. But try as she might, Karin can't make out the scene of where they are, where they will call home, perhaps where their babies will be born. Will it be dull, or bright? Will they feel free? And whose version of 'free' will that be? And now, since seeing Jutta: East or West?

The hands of her clock signal 4.45 and she wills herself

back to sleep, keen to be alert for the day ahead. There will be no lengthy shift at the hospital wielding her cleaning cart, not today. But she'll go through the motions of preparing for work, hoping Otto will leave for his office before she normally does, so she can get ready. Inside, she is conflicted. How can excitement sit alongside fear, when she's thinking of her own sister?

Otto seems not to suspect as he prepares for work, making coffee and eating the rolls he brought the night before, then kissing her tenderly on the lips. 'Have a lovely day,' he says on leaving. 'Keep safe.'

Does he normally say that? Karin thinks back. *Or does he suspect something different?*

There's no time to ponder, though. She scrapes back her hair in the bathroom mirror speckled with age and opens the carton she's brought from the shop, costing almost a third of her week's wages and an hour's queueing time.

33

Differences

Jutta spots Karin's familiar gait skirting the edge of the sprawling Alexanderplatz and notes her sister's contented expression. By contrast, her own face turns to wide-eyed surprise.

'My God, Karin! What have you done to your hair?'

'I dyed it.' Karin pulls off her peaked beret to reveal the near white blonde of her bob, her sharp and freshly cut fringe trimmed in the mirror. 'Do you like it?'

'Well, it's certainly different,' Jutta ventures. 'And it makes us look distinct.'

'That's the whole point,' Karin replies. 'We couldn't spend the day walking around like a mirror image of each other. That would attract attention.'

Jutta doesn't like to point out their resemblance is the least aligned at this moment, and not due to any dramatic hair transformation. Karin's drawn features make her instantly different. *Or am I being too judgemental?*

But Karin isn't wrong – as they link arms and head

purposefully out of the square, Jutta feels a short blonde bob next to her long black hair makes them distinct enough. Unless anyone cares to look closely, they are not the twins of the past.

'How was the crossing?' Karin asks

'Surprisingly all right,' Jutta says. If she discounts the hammering heart and grating nausea, today's passage through the house was uneventful. 'Easy' would be going too far. Again, there were few people about to hear her footfall in landing on East German soil, and she had swiftly brushed herself down and walked with false bravado through the alleyways into the main street. One of the Vopos had even smiled at her again, and she'd returned his friendly look, flooded with an inner satisfaction.

'So, where are we going?' Jutta asks.

'There's a large park about twenty minutes' walk away,' Karin says. 'It's got a woody area, and a small coffee booth. I've brought a few bits for lunch.'

'Me too,' Jutta holds up a linen bag triumphantly.

'Then we're all set.'

For a second, it's like being twelve years old again and marching towards the Tiergarten for a Sunday treat in one of the cafés hugging the small lakes. Until a green and white Wartburg rolls by on the street, its side emblazoned with *Polizei*, and Jutta feels Karin's grip tighten. Her sister's eyes dart left and right without the slightest shift of her head, and only when the patrol car turns the corner do her fingers relax on Jutta's arm.

The park is large and sparsely populated, though they steer clear of the clusters of mothers with small children and head into a small copse of trees, where the sun fights its way through the branches, creating a mosaic of colours on the mulchy floor. They spread out a thin sheet and, with the finesse of a magician pulling a rabbit from a hat, Jutta produces a large slab of Gerda's dense fruit cake from her bag.

Karin's eyes are as wide as any child's, her smile from ear to ear. 'No!' she cries. 'I've been dreaming of Gerda's cooking for so long.' She marvels at all the dried fruit before pushing it into her mouth, spilling crumbs with her fervour.

'And now, for my next trick . . .' Jutta rummages for a large orange, holding it in the palm of her hand and readying to peel it.

'No, no!' Karin stops her, girding it with her hands. 'Not here.'

'Don't you want it?' Jutta's voice betrays a slight wounding.

'Of course I do, but if anyone should smell it . . .' Karin looks almost embarrassed. 'We shouldn't attract attention, that's all. I'll enjoy it later.' And she goes back to devouring her cake, washed down with the insipid, frankly foul coffee they bought from the booth at the entrance to the park, though it's still the best picnic both of them can recall.

'Oh Karin, what are we going to do?' Jutta pitches the question lazily into the rustling trees. Their picnic is just crumbs and Karin's newly blonde head is lying on her flattened belly, Jutta twizzling the thin strands in her long fingers, sensing the thread between them grow stronger again as Karin's sinews melt into hers. Their dilemma is not about now – the day is already planned out, and they will lie here and talk and reminisce until Jutta begins to feel slightly feverish about the journey back through, and then their time will end. The bigger issue remains: can they keep doing this until Karin is ready to leave? Is it plainly stupid to not expect the portal to be bulldozed in the next few months? Or worse, discovered?

But Karin's silence says she can't, or won't, face it just yet, her breathing steady and relaxed against Jutta's abdomen. It's clear there's only one other person who can make Karin feel so content inside – and his life is here, in East Berlin.

Jutta, though, wants to understand Karin's choice. She needs to. 'So, where did you meet Otto?' she begins.

'At the hospital ironically,' Karin says. 'He almost bumped into me while visiting his papa.' She smiles at the memory. 'I think he must have some magical ability to see beyond the surface, because he asked me for a drink, despite that dreadful overall and me in a shocking state.'

A short pause.

'Is it the real thing?' Jutta says.

Karin's head shifts, and she laughs; the two of them spent hours talking as teenagers in the dim light of their bedroom about which man would represent 'the real thing', someone to relinquish everything for.

'Do you mean will I have his babies and live happily ever after?' Her playful tone only just disguises a hardness that Jutta can now hear, that her sweet sister Karin has become worldly-wise.

'Well, will you?'

Another pause, shorter. 'Yes, I hope. Probably.' She twists her head to look up at Jutta's face. 'But we are careful now.'

Jutta feels the knot in her stomach roll against Karin's head. To her knowledge, Karin hadn't slept with anyone before being engulfed by the East. Boyfriends, yes, kisses probably, but no one she felt ready to give herself to entirely. Otto must be different. Truly the real thing.

'What about you?' Karin asks. 'Any nice academics at the university?'

171

'No, they're all very intense and take themselves far too seriously.' For a second, she holds back about 'her American', as Hugo has labelled him, then feels embarrassed at her own arid love life. 'But I have met someone recently.'

'Oh yes?' Karin sits up, suddenly curious.

'Just once. He's nice, so far.'

'*Nice?*' Karin wrinkles her nose and Jutta can see plainly why this Otto has fallen in love with her. 'Come on, Ja-Ja. Spill!' Her eyes sparkle with intrigue.

'All right. He's American. Military.'

Karin throws back her head with glee. 'Oh, what a pair we are with our men! Between us we've got one dreamy socialist and an all-American Red-hater. Should we make up a foursome, do you think?'

Jutta surveys her sister. She *has* changed, her humour still playful, but it's developed a sharper edge. Is it any surprise, considering what she's been through? Karin, of all people, has every right to be cynical.

They lie for hours under the trees, Karin hungry for information about the family, and talking of all the letters they've written and never received, before moving on to Hugo and his new confidence at the radio station.

'Ironic, isn't it, that the Wall has given him that?' Karin says, though without bitterness. 'Robbing so much from so many others.' Jutta is urged to give a blow-by-blow account of Kennedy's visit, and Karin lies with her eyes closed, so obviously stitching together each description in her mind; more than ever, it's the way she sees the world now, weaving dreams inside her own head.

'Has your American got lots of hair and a big smile like JFK?' Karin giggles to herself, causing Jutta to pinch her in response. 'Ow!'

But Jutta isn't deterred by her sister's teasing. Strangely, she can only recall Danny's eyes, deep and ice blue, and she forces herself to think. 'No, but it's a nice smile. Listen, Karin, it's not true love, I only just met him.'

Then it's her turn to pump her sister for information over the beloved Otto. 'Have you been introduced to his parents yet?'

Karin shifts and deflates slightly. 'He lives with them for now, so yes.'

'And?'

'They're nice enough people, though entirely duped by, or afraid of, the regime.' Karin fidgets, sits up and looks at Jutta face on. 'They have no oomph, Ja-Ja. I understand how people want to be cared for, how the system makes them feel safe in one way. But it's like they're wearing blinkers . . .' here Karin swivels her head side to side, in what's become an entirely automatic move when speaking such words '. . . and they don't even see that they are. I know they think I'm bad for Otto, for his future in the East. The truth is, they're just hoping that we'll tire of each other.'

Jutta doesn't punctuate the silence.

'We won't, you know,' Karin adds defensively. 'Get fed up.'

'I didn't say you would.'

'But you thought it. You might even want it.' Karin looks hurt, crestfallen. Jutta reaches out and clasps both her hands, noting their roughness, the calluses in different places to the ones caused by hand-stitching. Wizened work hands.

'Oh Karin,' she sighs. 'I'm trying to understand, really I am. But it's not just for me – although God knows I miss you like crazy. It's for Mama and Gerda too. I haven't told them yet, about seeing you . . . I wouldn't know how. You can see how they might struggle to understand the delay, can't you?'

Karin nods silently, causing two lines of tears to dislodge and roll down her face, nestling on the rim of her lips. She moulds into Jutta and they hug and weep together under the dappling leaves. It isn't what they'd planned for the day, but perhaps what they need at that moment.

'Oh, I wish you could meet him right now, Ja-Ja,' Karin sniffs. 'You would see why then. I know you would.'

They both know it's too soon. Poor Otto, to be faced with the shock of his girlfriend's doppelgänger, no mistaking the likeness up close. People have told them time and again they even sound the same.

'Soon enough,' Jutta says, and she feels the tension run through her sister at the challenge she faces.

They pack up at 3.30, Jutta again keen to avoid the work crowds when slipping back into the alleyway. They make an exchange before reaching the streets – Jutta hands over American dollars, worth far more to Karin on the black market than the hollow Ostmarks, and Karin gives out Eastern currency for Jutta to buy train tickets or for use in cafés. The amount is a fraction of the dollars, but it may prove priceless in helping her to blend in.

They part in the narrow streets just north of Alexanderplatz, hugging so tightly it feels as if their bodies are truly blending. It reminds Jutta of the time when one of them would crawl into the other's bed for comfort, body parts slotting in like puzzle pieces and where Mama would find them in the morning, in exactly the same position.

They decide on twelve days until the next meet, co-inciding with Karin's day off so as not to arouse suspicion among the hospital staff.

'Keep safe,' Jutta breathes into Karin's hair, drawing in

her smell, mixed with the pungent ammonia from the cheap hair dye.

'It's me who should be saying that,' Karin replies. 'Listen, Ja–Ja – don't compromise yourself, ever. If it looks wrong, walk away. Don't come. Somehow, I'll find a way to get a message to you.' She pulls back from Jutta and a look passes between them. Karin's is a solid, strong expression. 'I will survive. I have so far, haven't I?'

'I've no doubt that you will,' Jutta says. 'But I also want you to live.'

34

The Real Thing

Karin watches Jutta descend the steps into the S-Bahn on Alexanderplatz, having warned her sister to keep aware and put her nose in a book, especially when they stop at stations; the Trapos transport brigade are peppered with Stasi all too adept at spotting potential 'jumpers'.

Suddenly restless, Karin needs somewhere to direct her energy and thinks of trawling through second-hand shops for cheap material. Strangely, though, she has no appetite for it. Besides, the dollars she has from Jutta are for essentials and shouldn't be spent on luxuries – although making dresses out of musty old curtains feels anything but luxurious. She's swilling in her own indecision, exactly how she felt the last time she and Jutta parted. She needs grounding.

Karin makes her way north of Alexanderplatz, snaking through grey streets and past buildings that form a sharp contrast – either dilapidated by the war, or sporting the crisp lines of the new communist style, ordered and functional. Once, it seemed almost like another country to

Karin – *was* another country – but now it's all too familiar. Should she be worried or comforted that she feels strangely at home in East Berlin now? And for how long?

The building she arrives at is an ornate, pre-communist structure, though made more tolerable to the GDR by the bullet holes pocked into the stone from the 1945 battles, giving it at least a history of struggle alongside the opulent architecture. The GDR flag sits stoutly at the entrance, and Karin tries not to feel cowed by it.

Gingerly, she climbs the steps into the echoey, high-ceilinged reception, not unlike the Charité, though with no odour of the Lysol that's now so familiar to her. The fierce Frau at the desk tries to ignore her, but in having to square up to the Charité's own severe receptionist from time to time, Karin is more than a match. She smiles sweetly, draws back her shoulders and pushes forth an air of impor-tance.

'Otto Kruger. Would you be so kind as to call his office please?'

'And you are?'

'A colleague,' Karin lies. 'From the Housing Ministry.'

The sentinel looks her up and down, drinking in Karin's casual shift dress.

'I'm on my day off,' she explains. 'And I'm very short of time. So, if you wouldn't mind?'

There's a huff, followed by the sound of a number being dialled. 'He'll be down shortly,' she grunts dismissively. 'You can wait over there.'

Karin sits opposite the once grandiose stairway, now moulded into functionality by a dull, metal bannister. She ignores the bodies toing and froing and scouts for one sight only. *I'll know*, she thinks to herself. *When he comes, I'll know. If it's worth the risk.*

When he does appear, at the top of the stairway and squinting towards the floor below, Karin is sure. She's certain because her heart floods with a tidal wave of scarlet lava and, even though she's sitting down, it flows at breakneck speed, hot and urgent. Firm in her decision.

'He's the real thing, Ja-Ja,' she mutters under her breath.

Otto looks quizzical as he descends the steps and finds Karin at the bottom. 'Hey, were we supposed to meet, have I forg—?'

'No, no,' she reassures. 'I got off early, that's all. Thought I'd surprise you. Can you get away now? We could sneak off and see a film.' She grins, knowing how much he loves her spontaneity.

He's pleased, clearly, but also torn. Otto takes his time-keeping seriously – in anyone else it might seem servile or geeky, but with him it's more often about how much he can get done, how much he can achieve for others. And she has to remember, he grew up in the East, in the Soviet zone since the city was divided up in 1945. Then, it was one city, but with boundaries which some were loath to cross, his parents especially. Otto is a child of the East, as much as Karin is a product of the free West. Or was.

'Listen, I've got half an hour's work to do,' he says. 'I'll meet you in the café on the corner of Lottumstrasse. Thirty minutes, promise.' He grabs her hand and squeezes, all too aware of the fierce Frau's beady eye on them both.

The café is one she's never been to before, populated with office workers and a few old men drinking schnapps. It's not like her favourite haunt of the Presse Café, alive with student talk and a backdrop of amateur bands and folk singers, painstakingly learning songs from beyond the Iron

Curtain. If she's honest, she likes the Presse because it reminds her most of cafés in the West.

With her mouth still sour from the bitter coffee in the park, Karin orders a Vita Cola and sits looking at the bottle – the GDR's own, poor substitute for Coca-Cola, although she has become oddly accustomed to its citrusy taste. Or is she kidding herself? Swiftly, she banishes any creeping thoughts of sitting on Kranzler's top tier, sipping an old-style 'Coke' and blissfully people-watching with Jutta, admiring the fashionable women sashaying through Berlin's vibrant centre. That life is distant – but can she make it return?

Otto is on time, as promised. He's smiling as he sits down and orders a beer, grasping at her hands across the table and stroking her fingers affectionately. He's already loosened his tie, and his blond hair is ruffled from a hasty walk. Unlike Jutta, he doesn't notice the calluses on Karin's fingers, given that they're so like his mother's. They register merely as women's hands, a proud symbol of equality in East Germany's working classes.

'How's your day been?' Otto is always eager to hear about her time at the hospital, just as Karin is endlessly fascinated by the work he seems to carry in his head, designing functional but quality homes on the scant budget he has, toiling to make them less like the barren concrete blocks he secretly loathes as an architect.

'Fine,' she says. It's not a lie, since the day was more than fine, just not at work. She tries to push away her guilt. 'You?'

'Good.' He takes a gulp of his beer. 'Ernst called me into his office today.'

'Oh?' Karin tries not to sound alarmed, even though Otto is smiling.

'It's amazing – I've been given a large block in Leipzig

179

to design. Four hundred homes. I'll be the senior architect, my first lead.'

'That's great, but Leipzig?' Karin is mildly panicked since it's more than 150 kilometres further south. 'Will you need to leave Berlin?'

He shakes his head. 'Only for a few days at a time, once or twice. Maybe we can take a trip together. Have you ever been?'

'No.'

'It's very rundown but still nice. Old and quaint. I have an uncle there.'

Now is as good a time as any. 'Do you think you could ever live anywhere but East Berlin?' Karin pitches casually.

'Hmm, possibly. There are some lovely places further East. Perfect for a young couple like you and . . .' There's a playful glint in his eye then. 'But hey, don't say you're thinking of leaving me already?'

She dismisses his blithe suggestion with a firm shake of her head, mouth firmly closed to hide the deceit, and Otto rambles on about Leipzig and family holidays, while Karin's mind feels static against her task. Already, she feels herself drained of hope.

'Karin?' Otto's voice cuts through. 'What's wrong? You've gone as white as a sheet.'

'Nothing.' *Nothing that a new life – a new world – won't fix.*

35

The History Man

14th July 1963, West Berlin

The very chic bar at the Hotel am Zoo has a younger
crowd than the Hilton, which makes Jutta feel a little less
jittery, but she's never been at ease waiting in such places.
She's early though, and slips behind a corner table nestled
in the shadows, filling the time by squinting through stylish
but not very effective lighting. As she scans the crowd, her
eyes are drawn to the fashionable women with lean bodies
and stiffly sculpted beehives, making them appear like
walking lollipops. She watches as they bat huge kohl-lined
eyes at stocky East German businessmen who have
somehow ghosted through the Wall on a whim – Jutta is
damn sure *they* don't scrabble through their own dusty
rabbit hole to reach the West. Money speaks, clearly, if you
know which border guards to bribe on a regular basis.

'Hello there.' Right on time, Danny slides into the seat
next to her, wearing a look of concern. 'Am I late?' He
smooths down his dark brown hair, perhaps as a way of
centring himself and checking his flushed face doesn't sport

any sweat. He flicks his fingers at the bartender and orders Martinis.

'No, it was me, I was hopelessly early.' Jutta is pleased to see he's not wearing uniform this time – a neat blue suit, expensively and expertly cut (tell-tale signs that she's picked up from Karin), and which shows off more of his broad shoulders and honed body. The tone matches his eyes, still a glowing blue despite the shadowy lighting.

'You look lovely,' he smiles.

'You too,' she counters, and finds she means it.

'Oh, this old rag,' he jokes back. 'And there's me thinking I didn't have a thing to wear.'

His humour breaks the ice perfectly, and Jutta eases into the conversation and the evening. Danny had suggested they meet on calling her at the library two days before – she'd hesitated for a few seconds on the end of the receiver, then quickly recalled how ungenerous her spirit had been towards him. *He's just being nice, for goodness sake.*

'Yes, that would be lovely,' she'd said finally.

On the phone, they planned on drinks only, but neither has eaten and they walk from the Am Zoo to a small Italian restaurant just a few streets away. 'Every guy at the base craves Italian food,' Danny says as he leads the way. Once or twice, she feels his fingers make fleeting contact with hers, then the air as his whip away into the space between them.

The house special carbonara is delicious, preventing Jutta's head from spinning with the white wine Danny orders.

'So, tell me about your family,' he smiles, expertly twirling and forking the pasta strands. Those eyes are on her as she swallows to hide a sudden, heavy pulse in her chest. *Is this when I deny my sister's existence entirely?*

'Um, I live with my mother in Schöneberg, and my

aunt and uncle, and their son, though he's more of a brother to me really.' Jutta pushes it all out in one, swift sentence. *Not forgetting my twin sister who is a prisoner of the GDR and it's breaking my heart.*

'And your father?'

'Killed in the war, the Battle of Berlin,' she says quickly.

'Oh, I'm sorry.' There's a downturn to his mouth, as if he alone shoulders the guilt of his country.

'It was a long time ago.' She smiles, eyes alight under her dark fringe. 'I promise – we don't hold grudges.'

'Phew, that's a relief.'

His family is from small-town Connecticut, he tells her, which is why he's been drawn to the excitement of Berlin, with its easy access to the rest of Europe – Paris, London and Rome. 'I figured if I was going to travel, then this would be the best posting.'

'And your job, isn't that a good enough reason?' Jutta asks, though stops short of probing any more. From experience, she knows it's pointless to enquire precisely what anyone in the military does for the mighty United States of America.

'It's okay – for now,' he shrugs. 'But paper-pushing isn't my forte. I'm far more of a people person.' He looks up. 'Though that's for other people to decide, I guess.'

'So what is in your heart then? Where will you end up after your wanderlust?'

He glances up, looks at her as if she's enquired into the well of his soul and sits back in his chair. 'You might be disappointed,' he says.

'Maybe I won't.'

'Well, when I say people, I mean dead people.' He laughs. 'And no, I'm not a pathologist, or some strange guy who hangs about in mortuaries. It's history, though not your

183

dry dates kind. I'm fascinated by the way everyone in the past lived, ate, made babies, died. What I believe the Brits generally call the "nitty gritty".'

'Isn't there a good deal of paper-pushing in that?' Jutta pitches. 'Quite dry and dusty paper?'

'Ah,' he says, elbows on the table and hunching his shoulders forward. The light in his eyes flickers. 'That's where everyone is wrong. If you rummage around for the right documents, then the people come alive, they pop out from the page.'

Jutta can see it there in his face – a lifelong passion. 'And so where would you do this living history, your *rummaging*?' She's humouring him, enjoying his zeal. Being bookish herself, she finds it wholly appealing.

'I've got my eye on a fellowship at Columbia,' he says. 'Entirely selfish – I get to live amid the buzz of New York, bury my head in books, and teach a few students when I feel the need to be with living, breathing people.'

'Sounds perfect,' she says. 'Just the military to get over first.'

He shrugs again. 'Uh, I can wait,' he says. 'Being here is more than enough reward. It's not many places where you get to see history being made in front of your eyes.' He holds back then as Jutta's eyebrows twitch, wary he's made the same mistake as on the aborted date at the Hilton. 'Oh, I didn't mean . . . Christ, I'm not being very articulate, am I?'

Jutta cocks her head, though, seeing this side of him, she isn't offended. In fact, he's becoming more attractive by the minute. *Tell me more*, her gesture says.

'It's what I was talking about: a living history,' he goes on. 'I love witnessing how people get by day to day, in the middle of war or unease, when their cities are under siege

184

– how they find stuff to eat, feed their children, socialise. Keep whole.'

They don't always, Jutta thinks.

'Do you really think that Berliners are under siege?' she says instead.

'Yes and no,' he replies. 'Coming from where I do, I wonder how people live in a relatively small space, like a limb out in an ocean. And yet, from what I can see, people here don't seem constrained. I detect there's anger at the Wall, but not a sense of frustration in their own portion of the city. Quite the opposite.'

'You learn to live within your confines,' Jutta tells him plainly. 'I've always lived on this island.' She considers telling him she's only ever been outside of Berlin once in her twenty-six years, to Frankfurt to see a distant relative; the sensation of driving down the autobahn connecting Berlin to West Germany, and feeling . . . how does she remember it? Exposed. 'I'm sure I speak for a lot of West Berliners – we're not living in a fishbowl, desperate to swim out.'

His shoulders slump. 'I hope I've not offended you again. Because I really don't mean to. And I don't want to study you, either.'

This time she doesn't curb her laughter. 'Well, that's good, because I'd be a very poor subject.'

'But I would like to get to know you. If you'll allow me.' He puts down his fork and pushes his hands across the table, making a fleeting connection with her skin. He doesn't grasp, clasp or grab. He just makes human contact and, inside, Jutta starts. Surprises herself at how welcome it is, how much in her constant state of unease that she needs it. Friendship. There is no hope of confiding in Danny about Karin, or her furtive slipping through the Wall. But to have something in her life, aside from what

185

feels like a suspended existence on one side and ghosting briefly to another . . . it's enough.

'I'd like that too,' she says.

'Then I promise, hand on heart, that I will not put you under my historian's microscope, or scratch you into my dusty books.'

'That's a deal, as you Americans say.' She puts down her fork and inches her fingers towards his. Another touch, to seal their understanding.

His grin is wide and pleasing. 'Then let's celebrate! They have *the* best gelato here, better than Greenwich Village, though I can't vouch for the whole of Italy.'

Afterwards, they meander down the Kurf'damm, faces lit by the bright neon, and this time he searches the space for her hand and Jutta doesn't resist. She glances at men and women similarly linked and, although she is a long way from thinking they are a couple, she's pleased at the belonging, the sense of sharing the evening with someone. Once it was Karin, but Karin has Otto now. She's sharing *her* dreams with him. Perhaps it's time for Jutta to branch out.

She points out some of the clubs and cafés to go to, and those that are better avoided; they look in the right shop windows and laugh at what he calls the 'kookier' displays, mannequins in odd contortions. It's getting late and both have work in the morning, but neither seems keen to signal the end of the evening.

'We'll get a cab and I'll drop you home,' Danny says at last. 'Are you free next Saturday? Afraid I have a reception in the evening, but I'm free all day.'

Inside, she lights up, then remembers Karin. *No thanks, Danny, I'll be risking life and liberty to see my sister, hopping into the communist state next door.* How ludicrous does her life sound then?

'Um, I've got a family occasion on Saturday,' she says, only glad it's not an outright lie. 'But any other day after that.'

Ruth and Gerda are still up, pretending they're clearing out the sewing box instead of waiting up for the merest detail of her evening. Hugo has clearly let slip about Jutta being on a date.

'Nice evening?' Gerda mutters, pins splayed between her teeth. Bless her, she's trying to sound casual, though inside Jutta can see she's burning with curiosity.

'Lovely, thanks.'

'Go anywhere nice?' Ruth chips in.

'Hotel am Zoo.' At which two sets of eyebrows rise up. To them, it means class, and money, if not entirely the best of taste, though she resists the way their expressions are urging her to sit down and tell. 'I'm very tired though, goodnight.'

Jutta is smiling as she leaves her mother and aunt in the parlour, with eyes like saucers and conjecture bubbling from their lips in low whispers. She slips under the bedcovers, reflecting on a near-perfect evening. There's only one thing that would make it complete and that's for her sister to be lying in the bed opposite, her head pushing up from the eiderdown. 'Come on, Ja-Ja, how was it?' she would urge in days of old. 'Tell me everything.'

But there's no voice from across the room. Only silence.

36

Another Ghost

20th July 1963, East Berlin

The sisters meet again in Alexanderplatz, on the south side this time as arranged, and Karin glides by and takes Jutta's arm as if they're in the midst of a usual weekend sojourn back home. Jutta would like to think the journey – from one universe to another, it often feels – had been as seamless, but in reality the thought still makes her tremble and the actual transfer is always hot with anxiety. Each time she goes through, she's increasing her chances of being caught, of someone seeing and not turning a blind eye. A betting man would not give her good odds.

Today, her heart had sunk at not seeing the mama cat and her brood in the garage-house; they've obviously decamped in search of more food than Jutta can bring. A sadder sight is left in their wake – a tiny, furry body curled in the nest, sleeping for eternity, perhaps the runt of the litter and never destined to survive. She's never been superstitious, but Jutta hopes it's not an omen for today, or any subsequent trips.

Karin is in a buoyant mood, leading her away from a steady stream of people going to and fro and walking south down the wide, sweeping Karl-Marx-Allee, the GDR's opulent version of a grand boulevard to rival any capital. The city's most luxurious shops and apartments are housed in opposing lines of the vast, buttery-beige stone buildings, under box-like balconies and intricate stone façades, the sun glinting off gold-style window frames.

'Where are we going?' Jutta asks. 'I thought we were headed somewhere discreet?'

'There's a little gem I want to show you first,' Karin says proudly. Finally, she stops abruptly at a streetside café, with a huge yellow sign in modern neon lettering: Café Sybille.

'Should we?' her sister queries. It doesn't seem as private as the Presse Café near the hospital, and much less of a student hang-out. 'I mean, what if someone spots us?'

'Don't worry,' Karin says, and pulls at the band tying Jutta's ponytail, leaving her thick dark hair to fall each side of her face and mask the outline of her jaw. With Karin's shock of blonde bob and a coating of pale pink lipstick, anyone would have to stare hard to pick out anything more than a family resemblance. 'There – you could easily be my cousin,' Karin adds. 'Come on, the coffee is too good to miss.'

Jutta can see immediately that it's Karin's place – a light, high-ceilinged café behind carved stone columns, with designer furniture and quirky hand-painted images on the walls. What's more, it's populated by lean, chic men and women in fashions often seen in West Berlin. Karin is wearing one of her own creations, a shift dress with sharp lines in her distinctive style, and she looks stunning. By contrast, Jutta feels dowdy in a dark, plain tunic nipped at

189

the waist, having purposely taken steps to avoid standing out.

'They named the café after the magazine,' Karin says breathlessly after ordering coffee, and points to a stack of *Sybille* copies on the side. 'It's the bible for anyone who loves fashion. Well, it's become my bible, really.'

Jutta picks up a copy of the glossy periodical and leafs through. The content is modern and the articles clearly not entirely in line with the austerity of socialism; the ethos is challenging and she wonders how difficult it must be for them to publish in such a climate. And how long it might last.

'They have fabulous patterns,' Karin goes on. 'It's the only way to stay up to date.' She flushes with excitement and delves into her large shoulder bag. 'Here, I made you this – it's from a *Sybille* pattern.' She pulls out something folded, which, when she holds it up, unfurls to reveal a short raincoat fashioned from clear plastic. In any other design, the material might be something a maiden aunt would wear, but the pattern is modish and the patch pockets expertly sewn in black thread, with a plastic zip running up the front and two outsize buttons on the wide collar. It's what Jutta has glimpsed on the front pages of the latest fashion magazines in West Berlin, and reminds her of one designer that she mentioned to Karin in passing at their last meeting.

'Oh Karin!' Jutta cries. 'It's amazing – how did you . . .?'

'I caught one of the porters throwing out a load of plastic at the hospital, and I nabbed it. It's not real Mary Quant, I know, but . . .'

'But it's beautiful,' Jutta says. 'If it wasn't so hot today, I'd put it on now.' She fingers the perfect stitching against the unforgiving plastic and can only imagine how frustrating it must have been to push it through any sewing machine. 'I hope you made one for yourself?'

'Of course, I had oodles of the stuff left.' Karin's eyes go left to right, and she lowers her voice. 'We'll just have to be careful not to wear it on the same days.'

'You're a genius, Karin. You know that?'

'Hardly, but I have gotten more careful with my material. You know some women here even make clothes out of nappies and shower curtains?'

A pitying look flashes across Jutta's face before she can control it.

'It's fine, Ja-Ja,' Karin counters, only half-forcing a smile. 'In the end, I will be a better seamstress and make my name, if not my fortune, from a collection entirely of scraps. You never know, I may even get some of my designs in *Sybille*.'

'Well, they'd be fools to turn you down.'

Karin is entirely right about the coffee – the best they've tasted in a long time – and they linger over the pastries. Jutta watches Karin handing over her precious Ostmarks to pay, likely the equivalent of a day's wages, and she's glad to have brought more American dollars for her, to at least lessen the cash burden of their meets. She hasn't dared change up any currency herself, to avoid any suspicion.

Outside, they hop on a bus, a short ride that leaves behind the splendour of Karl-Marx-Allee, through increasingly dour residential streets and on to where the houses and factories space out, arriving on the edge of the Rummelsburger Lake. In the open, grassy spaces, Jutta studies families enjoying the sunshine, carefree and laughing against the glittering water: is everyone here trying to forget the misery of their daily lives? Or is this 'misery' only what the West imagines, a construct to create heroes and villains in the politicians' Cold War? And then she thinks of the Wall-jumpers and the helpers, and those who risk their lives to go over and under the Wall – men, women and children. That people are prepared to die for it. There must be *something* to escape from, she thinks, and a sight from their bus ride sidles into her brain: a wall graffitied in bold, scrawled in either Greek or Latin: 'TYRANNOS'. But the meaning is obvious: *Tyranny*.

They settle in the shade of a tree again, laying out a thin blanket on the bumpy grass. Jutta has brought more of Gerda's cake, dodging her aunt's surprise at how quickly the loaf has been devoured and her dark frown at Oskar, who could only shrug his shoulders in innocence. She pulls one more slim parcel from her bag and hands it to Karin. At Café Sybille she'd been dying to reciprocate her sister's gift, but thought it easily recognisable as an item from the West, and best given in private. Karin's reaction is worth the good half of the weekly wage it's cost Jutta; the bright bold colours in a block Matisse-style, printed onto a length of thick silk.

'Jutta!' she squeals. 'Where did you get *this*?'

'Hmm, I happened to pass by KaDeWe one lunchtime,' she teases. She hadn't, of course – it was a special trip to Berlin's most expensive department store, where she'd made a beeline for the haberdashery. 'I thought you might be able to whizz up a dress for yourself, and perhaps one to show to a design house.' *Anything to help realise your dream.*

'Oh Ja-Ja, it's perfect,' Karin breathes, hugging the fabric to her chest. 'It's exactly what I would have chosen.'

'Well, isn't that the advantage of being twins?'

With their feet dangling in the cool water, they talk about the week or so gone by and details of their days, about Otto's new housing project, and in turn Jutta is pumped for every detail of her second date with Danny. They don't venture into the near future and how long these days might go on for. This summer seems endless, the sun is beating down and it's too nice for life-changing decisions or disagreements. Just being together is enough. For now.

Karin, though, in her new-found flush of confidence, has one more surprise to reveal. 'I've decided,' she says firmly. Defiantly. 'I want to come through.'

A gasp escapes Jutta's lips; the words she's dreamed of hearing since their reunion. Her sister has seen the sense in not waiting for six long months.

Before it can magnify, though, Jutta's optimism is quickly tempered. 'Just for one day though – a surprise for Mama's birthday,' Karin adds quickly. 'What do you think? Is it possible?'

Jutta nods slowly, shock and disappointment combined. It's feasible, with the keyhole they've created. The question is: can it be wise, for Mama? Though even if it isn't, has she the right to deny her sister the opportunity?

Karin, it seems, has been thinking long and hard over it. 'It's not for two weeks, so plenty of time for us to plan,' she runs on enthusiastically.

'Plan what?' Jutta says. For her, it's a simple case of drawing a map in guiding Karin to the entrance in East Berlin, where Jutta will be waiting to take her back home. Together, they will face Mama's shock, then delight, followed by inevitable and crushing distress as Jutta leads her back to the rabbit-hole entrance at the end of the day, until she can make the break for good – with or without Otto.

'I don't think we should do it together,' Karin says.

'What do you mean?'

'That I can't chance being missed in East Berlin.' She waits for Jutta's reasoning to catch up with hers.

'You mean you want us to swap?' Jutta is almost laughing at the sheer idiocy of the suggestion.

'Yes,' says Karin, as if it's the most obvious solution. 'We've done it before – do you remember when you pretended to be me all the way through the school Christmas play?'

'We were *eight*, Karin!' She checks the volume of her voice as a couple glance over, lowers it almost to a whisper. 'Why can't you just disappear for a day? People do, all the time. They visit friends and relatives.'

'Not me and not here,' Karin says gravely. 'My neighbours hear everything; the woman downstairs especially – she rarely goes out and she knows what everyone is doing. She's our block monitor and almost certainly spying for the Stasi.'

Karin is probably right. Jutta knows there are thousands of informants across Berlin, largely in the East, but some in the West too; civilians who act as the eyes and the ears of the notorious secret police, snuffling out potential Wall-breakers and dissidents. Some do it out of a genuine belief in the GDR, others purely for money, but a good many are forced by blackmail, and a fear for their own families, to turn the tables on their own countrymen. It makes the Stasi one of the most successful surveillance organisations in the world, and gives them a formidable reputation. The beady eye on East Berliners has forced Karin to be wary. And while Jutta imagines that Karin could easily disappear for a few hours, she knows her sister's plan is driven by a well-founded paranoia.

Jutta pulls up a strand of her hair and gestures at Karin's white-blonde bob. 'But we look nothing like each other now,' she points out.

'But I could dye my hair back to your colour and you could . . .' Karin leaves the most obvious suggestion hanging.

'And if I agree to this – *if* – what am I going to do for a whole day being you?' Jutta can't believe she's even considering it. 'I can't work at the hospital. I wouldn't know what to do and I'm bound to be found out.'

'We'll do it on my day off,' Karin says. 'Mama's birthday is on the Sunday. If we make the swap on a Saturday, I would be off work, and you get to spend a day with her too.' She takes a breath, eyes shining, the most excited Jutta has seen her since their reunion. Karin has briefly thrown off her pasty complexion, and she looks alive. 'Think of it, Ja–Ja. Mama gets to see both her daughters. What better birthday present could we give her?'

Karin swishes the water into an eddy with her feet and grins, a look of certainty on her face, the one she always has when she's confident of winning her sister over. That expression has worked with Gerda almost every time, and more often than not with Jutta. As it does now. Karin has tugged on her sister's heartstrings and they have given way entirely.

'That still doesn't resolve the matter of what I will do?' Jutta sighs.

'Just hang around at my place,' Karin says. 'Go in and out a few times, bang the door hard so Frau Lupke gets to have a good nose, perhaps go to the café where I drink. Maybe the cinema – then you can appreciate what dire offerings we have.'

'And what about Otto?' Jutta is aware she's simply trying to invent excuses now. Being in the East feels relatively safe alongside Karin, but on her own . . .

'I'll tell him I'm busy for the day and he won't come by on a whim.'

this evening, it being on the Stasi radar, but it's among his favourite haunts, and there's a band playing. It's likely to be only cover songs and the delivery quite rough, but rumour has it they might chance playing some British and American tunes, some Elvis and perhaps even The Beatles.

'I'll just have time to change quickly after work,' Otto had said. 'Can you drop by my flat and we'll walk from there?'

By 'his' flat, he means his parents', and while Karin doesn't actively dislike Herr and Frau Kruger, she always feels uncomfortable in their company. It's abundantly clear they think she's not good enough for their son, since being good socialists doesn't mean throwing off prejudice entirely. So time spent at Otto's place is always best kept to a minimum.

'Evening Frau Kruger,' she sings as she enters their small living room, the air heavy with the staleness of boiled pork and cabbage. 'Dismal' is Karin's assessment of the Kruger colour scheme each time she visits: the brown armchairs, a dark wood sideboard coupled with the yellowy lighting and the predictable lace doily laid neatly in the centre of the dining table. Otto's mother turns her head away from the tiny television set for no more than two seconds, glued as she and her husband always are at this time in the evening to *Aktuelle Kamera*, the GDR's daily news reports, a man or woman against a starkly empty backdrop, barking out ways in which socialism is triumphing over all. In her musings, Karin likes to think it's all for show and, as soon as she exits, the Krugers will hurriedly switch channels to the illicit West German news and some genuine content, as so many households are said to do. But looking again at Frau Kruger's pained smile and slavish attention to the screen, she doesn't think so. They are true believers, a framed picture of Walter Ulbricht and his goatee beard staring down from the mantelpiece.

'Oh, there you are,' Otto says as he comes in, slipping on a light jacket. 'See you later, Mama.' He nods at his father. 'Papa.'

'Don't be late,' Frau Kruger calls behind him, in her characteristic monotone.

He's twenty-seven for God's sake! Karin thinks bitterly, then recalls it's exactly what her own mother said each time she and Jutta ventured out. And she never minded, always revelling in the emotion wrapped around such an everyday comment. Mama. There she is again, the image of her. Swiftly followed by the grey spectre of the Stasi capture-wagon.

The Presse is packed and buzzing with anticipation. There are no posters or leaflets advertising the band, but word of mouth has gathered the crowd, and the drinkers leave a small area free in the corner of the room, though it's a stretch to call it a stage. Karin and Otto grab a small table to the side with their drinks and Otto's eyes are immediately dancing, feeding off the buzz of the room.

In time, the general hum of conversation rises slightly and four young men – boys really – shuffle into the space with their guitars and amplifiers, each clutching one part of a small drum kit, and set up with breakneck speed. Within minutes, they are striking up the first chords of a song Karin recognises from the tiny transistor one of the porters keeps in his storeroom, tuned into Radio Free Berlin: The Beatles' 'Love Me Do'. It's raw and unpolished but well received by the audience, and they follow it up with the latest Elvis hit, 'Return to Sender', and then a nod to Peter Kraus, the West German equivalent rock'n'roller. The young singer in front of them fancies himself in the same league, but Karin can't help loving his bravado, the way he struts in the tiny space he's afforded, perhaps imagining himself cool in a genuine leather jacket and carving out his own plinth in the middle of the floor.

She looks at Otto enjoying himself immensely. She is too, and yet there is a small but deep-seated seam of sorrow dragging her down, that this amateur band of hopefuls is what the entire room considers a good evening's entertainment, the most they can aspire to. Except she's seen far more on the other side: there *can* be better. And now she has the opportunity to see it again. With Otto. If only he will forego everything else in his life, including his ageing parents, his unwell father especially. She looks at Otto, tapping away to the music, and he smiles broadly in her direction; instantly, she's wrenched back to the truth she's been trying to hide from herself: she can't go without him. Thanks to Jutta, she has time to make him see, to paint a picture of the West as a good future. *Their* life.

The music stops as abruptly as it began. A sense of unease ripples through the crowd until the bar owner strides across and pulls the plug from the wall, and with nimble efficiency the band packs up and disappears through a door in the back, the drinkers instinctively flowing into the space. The jukebox, with its more traditional music, sparks up and the chatter resumes as if nothing has happened, just as the door opens and two men walk in and up to the bar. Casually dressed, they look like everyone else in the café, but the word is Stasi, clearly. There's still noise, but the easy conversation is at an end.

She and Otto leave soon after, linking arms as they walk towards Karin's place.

'Shall I stay tonight?' he says once they reach the entrance to her block. He doesn't always mid-week, but Karin is pleased to see a real desire in his eyes. She needs him too, close by, a hand-stretch away across the lumpy mattress as a consistent reminder that she's doing the right thing by delaying. Because it's for no one else but Otto. When she's staring at her own meagre flat and the peeling plaster, with frequent black-outs in the electricity supply and hours without water, she questions why. Especially now, since Jutta, since the door back home has been left ajar. Why on earth stay?

But as she lies awake in the glow of the street light cutting across Otto's lean chest, rising and falling while he sleeps peacefully after making love, she can find a good reason.

'I think I can bear anything with you,' she murmurs into his skin, her hot breath causing him to stir and his hand to probe for her presence.

'I love you,' he mumbles, only half-conscious, kissing her hair and cloaking his arm around her, sinking back into a deep slumber.

'Anything,' she repeats, and closes her eyes.

38

Distractions

25th July 1963, West Berlin

After several days during which emotions in the apartment had run high for no apparent reason, Jutta is relieved when Ruth leaves for work early, giving her time to think on her walk to the university. To ruminate properly, away from the house and the sight of relatives she feels certain she wants to see for years to come – Gerda, Hugo and even Oskar. Not to mention Mama. Eyes to the pavement, she has to face her own dread then, entirely separate to Karin's but no less terrifying. Jutta has appreciated the risk and the gravity every time she moves through the Wall; her racing heart and the fleeting odour of her own sweat is a giveaway. So far, though, her hours in the East have felt like a day trip almost. What Karin suggests is only a few hours more, but seems like giant leap towards the unknown, a potential abyss. She balances the scales in her head, weighing the risk against Karin's need and Mama's elation. In every calculation, Jutta's own sacrifice is outweighed by her family's continuing loss.

There's no question: she has to morph into Karin, a captured East Berliner. And she has just under two weeks to prepare; plenty of time to overanalyse and breed her anxieties.

She confides in Hugo again, because she needs to share her burden and because she'll need his help in making sure Mama and Gerda stay put in the apartment on the appointed day for some spurious reason.

'Is she crazy?' he asks, as they talk from the safety of their rooftop. 'More to the point, are you?'

Jutta groans, knowing he's right. 'But what else can I do, Hugo? I can't deny her the chance, when she's prepared to take it.'

'Hmm.'

He must genuinely think them crazy, because Jutta knows he misses Karin like a sister and feels her absence sorely. He will lap up Karin's company when she's in front of him, and so his resistance to the very idea speaks volumes. Should they heed his caution?

'Everything all right?' Danny pushes the drinks in front of her and sits opposite. 'Do you want to go somewhere else?'

'No, no, here is fine,' she says, and picks up the bottle of Budweiser he's set down, matching hers to his with a chink.

'Sorry, no glasses,' he shrugs. 'Not quite the Hilton.'

'I like it,' she says, staring beyond Danny's shoulder around the busy American base bar, a testament to all things US: from the drapery of the Stars and Stripes across all four walls, to the hatches serving burgers and buffalo wings, another for ice-cream alone.

'I liked the film, too,' she adds. 'You can't go wrong with Steve McQueen on a motorbike with that gorgeous smile of his.'

'Even if it's where the Americans and the British win out over the evil Germans?' he pitches.

If Jutta was affronted by *The Great Escape* as the base's popular choice of film, her mood is not showing it. She laughs, takes the hand not clutching his beer bottle. 'Listen, if I was sensitive to every quip about Nazis, I would have jumped ship long ago. You get used to it, and besides, my father might have been a soldier, but he was never a Nazi. I do know that for sure. I'm having a really nice time, Danny. Looking at Steve McQueen for the entire evening is not exactly hard work.'

'Oh, so you like them rough and rugged?' He matches her flirtation.

'I'd like him just as well if he was clutching a textbook with glasses perched on the end of his nose.'

'Remind me to get my glasses out then.'

The feeling between them is buoyant and the evening over too quickly; Jutta is trying to decide if Danny is simply a distraction from other parts of her complicated life, or something more. Perhaps it's the kiss to end their evening that causes her to settle on something more. It's not her first per se, but the only one for some time, and by far the best. Yes, definitely more than a simple diversion.

He'd called a taxi to the front of the base and climbed in with her. 'You really don't have to come with me,' she'd said, though hadn't resisted too much.

'But I want to.'

As they drew up at the Schöneberg apartment, he'd squeezed at her wrist. 'I had a great evening,' he said. 'And I'd like to do it again.'

'Me too,' she nodded.

Lying in bed later, Jutta is unsure who had made the first move. She wasn't aware of her mouth drifting towards his, but there it was. She laughs, in that, looking back, it felt almost like two pieces of a jigsaw slotting together: their lips perfectly aligned. He tasted lightly of beer, both of them pressing in and moving gently away, only to drift together a second time, and a third, an impromptu cough from the cab driver putting an end to the pleasure. They drew back like two embarrassed teenagers and Jutta even heard herself giggle.

'I'd like to do that again, too,' Danny whispered as she opened the taxi door, finally letting go of her. 'I'll call you. I'm out of Berlin until next week, but as soon as I'm back.'

'I'll be here,' she'd said. *When I'm not somewhere else.*

39

Into the Cleft

3rd August 1963, the Wall

Karin steps closer to the looming shadow of the Wall; she's not aware of a conscious effort to avoid it, but these days she rarely glimpses the stark, rough concrete and the barbed wire. Or maybe her routes around the city are like sleep-walking, an unwitting effort to blinker herself from the painful reality which can only remind her of home every time. Now, though, there is no circumventing, and from under her fringe she counts each Vopo casually patrolling. Is there a higher concentration the closer she gets, or is it just her imagination?

She's done her best to memorise Jutta's map, and reaches the point between two buildings where she thinks the narrow alleyways might begin. But then nothing – her mind is blank. A sheet of white, black, it doesn't matter; it's still a complete absence of detail, of anything. She dives into a nearby corner shop and buys a copy of *Neues Deutschland*, then sits on a bench with her back to the Wall, casually sliding Jutta's hand–drawn map between the paper's open pages and keeping it close to her face, though not too close, like a very inept spy. She stares at the detail, willing it to imprint onto her memory, feeling her fingers start to shake and having to rest her elbows on her knees, so the edges of the flimsy paper don't betray her with their tremor. With several deep breaths, and waiting for a passing Vopo to walk by (*big smile, Karin*), then disappear around a corner, she rises from the bench, hoping her legs will carry her suddenly weighty form forward.

Eyes flicking left and right, Karin slides into the cleft of the alleyway. 'For goodness sake, don't hesitate and don't look back,' Jutta had told her from experience. 'If there's anyone following, it's quiet enough that you will hear them, and you'll just have to fake getting lost.'

In her disquiet, Karin overcompensates, launching herself forward at a near run and almost missing the pile of bricks acting as a marker. Is this the right place? Where *is* she? Her nerves are at fever pitch.

It's worth it, she chants to herself in moving forward. *To see Mama. It has to be.* It's then she thinks of the sacrifice Jutta has made all these weeks, the nerve she's kept. Would she have been able to do the same in her sister's shoes?

40

The Swap

3rd August 1963, the Wall

Jutta steps onto her makeshift pallet ladder and checks her watch again, the top of her head just breaching the bottom of the grubby window frame, looking out into the alleyway of East Berlin. Two minutes to ten and she's already sweating, more than usual when she's about to leap into the abyss. Ordinarily, she would take a breath, check the way is clear and force her heart to suspend its clamour as she climbs through the window and across her own tenuous border. Today, though, the wait is worse.

One minute past; Karin isn't usually late, always a stickler for timing. Has she interpreted Jutta's map properly? Did Jutta explain every detail of the turning, the stack of old bricks left in a pile by the first corner, a roll of tarpaulin abandoned by the second building? They'd met six days before, on a Sunday as has become normal, to go over the details. Under the shady cloak of tree branches, Jutta exchanged her hand-drawn map for details of Karin's apartment, plus a few tips on good places in the neighbourhood to linger and be seen. The swap today is a Saturday, the day before Mama's birthday, and so more shops and cafés are open on both sides of the city. More chance to blend in, Jutta hopes.

There's a faint scrabbling below the window, and Jutta's eyes peep over the peeling frame; she spies a grey peaked beret heading towards her and squints to see who or what is underneath. At that moment, Karin's face tips upwards to hers, fear fixed on her features but the colour in her eyes suddenly alight with joy at finding the right place, that her sister is there to greet her instead of a Vopo with a gun and the keys to jail. Jutta reads her sister's lips muttering: 'Thank God.'

In a heartbeat, Jutta's hand is out of the window and pulling on Karin's slight frame as her feet slip and slide initially on the concrete wall.

'Slow down, do it slow,' Jutta whispers urgently, until Karin stops panicking and gains a foothold, and in one fell swoop she's through the window and they both reel backwards and just manage to avoid tumbling from the pallets onto the filthy floor.

Panting, the relief is somewhere between a silent laugh and a cry. Karin rights herself eventually, and her expression says it all: *Lord, Ja-Ja, how on earth do you do that, time and again?*

They each take stock and slow their breathing in a tense embrace. There's no hurry, they both tell themselves. With some bogus excuse, Hugo has seen to it that his mother and aunt will be at home for the entire morning.

Karin pulls off her cap and Jutta gasps at another transformation – the white-blonde strands have returned to a black crown of hair and, in truth, she looks like the old Karin again. In turn, Karin fingers her sister's new cut – it's virtually identical, as they'd planned. Jutta had gone just a few days before to a new hairdresser a short distance away in the Wedding district and showed the stylist a picture of Karin before her switch to blonde and said, 'Like that, please.'

'It's perfect,' Karin confirms. 'I dyed mine back to dark three days ago, and I've made sure Frau Lupke has seen me going up and down the stairs plenty of times since then.'

Wordlessly, they exchange clothes, Jutta noting that Karin's don't quite hang off her frame with the same ease, her sister's bony ribs and her meagre covering of flesh obvious as they undress. She's glad then that Gerda will be sure to fatten her up, if only for the day.

Karin hands Jutta a roll of Ostmarks, explaining she's exchanged a few of the dollars 'with someone I know'. They swap the contents of their bags, too – Karin's East German ID card, and a pack of Karo cigarettes with its distinctive black and white chequered design; neither could tolerate smoking the rough 'lung torpedoes', but plenty of women do and carrying a pack will make Jutta a more convincing East Berliner if she's searched.

'Ready?' Karin says at last, and it's then they both laugh at the ridiculousness of the entire scheme.

'Well, it'll be something to tell our grandchildren.'

'If we make it that far,' Karin shoots back, too soon to stop herself.

Jutta shifts Karin from further dark thoughts by tugging at her hand. 'Come on, I'll show you where to go.'

They snake wordlessly through the corridor to the house, stopping in the kitchen before the wooden cabinet and Karin's opening to a brief freedom.

'Just listen out for any movement before you launch out,' Jutta counsels. 'You can usually hear anyone clipping on the broken paving. After that, be swift.'

Karin only nods, the tremor in her fingers evident. Jutta

clutches at them, hoping to absorb the fluttering and trying not to increase it with her own fresh anxiety.

'So, six o'clock back here?' she reiterates.

Karin's lips barely move. 'Yes, six o'clock.'

Jutta draws her in for another hug and feels more of the old Karin she remembers, the sense of her sister beyond her hardened sinews. She releases and stands back, cranks out a smile. 'And hey, enjoy it? It's for you as well as Mama.'

Karin nods again, swallows hard. 'Thanks, Ja-Ja,' she says, her voice croaky and weak.

'Okay, now's as good a time as any.'

They scrape back the cabinet to reveal the brown tarpaulin that Jutta has recently taped on the inside of the hole, the colour chosen to blend in with the brickwork. It means any curious eyes need to be very close to the hole to notice any breach. Jutta stares, heart thumping, as Karin crawls onto her knees, her ears pricked for any traffic in the other country beyond the thin boundary. For Jutta, it's like watching her own actions from outside herself, and it strikes her how ridiculous the whole thing looks – needing to scrabble on your knees, like a criminal, just to hug your own mother. Despite living with the Wall for just under two years now, it hits home in that moment how utterly pointless and stupid it is. Absurd. And that it's not her or Karin who are the criminals, but Walter Ulbricht and his cronies, the Soviet leaders who give credence to it, the Western politicians who refuse to tear it down. It needs breaching. It needs Wall-ghosters like them to prove what a waste of human breath it is.

Karin is gone in a second, lithe as she exits and disappears without hesitation.

'Good. Don't look back, Karin,' Jutta murmurs. *But will you come back?*

211

41

Being Karin

3rd August 1963, East Berlin

Jutta sits for a time in a dusty old armchair left in the corner of the kitchen, feeling tempted to simply stay put for the entire day, whiling away the hours with the book she's crammed into her small shoulder bag – something by Eastern writer Anna Seghers, safe and acceptable to be seen with. Her stomach, however, gives off a grinding complaint; she'd managed to force only a piece of bread down at home, unable to face any more, and now her body is protesting. She needs to go and play her part, being seen in the GDR, as if all is completely normal and routine in the life of Karin Voigt.

Smoothing down Karin's dress – *her* dress for now – she fingers the expertly sewn seams and the keyhole pockets, notes it's the same short, waist-less style Karin favours now, and wonders if her sister wears it to hide the lack of meat on her frame. But then these dresses are in fashion too, though in West Berlin they are made from distinctly lighter and more breathable material; Karin's

212

creation is a patchwork of beautifully matched offcuts, but throwaway all the same. Some parts of it itch against Jutta's skin and she wonders how long it's taken Karin not to notice the cheap, nylon fibres rubbing up against her.

It's almost eleven by the time Jutta heaves herself through the window and out into the alleyway, perching Karin's cap on her head, pushing back her shoulders and sucking in a large breath. *I am Karin. Karin Voigt. I answer to Karin. I am Karin.*

She decides on walking towards her sister's apartment, which – Karin has assured her – isn't far from the Presse Café. It will waste some time, and she'll become more familiar with East Berlin, in case they do this again. She feels a slight panic at the thought – will they? Will this become a routine for months on end, until Karin makes the final break?

Beyond the alleyways of the industrial area, people are out and about doing their Saturday chores; the queues at several of the state-run Konsum stores are lengthy, and Jutta decides to join one of the lines, feeling that she's far enough away from Karin's place not to be recognised by one of her neighbours. It's a chance to satisfy her genuine hunger, as well as an appetite for stories and conversations while they wait, and for a fleeting minute she thinks of Danny and his similar fascination for the 'nitty gritty'. Danny – what she wouldn't give right now to be in a beer garden with him, on the edge of a lake in the Tiergarten, his fingers linking into hers, conversation free and flowing. Free to do anything. The sky is blue and the sun is shining in East Berlin, but the ceiling of oppression looms suddenly dark and low over her.

The chatter in the queue is both sad and heartwarming; little ones with their mothers are endlessly patient, amusing themselves with little games and singing songs, and Jutta wonders whether infants of the West ever display such tolerance, instead of hanging from their mothers' skirts and whining of boredom. For these children, waiting clearly becomes second nature from a tender age.

The lines are made up mostly of women, and the talk is chiefly of which shops are currently stocking hard-to-find groceries. 'Someone over near Spittelmarkt managed to get some lemons – did you ever hear of it?' one woman says, though there's no bitterness in her voice, merely surprise. Jutta senses only one snippet of near dissent, when the woman directly behind lowers her voice and tells her line neighbour of a raid in her block the night before.

'They took her away, screaming, in front of her children,' the woman whispers gravely. 'You'd think they would wait until the kids were at school, wouldn't you? Poor children, the last sight of their mother, like that.'

'What for?' her neighbour says.

'No idea,' the first woman says. 'Her husband is a Party man, too. But he was nowhere to be seen. Makes you think.'

The conversation drifts as the line moves forward, and Jutta is soon through the doors of the shop. She's determined not to compare it with the brightly lit stores of West Berlin, not to judge harshly, but it's hard when the atmosphere is immediately dour, with its yellowy strip lighting fizzing as if there's a fly caught in the filaments, stuttering above and threatening to cut out completely. The women alongside seem not to notice and plough towards the bread counter.

Jutta is conscious of simply meandering but, in all truth, there's very little to browse for. Jars are spaced out on the shelves to help make them look less empty, which is difficult when compared with the plentiful supply of Spreewald

214

pickles, a speciality of the East and something Oskar is partial to. Somehow, though, she doesn't think a souvenir is appropriate today.

The bakery counter is swamped with yet another queue so Jutta picks up a packet of dry-looking biscuits; they will sustain her until she can reach Karin's flat.

She pays automatically, and then freezes on seeing the frown of the till girl, instantly cursing herself. The girl's hand closes over the coins slowly, her wide eyes carrying an added weight to her expression. Will she shout or scream, waving her hands about to signify a capitalist spy in their midst?

Instead, she merely says: 'Have you got any other change, Fräulein?'

'Yes, yes, I have,' Jutta stutters, and pulls out the right coins – East currency, instead of the West she's handed over. *Stupid, stupid mistake!*

'Thank you,' Jutta says, her own look relaying intense gratitude, and hoping it's not misplaced. Her entire fate now rests on this young girl's reaction; mercifully, she moves on to the next customer without a second glance. Still, Jutta's nerves are drawn tight as she strides away from the Konsum, bracing herself for the heavy footsteps behind that might yet come. Only they don't.

You were lucky, Jutta. Don't push it.

Wearily, she trudges north in the midday heat, still unconsciously avoiding any groups of Vopos hanging around on street corners, pretending to patrol when they're simply eyeing up pretty girls. She checks her whereabouts twice on a street bench by taking out the copy of *Sybille* that Karin has lent her and hiding the map inside. So far, so good.

The Presse Café's imposing, stone columns are a relief, and she makes a decision to divert there: the biscuits have left her with a raging thirst and she needs both the coffee she missed out on at breakfast and several glasses of water, plus Karin's shoes have started to pinch – another element of identical twins that is not entirely exact. Once inside, she's also glad to see it's half full, enough to be seen and blend in, but not to stand out like a sore thumb as the lonely girl.

'Afternoon, Karin. Hot out there, eh?' the barman asks. 'What can I get you?' Shock and relief floods Jutta as at least one person is taken in.

'Oh, my usual coffee,' she ventures, 'and a glass of water.' She spies dishes of smoked sausage and potato salad on the counter behind him and her stomach rumbles again. Does Karin often eat in here? Can she afford to?

Jutta's nerves triumph over hunger and she decides coffee will have to satisfy for now.

The barman hands over the drinks and Jutta checks twice in giving over the right currency. Satisfied, he leans in close with the change.

'Hey, tell Otto there'll be another band next week – no date yet, but we'll get the word out.' She nods knowingly, and wires a message to her brain: *remember to tell Karin*.

Settled at a table next to the window, she pulls out her book and pretends to be absorbed, though the words swim past her eyes and she can't pin them down. Perhaps Seghers' tale about concentration camps isn't the best choice for today. 'Relax, *relax*,' Jutta half-mumbles behind the page. She sips at her coffee and there's some comfort in the thick, strong liquid. In minutes, she's beginning to calm down at last.

'Is that book as good as they say?' a voice pushes in; male, a little tentative.

'Sorry?' Her tone spirals up towards alarm.

'Your book. I was just wondering, only my sister is reading it . . .'

Jutta looks across at the table to her left. A young man – a grown-up boy really – is eyeing her earnestly. 'Um, I don't know really, I've only just started it.' She smiles weakly and cuts away, tries to slink back behind the page. Damn! Her plan is to be Karin's visible but largely silent alibi, with minimal contact. And this guy is not helping.

But he won't be thrown off, leans from his chair a little closer. 'Haven't I seen you in here before?'

Is that a chat-up line, Jutta thinks, or is he hinting at something else? He could simply be a nice soul. Lonely, and a little odd, but harmless. Or not; caution is by far the best tactic, especially today.

'Yes, I come here sometimes with my boyfriend,' she says. Firmly, but with a smile, then slices her gaze away a second time.

'You live nearby then?' he keeps prodding.

Jutta's nerves fizz. It's too much, even for an insistent suitor, and yet too blatant for Stasi – her guess is they would be more circumspect.

She swallows back the panic in her voice, forcing it to be still. 'Hmm, not far away.' *Surely he must get the hint soon, that I'm not interested?*

Finally, he seems to. He drains the last of his drink and moves towards the exit.

'Bye then,' he says as he passes. 'Enjoy your book.'

'Oh, thanks.' But there's not a single letter of text that's made it into Jutta's brain as yet. Her entire focus is on willing him to go.

Jutta watches him through the smear of the windows as he hesitates outside in the street, then walks off left. She's about to lose sight of him when he pauses to talk to someone on the street corner; her eyes widen with alarm as the man-boy stands alongside a Vopo, helmet removed but a gun hanging from his shoulder. The soldier is smiling and his stance friendly rather than challenging.

Who on earth is that young man? And why talk to her – as Karin? She's sure Stasi wouldn't be so overt or stupid, and certainly not foolish enough to waltz up to a Vopo and declare their GDR loyalty to all. Still, the episode leaves her disconcerted and thinking it's high time to hide away for at least a portion of this very strange day.

Karin's apartment is half a dozen streets away, though with each stark, square block that goes by, the area appears darker and increasingly drained of life; where there are plants in the window boxes, they've gone to seed, withered and brown. The few people on the street are hurriedly making their way into identical doorways, each with a fleeting glance back across their shoulder as they enter. Or is Jutta reading too much into a simple gesture of the head, as she's reading far too much into everything today?

Karin's building looks to once have been a dove grey painted over the concrete blocks, but it's now streaked with damp and seepage from various pipes, lending it the strange look of a striped animal from afar. Jutta can't help thinking it's a long way from the aged grandeur of the Schöneberg apartment.

The smell in the hallway is sharp rather than unpleasant; someone's been busy with a bucket of disinfectant. She bangs the door shut purposely and clomps up towards the third floor as noisily as she can. No need because, as she reaches the second storey, a door on the left opens a few inches and a woman's large, jowly face looms through the crack. Karin's description of Frau Lupke is spot on – 'Look

218

out for a rhino with curlers' – and Jutta has to stifle a laugh at the very sight in front of her.

'Good day, Frau Lupke,' she sings and sails on past. There's a grunt of acknowledgement chasing her up the last flight. Mission accomplished. Perhaps now she can relax?

The flat is as Jutta expects, though it takes her aback nonetheless; a small, rundown municipal apartment made quirky and welcoming by Karin's unique style, with swatches of fabric covering up the dark, damp patches and her sister's illustrations sketched directly onto the wall, the lines of peeling plaster incorporated into Karin's own meandering cityscape. It strikes her then how much she misses Karin's doodlings, often scattered on scraps of paper and café napkins in the apartment, or hidden under Jutta's pillow as a surprise.

Still, the apartment is tiny and in any other guise it would be entirely depressing. There's a minute galley kitchen, pipe-work obvious and ugly above the stained sink, and a bedroom–lounge, the window of which looks out onto a similarly miserable landscape of grey blocks, each draped in washing fluttering in the slight breeze, which at least offers some colour. The concrete seems intent on obstructing the sun's rays from making their way into the room, and Jutta thinks foolishly: is the light in East Berlin banned?

On the single, small table sits Karin's beloved sewing machine, surrounded by a dressmaker's tools of pins and thread, and rough pattern pieces she's made from old copies of *Neues Deutschland*. One cut mark slices straight across a picture of Walter Ulbricht and Jutta laughs aloud at Karin's effrontery.

On the bed, she finds a parcel, wrapped with old newspaper and bound by a strand of wool, a label on top in Karin's script: *For you*. Unwrapping it, she finds another of her sister's masterpieces, holding up the cotton-like fabric to reveal a straight shift dress of a style Jutta has glimpsed only in magazines, one that has caught her eye time and again. It's Quant, but essentially Karin too: the sleeveless block of maroon colour contrasts with vents in the skirt of a light red, matched on the collar trim, and triangular patch pockets of a deeper purple, each expertly appliquéd with two black stripes.

In a second, Jutta has pulled the curtains across the window and cast aside Karin's dress in favour of the new one. It fits like a glove, falling from her small breasts past her waist and just brushing her hips as she swivels inside. With the swish of her new bob – which she's beginning to like more and more – Jutta parades in the few feet of space around the bed, prancing like a leggy Quant model on a catwalk somewhere in London or New York, and her one wish is that Karin was here to see her right now.

She flops back on the bed, runs her fingers along the cool cotton of the dress – a rarity in East Berlin, she imagines – and wonders how much Karin sacrificed for it. Jutta draws in the scent of her sister on the pillow though, seconds later, there's a jarring, unfamiliar aroma; it's distinctly unfeminine, and Jutta is pulled back to a harsh reality. She is not in some faraway capital, but in a dingy apartment in the prison of East Berlin, taking in the scent of Karin's lover, while her sister is somewhere across that infernal boundary. She feels confined, hemmed in after only a few hours, and so how does that make Karin feel, living it each and every day?

For the next few hours, she reasons there is at least a door between her and the steely scrutiny of Frau Lupke, the Vopos and, she hopes, the Stasi. For now, she can feel relatively safe.

42

Being Jutta

Karin launches herself from the opening and onto the grubby cracked paving near Harzer Strasse, instantly reminded of a friend's pet when she was younger, a grey rabbit whose talent was in popping his head in and out of his hutch in response to their encouragement. With everything else swirling around her head, she can't imagine why she thinks of it now.

Swiftly dusting herself off, she scouts around, relieved to see there's no one else about. This part of Berlin is largely unfamiliar to her, but straightaway Karin is at home, on safe ground. Everything feels different, more solid almost. She hurries towards the nearest U–Bahn, keen not to waste time on a long walk to Mama. After almost two years, it's the faces on the platform and in the carriages that strike her most as unusual: their features are open and alive, a general chatter between friends unafraid of their conversation being overheard, in contrast to those in the East – closed, guarded expressions sculpted into a flat nondescript

221

look. And yet she's become so attuned to it, she's hardly noticed until now.

When she finally exits onto the streets of her childhood, Karin's nerves mesh like tangled wool. Before today, it had been a long wait, a happy anticipation, the thought of Mama's face when she opens the door. Now, there's unease nudging into the mix, of what she will say, how she will explain her need to go back East, to be with someone Mama and Gerda have never met.

She spies Hugo's face from the street, keeping watch from his bedroom window, and gives him a cursory wave as their eyes meet. Lovely Hugo – her best ally alongside Jutta, as a child, and now. A potential cushion against their mothers' combined confusion.

He opens the door and ushers her in, holding a finger against his lips. She hears Gerda's chatter and her mother's laughter from down the hallway, the sound of which springs immediate tears, and has to work hard to rein them in. *This is a happy time, Karin. Happy.*

Karin walks into the parlour behind Hugo, and he peels to the side.

'Jutta, what are you doing back? I thought you'd gone . . .' Ruth's words are held aloft, like dust on a warm breeze. It's said that every mother knows the cry of her own child, like a pin drop in a clamour of sound, and the same is true of twins; since their very first hour of life Ruth has been able to distinguish one daughter from another, almost by smell alone. This time, her eyes sense the difference. Karin is in Jutta's dress and with the same bob of dark hair – even Karin thought they had contrived well to look alike today – and yet the recognition is instant. Mama always says Karin possesses an extra, subtle curl to her lip, invisible to everyone else but a beacon to Ruth.

222

She was half-standing, and now she is static, frozen in disbelief. She glances at Gerda for confirmation, as the only other person who can identify the girls instantly, and, when Gerda's face displays equal astonishment, Ruth moves towards Karin.

'Oh, my love,' she murmurs, fingering her daughter's tear-streamed face. 'My darling girl, you came back. Karin, you're back.'

There are tears then on all sides – of joy at that point. And then, when Gerda has provided coffee and more cake than Karin can contemplate eating, some explanations are needed. Ruth is perplexed and fights hard to hide a deep disappointment about the contact Jutta has been keeping from her.

'But, Mama, if she'd have told you, it would have put us all in danger,' Karin insists. 'She had to make sure it was safe before I came. And in all honesty, it's been *my* fear delaying this visit, not Jutta's. She's the brave one.'

From the sidelines, Hugo nods, and his own mother shoots him a knowing look that says: *I'll deal with you later*, though it's far from menacing.

'But I'm here now,' Karin adds.

'Now, we can be a family again,' Ruth says. 'A proper family.'

Karin knows now would be the time to correct her mother, but finds she can't. Not yet. 'And look what I've brought for your birthday . . .' she rattles on instead, pulling out a wrapped parcel containing a handmade bag she's stitched from her best scraps.

Later, up on the roof, Karin sits in Jutta's chair, recovering from Gerda's swiftly prepared but huge meal. She draws on a rare cigarette of Western quality that doesn't make her cough violently, noting from the corner of her eye that the third chair in their old circle has been folded flat.

'So?' Hugo punctures the silence between them.

'What?'

'How is it? Living in the East?'

She lifts her head and looks at him – cousin Hugo all grown up. 'What else but tolerable,' she sighs.

'Hmm.'

'What do you want me to say, Hugo? It's like living among a fascist dictatorship where no one can move without state approval?' Except she says it languidly, almost bored of the question.

'And is it?'

She laughs then. 'Yes and no. Life goes on. If you replace fascist for communist, that's pretty much what it is. But, like I say, people go about their business.'

'So . . .?'

'Why go back now?' she pre-empts him. 'I know Jutta's told you why. Otto. Love. Plain and simple.' She smiles with resignation, and it's Hugo's turn to look on his cousin as older and wiser.

She takes another drag. 'Have you a girlfriend, Hugo?'

'One or two so far. Nothing serious.'

'If it does become serious, if it becomes love, then you will know why. I promise.'

'But it's so much to give up, to sacrifice,' he says, bending his own head forward earnestly and meeting her gaze.

'And so much to gain too,' Karin says quietly. 'Have you ever thought of that? Politicians aside, East Berliners are just Berliners – good people. They have their doubts, but they also have to survive.' She thinks of Walter and Christel and their steadfast kindness. 'And they have faults

224

and foibles, like most of the world's people. Unfortunately, it's those that get exploited.'

'But can you live like that, when you know there's an alternative?' Hugo pitches, his eyes wide with wonder.

'For as long as my love holds out, then I think, yes.'

Karin sighs again. When she's with Otto she doesn't need to convince herself of a life's direction with him, but being here, it's harder. She's left her tiny photograph of him at her flat, for safety, but she yearns to see his face now. For certainty. Ghosting back through the Wall today means no going back on promises, at least until she can win Otto round. For now, she has to convince Mama and Gerda of her choice.

'Hey, time's getting on,' she says. 'I'll need to head back soon.'

'You've got a bit longer – I'll give you a lift on the bike,' Hugo offers. Pauses. 'It's been great to see you, Karin. But please, be careful.'

This time she laughs loudly, the wise old cackle of a veteran dodger. 'I live in the East, Hugo. For us, caution is like breathing.'

43

A Close Encounter

3rd August 1963, East Berlin

Jutta wakes with a start to shouting out in the street beyond Karin's window. She'd made herself some tea and lain back on the bed with her book, closed her eyes . . . in the next moment the noise is causing her heart to bound towards the ceiling. Her eyes snap to her watch as she springs from the bed. How long has she been asleep? It's only nearing four o'clock, thankfully.

Squinting through Karin's thin veil of curtain she scans for anything suspicious, soldiers perhaps, but there are two women in view scrapping like cats outside the building opposite, neighbours beginning to swarm at the suburban spectacle, some goading, some trying to pull them apart. Jutta breathes relief: normal life happens everywhere – love, hate, acrimony and affection. Wall or no Wall.

She refreshes herself in the cramped bathroom, irons out the imprint of Karin's pillow on her cheek and practises a smile in the mirror. *Keep going – the charade is nearly over.*

Karin has little in her cupboards and Jutta is loath to use up the precious supplies. Besides, she needs to be visible as Karin again before heading for the rabbit hole. She leaves the oranges she's carried from home and a little note – *Thank you* – with an inadequate drawing of a little stick woman in a triangular dress, knowing Karin will understand its meaning and smile at her sister's poor excuse for a cartoon. She's back in Karin's dress, the new creation neatly tucked inside her bag.

Jutta bangs the front door shut and, as expected, feels the subtle suck of air as Frau Lupke's door opens a few centimetres as she descends to the ground floor. Good old Frau – she doesn't realise what an asset her snooping might yet prove.

It's cooler outside and the sun is disappearing westwards, as if drawing her home. Somehow, Jutta feels slightly more relaxed – the sleep has done her good, after a relatively unsettled night. But she's thirsty again, needs coffee to propel her towards the day's last hurdle, and yet the Presse Café twice in one day may be too obvious. Suddenly, Jutta thinks of Karin's other favourite haunt: Café Sybille. She can walk south-east to Karl-Marx-Allee and then take a bus or a U-Bahn to meet Karin. Perfect.

The streets are well populated, allowing Jutta to melt into the general shoal of bodies as she skirts Alexanderplatz and heads down the faux Parisian boulevard. Jutta quickens her pace, her mind blinkered to reaching the smell of good coffee and perhaps even a pastry.

'Karin . . . Karin!' A voice cuts through her invisible barrier. In an instant, she assesses the threat: it's a sharp tone, though not challenging. A Vopo? Or worse? One temptation is to stop, turn and acknowledge, show the identity card of Karin's that's in her bag. Prove that she is

Karin Voigt. 'Look at the picture,' she'll gesture to the face in a uniform. 'That's me.'

But everything else screams. *Keep going, pretend you didn't hear, try to shake it off. Only don't walk any faster.* It's Karin who told her that unequivocally: 'Don't ever run, Jutta. It's incriminating, and they have guns. They will use them.'

'Karin . . . KARIN!' The voice is closer, almost pleading her to stop, footsteps quicker and closing in. *Turn and face up. Smile.*

Jutta spins and scans in quick succession. No uniform she can see, but a casual, collared T-shirt, close-cropped blond hair. More importantly, a friendly expression. And thankfully, one she recognises, if only from a static image.

'Didn't you hear me?' Otto pants as he reaches her. 'I've been calling your name for ages.'

'Sorry, sorry – in a world of my own,' Jutta manages. *Oh Christ, how to play this?*

'I went to the flat, but you weren't there,' he says breathlessly, falling into step as she continues walking. He links his hand with hers and she has to remember instantly not to pull away. For a split second, it's Danny who springs to mind, the two of them walking down the Kurf'damm. If only she were there now, with him.

'Uh, no . . .' *Think Jutta. THINK.* 'I've been with Walter, choosing a present,' she says. It's the only name that pops into her head, but what the hell is his wife's name? Karin has spoken of them often enough. Why won't it come?

'For Christel?' Otto offers helpfully.

'Yes, Christel – it's some kind of anniversary. But it's all hush-hush, he wants it to be a surprise, so don't mention it if you see them.' Jutta is thankful they're walking, avoiding any need to look him in the eye while she's unashamedly lying.

'My lips are sealed,' and he gives her hand a friendly tug. 'So, no need to ask where you're heading. How about coffee and cake at Sybille, on me?'

'Oh, and what's the occasion?' Jutta asks playfully, trying to imagine how Karin would be with him, and yet finding herself not knowing. For the first time in all their years, Karin seems totally out of reach. She feels their thread pull and stretch. Intact but under intense pressure.

'No occasion, only that I love you,' Otto says, and leans in to kiss her cheek. It's fleeting enough that Jutta doesn't have time to recoil, and it's a blessing. But he smells fresh, and his kiss is loaded with affection. That much she can tell. And that Otto seems nice. No wonder her sister has fallen for him.

Café Sybille is busier than on her last visit, and Jutta is grateful to know the layout. Her heart is still on double time, though. What is it that Karin likes most and had when they were last here? The choice of coffee is easy, but the cake? Her memory is a vortex, churning and twisting, sucking everything down and offering up nothing.

'Your usual, then?' Otto asks, eyeing the menu as they sit.

'Oh yes, my usual,' she says with relief. Otto is blindly guiding her, almost as if he knows. Does he? He can't, surely. His expression shows nothing but contentment. And love. And Jutta has to do the same.

Once she is furnished with coffee and a slice of plum torte, he dives hungrily into his own pastry.

'So, are you finished with being Walter's shopping expert now?' He looks up, pale blue eyes directly on her. 'Can I poach you to come and see a film with me?'

Jutta's brain spins again. Oh Lord, another excuse.

'Um, maybe later, this evening perhaps. I said I'd go and help out a girl from work with her wedding dress at six. Some alterations.' She dredges it from somewhere deep in her psyche and forces a smile as she chews the cake that has developed a sour taste. 'But only for a couple of hours.'

'Well, I can hardly deny the woman your expertise, can I?' Otto says. 'She's lucky to have your skill at hand.' He pulls at her wrist affectionately, runs his fingers over hers and squeezes her flesh gently.

Perhaps because of the injection of caffeine into her system, Jutta is galvanised to play more of a part – it's not enough, she reasons, to sit and nod and smile. It's clearly not what Karin would do. His Karin. Otto has to be convinced or this double life cannot continue, though she doesn't relish any more encounters.

'Hey, I was at Presse earlier and the barman says there'll be some more music next week,' she offers, laying some groundwork to the lie.

'Oh yes, did he say which band?'

'No, nothing certain, but he'll get word to you.'

'Oh, great.' He swallows the last of his coffee. 'Was that Dirk?'

Jutta hides a blank look behind another forkful of cake.

'Behind the bar, I mean?' Otto nudges.

Is he testing me? Or just making conversation? 'I think so,' she lies. 'He might be new. He recognised me anyway.'

Otto nods, seems satisfied, and Jutta's cake is finally able to slide down. She needs to move the conversation on, focus on him. 'So what have you been up to today?'

'Oh, Mama nabbed me to run an errand – she'd heard they were selling bananas from a stall up in Pankow and made me hotfoot it over there.'

'And did you find any?'

He shakes his head. 'No, a very long queue but not a banana in sight. But it was a good walk and I spied some beautiful buildings tucked away, parts of old Berlin left standing. Makes me certain we can build it back up again, a great place for people to live. And breathe.'

He smiles into the table, half of his mind elsewhere, perhaps in some layout he's already drafting in his head. Jutta looks closely at him, thinks that he seems genuine, and she realises then how her sister has nurtured a love for this principled, honest man. Why she cannot bear to leave him, and what huge sacrifices Karin is prepared to make. And as her sister, how proud that makes Jutta feel. And how sad.

At the back of Jutta's mind, though, a nagging doubt endures: how on earth is Karin to persuade Otto that life in the West can be better, to shed his lifelong principles? Will their love survive that particular divide?

'Oh, look at the time!' Jutta's eyes stray over her watch, the same one she and Karin had been careful to swap at the changeover – and mercifully so. 'Otto, I've got to go. Where shall we meet later?'

'The Kosmos, in the lobby? There's a showing at eight.' She nods, committing it to memory and the lengthening list of things she needs to tell Karin.

'I love you,' Otto says as they part outside the café.

'I love you too,' she says automatically, though it sticks on her tongue. It's clear he's hovering, expectant. She turns her face upwards as he proffers his cheek, and she plants a light peck on it. His skin is soft and a minute wisp of something – taste perhaps – is left on her lips. He kisses her hand and is gone, his long legs striding in the opposite

231

direction, head up and scrutinising the mock splendour of Karl-Marx-Allee.

Jutta almost crumples with relief, something she can ill-afford to do as she needs to walk quickly towards the U-Bahn, in preparation for another encounter in the belly of the Wall.

When will this day end?

44

Return to Life

3rd August 1963, the Wall

This time it's Jutta who's late in reaching the inner sanctum, having misread the changes on the U-Bahn, though she's loath to hurry too fast towards the workshops, careful to slow her steps and almost loitering as she gauges any activity. There's an uncomfortable feeling hovering inside her that she can't shake off – one more to add to the day's tally – that it's been too easy so far. The day has been a series of challenges for sure, but nothing dangerous or threatening. Yet. She can't help feeling it's like picking at the petals of a daisy; pretty soon there won't be any more left to protect the stem.

Sensing the way is clear, Jutta strides towards the alley-ways, head slightly down but eyes everywhere. Still nothing amiss. She reaches the window and, with the benefit of practice, pushes herself up and into the opening. Her eyes scout for Karin, but there's no sign. Wary of crying out, she scrabbles up and into the corridor leading to the kitchen, willing her sister's form to appear and yet only inching forward, braced against her first sight being a Vopo and his gun, Karin in his clutches and looking terrified. A siren screams from behind her, on the East side, and she is static until it fades into the distance. But there's only silence from within the cavity of the Wall.

It's ten past six and there's virtually no sound as Jutta hovers in the empty kitchen near the wooden cabinet, wanting – needing – to recognise the sounds of Karin pushing against the tarpaulin. They've both agreed that if either doesn't show by 6.30 to carry on back to their own side. And yes, a large part of her hopes Karin will have undergone a dramatic U-turn and decided to stay at home today, for good. Strangely though, Jutta finds herself torn; she has none of her sister's passion or allegiance towards Otto, but she hopes his loyalty and love won't be crushed by loss. Having met him, even briefly, she feels he doesn't deserve that.

Why oh why does this inert, hostile blockade have to divide and rule their lives like a concrete cosh?

She sits in the armchair, twitching. One eye is on the hands of Karin's watch ticking slowly, the other on the rabbit hole. 6.14 . . . 6.15. It's her ears that prick first, alarm running through her veins. She's up and out of the chair, looking for something substantial to hit out at any Vopo who comes near. But Karin's head appears and the rest of her wriggles through quickly, twisting sharply and replacing the tarpaulin. There's a large grin on her face as she stands to face Jutta.

'All right?' Karin pants.

Jutta releases a large breath. 'Fine. You?'

'Yes, good.'

Jutta frames the inevitable question. 'How was it, with Mama?'

Karin nods repeatedly towards the floor and Jutta knows it's to stop her emotion breaking free. 'It was lovely.' She swallows and smiles with the recent memory. 'You should have seen her face! It was a picture. And she didn't keel over from the shock, so you know, the best we could hope for. And I'm stuffed with Gerda's cooking.'

Karin pats her slim belly, which is only slightly distended, then busies herself to swap clothes again, but Jutta won't let her cloud the issue.

'And the goodbye?'

'As you'd expect,' Karin mumbles, head still to the floor.

'Is she angry? Disappointed?'

Karin looks up then, faces her sister, lips stretched thin. 'Both. And at both of us, although me mainly. She doesn't understand why I have to go back for a man.' She shrugs. 'Our mother, who would have followed our father to the ends of the earth if she'd had the chance.'

Jutta grips at Karin's hands, sensing the thread weave itself. Strong again.

Karin's lip trembles. 'But you understand, don't you Ja-Ja? You know why?'

'I'm beginning to.'

It's the cue Jutta needs, to relay details of her day to Karin, recounting where she's been, who she's seen – Frau Lupke, the barman at Presse Café. And Otto.

'You've seen him?' Karin's eyes are wide and white with shock. 'I told him I'd be busy all day. He's never come looking for me at Sybille before.'

'Well, just remember you were shopping with Walter, and then with a friend adjusting a dress. And it's the Kosmos lobby at eight.'

'You're a genius, Ja-Ja – definitely missed your calling as a double agent.'

'Not me. I'm exhausted. I couldn't keep that up for long.'

They dress again, breathless, though with no real urgency now, aside from Karin's cinema date.

'All right, so three weeks tomorrow?' Jutta suggests. 'Just for me to come through, for us to spend the day together?'

Karin's face can't hide a slight disappointment at the lengthy wait.

'I don't think we should push our luck, that's all,' Jutta explains. 'And it's time for you to . . . well, be with Otto.'

Karin's fretful look says she catches the drift: to work her charms, to persuade him the grass really is greener on the Western side.

They face one another, each aware they share the same thought – not only about the bizarre nature of the day, but how creative and crazy their lives have become. And simply because a bunch of old men in suits decided that walling off an entire city was good for their portion of humanity.

'Go on, you should go,' Jutta urges, with her hatred for lingering goodbyes.

There's a final hug and a kiss, and Karin is gone. Jutta thinks about waiting for a few more minutes, but she's desperate now to be on home soil, not to be part of the East anymore. To breathe again.

She takes time to listen though, cocking her ear to the tarpaulin, and slipping between the smallest space possible behind the cabinet, feeling more and more like a contortionist.

Back in the West, she has the luxury of laughing at the sheer insanity of it all, walking away from the strange nature of a covered rabbit hole in a brick barrier to another world.

With each step away, Jutta feels the tension falling away, taking in the sights of an early Saturday evening, of people milling about, home from shop work or heading out for the evening. Blissfully familiar and normal. But she doesn't stride towards her own home. Not yet. There will only be the inquisition waiting, with the inevitable guilt and angst, and for now, she needs a different kind of contact. Jutta had surprised herself in how much she craves it as comfort, how much it's pushed its way into her thoughts through the day. She walks towards the same bar where she'd sunk a much-needed brandy after that first, nerve-wracking journey through the Wall. Now, she orders a beer and asks for change for the phone, tapping out the number that she's memorised.

'Hello.' The voice on the other end isn't his, presumably his flatmate.

'Is Danny at home?' she says in English. *Please let him be there. I need him to be.*

'Hey, this is a pleasant surprise.' His voice comes on the line, exuding delight, and it's what Jutta needs to calm the doubt twisting slowly within her. 'Is everything okay?' he goes on. 'Nothing wrong?'

'No, everything's fine,' she breathes into the receiver. 'I just wondered if you were free, either tonight or tomorrow, to do something?' There's a slight pause, opening up a sinkhole in which her confidence plummets. 'I mean, don't worry if you can't. We can always . . .'

'No, no, I'm just thinking,' Danny says hurriedly. 'There's another darned reception this evening. But I can show my face for half an hour and leave.'

'No, really if you're busy . . .'

'I'd rather be busy with you,' he cuts in. 'Believe me.'

It's exactly what she needs to hear.

45

Shadows of a Changeling

3rd August 1963, East Berlin

'You look tired. Was all that dressmaking a lot of hard work?' Otto teases her in the dim glow of the cinema.

She raises a weak smile in return. Can he really see her fatigue in the darkness, waiting for the inevitably grim film to begin, the one written by an earnest socialist and approved by some GDR ministry as being Good For Morale? Still, if you see enough of them, you can glean some light amusement from the perfect, clichéd life of a good socialist, as she and Otto have discovered. But yes, she is weary, though happily so, given what the day has brought.

Karin's journey back to the East side (back home? she wonders now) had been marred only by a slip as she lowered herself from the window, the splintered wooden frame scraping on her upper thigh. She'd bitten down on her lip to suppress the sharp sting and rubbed away at tiny bobbles of blood sprouting on her grazed skin. The rest had been uneventful, and she'd surprised herself at how normal it felt to be back pacing through the streets still in half ruins from the war. She'd noted a familiarity in the faces, slightly pinched in comparison with the pink and abundantly fed West Berliners, though her stomach was more than full and she'd filled with guilt at the sight of a skinny little lad running in front of her, his big head on a waifish body and spindles for legs. Or is that just how some children are before they begin to fill out? In one day alone, she'd felt her reasoning becoming slightly skewed, the lingering shadows of a changeling.

At home, Frau Lupke had been out on the landing, fussing with the plants she pretends to keep alive.

'You're busy today, Fräulein Voigt,' she'd said, though not casually enough. 'In and out a lot.' The old woman likes to regularly allude that she's on the lookout, keeping everyone guessing whether it's official Stasi business or just innate nosiness.

'Yes, Frau Lupke,' Karin had sung. 'It's been such a lovely day, and lots to do.'

If only she knew.

Inside, Karin had time only to sponge off the grime and the sweat of angst, washing the graze on her leg that felt increasingly sore and applying the GDR's home-grown panacea of Nivea cream. At least the wound sits high enough on her thigh to be hidden even by a short dress.

She'd unfurled two old dresses brought from Mama's and laid them on the bed, but in the two years since her leaving they'd become out of date, at least to Karin's fashionable eye. She resolved to enjoy picking them apart later and recreating a new outfit.

It *will* all work out, she schooled herself firmly, purging her doubts into her grimy bathroom mirror: 'This is your choice, Karin Voigt. Live with it.' And it was okay, wasn't it? She'd seen Mama, Gerda and Hugo, had some small fix of their love. And now there is Otto. His love. And their life. Wherever it might be.

It's dark when they emerge from the cinema and Otto doesn't suggest going for a beer, as they often do afterwards.

'I'm thirsty for you,' he whispers into the strands of her hair, a move guaranteed to cause a tweak of desire in her pelvis, enough to ensure frantic lovemaking the minute they break through the door of her apartment.

Karin is weary, and part of her wants to go home and rerun the day under the strands of sulphury street light casting across her pillow, alone. But another part of her needs Otto next to her, as a reminder of why she is back in East Berlin and not in Schöneberg, under her duvet next to Jutta, in comfort and safety.

'Then let's go home,' she says to him.

His hunger is evident and they are undressed by the time they reach Karin's bed, though Otto woos her slowly, gentle and considerate as always. Again, she has to bite back the pain when he sweeps a hand unwittingly over the graze on her thigh, now angrier and more raw than she's felt so far. After, as they lie panting and turned towards the ceiling, he reaches out and runs a finger innocently over her skin's scored surface, and Karin can't help flinching.

'Where did you get that?' he quizzes, pushing himself up on his elbow and facing her. 'It looks painful.'

The skin is pulsing, and Karin is sure now she needs more than Nivea cream to calm it. 'It's nothing,' she lies, 'something I did at work. I had a reaction to something I put on it, that's all.'

Otto looks concerned, though whether it involves suspicion, she can't tell. More so when he weaves his fingers into hers and pauses.

'Is that a new watch?' he asks.

Her heart stops. 'Um, yes, mine broke, so I borrowed it from the friend I saw today.' Karin winces inside at her bad lie, feels her stock of untruths well and truly used up. 'Hey, look what Walter and I found today!' She springs off the bed and holds up an orange in each hand. 'You may not have found any bananas, but we tracked down these.'

'You dark horse!' Otto's eyes are alight in the gloom.

'I'm happy to share my treasure, but it'll cost you,' she goads him impishly.

'Oh yeah? What's your price?'

'Two coins' worth of kisses and a whole hundred of pure love.'

'Well, it's a good job I have plenty of that in my wallet.' Her flirtation seems to have distracted him successfully from the watch. 'So you'd better come here while I count out the amount.'

'I think that's a very fair deal, Herr Kruger.'

46

Champagne and Pleasure

3rd August 1963, West Berlin

Jutta falls back onto the sheets, breathless and satisfied, as Danny does the same, the sweat and pungency of sex oozing from them both. In unison, they laugh, both from a delicious release and partial embarrassment – that *look where we ended up* type of noise. Surprise more than regret, or at least that's what Jutta hopes.

He rolls his body back to face her, reaches down for her hand and cups it in his still hot palm. 'That was wonderful, Miss Voigt.'

'And I liked it very much, Lieutenant Strachan.'

She won't tell him it's only her second time, and a great improvement on the first – a frantic, panting fondling from her student days that in hindsight went way too far. Consented but unwise, she later reflected. She never saw the boy again and was relieved.

Danny leans towards the phone on the side table and dials one number. 'Oh hello, can I please have a bottle of champagne?' he says into the receiver. 'Room 214. Yes, that's perfect. Thank you.'

She laughs again. 'Extravagant, Mr Strachan.'

'It is a very special occasion,' he says.

'Making love to a woman in Berlin?'

But he clearly senses she's joking, Jutta squealing as he digs at her playfully.

'You doubt me, Miss Voigt,' Danny says. 'It's making love to *you* – not just any beautiful woman. Being with you.'

She's sure then, looking at the animation on his face, that this is not a recurring event in the life of Danny Strachan. She does feel special, and he's responsible. After all, it's not every week or month that she ends up in bed with a man she's known for a handful of dates. Far from it.

He gets up to answer the door to room service, casually taking dollar bills out of his trouser pocket to tip. Jutta exhales heavily – a good sigh, though. A satisfying end to an altogether bizarre day.

After calling Danny from the bar, she had braved the brief trip home to Schöneberg, tentatively pushing her key into the door. She heard Mama's crying on walking down the hall, saw Gerda's sideways glance as she entered the parlour.

There was no row, though that might have been preferable, and she'd been ready to noisily defend her duplicity in working towards the longer plan – today's swap, for instance. Instead, Mama had drawn her into her hold, and she could smell the tang of dried and fresh tears, delight and regret.

'I'm sorry, Mama,' she said. 'I did what I thought was best.'

As Karin had already hinted, Ruth's disappointment proved harder to absorb, that her girls had conspired against her, albeit for the good of the family. Gerda's hurt, too, was evident: 'I thought you might have said *something*,' she hissed through gritted teeth, kneading the next day's bread as if it were the enemy. Even Hugo hadn't been there, to take her up onto the roof and reassure her that she'd been right to keep it under wraps. After all, what other option had there been?

As she slunk to her room, the hole left in Jutta's chest was replaced in part by a fresh irritation, that she'd risked everything, sweated and sacrificed to bring them one day of Karin. And for such a reaction, almost ungrateful. She knew their sorrow was fuelling the frustration, and that Mama and Gerda would see sense in time, but it did soothe her guilt about going out again to spend the evening with Danny.

'Where are you off to?' Mama had quizzed, surprised and perhaps affronted again.

'Out with a friend,' Jutta muttered. 'I need to wind down.' And then honestly: 'It's been hard for me too.' Emerging from the kitchen, Gerda extended an arm, a white flag, nodding her apology. Their eyes and understanding met briefly before Jutta disappeared through the door to her respite.

She'd meant it to be a straightforward date, had no intention of ending up in a nearby hotel room with Lieutenant Danny Strachan of the US army. And it was no seedy hotel, either – it was a four-star affair that he led her to, though not so confidently as to suggest that he had predicted or expected it. The talk at dinner, and the laughter, sometimes at himself – it all stripped away the anxiety of the day. He made her feel lighter. Jutta was relaxed, and deeply attracted to Danny in every way.

It was she who had hinted over the table with her eyes locked on his and her fingers crawling for his hand that the night wasn't to end with kissing in a cab. For a second, she'd imagined herself in another world, inhabiting another body, someone else mouthing the words. But no, it was true – *she* wanted to be intimate with him, craved his body close to hers. His eyebrows had gone up, in surprise and delight, Jutta hoped. She'd made a call home in the hotel lobby and unusually Oskar was the one to answer, his voice slurred by alcohol, as it seemed to be every Saturday night now, and more. Ruth and Gerda had gone to bed but, yes, he would pass on the message that she was staying with a friend. It was the truth, Jutta justified to herself. Perhaps with shades of a white lie to protect Mama, but not outright deceit.

And then they got in the lift and went upstairs.

After it pops and fizzes with celebration, the champagne is nectar. Danny turns on the radio and tunes into a music station, twirling with his glass now that he's put on his boxer shorts.

'I feel like I'm in a Doris Day film,' Jutta giggles.

'I'm very glad to announce you are a lot sexier and less chaste than she is,' he says, planting a kiss on her cheek and running his hand over her taut belly.

Am I sexy? Jutta thinks. She's never allowed herself to imagine something so real before, content to be happy in her work, though her thoughts of any kind of future have been interrupted by Karin. By that blasted Wall.

But finally, she senses some light pushing through the cracks of her life. Is this how Karin felt when she first met Otto? Light and love when she needed it most?

PART THREE

47

Red-Handed

5th August 1963, West Berlin

The glow had stayed with Jutta throughout the weekend, even after she'd crept back into the apartment at lunchtime on Sunday, trying not to radiate guilt like the cat that had spent the night on the tiles, though lying outright that she had stayed with Irma. Mama, for her part, was intent on building bridges with her daughter, referring to Karin's visit with a new optimism rather than loss.

'Your sister seemed to think we'll be able to do it again,' she babbled while chopping vegetables for dinner. 'Maybe meet her on and off, until these politicians see sense at least and tear down that monstrosity.'

The room was still for a second, Jutta catching the knowing looks traded between Hugo, Oskar and Gerda: *the Wall is concrete, and so is the GDR's conviction.* Though Ruth is no fool, either. It was simply wishful thinking, her self-protection from the unthinkable: that it might conceivably be forever. It makes Jutta wonder if Karin made any mention of her pledge – six months to convince Otto.

'Let's see, Mama,' was all Jutta had said in response. 'We have to be careful. In the meantime, we can swap letters now.'

'Yes, yes, of course,' she'd agreed. 'But it was the best birthday present, just to see her . . . and I know how much you helped. I do, my darling.'

Now, walking towards work, Jutta has time to properly take stock of the weekend and its black and white nature – the hazards of ghosting and potential capture, alongside Mama's joy and the unexpected pleasure of Danny. She thinks of his parting words as he kissed her goodbye: 'That was fantastic – please can we do it again?' She'd barely suppressed the sparks threatening to leap from every pore, nodding in agreement. *Absolutely*.

Jutta is dragged from her musings by a shadow falling into step beside her as she enters the university campus, the bulk of a body soon catching up.

'Morning, Jutta,' the man says. 'You've got a real spring in your step today.'

She snaps up her head to see that it's Axel Walzer, one of the crowd she often sits with in the refectory, the unappointed leader of the *fluchthelfers*. He's never spoken to her directly before, always seeming quite aloof – an older graduate student cultivating that rock-star aura around himself, both in his dress and manner.

'I'm just thinking about a nice weekend,' she says.

'Any reason for that?' he asks. There's an edge to his tone which makes her turn, and his smile switches to include a hint of something darker.

'No, it was just pleasant, that's all. Busy.' She's trying not to sound guarded or defensive, but his manner and approach have already set off a dozen alarm bells inside Jutta's head.

'And how *is* your sister?' Axel delivers the leaden query with an upbeat innocence.

'I wouldn't know, since she's in East Berlin.' *Keep walking. Don't stop. Don't face him.* 'Surely, you know that?'

This time, he pulls at her arm, not forcibly but enough for her to stop and face him.

'Then I wonder why she was in West Berlin on Saturday, at your mother's house. Pretending to be you.' His brown eyes look straight into her, heavy brows crinkled. Waiting. Then a twitch, prodding for a response.

'You're mistaken,' Jutta says flatly. Regardless of Karin's praise on Saturday, this is way beyond her skills at subterfuge, but she presses her point: 'We're identical – we were always being mistaken for one another. You know full well she's trapped behind the Wall.'

Instantly, it's plain to see Axel has something else up his sleeve – he's not simply fishing. 'I would believe you, had I not seen with my own eyes the two of you popping in and out like a couple of jack-in-a-boxes,' he says finally.

No amount of self-control can quell the gasp escaping from Jutta's lips. Automatically, she scans left and right, calculating for the half-second it gives her, feeling a plug being pulled somewhere in her body and every ounce of her being, along with Karin, draining away. There's no point denying it; the best she can hope for is collusion, for them not to be betrayed. But she can't fathom Axel's motives from his expression – he's a perfect *fluchthelfer*, showing little on his face. A consummate liar.

'I'll be late for work,' she says irritably. 'I'll meet you at lunchtime, twelve fifteen, in the gardens behind the library.'

He nods, though doesn't smile. 'I look forward to it.'

★

A Monday morning has never seemed so sluggish. Every student querying a title or stopping her to ask a question is like someone poking at a raw wound, and once or twice she flashes irritation, then remembers it's not their fault. It's she who has been caught, been somehow slapdash. It's she and Karin, and Mama and Gerda, who will suffer now, at the very least with their precious contact being severed. She tries to stop herself thinking of the worst. What could be Axel's purpose? Isn't he supposed to be on their side? The possibilities circle her head like tumbleweed in slow motion.

By lunchtime, she's already swallowed two aspirin and is in need of more. As she walks towards the gardens, the summer breeze is of little comfort and only pushes strands of hair into her eyes, scratching at her raw patience. Axel is sitting on a bench backing onto the library, looking out on the student traffic passing to and fro.

'Busy morning?' he asks casually, as she sits at the furthest end.

Jutta's throbbing head means she is in no mood to tolerate any polite preamble.

'What is it you want, Axel?' she snaps, only just refraining from barking the words. 'I have no money, and neither does my family, if that's what you're looking for? Or are you paid by the Stasi for such information?'

He shuffles sideways quickly and lays a hand on her arm – Jutta is stopped from snatching it away only by those walking by.

'Hey, that's not it,' he replies, his face contorted with hurt. 'I am *not* a Stasi informant.'

'And I'm supposed to believe that?'

'If I were, do you think we'd be sitting here now?' Axel says. 'They have a track record of acting swiftly. Even on the West side.'

He has a point, but then Jutta has little experience of how the GDR secret police work, other than what she's heard. It could be a double bluff. *How am I supposed to react now? This is not me, or my life.* The thought rattling around Jutta's head over the weekend returns in large, red letters: IT WAS ALL TOO EASY. This is the payback.

'So what *do* you want?' she presses.

'Only your access.'

She feels her heart fall away from her body – it's over. The portal for contact with her beloved sister snaps shut in an instant. It's followed quickly by a scarlet mist of anger, that the entryway she discovered and risked with each trip is so easily snatched from them, and yet Jutta is deflated enough that she has no zeal to argue. Only the line of her mouth shows the fury inside.

'Hiding escapees in cars and trucks is becoming more and more dangerous,' Axel explains. 'For every tunnel dug, the Stasi discovers another. So we need to find alternative ways to get information and false papers across. Then, the Easterners can simply walk across the border in plain sight.'

Jutta lets out an extended sigh of defeat. 'Who saw us? Were we that obvious?'

A smile creeps across Axel's wiry face for the first time. 'Not at all,' he says. 'In fact, quite the opposite.'

'So how?'

'It was a complete fluke. I happened to be over in that part of town visiting a friend, and I saw you walking towards Harzer Strasse. Doing what I do makes me naturally curious, so I followed you.'

'For how long?' Jutta shudders at the thought of Axel's eyes not being the only ones to spy. Of her and Karin being blissfully – and dangerously – naive, and under surveillance the whole time.

'Only that day, two days ago. Imagine my surprise when you popped back out a short time later. It did take me a little while to work it out, though: that it was your sister I was following then, dressed as you.'

'And how *did* you work it out? We were careful.'

'You were,' Axel agrees. 'The attention to detail was good. But another fluke – I'm a twin myself, identical. Takes one to know one, and my brother and I played the same trick many a time.'

Exasperated, Jutta pushes her head back and stares at the blue sky above. Any other day she might be out here eating her lunch and thinking life was good, what with Karin and Danny. Prospects. Except the puffy clouds dotted about seem threatening, sinister as they scud with the breeze.

'Will you allow me one more trip?' she says. 'I have to warn Karin. Surely you wouldn't want her to be in danger? If what you say is true?' *If you're not Stasi.*

Axel pulls himself up. 'Oh no, you misunderstand, Jutta,' he says. 'I don't want to stop you going through. Far from it. The opening is needed long-term – if we push people through in bulk, it will be discovered in no time. For now, it has a much more useful purpose.'

'Then what?'

'You can use your doorway to the East as much as you like, and we won't interfere, I promise,' he states plainly. His pause is intentional and carefully timed. 'In return for something.'

'Yes?' Her eyes narrow with suspicion. Of course, there has to be a forfeit for anything good in this world. How could she be so stupid to think otherwise?

'You act as the go-between. Be our messenger across the Wall.'

It feels as if Jutta's entire body calcifies. 'And if I refuse?' she barely manages.

Axel shrugs. 'You lose the access, of course.' For one half-second, his thinned lips and narrow eyes signal there could be more of a penalty. Much more. Then, his face reverts to the blank of a perfect, practised liar.

48

A Father's Concern

5th August 1963, East Berlin

Karin hums as she swirls the mop around the hospital floor, only the strength of the bleach mixture in her bucket keeping her from sinking completely into her thoughts. Nothing, though, can tarnish her mood today, not after the weekend and the promises of life ahead. She and Otto had spent Sunday shopping at a few market stalls that were trading, then headed with their picnic to the lake at Rummelsburger, swimming, eating and snoozing, and then doing the same all over again until the sun dipped out of sight. He drew lines in the sand, laying out his latest idea for the Leipzig project, his eyes alive with promise. Her only regret was in not being able to tell Otto the basis for her own bright mood, how it was so good to see Mama, to feel the instant flood of freedom in the West. She knew, too, that lying across his warm body beside the water was the perfect time to float the prospect of a different life together, over there. But it was *too* perfect a day. Karin recognised her own fear: Otto loves her for sure, but still, she can't help feeling that years of loving his home counts for a great deal too. And she has months left to gently sway his mind.

'You look miles away.'

'Sorry?' Karin is startled out of her daydream and stands almost to attention with her mop, recognising the voice half a second later. 'Oh, Walter – you surprised me. How are you?'

'I'm fine,' he says, 'and unusually free for lunch. Are you due a break soon? My treat.'

'Yes, I'd love to. I can get off at twelve.' She looks past him to the window and the summer sun streaming through. 'But can we go outside? I could do with some air.'

He looks at the bucket below, catches the acrid odour and her drift. 'Good idea. I'll see you in reception.'

They walk just outside the Charité's grounds, Karin wearing a cardigan over her drab uniform and Walter having shed his white coat. Predictably, he leads her to a slightly downbeat café serving meatballs that he loves and others are forced to tolerate, but Karin doesn't mind the potato salad and bread. She's pleased just to sit outside, bathed by the sun's rays; it's pleasantly warm rather than hot. Even the smell of traffic and Trabis pushing out exhaust fumes along Schlegel Strasse is preferable to the stench of her bleach bucket.

'So, busy weekend?' Walter says, sipping at the coffee, which is superior to the food, in Karin's eyes at least.

'Yes, very good,' she nods, and her mind drifts away. 'Very good.'

'Any particular reason? Did you see your sister perhaps?'

She flicks up her lashes with alarm. 'Why would you say that?'

'No reason, other than that I know it makes you happy,'

he shrugs, though his tone marks that he's noted her anguish.

Karin groans. The act of seeing her family brought untold happiness, but stifling such a secret is causing her to feel like a frantically shaken bottle of Coca-Cola – ready to pop.

'Karin? Is everything all right?' Walters probes.

It's the tiny prompt she needs to tell him everything. Jutta he's met, of course, and likely guessed that Karin's twin has been through the Wall more than once. But their recent swap clearly surprises even Walter, and Karin cannot fathom if it's his naturally cautious nature, or because it was blatantly foolish.

'Just be very, very careful,' he says, uneasy enough that his meatballs are in danger of going cold. He doesn't need to say more – the word *Stasi* is left unsaid, hovering on his lips like a foul curse.

'I will. Oh, but Walter, it was so lovely to hug Mama and everyone else.' It's the memory she can't, and doesn't want to, quash.

'I'm sure it was. But you came back. How was that?'

'Hard,' she admits. 'In some ways. Not so much after seeing Otto.'

'And does he know of your trip?' Walter's eyebrows are almost knitted together with concern, his grey eyes focused.

'No, he still knows nothing. And you can't tell him either, Walter. Please.'

'It's not my business to,' he replies. 'But I wonder how long it can go on' – he hides his words in a forkful of food – 'before the breach in the Wall is discovered. Or worse.'

'I know, I know,' she moans. 'I will tell him in the right moment. Just not yet.' Yet she daren't tell Walter of her

258

pledge to Jutta, since it feels like a betrayal of the man who's only ever been loyal to her.

'And you'll carry on in the meantime?' he says. 'I'm just concerned, Karin, that's all. You know how much Christel and I think of you. Almost like a daughter. If we lose you it means your family has lost too. And for a long time.'

Again, she can only agree with this sensible, giving man. It is foolhardy to risk capture, and her liberty. Jutta's too. And in moments alone she wonders if it can endure for months – but when she's with Jutta, or Mama, forever seems possible. Then back in the East, there are Vopos on every corner, Stasi unseen and floating everywhere. How much longer can their courage hold out? How long will the Wall stand? How long is a piece of string?

'I will work it out. I promise, Walter.'

Arm in arm, they thread back through the string of hospital staff taking their own lunches in the shadow of the grandiose building. Nervously, Karin observes a Vopo who's been shadowing one or two steps behind almost since they left the café. She unhooks her arm from Walter's and makes as if to tie her shoelace, noting as she gazes upwards that the grey-green uniform stops too, hovering. Walter has met a colleague in passing and is deep in conversation a few feet away, and Karin rises and turns slowly, pretending that something has caught her eye in the distance.

He's young, almost pubescent under the bowl of his smooth helmet, with unblemished cheeks and chin. Her eyes skate over him and make a hair's breadth of contact with his – he seems to grasp at it, raising a smile along with an arm, though luckily not the one holding a gun.

'I thought it was you,' he says, striding towards her in a friendly manner.

Karin seizes control of her face, forcing it to be blank, though inside confusion reigns. *Who the hell is he? Do I know him?*

'How is your book going? Have you finished it yet?' But he's smiling instead of hectoring.

Out of uniform, Karin might think him either mad, drunk or making an awkward pass, but his uniform looks real. She's always avoided Vopos, for obvious reasons. And now she just wants to escape this one's attentions as soon as possible.

'Uh, yes, almost done,' she lies. 'It's not bad, just a bit slow.' *Isn't that what people often say about books? Something general?*

'I'll ask my sister what she thought of it, she's nearly finished too,' he comes back.

People are beginning to look, curious as to how and why she's engaging in friendly banter with a Vopo. Mercifully, there's a shout from across the street, some men arguing outside a bar, and his head swings towards them.

'Well, see you around,' he says and turns tail.

Walter peels away from his colleague and joins her, wearing a quizzical look. 'Someone you know?'

Karin shakes her head. 'Never met him before in my life.'

49

A One-Way Street

5th August 1963, West Berlin

Jutta is sweating as she strides out of the library at the day's end, despite a sudden chill nudging into the air while the sun dips low. The afternoon had gone . . . well, she doesn't know where it went, because her mind was entirely elsewhere, battling a horrific quandary while her body and her mouth performed tasks like a robot.

Bloody Axel! How dare he pretend to be so selfless in helping escapees across the Wall, and yet so heartless in his blackmail. Because that's what it amounts to – pure coercion using her precious access to Karin as bait, dressed up as a small sacrifice to help others. Except it's her damn sacrifice, and not his. Jutta seethes as she walks, the chill cooling her skin but the furnace inside ever more stoked. And yet, she thinks: not once did he ask her why Karin hadn't escaped the East when she'd had the opportunity, why she hadn't just skipped away from the portal and her life in East Berlin. Can he know about Otto? Or does he simply not care?

She's seen Axel in the refectory and around campus; his status on the escape committee is a poorly kept secret, affording him a kudos among the others in the group, and women who seem to hover around a glow of his own making. How much peril does Axel actually put himself in? she wonders. Why doesn't he want to simply take over the rabbit hole and run the messages himself? It's a question she would love to confront him with, spitting her anger. And yet, Jutta knows she won't. Because, as Axel so shrewdly observes, the gateway to her sister is too prized for Jutta to forego. If she refuses to run messages, access to Karin is cut to zero, along with the possibility of her sister's eventual, permanent return home. And can she trust that a quiet word in the Stasi's ear from Axel won't also see her arrested? Or Karin too?

Jutta weighs up her options, a perilous set of scales: carrying messages is dangerous, but it means she does get to see Karin. Crucially, it keeps the portal ajar in time for Karin to work her magic on Otto.

Jutta has got one day to decide; that's how she and Axel had left the exchange. In her own mind, she's made her choice, though is in need of a confidant, someone to tell her the decision is not utterly insane. And as much as she wants to share her dilemma – and her trust – with Danny, she can't. It will be the death knell for a relationship only just beginning.

She finds a phone booth and dials the number for Hugo's radio station, thankful to hear his cheery voice.

'Hugo, it's me. I need a drink.'

Her tone must be fraught because he's quick to answer, 'Fifteen minutes,' and gives her the name of a bar in Charlottenburg where they've met before.

*

She's already seated in the window when Hugo parks up his bike and strides through the door, a renewed confidence about him these days. He orders a drink and sits opposite.

'All right, the psychologist is in session,' he says, grinning as he sips his beer.

'Oh Hugo, don't be like that.'

'Like what?' he queries. 'I'm just saying. I always know that when you call me, it's because you need a sounding board for something.'

Jutta sighs. 'You're my cousin. More than that. I love you.'

'And I love you, which is why I'm here.' He holds his hands aloft in surrender, displaying his palms theatrically. And he's smiling. 'So shoot.'

'Well, this Axel is a real charmer, isn't he?' Hugo concludes when Jutta relays the exchange. 'If that's what he does to his allies, I wouldn't like to be his enemy.'

'What would you do, Hugo? Honestly?' Jutta feels backed into a corner and is looking for a sliver of light – like that first chink she glimpsed in the portal. Something to lead the way.

'I really don't know,' he says apologetically. 'I would want to keep seeing Karin too. But these *fluchthelfers*, you know, I'm hearing stories at work about some being quite ruthless, money changing hands for helping families escape.' He looks up from under his mop of dark hair. 'A lot of money.'

'I would never take so much as a pfennig,' Jutta protests.

'I know that,' Hugo assures. 'But he's charging you a good deal of currency in risk, each and every time you go through.'

'And if I could guarantee Karin's safety, I would stop going,' she says firmly. 'I really would. But if I do what they ask, then she's protected, at least until she makes it across for good. Do I have any choice but to say yes?'

Hugo only shrugs. At least he doesn't diagnose her as utterly insane.

The next day, they meet on a bench at the opposite end of the campus. Axel sits, throwing off the attentions of a girl – a tall, nymph-like bean he calls 'Bibi', who loiters nearby, smoking and hopping from foot to foot childishly.

'Well, I'm glad we have an agreement,' Axel says, as if they've just shaken hands on a new car.

Jutta turns and glares. 'I'm doing it purely for my sister. So I can ensure her safety.'

'And it will. As long as we're clear: no more twinny swaps. You can see her in the East, but she doesn't come to the West.'

Jutta opens her mouth to protest, until he stops her with a low growl. 'It compromises the opening too much. One-way traffic is enough. Take those terms, or we take over the access completely.'

Jutta glowers her anger. 'And how do I know you'll keep your end of the bargain? That I will be the only one to use the passage?'

Axel stands up and smiles, lights the cigarette that he's been holding and rests one hand on his slim hips. 'You'll just have to trust us, won't you?' He blows out a lungful of smoke. 'We'll contact you when we have the first message.'

He walks away and links hands with Bibi, who prances alongside like a queen parading with the glittering king she's snared, and Jutta's stomach plummets.

In reality, Jutta has little choice but to face another set of challenges she feels ill-equipped for. And in the midst of playing spy games, how on earth will she tell Karin that her brief spell of freedom was a one-off?

50

A Journey to Consider

9th August 1963, West Berlin

They emerge from the cinema into a dusky Berlin peppered with the stream of red and white car lights, the sun's glow retiring after a long summer's day.

'A drink before we eat?' Danny says.

'Can we go straight to the restaurant? I'm famished.' Jutta links her own hand in his without a thought. 'And I'm intrigued by what you say is the best Vietnamese in Berlin.'

'No pressure then,' Danny laughs. 'I hope it's good – a tip from a guy at the base, who is Vietnamese, after all.'

At last, Jutta feels the stress of her week falling away, having endured two sleepless nights and the weight of sheer exhaustion. Unwittingly, she's given herself a breathing space by agreeing with Karin the interval of three weeks before they meet again. She plans to slip through the Wall before the weeks are up and explain, but there is time to pick her moment, to delay Karin's inevitable sadness. She's glimpsed Axel in the refectory only once since their agreement and avoided sitting at the table he was holding court on. Fleetingly, their eyes met as she felt him tracking her across the room – a brief stare, no movement or nod of the head. But the flash in his sooty pupils spoke volumes.

The Vietnamese *is* the best she's ever tasted, and Danny's face shows pleasure, though he gently ridicules her lack of skill with chopsticks.

'We can't all be globetrotters like you, Strachan!' she chides back.

'Speaking of which . . .' he says, eyebrows arched with spirited suspense.

'Yes?'

'I've been charged with an assignment next weekend, out of the country – a highly specialised job of delivering some documents and waiting for the exchange.' He winks to show his mockery of the task.

'Oh.' She sags a little at the prospect of his absence, though senses a need to play along. 'And where might this secret mission be?'

He reaches across the table and runs a finger over her hand. 'If I tell you I could well be breaking United States law. But I figure if I take you along as my accomplice . . .'

'The latter is definitely preferable.'

He sits back, relishing. 'How about it, then? A weekend in Rome? I can swing an extra seat on the air transport. The hotels, I'm told, are very beautiful.' His eyes sparkle at the thought. 'And then there's the gelato.'

Jutta is speechless. Rome. Somewhere she's only dreamed of since reading endlessly about the Colosseum, the Pantheon and the ruins of a Roman Forum. The buildings, the history, food and the spit and hiss of genuine Italian coffee. Yes, of course she wants to go! And with Danny too. But how will she manage it, with her brain so crowded, with Karin to placate and Mama to prop up, not to mention Axel and his less-than inviting mission?

'I will have a few hours of work to do while I'm there,' Danny is saying, 'but since I am only a messenger, there'll be plenty of free time . . .'

'Only' a messenger. *You don't know the half of it.*

'You know, if it's too soon, I'm sure we can go together later in the year,' he adds tentatively. 'A special trip.'

'No, no. I'd love to go.' Jutta snaps out of her indecision. She needs something bright and light in her world right now. And she deserves it, doesn't she? For all the risk and angst. She's trying hard to convince herself, and the more she thinks of a whole weekend of true freedom, with Danny, the easier it becomes.

Then a thought clouds the brightness. 'I don't have a passport. I've never been outside West Germany,' she tells him sheepishly.

Danny seems unperturbed. 'I'll check, but I think your ID card will be fine. We'd be going through a military airport so, as long as I vouch for you, you won't need anything else.'

'And will you?' Now she's teasing, the exhilaration bubbling over. 'Vouch for me?'

'Oh, I think so, as long as you stand me an ice-cream.'

'As much as you can stomach, Lieutenant Strachan.'

The excitement stays with her through the next seven days, until the day of departure. But there are things to sort out, most of which are in her head. First, though, announcing it to the household – Mama often speaks of her 'getting a nice young man', but Ruth's plans likely don't involve a double hotel room with an American soldier. Jutta needs to engage the loyal Irma, who understands as she's hopelessly in love with her own military beau but hasn't yet been offered an overseas trip.

'I'm off to a weekend in the Lakes, though it's not to be sniffed at,' Irma says. 'You go, lucky woman! It's easy enough to cover for you if I'm out of town too.'

It's Hugo, of course, that she charges with guarding her true secret as they sit on the rooftop confessional.

'Rome, huh? Is it serious?' he says with a wry look, then away across the Berlin sky.

'Not sure,' Jutta says with honesty. 'But I do like him a lot.'

'Then it's not his US passport proving the big attraction?'

'Hugo! You've become very cynical all of a sudden.'

'Comes with the job,' he mutters. 'I see a good many women hanging on the arms of Allied men, all focused on escaping.'

Jutta looks at him intently, thinks of her time in the East. 'But we're not prisoners, Hugo. Not like Karin.'

'Aren't we?' His skinny shoulders slump and he takes another drag of his cigarette. 'Just be wary, Jutta. He's military.'

'I know, Hugo, but he's not like . . .'

'I don't mean that. He's probably very nice, and a fine upstanding man and all that. But he will leave, Jut. He will go back to his own home. And you will be left here, encircled behind this bloody Wall.'

Hugo sinks back in the deckchair, a puff of defeat in his movement. Jutta knows he harbours his own worries; he's never been especially close to his father, but Oskar's movements of late have been more erratic than usual, his mood either depressed or drunk. It's mirrored in Gerda's worry, spilling to anger when her husband rolls in at all hours, spreading unease throughout the apartment. They all feel it.

One more reason why Rome feels like a utopia that's suddenly within reach.

51

La Dolce Vita

Jutta fingers the delicate handle of her coffee cup and stares out among the garden terraces banking upwards, swathes of pink and purple bougainvillea dripping over the white stone balconies. She's in a fairy tale, or a film – something unreal either way. Having already pinched herself several times, she finds she's miraculously still here, in the middle of the eternal city, looking up at a sky that also seems unendingly blue. Cocooned by the large, ornate garden, she could well be in the courtyard of an ancient Roman villa, being tended to as the lady of the house. Faintly though, she can hear sounds of modern Rome seeping through the dense shrubbery; a soundtrack of hoots and toots, the buzz of Vespas whizzing and weaving between taxis on the ancient, cobbled streets.

She's thinking of how blessed she is, of her surprise when the taxi drew up the night before at the Hotel de Russie's grand but understated entrance. Danny had insisted on making the arrangements, though checking she was happy to share a double room. After their first night together in Berlin, why wouldn't she be? They'd already breached the precipice of their own wall. Jutta would have been happy to snuggle up with Danny in a small pensione in some back street, eat arancini from street vendors and great slabs of pizza as they marvelled at Rome's grandeur. So the luxury of the Russie, just off the Piazza del Popolo, caused her to gawp as she walked into the lobby, stock-still at the glamour. What was she doing in a hotel frequented by the likes of Jean Cocteau and Pablo Picasso in their day?

She'd thought of Karin in that moment, not least because she was thankful to be wearing one of her sister's designer creations, helping her to play the part, a pair of outrageously oversized white-rimmed sunglasses perched on her head.

'You look like a film star,' Danny had said a few hours after they'd arrived, standing at the top of the Spanish Steps. 'Now I really do think I'm in a movie.'

As they'd descended hand in hand down the ancient steps and drank wine in a small café at the bottom, people-watching the meandering tourists, it was absolutely true. How Karin would love this, Jutta thought then, with a warmth and a pang of guilt in unison. Was it fate or sheer luck that had marked her out as the chosen twin?

'Another coffee, Signora?' The waiter's beautiful, lilted English floats in. Confused, Jutta suddenly remembers that she is 'Signora'; for the purposes of the hotel register, Danny had signed them both in as 'Mr and Mrs Strachan' on his military passport. How odd it looked in ink. Could she ever imagine it in reality, let alone get used to it?

'*No, grazie*,' she returns. Danny is absent for a few hours on his 'mission', and much as she could spend an entire morning basking in the beauty of the hotel courtyard, Rome is waiting.

Jutta steps out under a fierce, glowing sun pushing high into the sky, feeling its intense heat on her bare shoulders. Wearing her most comfortable pumps, she heads for the ancient artery cutting through the city, the Via del Corso. She marvels at its firm direction – straight as an arrow – and Jutta wonders for a minute: if the Ancient Romans could engineer such things, why does the Wall need to twist and snake across Berlin in such an unruly direction, slicing through buildings as it does? Although, in another sense, she is inherently grateful for its wayward nature and her portal squatting in the Wall space. Inevitably, it reminds her of the tasks awaiting her back home and her bubble deflates just a little.

Don't think about it now. For three days, you're allowed to forget that damn Wall.

She's happy, though, for Karin to stay in her thoughts, each time she spies a woman in chic clothing, or a shop window that she's certain her sister would stare at in envy.

Three hours is swallowed in no time. She gazes at the intricate faces carved into the stonework, noting the Italian women who trip effortlessly out of boutiques laden with designer bags, wandering, stopping for the best coffee – Jutta is staunchly loyal to the robust German variety, but oh! The making of it is such an art – along with the theatre of street life as she sits under an umbrella sipping and watching the world go by. As much as she mocks Danny for his endless movie comparisons, she does feel a little bit like Audrey Hepburn.

They meet back at the hotel at lunchtime.

'Mission complete?' she teases.

'I'm the consummate spy,' he jokes. 'I even managed to

shake off my tail. Let me just change out of this uniform and then we'll find somewhere for lunch.'

The weekend flies by in a dream – they walk miles in sightseeing, Jutta hungry to absorb everything of the history, with Danny's fascination and knowledge an equal match. Under the stunning concrete dome of the Pantheon, they hold hands and marvel until Jutta's neck aches, at its beauty and engineering entwined; surely the Berlin Wall would never be such an eyesore if the Romans had had a hand in its creation? Together, they devour pasta and pizza to satiate their hunger from so much walking, and *the* best gelato only a stone's throw from the rush of the Trevi Fountain. Danny takes up Jutta's cone and pushes a lira coin in her hand.

'Go on, make a wish,' he says.

She closes her eyes as it plops to the watery bottom, a future that includes Karin and Danny amid the family, all in one frantic image.

'And?' he quizzes, kissing her creamy lips.

'I can't tell you,' she laughs. 'Or it won't come true.'

'Well, just a hint – does it include me?'

'That,' she says, feeling flighty and flirty, 'you may never, ever know, Signor Strachan.'

'That sounds like a challenge – I may have to entice it out of you, Signora. I am a super spy, after all.'

They fall into bed each night with sore feet and craving sleep, but knowing that their rest will be delayed. Making love enveloped by the four-poster bed is like something out of the romance novels Jutta consumed in her early teens, teased by Karin for their illusory storylines and settings. How false and fantastic is this now?

'You didn't have to spend so much on this beautiful

273

room,' she says, lying in the crook of his arm, the pulse of his heart merging with the thrum of Rome outside. 'I would have been just as happy in a small pensione.'

He draws in a breath. 'I know you would, but equally I knew you would love this too. And I *want* to spoil you, to show you the world. I see in you a hunger for so much more, Jutta. For everything.'

She's flooded with satisfaction, recognising his generosity for what it is. 'Sadly, though, Danny, you can't rescue everyone from behind the wire.'

'It's not like that,' he says quietly. 'I do this for you because I want to. Because the US army pays me enough money that I can spoil us both, sometimes. Because it's nice.' He lifts his chest and her with it, takes her chin between his fingers. 'Jutta Voigt – please accept that Rome and this hotel room is all the more beautiful with you in it. And I don't believe for one minute that you need saving.'

'Well, that's all right then,' she says, kissing the hard edge of his jaw. 'And I do love this hotel.'

'And the man in your bed?'

She strokes his naked chest. 'Hmm, he's okay too.'

52

The Boy Vopo

The beat is fast and furious, the band in full swing again and playing for a full half hour without signs of interruption. Karin sees Otto's hand tap rhythmically on the table at Presse Café, and she loves that he's enjoying it so much, swigging occasionally at his beer.

When the foursome finish and pack up, having managed a full set, he turns to her, eyes glassy with delight and alcohol.

'That was better than some we've seen,' he beams. 'I love all that American stuff.'

Karin is suddenly hit with a distinct vision, of Otto cleaved in half – his respect for socialism (though minus its darker undercurrent), opposite the carefree and creative man with an intensely human heart. She knows he is not the only divided man in her midst, since Walter clearly suffers the same conflict. Maybe tonight, in private, it's the right time to broach a change, she thinks, then is struck by a rush of shame at her own guile, an eagerness to take advantage of Otto's pleasure.

'You should have been in a band,' she says. 'I can see you're desperate to get up there and strut your stuff.'

His lips spread with mischief. 'Who says I wasn't?'

'Were you? Really?' Her face lights with the idea.

He puts a finger to his lips. 'Shh . . . don't tell my boss. Lead guitar at university. I played a mean Buddy Holly in my day.'

'Otto Kruger, you're full of surprises! Have you still got your guit—'

'Hey, I wondered if I might see you in here.' Their exchange is capped off by a voice Karin half recognises, and she looks up to see the boy Vopo, minus his uniform and helmet. He appears even younger in his T-shirt and jacket, though old enough to have bought the beer he's holding.

'Oh, hi,' Karin manages, still combing her memory for any contact before their minor conversation outside the Charité. She senses Otto's body tense a little beside her, but he says nothing.

Oddly, the boy Vopo is not put off by Otto's presence. 'You like it in here, then?' he says.

'Yes,' Karin replies. 'It's a nice crowd.'

'And the music's good – mostly,' the boy says. 'Tonight's certainly was.'

There's an awkward half-pause where Karin wishes Otto would say something, but he's resolutely silent next to her. Has he seen this lad in uniform too?

'I would have thought this sort of place out of bounds for you?' Karin ventures. After their last encounter, she reasons it would seem odd to ignore his rank in the People's Police.

His lips spread and he laughs. 'Ah well, we are allowed time off.' He scans the room. 'And people do turn a blind eye sometimes.'

276

People? What people? Stasi? Karin's head is spinning. The boy Vopo is right, of course – the café is a known haunt for music fans so, if the Stasi were bent on preventing every gig, they could shut it down completely. Instantly. Therefore, it must serve some purpose, as a hotbed for gossip and informants probably. She's noticed that Otto tends to adopt a low profile in the Presse, his conversation muted. Still, Karin feels it's no worse or sinister than any other establishment.

'Well, I'll no doubt see you around,' the Vopo boy says finally, raising his beer aloft.

'Yes, no doubt.' Karin breathes a sigh of relief as he moves off into the crowd.

'Do you know him?' Otto's tone is cut with either jealousy or suspicion, though she can't tell which.

'I have absolutely no idea who he is,' she replies. 'He approached me outside the Charité when I was with Walter and seemed to know me then. Maybe he's seen me in the hospital, that's all I can think.' But as the words tail off, it hits like a thunderclap; the sudden flash clearing a path in her thoughts. Jutta. It's Jutta he's seen. Hadn't her day posing as Karin included a trip to the Presse? But what went on between them, and did Jutta know him as a Vopo on that day? Karin feels sure she would have mentioned it, had there not been so much else to fit into the day's breathless round-up.

Questions and cheap alcohol swirl around Karin's head, causing it to throb. Is it significant that he's a Vopo, or merely a coincidence? *Come on, Karin – this is East Berlin.* Few things happen by accident. By design or subterfuge, certainly. But she can't ask Jutta, not for almost another week. Until then, more indecision.

'Karin, are you all right? You've gone very pale again.' Otto's concern brings her back into the room.

She doesn't want it, but Karin swallows more beer to hide the choke that might crack her voice in that second. 'No, it's just hot in here, that's all. I need some air. Can we go?'

Back at her flat, they lie side by side in the darkness, her skin against his warm and constant flesh, a siren bleating faintly in the world beyond the window.

It's now or never. 'Otto, do you ever think of the West anymore? About how it is?'

His body shifts, though not tense. 'I think how you must miss it,' he says.

'And you don't?' Karin works at keeping her voice casual.

'No, not really. I didn't step across very much, to be honest. A couple of conferences.'

'Don't you like West Berlin?'

This time he does flinch, and Karin wonders if she's gone too far, too soon. What with her blunder over the watch, whether he might suspect.

'Uh, it's just not my kind of place,' he explains. 'Too busy, too commercial. It doesn't feel like home to me.'

'But aren't we all Berliners at heart?' She can't help her clumsy prodding, now it's begun.

'Hmm, I suppose. But now we have allegiances elsewhere too. To make life better for everyone, and a Wall is the least of our problems in that battle.'

Otto, normally so astute, is either fogged or made tranquil by the evening's alcohol, because he ignores the weight of Karin's question. Instead, he turns towards her, hungry for intimacy.

'All right?' He spreads his long arm around her shoulder in their familiar post-love stance, nuzzling his mouth into her hair.

'Yes,' she breathes. It's true. However much her nerves are jangled, stretched to breaking point by the secret that she harbours with Jutta, Otto's presence always seems to calm her. Again and again, she asks herself: if she can't sway his lifelong ethos to leave the East, can she face a future without him? Her intense desire to be free is tempered by the abyss of his absence.

She loves him, avidly. And having tasted it, is it possible to be happy again without the lifeblood of passion?

53

The Messenger

23rd August 1963, West–East Berlin

Approaching the portal, Jutta is more nervous than she's ever been, plagued with anxiety. Even the uncertainty of the first time had been dulled by the prize of finding Karin. Now, there is everything at stake. No pleasure ahead, with only anguish and disappointment awaiting in the East.

The memories of Rome have fallen away in past days, almost as if the trip was a true fable now etched on a page. Axel had the dubious honour of sweeping away the good in her life when he'd approached her the day after she and Danny returned to Berlin.

She'd recognised the shape of his tall, stringy form walk towards her desk in the library, his pretence of being a student on the hunt for a book. Except his engineering degree meant he would never step foot in the humanities section.

'Hi,' he ventured, and this time he looked to be coated in less bravado.

Still, Jutta was in no mood for niceties. Their exchanges were purely business now.

'What can I get for you?'

Checking left and right for anyone in earshot, he virtually whispered: 'I need a certain type of manuscript.'

Jutta almost rolled her eyes in disbelief. Did he have to play the spy quite so obviously? He was supposed to be good at this.

'Usual bench, twelve thirty,' she mumbled, then more loudly: 'Sorry, we don't have that in right now.' Her dismissal. To scarper. Get out of her sight.

She was irritated rather than afraid of Axel then, having had time to ponder over the terms of his blackmail. But as much as she continues to dislike him and his methods, she's forced to respect his power and the grim consequences he could pile upon the Voigt sisters.

It's mid-afternoon when she reaches the portal, Jutta having banked long hours since returning from Rome in order to leave work early, with her plan to seek out Karin and tell her the bad news. The streets around Harzer Strasse are only mildly busy and it helps to slice off some of the angst that naturally breeds on approaching the rabbit hole.

Now, with Axel's first task, she has two reasons to go: 'This job,' he'd said almost benevolently, 'is easy. Just a message to drop. No waiting around.'

He'd casually moved an envelope between them on the bench and whispered the address of a bar in East Berlin. For a second, Jutta had felt reluctant to even touch the paper, knowing it would almost certainly infect her; the minute she placed it in her bag she would be instantly snagged in the net of subterfuge. There's no going back, she thought. Then the phrase rankled: there's no going back for Karin. Not yet. *This is life now, Jutta.*

Strangely, the anguish causes her to propel herself through the tarpaulin with renewed bravado, barely stopping to listen out for sounds in the kitchen or the corridors. Whether or not it's for Axel, she's truly on a mission.

Despite the sunshine, the streets of East Berlin seem equally subdued and no one appears to give her a second glance. She makes her way north, having memorised where the bar drop is. The flimsy message sits like a weight in her bag, within a hastily made compartment in the lining, fastened together again with Velcro. Karin would have easily made a better job of it, and Jutta knows it's crude, but it could earn her vital seconds if she's stopped and searched. Vital to do what exactly, she hasn't quite thought out, but it gives a modicum of comfort.

She finds the chosen bar on the wide thoroughfare of Prenzlauer Allee, and is mildly surprised at how exposed it seems. But she's sure the address is right, and Jutta swallows hard as she steps into a large noisy room, crowded with men and cigarette smoke. The barman barely notices her and, when he does, she retrieves the chosen script from her memory.

'A Vita Cola please.' Smiles broadly. 'This weather certainly makes you thirsty.'

In silence, the barman reaches behind for a bottle, eases off the cap and places it in front of her. She waits for his expected response but he looks merely bored and eyes her for the money, which she hands over. This is not going smoothly.

'Have you a phone?' Jutta presses on with her next allotted line.

'It's broken,' he grunts, moving on to another customer,

and she's blindsided, sweating and dry-mouthed. She can feel eyes crawling on her: nosy regulars at best, at worst true suspicion. She takes several swigs of the cola and turns for the door, feeling the entire bar follow her every step, a low muttering from the corner. Outside, Jutta forces her head up, feet forward and into the tiny toilet cubicle of a friendlier-looking café, retrieving the crumpled piece of paper she's been told to destroy before today and peering at Axel's faded scribble. She had the wrong address! It's in a side street off the Allee. No wonder the barman seemed uninterested.

Oh Lord, Jutta, at least get it right! She wipes the sweat from her face, forces down a lungful of the stale bathroom air and resolves to do better.

Jutta's true destination is nearby in a crumbling alleyway, seemingly untouched since the war's end. It has an almost identical name, but is one of those fusty, ancient *kneipe* that old men are apt to use as their living rooms, only minus their wives. The door even creaks as she pushes it open, and for a second she is squarely transported into the film version of *The Third Man*, fully expecting Orson Welles to be sitting in a corner waiting for her, hat pulled down low.

Instead, there are one or two regulars planted on seats around the poorly lit bar. Grimy, lacy curtains at the windows make the room even gloomier, which is oddly more comforting for Jutta, as no one can possibly see in. She's the only female, and her presence brings the average age down by about forty years.

The barman at least has a smile for her. *Here we go again.*

'A Vita Cola please,' she ventures. 'This weather certainly makes you thirsty.'

'Yes, it's a good summer we're having,' he replies brightly. 'And they say it might go on into September.'

It's banal small talk, but music to Jutta's ears; on hearing the crucial words she can hand over the envelope, though not in plain sight over the bar.

'Do you have a phone?' Jutta ploughs on, taking unwanted sips of the sweet, sickly drink. The man points to a corner booth behind a thin wall, where she fumbles in her bag, back to the bar, cursing the effectiveness of Velcro for a minute and the rasping sound it makes as the lining comes away. Her reflex is to swivel and look for any reaction among the men staring into their beer glasses, but she works hard at keeping her focus. *Natural, Jutta. Act like you do this every day.*

As instructed, she slips the envelope between the pages of the dog-eared phone book and makes a play of picking up the receiver and dialling, then replacing it with a clunk.

'Thank you,' Jutta sings as she emerges from the booth, smiles and turns tail through the door.

'Have a good day,' the barman says.

It's done, and properly, but when the air hits her skin it's apparent that she's still sweating, the sheen on her forehead instantly drying to dust as she walks, perhaps too fast, away from the *kneipe*. Only when she's around the corner does she slow and force out the air kept hostage in her lungs. *Now I'm a criminal. Officially.*

Previously, ghosting through the Wall had felt like opportunism, sneaking behind the teacher's back. A crime in the eyes of the GDR yet morally sound.

Now, they – she – had entered a different world. A place where the captured suffer the full force of the Stasi's power.

Jutta takes a deep breath to steady herself. She wants a brandy, but coffee is necessary to combat a sudden wave of fatigue. There's still an hour or so before Karin finishes work – she's memorised her sister's rota, and even though she knows Karin keeps a spare flat key tucked in the second plant pot by the door, she daren't risk Frau Lupke's eagle eyes.

The Presse Café is the nearest, most familiar place to the Charité, and Jutta ploughs towards it, glad when the square, ornate entrance comes into view. The café is half full, and she orders coffee and a piece of apple cake that looks unappetising but will give her the sugar boost she badly needs.

Jutta buries her head in the day's copy of *Berliner Zeitung* with the pretence of being absorbed, though her mind wanders to various conversations in the tables alongside. On one, a younger and an older man are arguing the politics of the enforcement, whether the Wall is both moral and legal. She's surprised to hear the younger man arguing in favour of segregation, for the youthful GDR to be allowed to 'find its feet' amid the richer more powerful socialist nations, while the older man paints a nostalgic picture of his portion of the city. 'I think even under Hitler I felt more free than I do now,' he grumbles. 'The Gestapo were child's play alongside the Stasi nowadays.'

They banter back and forth while, on the opposite side, one woman tells another of her recent trip to Prague and how the shops were 'a dream compared to the dregs you find here. I found a pair of leather boots – real leather! Cost me a month's wages, but it'll be worth it in winter when they don't fall apart.'

Finally, it's twenty to four and time to head to the Charité. Karin has no office or department base as such, so Jutta's plan is to engage the receptionist (praying it's the fierce Frau's day off) and ask for Walter Simms. She reasons

285

that Karin's safety is important enough to call the doctor away from his duties.

Fate is on her side; the receptionist on the Charité desk is much less stocky and surly, with a softer air to go alongside.

'I'm a family friend of Dr Simms,' Jutta says, friendly but purposely assertive. 'Would you be able to put out a call for him, please?'

'I'm really not sure I can summon him away from his duties . . .'

'Trust me, he will want you to,' Jutta smiles, lips pursed in a *no compromise* expression. She watches for any sign of recognition in the woman's face, but Jutta has guarded against it with a pair of large, dominant earrings slipped on in the toilet, plus a thick coating of maroon lipstick. She knows that, at work, even the vibrant Karin looks dowdy in her uniform. The woman reads her tone and the lobby echoes to a loudspeaker message: 'Dr Simms to reception please', her words diffusing through the corridors.

'He should be here in a minute,' she says curtly. 'Unless he's with a real emergency.'

Jutta is genuinely sorry for having to draw the doctor away, but it's necessary, she reasons. It's all too necessary.

Within five minutes, Walter Simms is taking long strides towards the reception desk, a stethoscope flopping from the large pockets of his white coat. Jutta watches the receptionist point at her, and a range of expressions wash across his face in a matter of seconds: recognition, alarm and puzzlement.

She stands as he approaches. 'I'm sorry to call you like this, Doctor, but I need to see Karin. I've no way of contacting her, aside from sitting in her flat.'

His wrinkled forehead flattens and his eyes lose their alarm. 'Walter, please, and it's fine,' he says. 'It's just that when I catch sight, my brain still can't take it in, whether it's you or Karin – underneath all that jewellery and make-up. I hope there's nothing wrong, with your family?'

'No. It's something else.'

Like the near father he is, Walter clearly senses Karin will be upset at Jutta's latest news. He'll go in search of her, he says. 'Likely, she'll be near her locker at the shift's end. And I have a small room in the staff quarters for when I'm working overnight. I'll give Karin the key, and you can go up the back stairs to talk in private.'

'Thank you,' Jutta says, a hand on his arm. 'I hate to think where my sister might be without you and your wife.'

'She's a lovely girl,' he says, 'and I hope one day we come to know you as well. Through all this.' His eyes raise to the ceiling, but they both know what he means.

He gives her directions to a small bench behind the main building, and she waits with her face directed into her book and pulling her small curtain of hair across her features.

'Hi.' The voice, and the feet, she can see are all too familiar. 'Just follow a few paces behind,' Karin says in a low voice and walks smartly away.

They make it up the metal fire escape and into the doctor's room without seeing anyone. As the door is shut, Karin throws her arms around Jutta, almost squeezing the life out of her.

'Hey, what a wonderful surprise! I thought you were coming at the weekend?'

Perhaps she senses a stiffness in Jutta's body, or the small release of her sister's breath in her neck, but she draws away. 'Is everything all right, Ja-Ja? Is it Mama? Something wrong?'

Jutta urges her to sit on the bed. There's no delaying it. She tells her about Axel, his discovery and his conditions. The guillotine on all their plans.

Sadness and anger colour Karin's face. And then a look of horror, the realisation not of Jutta's sacrifice in coming, or the urgent task in persuading Otto, but of the damage already done.

'What does this Axel know?' she demands, eyes wide with alarm. 'If he's seen us, does he know any more? About me and Otto. What does he know, Ja-Ja?' Karin is trapped in a frenzy of paranoia, gripping at Jutta's flesh with her shaking arms. 'He could easily tip off the Stasi about Otto, and then . . .'

'Calm down, Karin,' Jutta says, forcing their eyes to lock together. It's when the thread is the strongest, the point at which they connect fully, though now it feels taut and strained. 'Axel has no interest in betraying us – he needs me.' He needs the portal the most, she thinks, but for now she and it go hand in hand.

'As long as you do what he says?' Karin hisses bitterly.

'Yes! And I know that. And I will. I'll do what he says, if it protects us – you, me and Otto.' Jutta stares hard into her sister's face. 'I will give him no reason to betray us.'

'But what if he has someone watching the entrance all the time, watching what you do?'

'If he has, then he will see just me going through,' Jutta asserts. 'No one else, won't he?'

Karin sniffs and nods, the years suddenly stripped back to when they were small and she would fold herself in Jutta's cradling arms each time she was upset. From birth, they took on and accepted their individual roles without question – Jutta as the more outgoing, seemingly stronger one, Karin as the caring provider, more sensitive, though with an iron will deep in her core. Now, Karin weeps with the full appreciation of not seeing Mama until . . . until she can achieve what still seems impossible right now.

For Jutta, cloaking her sister's thin body, a fleeting memory pushes up – no, not even a memory, the mere taint of an image, the flicker of a feeling. It could be entirely within her head, but Jutta has sensed it before, and now it seems more tangible, as if it really could become a proper recollection, were she to pinch at a corner and pull it properly into consciousness: that this is how they started, in their mother's womb, she wrapping her limbs around the baby who was to become Karin. And she wonders: was it strength or protection? And which one is it now?

54

Sacrifice

24th August 1963, East Berlin

Karin hauls her body across the paving slabs leading to Friedrichstrasse, forcing energy into her limbs. The prospect of meeting Otto usually gives her the sensation of floating on air, but not today. Not with what she is planning.

'Hey,' he says as she approaches in the shadow of the railway, kissing her on the forehead as he folds a long arm around her shoulder, nestling her against his tall form. 'You look amazing.'

He's being kind. She hasn't made much effort – quite the opposite – but Otto is ever observant of something she's rustled up on her sewing machine. A clasp pins back her hair to keep it out of the way, and her reflection in the mirror at home was appropriately stark. But he sees beauty in everything she does. He loves her, clearly, and that makes what she is about to do even harder.

'No! You don't mean it,' Otto cries, his whole solid and dignified being deflated in an instant. 'You can't.'

Karin nods, because if she speaks it will be only to agree. He's right – she doesn't mean a word of it, what's she just revealed to him: that they should stop seeing each other. That she doesn't feel for him anymore. Saying it once was hard enough, urging the false words out of her mouth. Now she can barely gesture her lie as they sit on the banks of the Spree, surrounded by noisy, happy children.

'I don't believe it,' he mutters, tears scratching at his eyelids. 'I don't believe *you*.'

There's silence in the space between them, against a backdrop of people going about their business, a family's joy invading their misery.

'You should,' she murmurs at last. 'I don't love you, Otto. It's as simple as that.'

He fidgets, scoffs, sighs and throws up his hands – a mosaic of reactions in his despair. 'But where has this come from? I don't understand, Karin. We've been fine, haven't we? Having fun. I thought we loved each other.'

We do. We really do.

He stops for a second and seems to consider, leans closer so that she can smell his clean, soapy scent and the familiarity of his fibre. Oh God, she wants to kiss him so badly, fully and on the lips. But she can't have him. She's not allowed. The GDR says so. Circumstance says so. Axel makes it so. That fucking Wall dictates it.

'Is this something to do with your family?' he quizzes in a low voice. 'Have you heard from them?'

She snaps her head up, though determined not to give herself away with a rash, swift denial. Looking him straight in the eye is the only way to deceive him fully.

'No,' Karin says, with a stiffness she conjures from nowhere. 'This is me, Otto, making my own decisions. I may be a poor alien on this side of the Wall, but I can do that. Think for myself. And this is what I think.'

He recoils at the gravel in her voice, while inside she's cringing at her own cruelty towards him. Otto of all people has always respected Karin's intellect, her skill and creativity driving towards her own little business, despite the ethos of the GDR in enforcing equality. She shouldn't have to return his total belief in her with this malice, to be so callous. But there's no choice, is there?

The night before had been long and arduous. After Jutta left the hospital, Karin retreated home to cry. Then, withered and dry of tears, she had worked through every scenario, though each avenue arrived at the same conclusion. Two and three a.m. had come and gone, the sulphur glow of street lighting streaming through her thin curtains like arrows. With a sense of urgency, Jutta had insisted that she try to sway Otto's thinking, for them both to make the border crossing as soon as possible. But Karin knows such a seismic shift to separate Otto from his family and life will take time – time they haven't got. Only one path now will preserve Otto and his family's status and safety. But first she will have to break him to save him.

'I won't believe it, Karin. I don't accept it.' Otto's badgering voice brings her back, his pain turning to indignation. 'I know there's something else here. Why won't you tell me? Don't we love each other, haven't we pledged ourselves?'

'It was a moment,' she says coldly, rising from the bench, her limbs suddenly cast in concrete. 'We got carried away. We had fun but now it's over.'

He grabs at her wrist, and she's crying and dying inside, desperate to leave and end this agony, and yet her feet refuse to propel her.

'Maybe now you feel this way, but I won't give up on us,' Otto says, his tears now evident and streaming. A woman walks by and her head turns at his distress; she slows and then walks on. 'Perhaps we need a break – we can do that,' he entreats. 'A week or so, two. See how it is then. Please Karin, give us a chance.'

How she wants to spin and tell him straight, to scream into his sodden face: that she has used up every chance of happiness by protecting him from the knowledge of Jutta's gateway, by not going back when her sister begged her, by living this shitty life now so they can exist in a better one in the future. But now there is no future, for them at least. Not when Axel and his like have a stranglehold on their truth. Axel's watchers might know of Otto already, and if so there's the potential for him to be annihilated in one fell swoop, in one call to the Stasi. She will slip through the portal and go back to being a Westerner, misery or no.

'Goodbye Otto,' she says and wrenches her body from the spot.

'I won't give up,' he says weakly, but doesn't follow. His sobs track her to the edge of the park and then fade into the buzz of traffic.

Karin sits in a café, at a table tucked into the corner, to hide her distress. But it won't come. She's devoid of tears, feels what she's done has wiped away all emotion. 'I'm barren,' she thinks. *Dry and grey as the bricks on that bloody Wall.*

55

Needing and Loving

24th August 1963, West Berlin

It's a sensation Jutta is ill-used to, and it sits awkwardly within as she walks with hurried steps towards Kranzler's. It's taken her a while to work through her unease, but deep down she knows the answer. It's need. Throughout her life, she's had need of her family, work, and Karin, of course. But never a man. Until now. Today she finds herself almost breathless with her pace and the anticipation of seeing Danny, desperate to make contact with his body, even if it's in a crowded café, and to hear his American banter, his grounded take on life, when hers feels anything but stable. So, is that need, or love? Just the mere thought – the L-word – causes her step to falter.

Leaving Karin the day before had been worse than usual, in the confines of that small, soulless hospital room. Her tears had stopped but there was no end to her despair, like giving a child a toy and then revealing it has to be kept boxed on a shelf, never to be played with or enjoyed.

There were also practicalities to deal with. Jutta would

likely get scant notice of her trips across the Wall for Axel, and the sisters needed a reliable conduit for messages on days when Jutta crossed. Handing in a sealed envelope at the Charité reception only risked it being passed to the Stasi by an observant worker on its payroll. Karin had come up with a hidden niche in the brickwork, behind the hospital bench they'd met at, accessible to Jutta and somewhere Karin can check easily every day. It's not perfect, or speedy, but the only option if they are to avoid Karin's apartment and the hound dog that is Frau Lupke. More than ever, they will be forced to play it by ear. Take chances. What else is new?

'Hey, you look flushed, have you been running?' Danny stands up from the table and kisses her neatly on the cheek. Then, sensing something else, he moves his lips to hers and presses firmly. 'You smell good,' he whispers into Jutta's ear before drawing away, and she's giddy with him already.

'I just left late, and I didn't want you sitting here like you've been stood up.' She laughs to hide the embarrassment of her lie.

'Very considerate of you,' he bounces back. 'I've got coffee and pastries on order already.'

They sit looking out from under the Big Top awning of Kranzler's top floor at the people moving along the Kurf'damm – among Danny's favourite places because, he says, the red and white stripes remind him of being at the circus as a child. Jutta watches as his vibrant eyes flick back and forth over the traffic of people and cars. With work commitments, it's the first time they've met since returning from Rome, and she's hungry for him, in every way. So when he says: 'What do you fancy doing today?' her mind goes to more than a walk in the Tiergarten and beer by the lake.

He spies the desire rippling across her features. 'Jutta Voigt, you are incorrigible!'

They do walk in the park, but only sandwiched between a small hotel on the outskirts, and lazy, protracted daytime sex.

'We can't keep doing this,' Jutta pitches as she lies in the crook of his arm.

'What do you mean?' He flashes concern.

'In hotel rooms,' she qualifies. 'You'll be bankrupt, and then they'll send you back . . .' She stops herself. It's the first mention of him leaving, by either of them. It's too scary to address that now.

'Well, short of my meeting your mother and we disappearing into your room . . .'

'Hmm, not a good prospect,' she cuts in.

'. . . there's only my place. I didn't think you'd want to, with my roommate. Though he's quite often away, with his girl in Frankfurt. In fact, he's going next weekend.'

'I don't mind,' Jutta says. 'I really don't need wining and dining all the time, Danny.'

'I will tidy up,' he promises. 'I'll even change the sheets.'

'Well then, Mr Strachan, I hereby formally book a room for next weekend. You provide the bed, I'll bring the breakfast.'

'Deal.'

Later, Jutta stares at the shadowy outlines on the hotel ceiling as Danny sleeps soundly beside her. How did she get here – to this place in her life, with its layers piling on top of one another? Common sense tells her the pile will teeter and topple eventually. But how to stop it growing higher and higher?

The toughest but softest tier is lying right beside her. Surely, it's the one she won't be forced to forsake?

56

The Blacklist

13th September 1963, West Berlin

To Jutta's surprise, Axel doesn't demand her courier services for almost four weeks, and although she's desperate to see Karin and hear of the progress with Otto's persuasion, they had both agreed it's unwise to cross any more than the messages dictate. Those lazy days of idling in the park are long gone, both sisters realising that contact has to take second place to self-preservation.

As with their previous liaison, Axel approaches Jutta in her library department and they meet in a different part of the campus. Her reaction to him is civil but distinctly cool.

'How's your sister?' he asks, drawing casually on his cigarette.

Jutta's face snaps towards him, flashing immediate suspicion.

'Hey, relax,' he shoots back. 'I'm only asking – it's not a veiled threat. Believe it or not, I do care about those over there. That's my purpose, remember?'

'Yes, well, you have a funny way of showing it.' Jutta struggles to breathe any warmth into her encounters with Axel. He's still impossible to read and not above her suspicion.

'Needs must,' he prickles. 'It's all about making sacrifices for the greater good.'

'And what might those be on your part?' Jutta bites back, eyeing the spectre of Bibi hovering nearby like a determined limpet. He follows her gaze, but doesn't answer. 'Don't worry, I am keeping to my side of the bargain,' Jutta mutters.

'I know you are,' he says pointedly and grinds his stub into the dirt, before sliding over an envelope and walking away to link hands with the limpet.

A note inside says he wants the message delivered as soon as possible, but not on a weekend, and Jutta has to hastily arrange another day off for Monday. At this rate, she's in danger of running out of holiday. For a brief moment she considers fabricating an illness at home to warrant more time off, but decides it might only tempt fate or add another layer of deceit to her life that she can't control.

As it happens, there is no lack of drama elsewhere. Jutta arrives home on Saturday afternoon after a lunchtime date with Danny to find the apartment in disarray. The hub of the noise comes from Gerda and Oskar's bedroom, but she can tell someone is hurt, with a spread of Gerda's medical supplies on the parlour table, surrounded by abandoned, bloodied gauze.

'Mama, what is it?' she pants, seeing Ruth emerge from the room, her face pinched with worry. 'Is Gerda hurt? What's going on?'

'No, it's not her,' Ruth sighs bitterly. 'It's Oskar.'

Her tone signals that, as far as Jutta's uncle is involved,

it's not so much a tragedy or an accident as an inevitability. The company and the hours he keeps, as well as the dark, basement clubs he frequents. More and more of late, arriving home drunk and contrite, only to repeat the cycle again.

'Is he badly hurt, Mama?'

'He'll live,' Ruth scoffs. 'It's Gerda I care about, worrying herself to death over him.'

When Gerda reappears, her face grey and drawn against the crimson smears on her dress, she confirms her husband has one or two broken ribs, alongside a bloodied face that she's patched up.

'He's adamant that he won't go to hospital,' she says, 'so I suppose I'll have to nurse him here.'

'It's not fair on you!' Ruth blusters, bashing about the kitchen angrily. 'You shouldn't have to put up with this worry, Gerda. He shouldn't do this to you.'

Gerda is unusually subdued, and Jutta can see the wind has been sucked out of her aunt's normally sturdy sails, though she remains intensely loyal to her husband.

'And wouldn't you do it for Rolf, if he was here?' Gerda says quietly, silencing her sister with a question they all know the answer to. None of them doubt Oskar has been involved in some dubious dealings over the years, moving black-market goods, but at times it served the family well in the blockade of '48 when the rest of Berlin went hungry. In the past, he was often blasé and even boastful over the status it gave him. Not now. Sitting in the corner of the parlour night after night, smoking endlessly, he's become a shadow of his former self. And when he does venture out, it's late and there are clearly dangers lurking.

'Stupid bastard. It was bound to happen eventually.'

'Hugo! That's your father you're talking about.' Up on

the roof, wrapped in blankets against the autumn evening chill, Jutta is shocked at her cousin's reaction, even if she suspects Oskar has likely brought the beating upon himself.

'Before the Wall, he could hop across the border to his heart's content, and even buy off the border guards to keep quiet,' Hugo continues spitting. 'Everyone turned a blind eye, especially when he was supplying the GDR elite. And making profit out of them. He should know better than to try it now.'

'What do you mean?'

Hugo turns to Jutta, expression grave in the dusky air space, perhaps wary he's revealed something he shouldn't. 'I only found out by accident – someone at work doing a story. A name came up, a good friend of Papa's caught supplying Western goods to the fortress over at Wandlitz.'

Even Jutta knows of the specially built compound on the woody outskirts of East Berlin where GDR leaders live in their complex of ideal homes. They claim to live like 'the people', but it's only the elite who have access to those nice houses and an array of Western goods. And Stasi protection.

'I guessed then that Papa had been involved,' Hugo adds. 'Which meant that as soon as the Wall went up, his business and his income all but disappeared.'

'Why didn't you tell me, Hugo?'

His eyes narrow, as the orange tip of his cigarette flares, ash dispersing in the wind. 'Oh, I don't know – why do you think, Jutta?' he comes back, heavy with sarcasm, though his voice is laced with guilt too.

It takes a second for the cogs of her mind to work out his meaning. 'Is that the reason we couldn't get a visa to visit Karin, because of Oskar's dealings in the East?' Just the thought makes her stomach roll. And her fury begin to swell. 'It's down to your father being on a Stasi blacklist?' She thinks of her frantic pleading in those first few days at the Wall border when the guards consulted their lists and came back shaking their heads, of her hopeful visits to the town hall in applying for visitation, utterly naive to the fact she had zero chance of success. The Wall might as well have been twenty feet high even then, for all the good her pleading did.

Hugo blows out his frustration in smoke. 'I can't be sure, but I think so.' He looks directly at her. 'I'm sorry, Jut. I didn't want to believe it, let alone know how to tell you. How much heartache it's caused you and Aunt Ruth. And my mother. I'm so sorry.'

She signals to him for a rare drag on his cigarette; she can't feel angry at Hugo, nor muster much rancour towards Oskar if she's honest, even if he damn well deserves it. Some contempt for her uncle's weakness, maybe, but Jutta has watched him wither as the Wall has climbed higher and more robust. Karin's hurt, and the family's pain at her absence – Oskar has seen it, assuaged his guilt in alcohol, watched his wife fret and his son lose respect. He is not unscathed. Since the Wall, everyone has lost.

57

Life of a Messenger

16th September 1963, East Berlin

For once, the sky seems brighter over on the East side and Jutta turns her face to the sun, hoping to absorb its energy; she's already exhausted, by both the atmosphere in the apartment and her attempts to appease her mother's anger at Oskar. It's normally Karin's forte, being the peacemaker, and Jutta finds it taxing stepping into her sister's shoes. Again.

She needs her wits about her today, as Axel's mission is trickier, and possibly riskier. This time, she's to deliver a message as before, but then return several hours later to a different venue for the reply. Her first port of call, though, is the Charité, where she will slip a note into the wall behind the hospital building, hoping that Karin checks it at the end of her shift, in time for them to meet afterwards. She prays Karin will have left a letter, too, to appease Mama's hunger for contact, a need that's beginning to wear Jutta down.

With summer waning, Jutta has brought a light scarf and a wide-brimmed hat so they can meet in a café and still appear distinct, though she suspects that, for once, she will look a good deal more stressed of the two. And if Karin notices, as she is certain to, how can she mask that it's Oskar's greed and stupidity which has kept them apart since the Wall went up?

The hospital grounds are sparsely populated, although Jutta has to linger nervously for several minutes in waiting for two nurses to vacate the bench behind the main building. Finally, she sits and, with no one in sight, feels the low wall behind, locating the loose, mossy brick which mercifully reveals a tiny envelope addressed to Mama. She pulls it out and replaces it with her own, folded note written in a simple code she and Karin have worked out. Leaving the hospital grounds, Jutta's heart spasms – so much duplicity even before the day's really begun! She draws in a long breath: task one completed, two to go, and then the wait to see if Karin has received the message and can meet her at Café Sybille. Already, it seems interminable.

It's perhaps not the best idea to stay in the same area as the Charité, but the Presse Café is in easy walking distance and her nerves are craving some familiarity. She can be certain, too, that Karin won't be there, so her visit is unlikely to cause any confusion with the bar staff.

By the time the hot, strong liquid licks at her taste buds, Jutta is persuaded she's made the right decision. Only it's reversed in the next minute, with an invasion into her private bubble.

'You must like it in here as much as I do,' a man's voice says.

Jutta controls the jerk of her head just in time, looks up casually instead – is she getting better, or just more experienced at this subterfuge?

'Oh, hello.' Again the tempering of her voice, returning his smile. He's only vaguely familiar. *Who is he? Is it me or Karin who knows him?*

'I see you're still on the same book – you did say it was slow going.' He nods at the Seghers novel in her lap and it's a nudge to the edges of her memory. She scans her brain furiously for recall of her previous visits to the café. Was he the one who mentioned a sister with a liking for books? And didn't she see him in the street afterwards, talking to a Vopo? So much has happened since then.

'Uh yes,' she manages. 'But it's just a quick stop for me today.'

'Well, in that case, do you mind?' He gestures at the empty chair opposite. 'It's pretty crowded in here today.'

It's not. The main cluster of tables are occupied, but behind the pillars a couple are free. He sits down before Jutta has a chance to reply, and every sense within her is immediately on high alert. Does he know something? Is he angling for information? She can't imagine why the Stasi would send in someone so obvious to probe, a man openly engaged with the authorities. It doesn't make sense, and yet her nerves are no less frazzled.

'Are you on a day off then?' he asks, sipping at his own coffee.

'Er, yes. A couple of days' leave,' she lies, pressing herself to stop fingering the rim of her cup nervously.

'My aunt used to work at the Charité,' he goes on. 'Sometimes I'd meet her in the canteen for lunch; they have nice wurst.'

Jutta thinks of the soulless lunchroom where she'd first laid eyes on Karin after almost two years apart, recalling it as anything but welcoming.

'Oh,' she says. 'Is your aunt still there?'

304

'No, she left.' He's murmuring into his cup. 'Got a better job.'

'Anywhere nice? Maybe I should think of following suit.' Jutta tries to make light, in treading water with her reactions.

The boy glances up, sadness swimming in his eyes. 'She went over the Wall.'

'Oh.' *Here it is. The prod. The test. And it's far from subtle.* 'I'm sorry to hear that.' Jutta follows it up by meeting his look firmly, determined not to shy away from the subject, which would only appear worse. *I am a loyal communist*, she is relaying, *and it's sad your aunt would want to shun the ideal we are creating in the GDR.*

'I sometimes wonder . . .' he breaks his own gaze, back to the muddy brown of his cup.

'Oh, look at the time!' Jutta cries. 'I said I'd meet a friend. I'm sorry, but I have to go. Good to see you again.'

'Yes,' he says, curling his lips weakly in raising a smile. 'See you around.'

Jutta is out the door, under the railway bridge and forging down Friedrichstrasse before her head has a chance to ignite any panic. She finds a public toilet and lingers so long inside the cubicle that a woman with a child knocks impatiently on the door and asks if she's all right.

The truth is she would rather spend the entire day sitting in the cubicle, among the sour stink of urine, than wander across East Berlin, exposed. For a moment, she thinks of abandoning the message drop and telling Axel it was simply too dangerous because of the boy Vopo. On reflection, though, she worries her handler will view it as a weakness, assessing the portal as having more worth on its own. Her only value to Axel is that she is prepared to use it, again

305

and again. The eternal ghost. And she has to keep it open, just until Karin can make that final break.

The drop is set for twelve noon, in a bar to the Eastern city boundary. Jutta wanders in and out of shops until the appointed time, finding little that she would want to buy, and then heads to the bar on foot, her ankles already feeling the strain of being on the move for so long. This time the bar is easy to find – though she checks the address at least three times – and reassuringly small and dingy. The waiter responds by bringing her the right box of matches she asks for, along with a Vita Cola. The message itself is smaller than an average envelope, which she slips under the bill, along with her coins. Then, there's three hours to waste until the reply, several blocks to the north.

At each point, each corner and every entry to a shop, Jutta employs different techniques to check she isn't being followed, pointers that she's picked up from her contact with the *fluchthelfers*, others that are simply common sense. Wearing lace-up shoes means she's able to legitimately stop and tie them, and she's left her sunglasses at home, allowing an excuse to shield her eyes from the sun, as if scanning the horizon in meeting a friend. Her only respite is reading her book on a bench, leaving just enough of the Seghers cover visible to be noted. Still, she's exhausted by three p.m. and the appointed pick-up.

Jutta's recurring fear is that, aside from her odd encounter with the boy Vopo, it's been too much like plain sailing. And so it proves. She gives her memorised request over the counter of a small hardware store; the proprietor forces a smile, at the same time wearing a decidedly nervous expression. Instead of handing her the spurious goods she asks for, he says no, he hasn't got that type and he'll go into the back to look. Can she wait? His eyes flick left and right, and his nostrils twitch impulsively.

It throws her, and Jutta shifts from foot to foot. Does she stay and risk it being a trap, with Stasi waiting to pounce in the back of the shop, or turn tail and have some chance of escape?

The questions roil, seconds fall away and Jutta's mind swings with every tick of the wall clock: Stay or go? Risk or bail? There's an old woman alongside, mulling over which type of rat poison to buy, and the shopkeeper returns, hovering anxiously. Now, he has a glint in his eye, but is it his own fear of Stasi capture, or that he's consciously leading a lamb to the slaughter? Jutta's indecision is agony, and she has to fight every instinct not to retreat through the exit. Only a desperate need to satisfy Axel – to keep that portal door ajar – fixes her to the spot.

After what seems like an age, the old woman leaves, clutching her poison. The shopkeeper's sigh of relief is audible, and he quickly switches on a noisy key-cutting machine and motions for Jutta to step behind the counter. Again, what choice does she have?

His forehead glistens with sweat as he whispers into the conch of her ear: the reply hasn't arrived, but there's word it's not far away. Two minutes, five at most. The man looks beyond her to the outer shop. She needs to wait, he urges. 'There are so many depending on it, Fräulein.'

Again, it's the emotional blackmail Jutta finds hardest. She'll discover soon enough if she can trust him: either she walks out of the shop and freely down the road, or is forced into the dark alternative – the back of a Stasi van. But she will never truly know the importance of this message, whether its passage will help one person or fifty, one family or twenty. But do the numbers really matter?

If the roles were reversed, she would heap gratitude on anyone willing to help her one and only sister across the Wall. If only Karin would go.

The seconds bleed into minutes, the man gesturing above the grinding noise for her to sit on a hard wooden stool alongside his workbench. He looks old and weary, and she wonders why he does it, endangers his livelihood and his shop. Can she trust his motives? As if reading her mind, he points to an old dog-eared photo pinned on the wooden surround – a young woman and her two children posing in a garden – and he nods. It's for them. Maybe he's working his ticket, gaining favours rather than paying the large sums often demanded to move whole families across, in the boot of a car, or with new passports. Jutta eyes the ceiling-high shelves lined with boxes of nails and screws, the backlog of stock he's amassed over the years, and she's certain, just by this man's look, that he would leave it in a heartbeat to ghost across the Wall with his family in the dead of night, that he wouldn't once look back on all the hours and days he's spent in the shop making a world for himself.

That's the value of freedom.

There's a knock at the back door, faint over the drone of the machine, and he hurries to answer it. Again, no words are exchanged but he arrives back at the workbench and slips a brown envelope into her hand, cocking his hand to signal her to go out the front of the shop. Axel had indicated the same – if any place is under routine Stasi surveillance, they will count the customers in and out, with suspicions raised if the numbers don't tally.

Sour bubbles of hot breath erupt in Jutta's throat as she steps outside, gripping a bag of nails the man has thrust into her hand for show. She can't help that her eyes sway left and right in searching the vehicles on the road; a

Wartburg motors goes by in the bright green livery of the Polizei, but the driver looks to be making a routine sweep, and there's no hint of an insidious laundry truck trundling behind. Head high, she moves nonchalantly away from the shop, counting each step until she reaches another public toilet and vomits every morsel inside her stomach.

The wait at Café Sybille is made less arduous by good coffee and the *schokoladenkuchen* that Jutta not only desires but needs; she hasn't eaten much all day, and what she has consumed has either been purged or walked off. Before ordering, though, she counts out her Ostmarks in the bathroom – the amount is getting low and, aside from her desire to see Karin, she also hopes to exchange more dollars for Eastern currency.

Head down and facing the door, Jutta glances up each time the bell tinkles its opening – but no Karin. It's gone five and she's almost given up hope, the chocolate cake reduced to crumbs and her coffee down to the dregs. She knows Karin finishes work at four each day, and it wouldn't take her long to walk or hop on a bus to Sybille. Maybe for some reason she hasn't checked the drop-off point today. After all, it's been empty for almost a month now.

Then, the slight scrape of a chair next to her and a pair of feet slip into view. She doesn't need to glance upwards, the thread instantly stronger. The relief makes her heart soar, and, for a second, Jutta feels she might just burst into tears. When she does look up, however, Karin's face causes her own stress to fall away instantly.

The prospect of Jutta looking the more strained of the two vanishes; Karin looks dreadful. Underneath her thin jacket, she's hiding her hospital uniform, which is drab enough, but her skin tone matches it, hair roughly scraped

309

back with grips. There's no style, and no verve in the smile she tries to muster.

'What's wrong?' Jutta half-whispers.

Karin's eyes dim, her lips waver and begin to crimp. 'Not here,' she burbles and turns, heading for the door at a pace, forcing Jutta to hurriedly lay down almost all the Ostmarks she has.

Outside, they link arms instantly and without a word Karin steers them both off the main thoroughfare and into a side street, at the end of which there's a small square with a bench. It's there that Karin crumples, sobs seizing her entire body while Jutta holds her tightly, absorbing the shuddering of her sister's distress.

Finally, the quivering subsides and Karin draws away, the wetness animating her cheeks a little.

'I'm so sorry, Ja-Ja,' she whimpers. 'It's just been building for weeks. Just the sight of you . . .'

'Haven't you been able to talk to anyone – Walter, or Otto?'

There's a slight shake of the head, tears threatening to flow again.

'But why? Surely Otto would understand?' Jutta probes gently.

'We're not . . .' Karin struggles to frame the words. 'We're not together anymore.'

Jutta is shocked. While initially sceptical of their commitment, she's come to see their love as constant, more so since having met Otto. Immediately, she imagines they've argued, that he's refused all talk of the West and turned his back on Karin.

'Since when? Why?'

'Weeks – the day after we last met,' Karin says. 'It's not Otto's doing. I broke it off.' The skin around her eyes is now dry and flaky, her voice cracked.

'I can't do it to him, Ja-Ja,' she rattles on. 'What with your . . . the demands on you, I can't put him anywhere near a Stasi spotlight, even for a short time. Risking myself is one thing, but him . . . He's much better not knowing me.'

Karin sags under the weight of her explanation and Jutta feels instantly deflated that she is part of the problem. Bloody Axel. Then, a light fights its way through the dense mood; without Otto, there's nothing to keep Karin in the East. She can ghost back over the Wall – for good. Today. No reason to have to kow-tow to Axel any longer and she can sever those ties. Though she still shoulders her sister's pain, happiness floods silently through Jutta's body, making her dizzy with anticipation at Mama's face, Gerda's unfettered joy.

She leaves enough space for Karin's sorrow to settle between them, and then says as much. That they will have to be careful, but it's possible they can do it now, collect some of Karin's most precious things, though Jutta wonders aloud if Karin will want to say goodbye to Walter and his wife, if it's safe to do it.

'Oh Ja-Ja, if only it were that simple,' Karin says, stroking at her sister's face. Jutta feels the thread jerk, suddenly rigid and uncomfortable. Sometimes, she wishes she didn't sense so much, certain that what Karin is about to say will put their cord under intolerable strain.

Karin coughs, her voice croaky. 'I don't know if I can come, Ja-Ja, as much as I might want to. I have to stay. Now more than ever.'

'But why? What on earth is keeping you here now?' Jutta's tone is strangled. She's fast losing reason – and patience.

Karin smiles and frowns in one half of a heartbeat. 'Because I'm pregnant.'

311

58

A Confession

Karin lingers opposite the square, municipal building, perched on a stone step that's already made the bones of her behind go numb. But then so much of her is deadened these days, it's a wonder she notices at all. The workers are streaming out at day's end, but Karin's eyes are focused for just one form.

At 5.05, there he is. Her heart jars at the mere sight of him casually talking to a man as they nod and wave each other goodbye. She pushes her weary body to standing and begins tailing him down the street, needing to walk and skip a little to keep up with his long strides, though noting his shoulders appear stooped. Over the last weeks, he's left a stream of messages for her, at home and at the Charité, all of which she's struggled to ignore. The tone is understanding, then pleading, his devotion eloquent on the page. It's taken every ounce of Karin's willpower not to reply. Until now. Until Jutta's wise words cemented her own thoughts. It was a selfless judgement on her sister's part, but Karin already knew it was the right thing to do; she just hasn't had the courage of her convictions until now.

As Otto slows and stops in front of a newspaper stand, Karin draws closer, near enough that she can almost smell him, even over the dense fug of exhaust fumes. Or is that her imagination? Her own intense longing?

'Hello Otto.'

He spins at the first syllable, almost rocking off his own axis, righting himself as he looks at her with startled features.

'Karin.' He stops. Stares. Pushes out a single, long breath through his nose, causing Karin to question this confrontation, as she has again and again, all of the previous sleepless night and the whole day cleaning floors in a daze, ever since she met with Jutta.

'It's good to see you,' he says finally. 'Are you all right?'

Clearly, she's not, and less so when he utters those words. Much like Jutta, Otto has the ability to stir emotions in Karin that she struggles to keep under wraps. Today, they won't be confined. Not when he's in front of her looking beautiful and strong, and so like the Otto she fell in love with. *Is* in love with.

'Karin, please tell me,' Otto says when they are seated in a bar nearby. He'd offered brandy, then coffee, but her stomach lurched at both and she's settled on a soda.

'I will,' she assures him. 'Just give me a minute.'

'Is it your family? Some bad news?' he explores gently. His hand hovers on the tabletop, inches from hers, itching to make contact.

Now or never. He has a right to know, doesn't he? Deserves to know.

'I'm having a baby.'

He cocks his head and she virtually sees his brain

313

spinning inside. Lord knows what's happening down in his chest.

'It's yours,' she qualifies, in case the pause is a question, his suspicion.

Another epoch ticks by, his hand frozen midway towards hers.

'Say something, Otto. Please.'

He eyes her, searching, penetrating. 'Did you know? When you ended it, with us, I mean?'

'No. No, I didn't.' She can see how it might look to Otto then, in the light of their recent break-up; having discovered she's pregnant, Karin has effected a swift U-turn, viewing the baby as her meal ticket, her automatic marriage to an up-and-coming architect, and a life made a little easier by the little privileges his position brings – despite the so-called equality of the GDR. His expression in that moment seems fogged with confusion and shock. But is he angry, too? That she should come to him now, after leaving him so cruelly?

'I don't expect anything from you, Otto,' she assures him. 'Really I don't. I just feel you have a right to know. And to see your child. I couldn't keep that from you.'

Try as she might, Karin can't hide the look that says it's love as well as duty driving her to seek him out. That she does crave Otto for himself, and not simply paternity for their child.

His finger twitches and moves across the rough wood made sticky with use. Now she sees only delight dawning on him, and no flicker of anger.

'It's *our* baby,' he says, quietly but firmly, raising his eyes up to hers to gauge a reaction. 'I don't want a child from afar, Karin. I want it with you. I've never *not* wanted to be with you.'

The relief inside Karin is instant, swilling alongside the day-long nausea that has dogged her since a week after she walked away from him, the first sign to alert her of something other than sorrow inside her. They were always careful, but accidents happen. Children are tenacious and life is determined.

She walks her finger to link with his, and issues the first real smile to cross her face in weeks. Her courage mounts and she thinks now is the time to broach it – raising their child in the West, telling him of Jutta's access and how easy it would be. But Otto's excitement can't be capped, and he's already bubbling over with plans.

'My parents are going to be so delighted – to have a grandchild nearby,' he says, clasping her hand tightly. 'I would have asked this anyway, in time – I promise you. But, Karin Voigt – will you marry me? Please?'

Karin's nerve shrinks, both with surprise and her own deluge of joy. It's not the proposal either of them dreamed of, but it is heartfelt and real, in the smoky, ugly bar. Karin knows she will always harbour the worry, the danger she poses to Otto by association, and she will have to live with it, nudging at her now tumbling heart, jabbing at her sleep in years to come. But life has decided – the tiny bean nestling in her belly has chosen for them, that love, or circumstance, or the sheer bloody-mindedness of survival, will keep them together. Wall or no Wall. East or West.

'Yes, Otto Kruger, I will marry you.'

59

The Right Thing

18th September 1963, West Berlin

'Oh Christ!' The rooftop sessions with Hugo have come to resemble a perpetual confessional; each time they steal away, Jutta seems to have some new drama to reveal. Hugo's reactions are rarely muted – and they aren't now – but he is the only person she can unburden herself to with such momentous news. What with work and life, she's already kept Karin's secret inside for a full two days and it's burned a hole in her resolve.

'What on earth will she do now, and you?' he asks.

'I don't know,' Jutta sighs. 'Karin plans to tell Otto. It's only right, but I have no idea what his reaction will be.'

'Do you think he'll do the right thing?'

'And what would that be, Hugo?'

'Firstly to marry her, of course.' Her cousin's face distorts, signalling any other route would be complete madness.

'But is it?' Jutta questions. 'Even if he chooses to stay in the East, she can come back. Women do it, these days. Have children on their own.'

Hugo stares his disbelief. In the darkness, his eyes widen. 'And you know how they live, Jut. Shunned. Ignored. Sure, women are pushing at the boundaries in a lot of ways, but they haven't bashed through the gate yet. Not to mention what it does to the family.'

'Mama and Gerda would stand by her, I know that for certain,' Jutta pushes.

'Yes, they would,' Hugo agrees. 'But at what cost to them?' He pauses. 'Not forgetting the other element.'

'Which is?'

'She loves him, Jut. She loves him a lot. Even I can tell that.'

Jutta lays her head back on the hard edge of the deck-chair and blows out a breath with enough force to move the stars above. For someone young, male and just dabbling with his first girlfriends, Hugo talks a lot of sense. He sees the harsh side of life in his job, the struggles that others face. But there's a yearning inside her own self which makes Jutta think it could all be possible: Karin as the mother at home, she as the dedicated aunt. Doing it together, they could put up with idiots looking down their moral noses. To have Karin near her again. It's selfish, she knows, but she can't help it – it's what she dreams of.

And then Jutta thinks of being in Karin's shoes and having to make that decision, possibly to leave without the man she loves. It pained her to say it, to side with Karin that Otto has a right to know about the baby, but on reflection it is the right thing. It's his baby too. Saying goodbye to the East is easy for her sister, waving away Otto another thing entirely. In the same way she might have to part from Danny at some point. Soon? He's never said for certain how long his posting will last, more that it's 'flexible'. But some day, she might be in Karin's unenviable shoes. And how will she feel then?

Why does this life have to be so damned messy?

'Look, we don't have to go to the movies,' Danny says, fishing for her hand as they leave the restaurant.

'It's fine, I'm happy to.' Jutta is realising her acting skills have a limit, with Danny especially. She is delighted to be with him and finds his company both enticing and soothing, but Karin hovers inside her twenty-four hours a day, an image just behind her eyelids, tapping at intervals at her insides, rolling in her stomach, much like she imagines the tiny dot of a child somersaulting within her sister. Jutta has never believed in all the talk about twins feeling each other's pain or instinctively sensing danger, but for a brief moment it does cross her mind. Then, she dismisses it. It's simply worry. Pure concern for her sister who is pregnant and separated from her by a deadly concrete divide.

'Sure you're okay?' he nudges. 'You just don't seem yourself.'

'No, I'm fine really,' she lies again. 'Probably just a cold coming on, Mama's had one brewing all week.'

What makes it worse is that she feels Danny trusts her to be herself, to be what's in front of him. And the more involved they become, the bigger fraud she feels. She's a walking deception. There are only two options open to them, and both painful: that he will be recalled to the US and they will say a tearful goodbye at some draughty airfield, or that he discovers her mendacity and ends it, hurt and wounded. Somehow, the former seems less painful to all.

'Hey, I forgot – I have a surprise for you,' Danny says as he walks her home after the film. It's chilly and late but Jutta has waved away the offer of a taxi, eking out their time together.

'Oh, and what's that?'

He pulls out two slips of card from inside his jacket. 'How do you like opera?'

'I haven't seen a great deal, to be honest, but I'm always keen for something new.'

'Next week, good seats.' He waggles the tickets in front of her, with gleeful anticipation. 'I can borrow a base vehicle and we'll cross on my pass.'

Cross? Did he say 'cross'?

'Oh, where is it then?' Jutta frames it casually.

'State Opera House, just over the border. Wait until my mother hears I've been there, she'll be so jealous.'

'You do know I have no entry pass to the East, Danny?'

'Yeah, but it won't matter if we have military plates. They have no right to check credentials with an Allied vehicle.'

Danny wasn't in Berlin when the same petty issue over documents almost brought the entire world to the brink of conflict back in '61, with US and Russian tanks nose to nose at Checkpoint Charlie, their heavy guns trained on each other in a tense stand-off. But he's right in that, nowadays, vehicles with diplomatic and military plates roll across the border frequently without rigorous checking. Very possibly with Eastern fugitives hidden in a secret compartment in the back, but that's another story.

The question is: how will Jutta feel about crossing in a legitimate way? Strange, certainly. And if she's spotted, it could compromise her work for Axel and impact hugely on Karin, at a time when it's crucial to keep the portal active. Jutta is furiously calculating for valid excuses when Danny squeezes her hand tight.

'I'm so glad you can come – it'll be my best birthday yet.'

60

Happy and Free

21st September 1963, East Berlin

Otto's finger traces a delicate line around Karin's belly button, lightly touching her skin, as if afraid to push down any further. Already he's questioned if they should have made love, but Karin has combed furtively through textbooks in the doctor's rooms to reassure herself it can do no harm. Besides, she feels this baby has a tenacity that almost nothing can blight. This child wants to survive.

He plants a tender kiss on her abdomen. 'When did you know?' he questions. 'I mean, not in the obvious way, but inside yourself? When did you feel it?'

She strokes at his tousled hair lying alongside her hip bone, sighing with satisfaction at his touch. 'Well, the throwing up was a good clue . . .' he flicks a finger at her thigh in a playful reproach '. . . but before then, I suppose I felt something like an itch travelling up and around. No, not an itch. A presence. It's hard to describe. I wasn't certain until the obvious clues.'

'And then?' He pulls up his head and looks at her, an innocent craving on his face.

'Happy, sad. Scared, desperate. Delighted. All those things.'

'And now?' Otto has been ravenous for all of her since their reunion, the physical and emotional, as if clawing back those lost weeks.

'Happier,' Karin says, noting her voice does not commit to the emotion entirely. Over the weeks, she has thought long and hard about having a child on either side of the Wall. In the East, there will be good, free childcare, enabling her to work, as per a good socialist citizen. As a couple, they will have free healthcare, a home, and more likely one that Otto has a hand in designing. They will be provided for, possibly better off than some. But with the cocooning, there are caveats; does she want her child to learn its numbers by counting toy soldiers, or trained in throwing with the aid of fake grenades? Does she want them to grow up alongside the spectre of the Stasi as normal, schooled into looking over their shoulder from infancy?

In the West, there is liberty to move and think freely. And her family, of course. But possibly no Otto. With the strands of his soft hair under her fingers, teetering in her mind on the top of that concrete blockade, she is resigned to the fact there's only one way – if pushed – that she will jump.

Now it's her turn to delve. 'Otto, what do you dream of, now this has happened?'

He traces another contour with his finger over her flesh, rolls onto his back and props his head on his elbow. 'Oh, that we're in a house, somewhere green, maybe not in central Berlin, with our children . . .'

'Children!' Her eyes widen in faux alarm.

'Maybe . . . and we're happy, always. We have enough

321

to eat and live, and we're fulfilled in our jobs.' He pauses. 'You're an amazing designer who's in demand across the whole of the East, of course.'

'And that we're free?' She can't contain the question.

His brow wrinkles. 'Yes, free. Of course. Free to determine our destiny as a country. To prosper, make things better.'

She grabs at his hand and weaves her fingers into his, in part as a way to end the discourse. She knows it now, for certain; he still believes. It's not like Santa Claus, where children are bound to discover the truth with age and over time. Some who don't know Otto might label him credulous, the product of propaganda, but Karin only sees belief in this clever, loyal and beautiful man. Possibly, he's misguided, but, like a child with innocent dreams, it seems almost cruel to face him with the stark reality. He loves the only country he's ever known, and he's neither duped nor blinkered: merely a hard-working man who believes in the good of others. How can she love him as anything else? Or force him from what he loves?

'How will we tell your parents?' Karin ventures later, as they make supper in her tiny kitchen. The Krugers are traditionalists, and there's the question of not being married yet.

'Perhaps I should say something first,' Otto offers diplomatically. 'They'll come round but, you know, they're not so used to change. They will be delighted – they've always wanted grandchildren. And since he became ill, my father talks of it more and more.'

Karin is warmed by Otto's faith that his parents will come round, learn to like and accept her. But there's another hurdle only she can face. How to tell Jutta that, without a sudden and dramatic turnaround in Otto, her life could be here, on this side of the Wall? There's still time for persuasion, but like sand in an egg timer, that opportunity is disappearing, faster and faster each day. How much should she push for her own ethos, that the West is the better option? She feels doubly selfish then – for Jutta's sacrifice and the peril her sister is enduring, and for putting her own desire and happiness with Otto first. Inside, she's physically torn in two.

Anger, too, twists in Karin's breast, not towards Otto or Jutta, but the faceless bureaucrats who fail to see the resulting pain of their politics – pain suffered by their own people. Families continue to be sheared apart by an ugly canker, so that heartless men can score points over each other. Arrogant and unfeeling is how she sees them. And yet still powerful enough to hold her happiness in their palms.

61

Into the East

The throaty engine idles noisily, throwing out clouds of exhaust smoke as the car sits behind another at the Friedrichstrasse crossing, otherwise known to the world and its media as Checkpoint Charlie. Jutta gazes purposefully into her lap. She feels exposed in the front seat next to Danny, her face visible through the side window and the vast windscreen of an American sedan. It's more than two years since she pleaded and pestered the border guards for access to the East and Karin, lying unwell at the Charité. But these men are trained to remember faces, and she keeps her eyes lowered, pulling her arms tight to her chest both to stop her heart from bounding outwards and to hide the visible quiver of her hands. The ghosting is bad enough, but now she is crossing to the East in plain sight, and it feels worse. Surely, her picture is on a list somewhere? Her mugshot – one not to let through, to detain, retain. Imprison.

But Danny was right; there are no guards leering into

324

the windows or demanding passes, and they trundle through with ease, like crossing a set of traffic lights. As if it is one city after all.

'Do you know this part of Berlin at all?' he asks casually.

'No, not really,' she lies. Again. 'I barely came across after the GDR was formed in '49.' The memories of pounding the dowdy streets in recent months are swallowed back with her guilt.

Several of Danny's work colleagues are already waiting in the lavish lobby of the *Staatsoper* and they make general chit-chat; only one of the officers' dates is German, the other French, but Jutta's English has improved in Danny's company and she follows the conversation with ease. She's beginning to relax a little, though the sight of military uniforms from both sides reminds her to be on alert, so too the thought of Stasi mingling among them in everyday clothes, an invisible vapour curling around their ankles.

Danny's enthusiasm, however, steadies her mood. He looks handsome and charming in his evening dress, and his face is glowing with expectancy as the curtain opens up in the grandiose theatre. At the interval, they collect as a group in the bar for a drink and she breaks away to the bathroom, eyes down as she's accustomed to doing in the East.

'Hello, what a surprise to see you here.' She daren't look up. The male voice is undoubtedly directed towards her; it's a sound that strokes at her memory, and her brain strives to identify it. The tone is too mature for the boy Vopo, but who else does she know? Surely one of Axel's contacts wouldn't dare approach her?

When she finally raises her gaze, it's into the face of Dr Simms, smart and smiling in his black suit.

'Oh, hello.' Her eyes move left to right in quick succession.

'It's all right – your secret's safe with me.' His own eyes light and Jutta feels quickly reassured. There's something about his even features and a smattering of crow's feet that makes him seem trustworthy, even without the knowledge that he saved her sister, both from death and an uncertain future.

They pause awkwardly. 'Have you seen her lately?' Jutta says at last.

He nods. 'Yesterday. We had dinner.' He nods again. 'She told us, my wife and I.'

Jutta's eyebrows rise. 'And how is she?'

'She looks better. More colour in her cheeks. I'll make sure she's looked after.'

'Thank you. Again.' She wants to ask if Karin has told Otto, to hear of his reaction and their plans, but she senses that Walter too is aware of the vapour, bodies sidling by, wall lamps that could so easily be listening devices.

He turns and leans into her, as if they are close acquaintances. 'She needs to be careful,' he mutters in a low voice. 'Now more than ever.' He says it with no hint of a threat, only concern.

'I know, and I would never . . .' Jutta begins.

'I'm sure you wouldn't,' he cuts in, and it's his turn to scan for any eyes levelled at them, dropping his voice again. 'Not intentionally. But you have to realise that they will not take account of a woman's condition. Humanity will not get in the way of their pursuit.'

'They' does not need qualifying. And Jutta already knows that the Stasi's motto perfectly encompasses the pursuit he talks of: 'To know *everything*.'

'I'll be careful, I promise, but with her and I . . . it's hard to explain,' Jutta attempts.

'I can see that,' he says, laying a hand on her elbow. His touch is warm, considered. 'It's clear to me the love between you is, well . . . I can't begin to imagine. But she also loves Otto. And he is a good man.' He shapes his lips into an apologetic smile. 'One day, she may have to decide.' And with that, he peels away.

The lurch inside her is barely controlled as Jutta reaches the bathroom. Staring into the mirror at a face that looks increasingly strained, she knows the truth of what Walter Simms says. He's a clever, sensible man. With a heart. But he's a doctor and a veteran of the GDR – he knows all about sacrifice too.

'All fine?' Danny says as she rejoins the group. 'Enjoying yourself?'

'Yes,' she lies again, and he feels for her hand while her heart hardens like the concrete on the Wall. Danny doesn't deserve this, she thinks. I don't deserve him. And yet the realisation of *not* having him, warm and solid next to her, is like the instant clearing of a mist; in that split second, she understands Karin and her dilemma. The love that can tear you apart and lead you at the same time, and she prays to never have to make that choice. One Voigt sister with a life ripped apart is enough.

The journey back into West Berlin is quick and uneventful, with no border delays, and Jutta is silent in appreciating the neon lights of the West. For the first time in hours, her body feels at ease, though her eyes droop with the strain of being on constant watch.

'Opera's not really your thing, is it?' Danny teases, pulling up outside the apartment.

'Always good to experience new things,' she says, kissing him full on the lips. *Oh for God's sake, Jutta – stop lying.*

327

'I promise, no more wailing women,' he smiles. 'See you Sunday? At mine?'

'Yes, and I'll have a belated birthday present all ready and wrapped.' She winks in a way that makes his eyebrows arch.

'And I do love opening presents,' he says.

62

Much Too Close

29th October 1963, East Berlin

Jutta pulls one foot up and rubs it against her calf, hoping to create some blood flow in her toes, since she daren't risk the noise of stamping to create warmth. It's eerily quiet from her position in the corner where two buildings meet. And freezing. The winter in Berlin is closing in and it's no time to be alone in an old brewery in the dusk, waiting for someone she doesn't know to crawl out of an equally dark corner. But here she is, at Axel's bidding.

It came out of the blue, a visit from him in the library just the day before, after a month during which she'd been required to cross with messages only twice, neither with enough notice to see Karin, only time to leave a note in the cleft of the brickwork and collect a letter for Mama, which contained no mention of the baby or her progress. Jutta is impatient to discover Karin's plan, but equally knows she needs time to work on Otto, with the added pressure of the pregnancy. It's just fortunate that newborns take time to nurture.

'I need a message moved across tomorrow,' Axel had said when they met on campus, pinching at his cigarette butt and throwing it down with force.

'Tomorrow!' Jutta couldn't disguise her indignation.

'Yes. Sorry, but it is urgent.' He did sound genuinely apologetic. 'And I don't have anyone else at such short notice.'

She knows from conversations at the refectory table that the group often call in messengers from outside Berlin – West Germans who can be issued with day visas – but that inevitably takes time.

'I'll need some Eastern money,' she told him firmly. 'I've run out, and I'm not risking changing any.'

He reached into his pocket and handed over a sheaf of Ostmarks, enough for use on the U-Bahn rather than the endless walk north. The drop, he said, was in the northern Prenzlauer Berg district and would be straightforward – no waiting, but it couldn't be made until six in the evening. It meant there was no reason to cry off work for the day, and little point in leaving a message for Karin to meet, though Jutta was desperate to see her, hug her sister's burgeoning body. She felt as if it would be another wasted visit, in missing out on Karin. Much like so many who are earning their illicit passage across the Wall with favours, she had to view it as useful in banking some credit with Axel, a valuable currency should she need to trade later.

Jutta had imagined the drop point of the Eastside brewery would still be busy at six, with different shifts overlapping, but it was almost deserted as she took up her place in the cleft of two adjoining buildings. The red-brick walls loom large over a cobbled courtyard, casting long dark shadows, and there's a gentle rattle of glass bottles that comes in a wave when the wind whips through the yard, stirring up the stale odour of yeast and sulphur. Still, it makes her thirsty.

She rubs at her arms through her coat and checks her watch. One minute past six. She's been told to stay hidden and simply wait for a signal: the sound of an owl hooting, which almost made her choke with laughter when Axel told her, as if an owl in the middle of a city counts as a normal occurrence. But who is she to question?

Two minutes past. Her eyes adjust to the gloom, but still she squints past the corner of the brickwork and into the yard. The air is sliced by a whistling of a tune across the way and the form of a body cuts across her vision, the clatter of crates being transported fading as the form disappears. Then nothing. It's ten past when she looks at her watch again; in five more minutes she has grounds to abandon, and part of her is willing the hand to move faster. Something about this doesn't feel right. Her heart is always fluttering during a delivery, but today her guts are grinding relentlessly. Two days ago she was happy and warm in the crook of Danny's arm in his flat, flirting and laughing and loving. The memories of it make her current whereabouts all the more precarious. She would even rather be at home suffering Mama's constant enquiries about Karin – when will they see her again? Why can't she have more than the letters Jutta occasionally brings? – than be here right now, cold and alone. Exposed, despite nature's dark and starless curtain.

A sudden noise demands Jutta's attention. Not the owl, but a constant scuffling, and she wonders if it's a stray dog nosing for food. She peeks around the brickwork again and sees shadows – possibly a person, or an animal, or her mind playing tricks. She ventures one foot forward. The

331

contact is late; perhaps they've forgotten the signal? They will want to be out of here as much as she does.

Then, a sound someway between a whistle and a bird noise. Possibly a bad impression of an owl? She's not so sure, but it's enough that Jutta's impatience makes her forsake the refuge of the shadows and step nimbly towards it. In the same second, the moon – previously couched behind a cloud – escapes its own cover and shines luminous over the cobbles, trapping Jutta in a virtual spotlight. The sound is easily distinguished then: a man's anguished cry. 'Run! *RUN!*' The words that follow are corrupted and mangled in his throat, clearly by force.

Jutta's shock acts like a kick-start to her frozen terror, pumping her legs not towards the imposing archway where she entered but further into the darkest corners where she's noted an outer stairway into one of the buildings. Over her own heavy breath she can sense and hear footfall behind her, closer, though no shouts. If only they would cry: '*Achtung!* Halt!' like in the films, then she could gauge some distance or direction. But this is no script playing out.

She reaches the foot of the wooden stairs and strides up, yanking on the handle and feeling relief when the door to the building opens, going from outer gloom to a double-height darkness, lit only by a weak bulb on the ground floor. She stops to listen, a wild animal sniffing out danger, nostrils flaring. The air is still, no wind here to jangle the glass, only packing cases piled high.

Jutta steps gingerly to the ground floor, skirting the warehouse walls and paddling with her hands for signs of a door. It's then she hears the whisperings on the other side of the thin divide, a jumble of partial words. There's no doubt of the intent though: not the cheery talk of brewery workers, or innocents passing through. That insidious vapour is evident, focused on infiltrating her space, finding her. Her throat tightens and she scans wildly for an escape.

Sheltering behind a packing case, heart crashing against her ribs, Jutta forces back the shrill sound inside her own ears, reaching for breath. She wills herself to conjure Karin, Mama, Danny, Gerda. Their softness. Anything but the sharp whine of a Barkas engine and the clanging of a cell door. *Be still and think.*

A door creaks open, a sliver of moonlight pushing into the darkness, the sour scent of bodies weaving into the room, and she can almost hear them signalling to each other. Like a game of childish hide and seek, she tracks their footsteps and moves stealthily back into the space they have vacated; the view from above is of two predators stalking each other in a maze. Two feet from the door, she makes a decision – and a break. Not since high school has Jutta run so fast. The scrabbling of bodies she hears, the stomp of their good shoes on cobbles, but she is already in the shadows, under the brewery arch and away, running, running, running, as if life and liberty depends on it. Which it does.

She is at least a kilometre away before she slows to a half-skip and then a walk, cooling her burning lungs before sliding into the dingiest *kneipe* she can find, partly for cover, and partly to order a brandy with the money Axel has given her. The shock of it hitting the back of her throat in one gulp stops her hands from shaking, and the barflies stare at her with curiosity and admiration. She's gone before they have a chance to ask any questions. Jutta is tempted to walk the entire way back to the portal, avoiding any stations where there are Vopos patrolling, but she knows time is of the essence.

Moving back through the portal is relatively easy, though she's ever careful to assess any movement around the industrial units, with no legitimate reason to be there under darkness. Once through the East side of the membrane and in the abandoned garage, Jutta feels a huge wave of relief, as if she's already home, when in the past it's always seemed a precarious limbo. Scrabbling out into the West, the full force of the danger she faced slams hard into her and she has to slow her pace to calm a recurring shake in her legs. That perpetual question rears again, knocking hard at her judgement: *What on earth are you doing, Jutta?*

'Something to eat, a mug of hot chocolate?' Gerda sings out from the kitchen when she hears Jutta come through the door. She forces herself to sit with her mother and aunt and to hear of their day, compelled to spout more fiction as to where she's been.

'With your man again?' Mama prods. 'When are we going to meet him?' She smiles with satisfaction; Jutta is pleased to be the cause of Mama's delight, then guilt-ridden that while Danny is no figment, the rest of her life in that moment presents as a dirty lie.

63

The Door Slams Shut

30th October 1963, West Berlin

Axel is apologetic and unusually contrite when Jutta finds him the next day, signalling with the stern look in her eye that he needs to tear himself away from the adoration of Bibi lookalikes and explain to her just what the hell went wrong.

'I'll admit it was rushed,' he says as they move through the campus. 'But we had no one else.'

'So it's okay to sacrifice me for some half-baked plan?' She's seething as she walks, her voice only just kept under wraps.

'No. And I'm sorry,' he says. 'It won't happen again.'

'It bloody well won't. Because that's the last time, Axel. I won't – I can't – risk it. For my family's sake.'

He slows and turns to her, irritation washing across his face. 'Clearly, you know the price of that.'

'Haven't I done enough?' she demands with fervour. 'You've said yourself, the opening will be compromised soon enough. It can't have much value for you.'

He continues walking, face angled at the ground, but his voice morphs to cold and unfeeling. 'Surely you're not that naive, Jutta? Your opening is gold dust to us as a group. Yes, it will be compromised eventually, but not before we're able to move scores of people across. In one day alone. You can't possibly imagine we'd just hand it back to you after you've done us a few favours?'

His fleeting look is almost pitying, and it stokes her anger even more.

'It's no one's claim,' she hisses. 'And I'd say having the Stasi hot on my tail is more than a few favours.' She's not unwise and knows that any access is prized, but still Jutta retains hope that, somewhere deep inside, Axel's humanity will push through.

He stops and lights a cigarette, draws on it heavily. 'You've done well for us, but it's not my decision.'

'Then whose is it?'

'The group as a whole. I'm simply a handler.'

'I'm not some fucking spy, Axel!' She feels her anger ricochet off the pavement below, and has to stop herself yanking at his sleeve.

'Aren't you?' But by the look on his face, he understands her fury all too well. 'Look, this has been coming for some time, anyway. There are those in the group not happy about us having good access, one without the need for an expensive tunnel, which is not being used to its full potential.'

Its full potential. How can they possibly know what it means to her and Karin? The entire family. Their life and hope?

'You have one more week,' he says flatly, scuffing the ground with his foot as a way of not having to look at her directly. 'We're already planning something after that, through your "rabbit hole". So if I were you, I'd persuade your sister which side of Berlin holds the best promise, bring her through and then steer well clear – for good.'

There's no point arguing, she knows. Axel is one face of the force that is ardent, some say arrogant, in its pursuit of freedom for Easterners. She daren't think of what this means for her and Karin, Otto, the finality of it. That's for her to grieve later, in private.

'You promise I have one more week – without interruptions?' Her plea forces him to look up.

'You have my word.' He throws down his cigarette and looks sideways, where the spectre of skinny Bibi is hovering like a perpetual shadow.

Jutta peels away. 'Thanks, Axel,' she says.

He goes to smile.

'Thanks for nothing,' she spits, turning her back on his falling face.

Jutta knows she has to act – and fast. There's an urgency inside to reach Karin and pull her out before their precious fissure closes over for good. At the same time, her actions have to appear as normal as possible, never mind that her insides are being squeezed in a mangle night and day, combined with the exhaustion of not sleeping, tossing and turning for an entire night after the encounter with Axel.

She works through lunch and leaves the library an hour early, taking the tram to Harzer Strasse and hovering longer than usual before approaching the portal through the day's constant drizzle. Now more than ever, she cannot be caught. Not before she reaches Karin.

There's a huge relief as she moves through the Wall for almost the last time. More and more she feels that her luck is bound to run out soon. Even a cat has only nine lives.

Once through, Jutta takes the tram north for speed,

avoiding the border of Friedrichstrasse station and getting off at Oranienburger Strasse and hotfooting it towards the Charité through a dreary veil of rain, matching her mood. It's already 4.30 and Karin will have finished for the day and likely already checked the hole in the wall. Jutta musters nerve that's in short supply and sits at their bench, hurriedly slipping in a note as hospital workers move to and fro. Karin should get it by the next working day, giving her enough time to make the necessary arrangements and allow her to meet Jutta early the day after. They'll likely need a whole day for what she is planning. She retraces her steps, walking this time to a U-Bahn one stop north of Friedrichstrasse, and again giving the area where border guards, People's Police and no doubt Stasi are in abundance a wide berth. She's striding with purpose, the persona of an office worker heading home towards a warm fire, a hot meal and their daily dose of propaganda on *Aktuelle Kamera*.

'Hey, hello, nice to see you here.'

Jutta's flimsy resolve sags. *Not again*. Much like in the Presse Café, the voice is clearly aimed at her and she looks up to see that it is the boy Vopo, complete with uniform and fishbowl helmet. The earnest smile is the same as he lopes towards her and she feels compelled to stop and acknowledge him.

'Oh, hello,' she mutters, wary of those catching a look as they walk past. 'Sorry, I was miles away.'

'It's that time of day,' he nods. 'People just want to get home in this weather.'

'Yes,' she says. And that awkward pause rears up. Whether or not he thinks she's Karin, what can he want?

'I haven't seen you at the café recently,' he says at last. 'I thought perhaps I'd bump into you.'

'No, I've been a bit under the weather lately,' she says.

'Holed up at home.' Please take the hint, Jutta pleads inside herself. 'But no doubt I'll see you there soon . . .'

'Erich,' he offers earnestly. 'Maybe next week, there's a band . . .'

'Yes, maybe,' she casts behind her. 'Sorry, I have to catch my tram.' And she effects a half-run towards the nearest stop, boarding an opportune carriage which pulls up sharply.

She watches him through the rain-spattered window as it draws away; he's making a play at patrolling and looking stern under the rim of his helmet. Is he friendless, sinister or simply a nice boy pressed into service? And why target her, or Karin, as he likely thinks she is? She searches her memory: did she tell Karin of her encounter with the boy Vopo on that crazy exchange day? Perhaps she didn't, with so much to remember. Thankfully, Axel's ultimatum means they won't have to dodge unwanted attention from any Vopos much longer.

Still, the feeling rankles as Jutta travels one stop and alights, pushing towards the portal and her own feeling of safety. Except it's not home she targets once through to the West side. Her very being needs lifting, and she stops in a bar near Harzer Strasse to use the phone.

'Danny, it's me. Are you up for some company tonight?'

64

The Last Ghost

2nd November 1963, East Berlin

They meet in a park in Wilhelmsberg, a good way east of the Charité, as extra insurance against being spotted together. The rain has stopped but the wind is whipping through the trees, and it helps that both sisters can legitimately hide behind scarves and hats. Karin's eyes, Jutta notes, still look dry and tired.

'How are you feeling?' she opens.

'Better,' Karin says. 'Only throwing up once a day, which is an improvement.' But underneath her scarf, Jutta can tell she's smiling, can only hope the reason is good.

They walk to a collection of benches near a playground and buy hot chocolate from a stall.

'I hate that I've gone off coffee,' Karin complains. 'I do want it, but then the smell makes me retch.'

'It won't last forever,' Jutta reassures. 'And it will be worth it.'

Amid puffs of steam, she cannot hold back. 'Did you

tell Otto?' *Will he come? Please say he'll ghost through to the West.*

'Yes.'

'And?'

'He's delighted,' Karin says, 'with the baby.' But her thinned lips are more telling, and Jutta's heart – against her better judgement – plummets. *You haven't convinced him, have you?*

'He proposed, Ja-Ja,' Karin follows on.

'Oh, wow. What did you say?'

'I said yes.' Karin turns and looks at her sister, her soulmate, her companion in and out of the womb, and the look is of apology. And regret.

'That's great, I'm so pleased.' Jutta is working hard to inject a dose of enthusiasm.

'I mean, it will have to be quick and I doubt anyone will get a pass to come over for the wedding,' Karin says. 'It will be a small affair anyway, but maybe you can make it in some way? I don't know where I'll get the material for a dress . . .' She's talking excitedly, with more verve than her sister has seen in months.

'No,' Jutta cuts in. 'I won't be there.' It's her tone which makes Karin stop mid-sentence and look hard into her sister's face.

Jutta tells her. About the timing and Axel's proviso, that their own portion of freedom – their *oxygen* – is certain to be capped off. And soon. In four days.

'So, you have to come soon, if not today, then tomorrow, for the both of you to make it through,' Jutta blurts. 'Have you talked to Ott—'

'I can't.' It's Karin's turn to slice into their future dreams. 'He wouldn't leave his parents, not so soon. And I can't

341

make him.' She looks intently at her rough, wringing hands, as if the stark truth and the finality of not seeing her family is bleeding through her, inch by inch. 'I'm sorry, Jutta,' she mumbles. 'I really am. I have to stay.'

From somewhere deep down, Jutta is oddly not surprised, though the whump to her innards still winds her. The brutality of the decision Karin is forced to make. But she won't permit herself to react; if she drops her hastily contrived mask, the truth will come tumbling out. No matter what *she* thinks, or the risks endured to free her sister, Jutta can't let her disappointment show. Karin has to be allowed to decide on her own happiness. She *deserves* it, for living the past two years, as some kind of recompense for what started out as pure misfortune. Otto is her redemption. Not the GDR or its false politics, but the man she clearly loves.

Karin's fingers search for her sister's. 'Jutta? You understand, don't you?'

'Yes, I think I do.' And this time, with her mind suddenly focused on Danny, Jutta means it. She does fathom how Karin can make such a sacrifice — because she has tasted that feeling and found it sweet. She has tasted love.

Being Jutta, though, she jolts herself back into the world and the moment; more than ever, they can't waste this day, or the precious time left. 'You know I can't come through again, don't you?'

Karin nods, bites her lip as she always does when deep in thought. 'Then maybe today we should both go through, to see Mama,' she says. 'I want to tell her myself, about the baby and the wedding.'

Jutta considers in silence. It's a crazy idea, but no wilder than every trip since prising open the rabbit hole. 'It's risky, like always,' she says at last.

Karin blows at her cup, sips and swallows. The seconds

tick by, wind swirling tiny dust bowls under their feet. 'I know, but haven't you taken that risk, for me, so many times?' Karin reasons. 'And I do owe it to Mama – to tell her she'll be a grandmother. And Gerda too. I know it will break their hearts, but more so if I don't go.'

'Then let's do it. Let's go home.'

Jutta would prefer to head straight for the portal but Karin pleads to go back to her flat and collect some gifts she's been making for the family, to hand over personally. It's still early in the day and time is on their side, although Jutta is aware that pity and sorrow are causing her to acquiesce; she will do almost anything to make it better for her sister, to ease the pain of what is likely to be a lengthy parting. If not a permanent one.

Mindful of Karin's fatigue in early pregnancy, they take a tram across town and get off just north of Friedrichstrasse station.

'Listen, we can't risk old potato face Lupke seeing us both in my block, so I'll go home and you wait in the Presse Café,' Karin says. 'I'll collect you there, come in with my hat and scarf, so no one will notice.'

While she feels uneasy about delaying their crossing, Jutta is already weary and craving coffee that at least holds a candle to that in the West. 'All right, but be as quick as you can. We need to get going.'

Karin's eyes sparkle in response – much like Jutta, she's not allowing herself to think of the long-term forecast, only the pleasure of what today will bring. The painful reality can wait.

The Presse is moderately busy for a Saturday morning, with a few faces Jutta's seen before, and the barman doesn't look twice as she orders coffee and sits in the window, keen to watch for Karin's approach. The first sip wets her lips, the second – even though it's weak by Western standards – gives her something of the kick she needs. The third, though, catches in her throat and she has to swallow back a bitter mouthful.

Christ! There he is again, through the window, the long, eager strides of the boy Vopo, out of uniform and walking towards the café. It's too much of a coincidence. He's everywhere she is – or Karin. Either way, it's not good. And today of all days.

Swiftly, Jutta heads for the women's toilets, hoping she can hover and peek out to spot which table he's at, then sidle past unnoticed towards the exit. It will be an uncomfortable wait for Karin outside on the street but what choice does she have?

Too late. She turns and he's there in her pathway, like the proverbial bad penny.

'Hello!' he says, his lips broad. 'There's a nice surprise.'

Jutta musters every ounce of energy to return his smile. 'Oh. Yes. Just a quick stop – lots to do,' she blurts. 'I was just going.'

He makes no effort to move. 'I wonder, can I talk to you first?' he says, eyes alight, still genuine, though his look is now more determined than innocent.

'Well, I am running late . . .' Jutta is inching sideways towards the exit. In the back of her mind, she considers making a run for it, but common sense tells her no. Under her coat, she's sweating.

'It won't take long,' he presses. 'I promise.'

He leads her to a window seat, and this time Jutta feels utterly exposed. Is there Stasi out there, looking in? How will she signal to warn Karin when she approaches?

'So, I'm all ears,' she says lightly, with every effort to contain the tremor in her voice.

He cranes his long neck towards the table. 'Well, this is difficult,' he begins. 'But I think I know where you're from.'

'Oh, do you? Um, my family's from Dresden,' she lies, plucking geography from the air.

He looks at her, rubbing the rim of his cup. Not scowling as such, but a look that says: *don't patronise me.* 'I know you're from the West side,' he murmurs.

'Well, more recently, yes. But I'm here now, to stay.' Jutta smiles – badly. *How? How does he know?*

'We have a mutual friend,' he says, a little sheepishly. 'A concerned friend. They asked me to keep an eye on—'

'Stop there!' Jutta hisses in a whisper. She feels heat and sour spit rising. Panic. 'Don't talk like that.'

'I mean I'm not going to say anything,' he runs on breathlessly, 'and I'm not spying. Really. I simply wonder if you know someone that can help, me and my family. Or that you might be able to? You know what I mean.'

Here it is. The trap. I'm the fly being led to the sticky centre of the Stasi web.

'Look Erich, you're mistaken. I don't know anyone, and I can't help you.' Jutta looks square into his young face to reinforce her barefaced lie. There's a few soft whiskers around his jaw, but he seems barely old enough to shave. 'Those words, thoughts even, could get us both into a lot of trouble, so please stop.'

The expectation in his face tumbles, and she can detect no animosity or malevolence. Or cunning. He looks genuinely sad. If he's Stasi, he's darned good.

'No, no, sorry,' he says. 'It was wrong of me, I shouldn't have . . . but if you could . . .'

'Goodbye.' Jutta summons the courage to rise, praying that Karin is approaching the café. Already the prospect of their joint visit to Schöneberg is fast disappearing, and Jutta feels eager to reach the rabbit hole as quickly as she can. Alone. And for the last time. But she needs to warn Karin first. Where is she?

Jutta senses the eyes of the boy Vopo burning into her back as she heads through the door and onto the pavement, instantly scanning for any sign of Karin. *Just let me get out, far enough away to run.* An S-Bahn train screeches on the bridge overhead as, with huge relief, she picks out her sister in a crowd of people crossing the road, eyes peering out from under her hat, her scarf hung loosely.

It's then that everything reverts to slow motion; frame by frame is how she will remember it.

Karin's face is the first to twist, as if it's suddenly made of molten wax, though she's not looking directly at Jutta, but beyond and at the space behind. There's a warning shout from what sounds like Erich, who's clearly followed her into the street. The noise of the road and railway make it hard to tell who he's shouting at. In the same second, she hears it – the unmistakable growl of a vehicle approaching; not the comical putt-putt of a Trabant, but a heavier workhorse sound. The vision of a green and white Polizei vehicle is alarming enough, but the second sight – a normally innocuous image of apples and oranges in vivid paint against metal on the side of a small, grey van – frightens her to the core. There's a squeal of brakes from one side and Jutta's head spins towards a human cry on the other; she catches his youthful face, warped with alarm, eyes ablaze, mouth contorted.

'NO! NO!' Erich is shouting, teeth flashing.

NO what? What does he mean?

The first grab is to Jutta's coat, the second on her arm, firm and unyielding. Wordlessly, two men in plain clothes push and shuffle her towards the van, she instinctively resisting and digging her shoes into the pavement, but their force is infinitely greater. As they move her, Jutta swivels again to catch Karin's face frozen in horror, body poised to run forward in defence of her sister. Jutta manages to yank hard on their thread, catch Karin's eye and their unmistakable connection is mercifully intact: *STOP!* Jutta's look pleads. *Please stop. Stay safe.*

Karin is static with fear, her mouth open slightly, and Jutta understands then every word and sentiment that would come tumbling out if they had the chance. Everything bound up in love, sacrifice, and sorrow.

Their thread goes slack in response to more protests from behind. Perhaps driven by the injustice, or even guilt, Erich is frenzied, physically pawing at the men manhandling Jutta and shouting indiscriminately. From somewhere, there's a glint in the grey daylight, and her eyes barely register what it is until the dull thud of a gunshot echoes around the street; the cries stop instantly and a second thud follows – this time, a body hitting the ground, after it folds in two in front of her, frame by painstaking frame.

She sees only one half of Erich's face before the heavy men bundle her into the side of the truck, but what portion she sees is lifeless, a solitary eye staring at the grubby ground.

65

Stasiland

2nd November 1963, East Berlin

There are no apples or oranges in the van, nor the smell of any rotting vegetables. No odour except the sour stench of fear that a good deal of pungent disinfectant has failed to dislodge.

The men don't utter a sound as they push Jutta inwards, plunging her into darkness, feeling their own way with ease. She's thrust into a space and made to sit, her knees bashing against cold metal, the chill pushing through her tights. Shackles claw at her wrists and close over with a ratchet sound, her feet fixed in the same way. It's followed by the resounding bang of the door and a lock twisting, acoustics that tell her she's not manacled simply to a seat, but in the tiniest of metal cells. In the second before the van door is slammed shut she catches a glimpse of the space she's in – grey and black peeling paint on steel bars, well-used, barely enough room to sit; anyone bulkier than she would be doubly uncomfortable. This is the Stasi finger-print, fitted out for the purpose – the capture-wagon, a concept surely out of a Grimm's fantasy. But no, here in the GDR it is truth. This is the reality of ghosting the Wall.

In total darkness, Jutta feels the van set off with a jolt, turning left then right again and again, swerving around corners so that her shoulders are pushed with force into the steel confines, making sharp contact with bone under the layer of her coat and her thin skin. After a few minutes she gives up trying to track their direction – it's impossible with no light and barely a sound breaching the metal prison on wheels.

Her neck begins to ache with the constant lurching of the van and her mind goes oddly to a rag doll still sitting on her bedroom shelf at home, a childhood toy precious to Jutta but one Karin would tease her with at times, shaking the doll's head until Jutta felt sure it would tear off. Karin . . . Karin. KARIN! She's jerked from her own shock and leans forward, hitting her head and dry-retching at the thought of what's happened to her sister. She could easily be in an identical van behind, plucked off the street with similar efficiency. A double triumph for the Stasi, though, if she's astute and quick enough, Karin will have turned tail in the confusion over Erich and walked calmly away. It's the most Jutta can hope for.

Erich. The boy Vopo. What was he doing? He's dead, she's sure of it. Unless it's an intricate charade to fool her, but his eye was inert, and it's almost impossible to fake that. Was he Stasi? Or simply a desperate lad who suspected she could help his family over the Wall, having somehow fallen upon their ghosting? It's already happened repeat-edly – border guards and People's Police sickened by their own system and taking advantage of their position to leap the Wall, or scurry through. They read of the successful escapes in the West, though Easterners hear only of cruel punishments for those failed attempts, fear being the Stasi currency. Was he courting her, or Karin, to help his family across too?

And how will the authorities explain an off-duty Vopo shot in cold blood on a busy street? They'll tag him a traitor to the communist cause, who brandished a gun and turned on the law-keepers, regardless of who pulled a weapon first. Something inside Jutta tells her Erich was intent only on protecting her, some kind of knight in shining armour, though she has no clue why and no energy to imagine.

They drive and drive. The spin of her head and the constant motion of the vehicle in pitch black creates a gnawing nausea and Jutta closes her eyes, a tidal wave of exhaustion flooding through every artery and muscle. She can't bring herself to think of Karin, or Mama, or Gerda. Hugo too. And Danny. *Oh my God, Danny.* Something tells her she'll have plenty of time alone to consider them later. Hours and hours. For now, she just has to concentrate on keeping upright and her wits intact.

'OUT! OUT NOW!'

Jutta shudders from a half-trance as the van comes to an abrupt stop, doors banging and shouts evident. They're inside, she can tell that much, with voices echoing off tall surfaces. The door opens and she shies away from a sudden shard of blinding light. A body scrambles in, unlocks the cell door and feels for her wrist. She thinks it's to unhook the shackles, but they are searching for her watch, and wrench it off in one tug. Only then do they release her from the metal bracelets.

Already, all four limbs have gone numb. Jutta wonders how many hours they've been driving and where in the world she is, how many kilometres from home, her family and the love of Danny. An arm drags her, and she stoops to walk unsteadily down from the van and into the glare of bright, artificial lamps overhead.

'HALT! HEAD DOWN! LOOK AT THE FLOOR! NO TALKING!'

Eyes to the concrete floor, she sees numerous feet, all in identical boots, struggling to calculate how many limbs or voices as they're all battering her at once. More shuffling and then she's led up several steps, chancing a look at what seems like a long corridor. The bleached yellowy bulbs cause her to shy away again from the brightness, burning sharply on her retina.

If Jutta isn't scared enough already, she is soon near catatonic with fear as the bottom of each door lining the long corridor comes into view. Grey, drab metal, heavy and thick, with a lock near to the ground. Cells. Prison cells. Each and every one. She's not sure of the sensation it creates, something close to an unadulterated terror, a pain so great in her insides that she would buckle and fall if not for the numbness alongside.

I'm in the heart of Stasiland, and no one, but no one, can help me.

She appears to be the day's only quarry because there's no one following, and she's nudged forward. Jutta can hear one or two cries from behind the doors, but they are soon muzzled by a fierce banging from a guard and shouts of 'SILENCE!' The voices obey.

She's led into a room, which has bars on the high window, but it doesn't seem like a cell as such. A woman is waiting there; the unattractive heeled shoes are a giveaway, and Jutta dares to flick her eyes upwards. Ordinarily, she would be glad to see one of her own sex, but the austere expression below the grey, wiry hair tells her this is no ally

351

to womanhood. Two guards follow and she gauges from the space they occupy and the size of their feet that they are men.

'102. Undress,' the woman says flatly. Jutta can't help turning towards the guards behind, as if she might ever so politely ask them to leave.

'102, face front!' the woman barks. 'They stay. Undress. Everything.'

Jutta feels her throat constrict and tears move rapidly towards her eyelids. *Do not cry, do not cry*, she chants inside. *It's the beginning of the end if you cry now*.

Shivering from fear and cold, she begins to peel off her layers and the stony-faced woman approaches. It's clear they mean to search her. Thoroughly.

Just don't flinch.

Being instructed to lie on the thin mattress in a cell comes as something of a bizarre relief to Jutta, after the violation of the search and the way it's sapped all energy from her body. That and the pain she feels from their rough treatment. They found nothing, of course – she's always careful to empty her bag of her West Berlin pass when she ghosts through the Wall, with nothing else to identify her. But they asked no more, not her name or where she comes from or what she is doing in the East. Perhaps it's because they know already, or perhaps they plan to simply beat it out of her.

She fingers the cheap nylon two-piece of loose trousers and long-sleeved top she's been instructed to wear, made of worn material and hugely oversized, with threadbare socks that bear the well-infused sweat of some other poor individual. She's cold, but daren't get under the thin, scratchy blanket because they told her not to, to remain instead on top of the bed. Every so often – she can't tell how long – a guard opens the hatch and peers in, a large red face scowling at her. She turns a little to her side to relieve the pain in her buttock and a mean mouth growls at her: '102, lie flat!' And so she does.

There is natural light in the cell, but no vision, even if she were to stand on the bed on tiptoe, because the 'window' is a mosaic of dirty glass bricks, distorting the unknown world outside to a blur. A small table nudges up to the bed, and there's a cracked sink and a toilet without a seat or flush handle. Jutta hopes her insides behave, though the unrest in her gut already signals they won't.

It's hours or minutes or . . . who knows. But her eyelids are just beginning to sag when the clank of locks jolts her awake and the door opens.

'102. Stand up. Eyes down to the floor. No talking.' It comes out in a series of staccato instructions, as if read by a particularly wooden actor.

In her socks, she's pulled from the cell and made to face the wall, the corridor empty, she thinks, except for one other guard. Head down, she's led along the hallway and through into what feels like another wing; the air changes noticeably, and it's warmer, a balm wrapping around her. Maybe they've changed their minds? But does that mean they'll go after Karin? That's worse. Should Jutta persuade them that she is Karin? Her mouth is stale and sour from no fluid since the two coffee mouthfuls at the Presse Café and her brain feels like a collection of brittle abandoned honeycomb, empty cavities where her senses once sat.

The comfort of warmth ceases on sight of the door she's led through – a heavy, lockable outer membrane of steel, with a wooden inner door. Padded. Her fear rises and her bowels threaten to mutiny.

The room, however, is an office rather than a cell; she's instructed to sit on what looks like a milking stool in front of a desk. Everything in it, aside from a grey plastic phone, is brown. The colour of dung: wallpaper and desk, curtains and chair. A cavern of shit, split only by the light from a window. The door clangs behind her and she's left alone.

Jutta's rear is aching and she's fidgeting when a door in the side of the room opens and a man in a suit walks in. Also brown, though his hair is sandy. He gives her a desultory smile and sits, placing a large buff file on the table. With the height of his chair against the low stool, Jutta feels as if she is at kindergarten all over again, an adult looming large over her as the tiny child.

'Fräulein Voigt,' he says, looking up.

So they know who I am. But do they know which one? She says nothing since it seems like a statement, as if she's just walked into a job interview.

'I'm hoping you will answer some questions for us?' In keeping with the general colour scheme, his teeth are nicotine yellow as he smiles. At least he's not barking at me, Jutta thinks, having already scanned the area for signs of tools used to inflict torture, or cupboards where they might be hidden.

'I . . . I . . . what . . .?'

'Let me tell you first what we know of you,' he interjects, 'and you can correct me if I'm wrong. How about that?' His tone is mildly patronising, but not threatening.

She gives a slight nod.

'We know that you, Jutta Voigt, are a resident of West Berlin, from Schöneberg, and that you live with your mother, aunt and uncle, and your cousin, who works for Radio Free Berlin. Correct?'

354

So they know I'm not Karin. There seems little point in denying the obvious truth, though Jutta hesitates. She needs to know more of what she's agreeing to, but he takes her silence as a yes.

'And until August 1961, you lived with your twin sister Karin in said residence. Until, in fact, the day when the anti-fascist protection barrier was erected.'

The Wall. If we're being honest, call it the fucking Wall.

He goes on: 'A sister who appears willing to stay in the GDR, with her boyfriend Otto Kruger. Sensible girl – she knows the GDR will give her a good life, in return for her loyalty and hard work.'

Still, there's no threat, only fact, but it doesn't prevent Jutta from sweating inside her pathetic pyjamas, a line trickling down her now aching back.

'The help we need is with your access,' the man goes on. 'A tunnel is unlikely, as you don't appear dishevelled – the mud of underground Berlin is a devil to shake off – and we know you don't go via a checkpoint.' He cocks his head, as if they are playing cards and he's bluffing out an ace, trying to spot the card player's 'tell' in her eyes.

Jutta remains tight-lipped. Despite Axel's disloyalty towards her, there's something about the portal she does not want to reveal. For the other ghosters, and for her. Though if they threaten to harm Karin, she will sing like a canary, without hesitation. It's not betrayal, merely survival, she reasons. In the meantime, she'll hoard her knowledge as her bargaining chip.

They go round and round for what seems like ages. He's smoking cigarettes and asking questions, but only half-heartedly, and doesn't seem annoyed when she gives no answers. He never once says she can go home if she reveals the portal, and so Jutta assumes she's not going home for some time, though she won't allow her mind to speculate as to how many days, months or years it could be. That's just too terrifying.

Finally, as her back is beginning to sting with the effort of staying upright, the man closes the buff file and takes his brown self out of the brown door, saying only, 'Until next time, Fräulein Voigt' and showing his yellow teeth.

Back in the cell, day becomes night, but only because the light fades through the glass bricks. Jutta hears voices crying out, but no sobbing or screaming; the guards clatter up and down, voices snapping orders as presumably other prisoners are taken out. Her bowels finally give out, and the guards leave her to marinade in her own stink before they flush the toilet from outside. The lights go off, although one luminescent bulb above the door switches on what seems like every few minutes and the hatch opens to reveal eyes, and sometimes a mouth. Soon, she even gives up raising her head to see.

That first night is long and varied. Quite apart from the gripe in her stomach, of emptying and then half-filling with a dry meal of bread and sausage, sleep is a rolling wave of horror and imagination, split by being pulled out of her cell and marched back to the nauseating brown room, where the brown-suited man is waiting, fresh as if he'd just had his morning coffee. The curtains are drawn and the bulb above is yellow and blinding, and Jutta has no idea whether it's two or five a.m. She squints to avoid the pain it brings to her eyes.

'Hello, Fräulein Voigt.' And he starts again with the questions. She gives no answers, while he dishes out facts about her family but never once issues a direct threat. Instead, there are throwaway comments, like sideways glances at a school dance, designed to entice. And endless, endless questions.

'Why do you hate communism, Fräulein? Have you ever been a member of a fascist organisation? Your father was a Nazi, wasn't he? How have you sought to infect those in the East?' But there's no invective in his manner, and he doesn't seem to expect any answer; there's only the sense that they're both simply biding time or playing a game. Round and round on an endless carousel.

Then, she's back in the cell: *102. LIE ON YOUR BACK! STAND UP! LIE DOWN!* Bark, bark, crash, bang.

Karin's face is ever present as Jutta stares at the grimy ceiling – her sister's horrified, helpless reaction as she was dragged into the Barkas outside the Presse. Karin's words, her fears when they were first reunited, cartwheel in Jutta's tired mind: 'I can't chance being caught, Ja-Ja. It frightens me to the core.' The Stasi wear everyone down in the end, Karin warned her then: *'Everyone.'* Now, Jutta would give anything for her other half to be nearby, but please, please not in a cell. Not here, in this alternate hell.

It's hard to even cry, as the tears squat in her eyes and she's afraid to turn her head sideways and let them fall freely, for fear of being shouted at. Eventually, though, they brim to breaking point and roll down her face, snaking into her ears so that even the sound of her own sobbing is distorted, like everything else.

The same again. And again. There's no breakfast or dinner – just one standard meal, pushed through the hatch, with metallic-tasting water or gritty, tepid coffee. Jutta sees no one apart from the guards' shoes and partial faces, and Herr Brown, as she's begun to call him.

He stops asking and begins suggesting, although Jutta

recalls enough of the Stasi technique to know that this is their speciality: never to use violence, but to employ the long game, to hint and cultivate doubt in the prisoner's vacuum. To erode her own soul. Herr Brown begins, slowly, to dripfeed the names of those who might have betrayed her – Axel is among them, so too Hugo, and Otto. Even Gerda and Oskar. Oskar, he tells her quite jovially, is well known in the East, a supplier of goods to the complex at Wandlitz, their leader Walter Ulbricht among the recipients. This knowledge that Oskar harbours means that he owes them favours. A lot of favours, Herr Brown reiterates darkly. There's mention of Karin and Ruth as the culprits, which Jutta dismisses in a heartbeat, and a few names from her library department, sure to be a bluff as they know nothing of the portal. But someone did. Someone betrayed her.

Then, Herr Brown begins suggesting. The words are mildly threatening, though his unwavering, steady tone doesn't falter. He mentions a castle in Saxony, though at first Jutta can't understand why he's talking of the beautiful scenery in East Germany.

'It's perhaps not your traditional castle,' Herr Brown adds drily, 'but it does do very well as a women's prison. Lots of space for inmates and very secure. It's where we send those guilty of espionage.'

She laughs then – she can't help it, a dry throaty cackle born of pure disbelief. 'I'm not a spy,' Jutta croaks, in the longest string of words she's uttered for an age. 'I was only seeing my sister.'

'You're from the West and you went through to the East, secretly and illegally,' he prickles. 'Of course you were spying.' Still, there's no malice, and he says it as if it's already proven and she is convicted. Perhaps she is.

On her next outing, she is pulled from her cell and a

half-sleep to a similar office adjoined to another by a window-sized hole in the wall, a metal grille separating the two. Jutta is told to sit by the grille, looking into the next-door office, with its regulation brown furniture and a typewriter as well as a phone. A different man, in grey this time, arrives. He sits upright behind the desk and tells her she is charged with espionage against the German Democratic Republic, and several counts of 'border viola-tions'. He mutters something about life imprisonment, but Jutta is entirely distracted by the window's metal bars, wondering if they will notice her resting her head and stealing a minute's sleep. There's dread, mingling with disbe-lief and the words floating over her, but mostly she just wants to close her eyes and drift.

Then it's back to her dates with Herr Brown. Once, he offers her a cigarette, which she takes warily, but only because he's smoking from the same pack. On top of an empty stomach, it makes her light-headed. Even so, she thinks it's a kind gesture. Herr Brown is nothing if not civil under his flat, slightly disinterested air. As he rambles, she ponders where he lives, what sort of wife he goes home to at night, and whether this is just a job, or if he actually enjoys it. How he explains to his children what it is that he does, every day at work.

At their next meeting, she's angry – livid at being plucked from an endless nightmare of waking in what feels like the small hours. She sits hunched on her silly stool and scowls. Herr Brown doesn't flinch, just carries on droning. This time there's a guard behind her, who prods her in the back when she drifts off as Herr Brown is speaking. She wants to spit at the guard and claw his eyes out, so he will leave her alone to sag and sleep, she doesn't care where. Just to sleep, perchance to dream. *Who said that? Is it someone I know?*

66

Thoughts

Sometime in November, Somewhere in East Germany

*There are four bricks across and seven down in the window –
that's twenty-eight in total. I've counted them over and over. What
is twenty-eight? Not my age, not yet. Will I even reach it? Days
in February, that's it. That's Hugo's birthday too. Hugo. Could
he have told them? He knew, maybe he was threatened – his job
that he loves. No, he wouldn't. Would he? There's Oskar too –
his odd behaviour, a black-market trader to the East elite. Poor
Gerda. Someone knew I was there, with Karin. Right there.
Erich? Then why would he defend me, go and get himself shot?
Who else knew? Walter? They haven't mentioned him. He's a
doctor, they might have threatened to take away his position, force
him into farm work – they can do that, can't they? And he loves
Karin, wants her to stay in the East. Maybe at all costs. Otto
too – he might be more loyal than Karin knows, a member of
the Party, one of them. A Stasi man. Karin said it herself – they're
everywhere. Was that a warning? Did she mean me to stay away,
does she mean it's her? It's not grumpy Frau Lupke who's their
block informer but her, the pretty flighty girl from the West being*

blackmailed. So many times Karin could have come home. And yet she didn't. Why? Is she just pretending? Now one of them? Enough to give up her own sister. No. Surely, not Karin. Not my Karin. Not to her Ja-Ja. But she might, for her own freedom with Otto. She just might. But then there's our thread. I know it's there. I can feel it. Can I? Really? Or is that me dreaming, wanting it too much?

Yes, I AM lying on my back. Just let me sleep. PLEASE. I will give you anything, the nylon shirt off my back, my blanket, my hunk of tasteless bread if you'll just LEAVE ME ALONE. Let me escape from these thoughts, shut down, roll over, curl up, let me sneak under my coverlet of dreams and smell the stale eiderdown on Karin's bed, draw in her scent so that I can fill my nostrils with joy and memories. Let me run a hand over her rounding belly, kiss the soft, downy top of her baby's head. But you animals won't let it happen, will you? You deny us, because you want something that we have, that you will never ever own. Because you want to know it all, but you will never know the love. The love that's possible, between sisters. Between people. Her and me. Her and Otto. Me and Danny. Oh Christ, Danny. He's so nice and yet I'll never see him again. I'm soured, tainted, forever to reek of this sweat-brown place and they'll keep me here until I'm old and wizened and my hair is matted and grey and I squawk like a mad old crow, and they can because there is another one of me out there and her name is Karin and so no one will ever know.

Oh Christ, when will this ever end? If I say anything and everything, can you promise to let me sleep?

67

Breaking

November (Possibly), East Berlin (Maybe)

In her lucid moments, Jutta can sense that she is mad. Or that it's creeping up on her. In one way, she feels it's a good thing to recognise when lunacy is imminent; it means she still has part of her mind intact. Part of the old Jutta remains. For now.

Sleep. She's never imagined it has such currency, that she could crave it so much, that she would have a waking delusion about being able to dream for a full eight hours. That she might actually trade her life for it.

They have her up again and out in the corridor, eyes down. If she is to be awake at least it might be to see Herr Brown, who is the only one who talks to her in words of more than one syllable at a time, who so far has not made any real demands other than she stay awake to listen to his stories and tales of her betrayal. Who calls her by her own name, and not a number.

'Hello, Fräulein Voigt, and how are you today?' he says, more cheerily than usual.

The dark welts around her eyes are the biggest clue, but at least he asks, Jutta thinks. And he's nothing if not consistent – same suit, shirt and tie, and Jutta wonders if he buys those beige shirts in bulk or whether they're issued by the Stasi, for the full dowdy, depressing effect.

This time, the stool is absent and he offers her a chair in front of his desk, like a bank manager. In fact, there is a piece of paper in front of her, with lots of typed words, much like a contract. Her vision is so skewed she can't make out the meaning, or even read the top line, but no matter, because Herr Brown is ready to help her in translating.

'I have enjoyed our little chats,' he begins. 'But I think, Fräulein Voigt, now is the time for us to come to some arrangement.' He looks up and smiles, exactly like a bank employee. 'We could go on doing this for a good while – I mean, I'm here most days, but frankly, it's exhausting.' He says this with no hint of irony.

'So what I'm proposing is that you sign this declaration, agreeing to give us what information you come across, and then you can go home.'

Home? Did he say home? To Mama and Gerda. To Hugo . . . and Danny?

The vision of her stepping through her front door in Schöneberg threatens to overwhelm, causes a hot brick to lodge in her throat. Then, in a flash of lucidity, Jutta sees beyond the vision, thoughts jangling and coming to a resounding halt, the true meaning. Herr Brown is proposing she tells him things: that she in turn betrays those around her. Becomes a Stasi informer. It's a club with a big member-ship, so Karin has hinted, on both sides of Berlin. She will report on Axel, Oskar and Danny and anyone else who is planning, proposing or even thinking against the East. And she also knows from Karin that everyone says yes to this proposal eventually. It might be weeks or days, but everyone caves in the end, Karin told her once with a grave face. Herr Brown's patience confirms it. So why not do it now? At least she'll be allowed to sleep before the madness crushes her.

The battle rages within; Jutta raises a finger towards the pen, forces it down physically with her other hand. The words on the page swim again, with no hope of reading or absorbing what it says, other than that she will be their slave. Again, she forcibly slaps down at her writing hand under the table.

A second flash of clarity. 'What about Karin?' Jutta says.

'Your sister? What about her?' Herr Brown's hands are clasped over the buff file like a church minister's.

'I'll do it, but I want some reassurances.'

'And they would be?'

'That Karin is left alone. With Otto. To live a good life.'

Herr Brown sighs with a hint of theatrics. 'But we have no way of knowing how loyal they are – surely you can see our dilemma?'

'She is loyal. Otto too – he knew nothing, I promise you. Not the access, or my visits. Or even that Karin has a twin. She's made a new life with him, and she *wants* to stay.'

He looks less than convinced.

'If she isn't in love with Otto, and willing to give up everything, then why is she still in the GDR?' she pushes. 'She could have left with me easily. Her *heart* is here.' Jutta wishes then the statement wasn't so, but she knows it is. Quite bizarrely, she's telling the truth to the Stasi. 'I will be your eyes and ears in the West, but my sister is part of the deal.'

Jutta sits back, lips pursed in defiance, though she is

bluffing wildly, with no aces – in fact no cards – in her hand. If she doesn't agree to sign they can simply keep her here, claiming quite rightly that she is a Wall-jumper and to be punished as such. She's banking solely on the Stasi needing legitimate spies in the West.

Herr Brown looks into her face directly and Jutta strives hard to match his stare, when her lids are screaming to droop.

Perhaps he's equally weary of this stand-off, because he says: 'This is not something I can agree to readily.' His voice is colder, more businesslike. 'I will need to—'

The grey phone next to him trills, and he stares at it for a few seconds, as if he's shocked it rings at all. That it's been a mere prop all along.

'Yes?' he says into the receiver, brow furrowed. 'Hmm, are you sure?' Irritated now. 'Wait there. I'm coming.'

Herr Brown is now not the human soul with a wife and child in their East German allotted apartment, with his beige shirts and brown suit. He is cold, hard Stasi, and he's just turned grey. 'Stay here, Fräulein Voigt.'

He disappears through the side door, and Jutta hears his voice, angry and raised at times, clearly talking into another receiver. The slam of it being replaced jolts her from sinking into a minuscule sleep and he's suddenly in front of her.

'Come with me,' Herr Brown says tartly and opens the padded door, where a guard waits on the other side. Instinctively, she lowers her eyes to the floor, though no one tells her to do it. Herr Brown leads them down the corridor, but not in the direction of her cell, and the guard follows silently. When they descend two flights of stairs, Jutta's fear brews again – she has no recall of climbing upstairs since her arrival. Or does she? To her, the bowels of any building conjure basements, dungeons, torture and death. Each word feeds greedily off the other, breeding images of blood and pain and horror.

Hold on. Hold on. Hold on.

They stop descending and Herr Brown walks the length of another corridor and, to her relief, Jutta can see daylight bleeding through, even glimpsing a slice of pure light in a clear window. He leads them into a large office, a brown desk spanning most of the vast window space, behind which is a man in a uniform, the gold braiding on his shoulders outshining the dull image of material and his stormy face combined.

'Good day, Fräulein Voigt,' he says icily from his chair.

Should she speak? Is she allowed? Jutta opts to nod instead, her blurred vision fixed on him.

'It seems there's been a development,' he begins. Instantly, she assumes they have Karin. And Otto too, possibly. The GDR now has no need of her, or her petty snippets of information from the West. She will disappear to that castle in Saxony, under the vast cloak of the Iron Curtain, a victim of the Wall like so many others. Jutta is stone-like, through despondency and fear and being schooled so well not to move.

'Fräulein Voigt?' The voice of the military man prods her back into the room.

'Yes?'

'It seems you have . . .'

It's then she locates a sliver of something, in or around the room; a shard of goodness and light amid the grim spectre of this entire mausoleum. A movement to her left, and she daren't believe it's anything other than a guard to take her away to a different hell, but she has just enough left inside to hope.

'. . . friends in high places.'

The faint scent marries with the sight to her side then.

'Miss Voigt.' He says it formally. That unmistakable Yankee lilt, the short dark hair, the tan trousers of his uniform.

He came.

'Colonel Strachan has made a personal request,' the military man prattles on, and she has to restrain herself from pushing her head into Danny's chest and weeping with relief. 'And in the interests of political relations, all charges will be dropped . . .'

The rest floats above her head, but she takes it to mean she will leave. Here, today. With Danny. But to where?

'We will call for Fräulein Voigt's belongings to be brought,' someone says.

'No, no need,' Danny says formally, diplomatically. 'You will appreciate her family is anxious to see her as soon as possible, and I have a car waiting. I'm sure there will be nothing she needs urgently. Am I correct, Miss Voigt?'

Through her haze of fatigue, Jutta struggles to read between Danny's lines. *Agree with me*, she thinks he's saying. She nods, dutifully.

'Very well. Colonel Strachan,' the military man nods, 'I hope we may conduct business again in the future.'

'I'm sure we shall, and the US government thanks you for this human act of decency,' Danny recites. It's all so surreal that Jutta half-expects him to nudge her in the ribs and start laughing, revealing the prankster he's suddenly become. Or the Stasi snitch. Then she can be marched back to her cell and begin her day of staring at the ceiling and counting the window bricks.

Instead, she and Danny are led out of the office and up a flight of stairs to an entrance, and then out into a court-yard, faced with a prison wall, a watchtower to the left and right, barbed wire coiling above the barrier, like the Wall she knows so well.

Even the bleak autumn sun on Jutta's face feels like fuel, and the breeze brings her round fully. The sky! She can't believe how much she's missed the definition of clouds as they drift in grey shapes across an infinite ceiling. Danny nudges lightly, herding her with his body and his pace towards the gate, where they pass through without delay. Can it really be this easy? That self-same doubt washes through her weariness.

Danny opens the front passenger door of a dark American sedan, slipping into the driver's side. She goes to speak, the temptation to fling her arms around his neck almost too much.

'Don't say a thing,' he says through clenched teeth, sparking the engine. Confusion tumbles inside Jutta, butting up against the torture of sleep deprivation and paranoia: is he angry with her? Why is he here? *How* is he here?

'I'll explain when we're out of sight.' Danny's gentler voice breaks into Jutta's bewilderment. It takes only a second's glance, his eyes on hers, she trawling his crystal blue for the truth, and even in her fog there is certainty. He came for her. Properly. Fuelled by love. She is safe now.

The huge engine revs and he pulls away, his eyes flicking nervously left and right, the prison walls falling away behind.

'Danny, how on earth . . .?'

'No time for that now,' he says hastily. 'Listen, we're in the north-east part of the city. Which direction is your opening? Please tell me it's not far away.'

Jutta's haze magnifies. 'We're still in Berlin? But surely we'll be going through the Allied crossing, Checkpoint Charlie?'

'Not when they discover who I am,' he says. 'Or rather who I'm not.'

Jutta looks at him then, at his uniform and the rainbow of braids across his chest. A dawning claws through the fog. 'Since when did you become *Colonel* Strachan?' she utters.

'Oh, about an hour or so ago, when I gave myself a rather hefty promotion, starting with my uncle's uniform. Then a fake phone call and a bit of precocious ranting to pull rank in high places.'

'Danny!'

'Well, what else could I do? Listen, no time for that now. They're not stupid. Any minute, they will put in a phone call to Allied command or the bush telegraph will begin to sing, so where the hell is that access of yours? From what I can gather, I'm fairly sure they haven't found it yet.'

Jutta has to concentrate then, physically shaking her head to hurl away the lack of sleep. She directs him south, using Karl-Marx-Allee to orientate herself towards the portal neighbourhood – the bright yellow sign of Café Sybille catches the edge of her vision and she forces herself not to think of Karin in that moment. Stealth now is everything. Danny's eyes are flashing, scouring his mirrors for signs of a tail.

'Anything?' Jutta asks.

'Not that I can see. Although if it's Stasi . . .' He doesn't need to elaborate. She's aware of his foot hovering over the accelerator, eyes roaming for Polizei or any other vehicle too close. Her mouth is sour and dry, pulse jabbing into her throat in double time.

Then it becomes faster, in line with their speed. 'Hold onto your hats,' Danny says suddenly, swinging the car around a corner, tyres squealing like a scene from a gangster film. 'We've unwanted interest.'

369

Jutta twists her head round – a black Mercedes is keeping pace, near enough that she can see the expression of the two men in front: dark and determined.

'Find me a side street,' Danny says, thrusting a map at her as he taxes the car's engine. She pulls the print close, struggling to pin down their position, then flicks up. On flying around the Nöldnerplatz near to a place where Karin once hauled her to a very dull exhibition, there's a sudden recognition. With relief, she spies a familiar café, then a bakery.

'Next left!' she cries suddenly, just as a long horn sounds angrily behind them and the Mercedes' pursuit is cut by a truck veering across its path. Danny seizes the chance and swipes the wheel hard left, and left again into a tiny side street, swerving into a dingy parking space behind a large parked lorry. He cuts the engine instantly, and they suspend breathing. Ten, twenty, thirty seconds. Beyond the lorry, they detect the distinctive throb of the Mercedes slowly trawling the street, searching. Air seeps from Jutta's lungs as they hear the car reverse, idle, and move off again. Silence then, save for their suspense; Jutta swears she can hear the thump of Danny's heart.

'Close enough?' he says at last, though in a whisper. And he's still smiling through it.

'I'll give it to you – this is some date, Colonel Strachan.'

Bathed in relief, they drive warily south towards Treptower Park and the Spree, two sets of eyes scrutinising vehicles and people as they go past. Thankfully, no one gives them a second look.

'Pull up alongside the park and we'll walk the rest of the way,' Jutta instructs. 'There's very little traffic here and it will look odd if we drive up.' She's aware too of the observation tower nearby – if the word is out, as Danny suspects, the guards will have been notified of the fugitives.

Danny reaches in the car's back seat for a plain, grey jacket and sheds his colonel's uniform, his tan trousers making up a casual two-piece. His military tie is also cast off, and he gives Jutta a pair of trousers to slip on, with black pumps that are slightly too large and a woman's button-down coat, the thick material hanging off her lean frame. It covers her Stasi pyjama top at least.

'Right, which way?' He grabs at her hand and she feels his warmth; Jutta is reminded of that early date on the Kurf'damm when she felt like they were a regular couple for the first time, and the comfort it gave her then. Now, there's more than a pleasant feeling at stake, and they have to be the perfect couple, or the GDR's ruthless shoot-to-kill policy will add them to the numbers of Wall dead.

The energy pulsing through their interlocked limbs is electrifying, but the couple focus on projecting a public calm: talking and smiling, lost in each other and meandering through the ruins of residential blocks. They could easily live there, be on their way home to cook dinner or make love in a post-war shell of an apartment. Anything but ghost across the Wall, breaking the law and risking life and limb.

Jutta is tightening her grip on Danny's fingers with one hand and gesturing that they're approaching the maze of industrial alleyways with the other, when he spies a Vopo casually patrolling on the opposite side of the road. Swiftly, he pushes Jutta into a tobacconist's, slips her a few Ostmarks, and she buys a copy of *Neue Deutschland*, rolling it up and holding it under her arm.

'Home to a warm fireplace?' the shop owner asks. 'Chilly tonight.'

'Yes, too cold out for me,' Jutta chirps.

They turn to leave, and startle uncontrollably – the Vopo is behind them, tucked inside the shop doorway. He smiles, though, and nods approvingly at Jutta's purchase.

'Let's not hang around now,' Danny says as they reach the pavement outside. 'We'll just go regardless.'

'Why?'

'I might be wrong but I think that Vopo spotted my collar buttons,' he says, fingering the star-shaped metal pins and pushing them out of sight, perhaps too late. 'Damn it, I should have taken them off.'

Jutta's instinct has always been to tiptoe towards the portal, but this time she strides with false confidence into the maze of dirt alleys; it feels like an age since she was last here and she still has no idea how long it's been, or what day it is. It's quiet, with nobody about, and she pulls Danny in her wake – one more left and right turn to go. Will the stone blocks be there to hoist them into the window? At least they have each other to lift and pull up.

'Hallo . . . hallo?' An echoey voice is a little way behind them, enquiring, though they can each guess who it is, military boots splitting the gravel underfoot with the heavy trudge of a march. They freeze instinctively, Danny flattening them both into the side of a wooden building under the eaves of a roof.

'Hallo, are you there?' Still friendly, but not to be put off. Now two sets of boots, mutterings evident between colleagues. The steps quicken, followed by a distinct click as weapons are cocked ready.

Jutta's eyes widen into Danny's: what to do? To bluff it out so near to the Wall, certain to be suspicious, or to scuttle silently towards the opening? Will they make it?

Danny reads her thoughts and the hand sign she makes – *it's left then right* – and nods. They push off as the two Vopos round the corner, their fierce cries signalling complete and utter dread.

'HALT! HALT! WE'LL SHOOT!'

They do – the initial shot ricocheting off the wall of the first turn, the second thudding into wood.

'Keep going!' Danny yells, as if they have any choice, and Jutta's too-big shoes flap around against her soles, slowing her up. She can hear the Vopos scrabbling behind them now, rounding the last corner at speed, and life goes into slow motion all over again as Danny pulls out a gun from inside his jacket, turning and aiming it towards the two grey uniforms. Only she sees his hand shake as he points the weapon directly at them, but the two young boys shrink back, their youth and fear overcoming any bravery in the face of a barrel.

Seconds, or more? What is time to Jutta after the past days? The brief respite gives her the chance to reach the blocks, thanking providence the pile is still there. She yanks open the window and vaults into the space, landing on the boxes on the other side, turning and shouting, 'Here! Here!' at Danny, as he sprays two shots into the air to create more time.

In the next moment, she's hanging from the window and, with strength that comes from nowhere, hauls Danny's arm up and through the portal. They tumble from the stacked boxes and land in a combined heap on the floor, and Jutta feels her ankle crack on contact. One frantic look traded and they're both upright, Jutta's foot searing with pain, though the sight of a Vopo face at the window overrides the agony. They glance at shoulders being hoisted through the window space; until she and Danny are through

373

the tarpaulin they remain on the East side of the Wall. Still targets.

Biting against the pain of her ankle, Jutta takes the lead through the corridor, crashing into the doors with enough force that the glass is ejected and smashes behind them, mixed with a cinematic ping as more bullets bounce off discarded metal. These Vopo boys are determined now on their glory of nabbing Wall-jumpers, and keen to avoid the punishment if they don't.

Danny is a hair's breadth in Jutta's wake as she half-runs half-limps into the kitchen. With the Vopos seconds away, Jutta squats instinctively behind the old sofa, jerking Danny down. Their lungs sting with fearsome breath as the soldiers clatter into the empty room.

'Shit! Where did they go?' one says in a panic.

'They must be here, there's nowhere else. Two rooms over there. Quick!'

Footsteps circle and then recede, though only to the adjoining room – one pair of boots thumps up the stairs. Without thinking, Jutta seizes the moment, kicks off her shoes and hobbles to the cabinet, lifting it with stealth to avoid any scrape and judging the space big enough to fit Danny's frame. He creeps from behind the sofa and she kneels down, feels his hands guide her hips as her face touches the tarpaulin with utter relief, the diver breaking the surface to suck in the precious air of the West.

On the pavement, Jutta scrabbles up and turns to see Danny's dark crown push through into freedom, then shouts from beyond the tarpaulin: 'Hey Hans! Here they are!'

A single shot follows, with Danny crying out in sudden agony. His head jerks, torso half in and half out, and his body slumps. Jutta heaves at his shoulders frantically, her ankle instantly numb but every other muscle screaming with the effort, and inside a voice pushes her on: '*Just one last time, one last time through.*' It feels an age until the sudden release of his deadened legs, she not stopping until his entire frame is pulled clear and is present in the West, along with a red river of blood seeping alongside the grey granite of the Wall.

Inside the ambulance, Jutta wills Danny's blue, blue eyes to open, but the smile she knows so well remains absent, his features slack. The pool of crimson creeps upwards from his foot and soaks through the bandages, while Jutta hears the medic muttering to the other about a big loss of blood and 'hitting an artery'. The siren screams through the streets of West Berlin and her own voice croaks: 'Stay with me, Danny. Please. Stay with me.'

PART FOUR

68

The Divide in Decline

11th November 1989, Friedrichstrasse Station – West Side

There is a discernible but low hum of expectation as Jutta cranes her neck to scan above the heads under the bright station lights. Brown, black, ginger and grey strands form a mobile wave of human hair. Hearts are on hold, tears held in abeyance, and Jutta's own, labile emotions match the general anticipation; excited, reticent, up, down, happiness mixed with a deep-seated sadness at so much time lost.

Time is a healer, so the saying goes. But Jutta has long since decided that it's more of a bandage – it can stop the bleeding, but the wound remains underneath, sore and scarred. Time, too, creates history, and plenty has occurred since her own wounding: in two and a half decades men have walked on the moon, girls driven to frenzy amid Beatlemania, JFK has fallen to a bullet, his brother too, and Martin Luther King lost to hatred. The world has endured Vietnam and famine, celebrated Band-Aid, Bowie and punk. Countries and governments have been created and destroyed, wars fought and lost.

In Berlin, the Wall has morphed over the years – stronger, higher and more fortified, rebuilt to repel more efficiently, with dogs, death strips and mines. The escapees, in turn, became more creative, using ever more daring tunnels as their conduit: the tiniest of bubble cars, hot-air balloons and even a fake, life-size cow; their determination never quashed.

More recently, and crucially, the Iron Curtain has shown its weakness, fading and fraying to sprout holes, with freedom-seekers picking at the fabric. And the holes became bigger, first at the borders with Hungary and Czechoslovakia, now in Germany itself. Communism is chipped and cracked, its own fissure unable to be cemented. Finally, the Wall is surmountable.

Which is why Jutta is here now, two days after those incredible scenes were broadcast to the world, people stopping and gawping through windows of electrical shops globally, surprised and smiling; the image of thousands scrambling up and over the Wall at the Brandenburg Gate, a convoy of comical Trabants hooting in a crazy symphony as they tootled over the border, and the hacking at the concrete as the GDR finally acquiesces and admits the Wall can no longer stand firm.

Heart in her mouth, Jutta had picked up the receiver and booked a ticket immediately, was on a plane the very next day.

Now, Danny squeezes her hand, kisses the side of her hair and whispers, 'All right?'

She pulls up her bottom lip, thinking that if she speaks, tears might ooze through the rift in her tight-knit resolve. The truth is, she doesn't know. How can she? Somewhere, in a throng on the other side of the platform, her twin sister will soon arrive, a full twenty-six years older. Greyer, probably, since Jutta needs to reach for the hair dye more often these days. How will her twin sister look? Will she be hardened by a life spent longer in the GDR than in the West, or will Karin's soft inner core have survived the future she chose?

Jutta feels her own life, by comparison, has been blessed. She still asks herself why, out of the two, she was the one chosen by fate to be on the West side, to have dodged the spectral shadow of the Wall, by a whole series of coincidences, dares and strokes of fortune. Why she was the one allowed to flee and be free.

And they did take flight quickly, once the injury to Danny's foot had been patched, the Vopo bullet ripping through his heel as he disappeared like a creature in a burrow. Barely out of surgery to repair the shattered bone, he'd faced up to the wrath of his uncle, the real Colonel Strachan; the fury of the senior American army man had been white-hot, not only at Danny's insubordination but also at the danger incurred by such a reckless plan. The injury, which still causes Danny to limp a little in the cold weather, proved to be a saving grace for him; a potential international incident was buried as an embarrassment by the East, the Allies in turn needing to showboat their gratitude for saving the life and liberty of a West Berliner. In the end, *Lieutenant* Strachan's reward was a quiet and honourable discharge from the US army and the chance to pursue his long-held dream of academia. Jutta fled with him, her own future in West Berlin judged as perilous with the Stasi lurking, prompted also by Danny's proposal of marriage from his hospital bed, which they still laugh about now.

They headed for New York and Columbia, with Danny sinking back into his own blissful past and working towards his professorship in history, buried in his beloved, ancient tomes.

Jutta never quite managed to be the archetypal professor's wife, instead gaining a PhD in modern languages and a student faculty of her own on the campus in Munich, where after fifteen years at Columbia they relocated as a family, and from where they're able to check regularly on Ruth and Gerda. The two older sisters are in their seventies now, and waiting tentatively at home in Schöneberg, with Hugo, his wife Lottie and their three children, for a full family celebration.

Jutta's children, Livvy and Thomas – native New Yorkers and Germans at heart – are old enough now to have flown the coop, with Livvy choosing to sample the edgy underbelly of West Berlin, and to stay for the time being. Jutta reasons she's probably high up on a section of Wall at this moment, raising a fist in defiance and clutching her own slab of history. Little does she know how much of her own past is set in that concrete.

There's only one piece of Jutta's self, her heart and her life jigsaw that is missing, now just metres away. Soon to be in sight, palpable, and within arm's reach.

69

Scaling the Divide

'Next stop Friedrichstrasse station,' the Tannoy announces, and a cheer goes up through the carriage as the U–Bahn prepares to stop in what was known to Berliners as 'The Palace of Tears', an underground border divide designed to split families from East to West across a dreary platform. For decades, it sought to separate. But not today.

Otto looks at Karin and nods, eyes wide with true delight; he's aged well, she thinks constantly, with his boyish looks intact and blond hair a little thinner but not balding. The faint lines around his eyes make him even more attractive. No wonder she fell in love with him, no mystery that she stayed.

It's Karin's first time in the West since that day when she ghosted through to see Mama and Gerda all those years ago, and she wonders how much of this Berlin she will recognise, if the pace and its modernity will unsettle her. Even the East side of the city feels slightly alien these days, she and Otto having spent most of the last twenty-six years in Leipzig, only returning recently to live in Berlin again.

A forced move was their punishment, of sorts, a kind of banishment the GDR liked to press upon its valued but wayward citizens. Typical of Otto that he saw it as more of a challenge, in working to rebuild the oft-forgotten war-torn ruins of Leipzig.

On that day when her sister was netted in front of her eyes outside the Presse Café to a potentially horrific fate, that poor boy Vopo gunned down in cold blood, Karin received her expected visit from the Stasi. But not before she'd managed to run to the only person sure to help then, the one who had the means and position to get a message across to Danny in the West; Walter, her constant, her father-figure to this day, a surrogate grandfather to her children. Then she was scooped up (much to Frau Lupke's joy), along with Otto.

Individually, they were interrogated, warned, threatened and sleep-deprived – for the umpteenth time Karin was split several ways: worry over Jutta, fear at never seeing Otto again, the growing baby inside her belly.

They couldn't squeeze out of Otto what was never there in the first place – having never known details of the portal – and so they were both freed, with the inevitable conditions, though Otto somehow resisted becoming an informant. Later, in safety, he admitted to suspecting something of Karin's double life, since spying the 'borrowed' watch on her wrist and detecting a change in her. He was never certain enough to confront her, but he laid plans all the same with the people he knew, those few in the GDR with power and humanity combined. So that when he needed it most, he called in the biggest of favours. For

Karin, the woman he loved. In the relative security of their own bed, he confessed the rest in whispers: his fears that Karin had got herself 'into some sort of trouble', and his attempts to protect her, using Erich as his eyes. Otto admitted then to knowing Erich from school, and of his boyhood friend's antipathy towards the regime, jaded by what he saw from inside his uniform. 'I wasn't spying, I promise,' Otto told his wife. 'I just didn't want to lose you in the worst way possible. I wanted to warn you if I could.'

The rest, he could only gather, was pure coincidence, coupled with Erich's own desperation to flee East Germany, along with his family, a reckless valour for the freedom he truly believed in. Though sadly fatal.

So, for the sake of their growing child, Astrid, and a second daughter, Sabine, the Krugers lived a model GDR life, providing for others and raising their children, never giving the Stasi cause to doubt. It was the only way they could survive, gratified to escape the horrors of a long imprisonment.

To any outsider it looked as though Otto upheld the ideals for several years, and only Karin was close enough to see that his former beliefs had been crushed by imprisonment and the ongoing regime. For years, they simply maintained the façade. But when the dissident demonstrations against the regime brewed first in Leipzig throughout 1989, Otto was there, watching and waiting on the periphery, not sorry then that his home country would be forced to implode, the GDR to admit that their utopia finally proved unworkable. Proudly, they were both in the crowd of 70,000 protesters marching through the streets of their adopted city on October 9th, as the first virtual block of the GDR was felled, followed a month later by the Wall itself.

Karin knows that Otto is nervous about adapting to new beginnings and a wider world, but they can start small;

she can show him the joys of her Berlin, the city as a whole. *Their* city.

As for her sister, Karin received scant word of the prison release and then escape to the US - enough to allow her to breathe again. There were pictures permitted over the years as the Stasi stranglehold loosened and the blacklist became old and dog-eared. She's fingered the photographs of Jutta's growing children more times than she can remember, hardly hoping to ever meet them in the flesh. Mama and Gerda were consistently denied the Christmas passes afforded to many West Berliners, but in recent years the two women have been permitted to visit Leipzig once or twice, though the journey is long and arduous for them. Karin was forbidden to attend Oskar's funeral in 1970, his body found sodden with alcohol in the Spree; no foul play suspected and no suicide note, though the family don't speak about why or how, for Hugo and Gerda's sake. Still, Karin suspects her uncle died of guilt, and that her aunt shoulders that burden now.

Now, she's fizzing with excitement at the thought of being back home, in the apartment, seeing Hugo and his children, her own daughters meeting their cousins for the first time.

Does she have any regrets? Only that it's taken so long for the world to wake up and act, for those in power to stand back and realise the ridiculous nature of splitting a vibrant, functioning city in two, slicing the fabric of families, causing pain and mistrust. But when she looks at her husband and her beautiful children, no. No regrets. And now Jutta. Karin daren't imagine the first touch, the words they will exchange, destined to be drowned in tears, no doubt. The train is slowing and coming to a stop, and Karin's heart is gathering speed, making up for the twenty-six lost years since one small slice of it has lain dormant.

70

Together

11th November 1989, Berlin

The crowd ripples with expectation as the doors slide open and bodies flood onto the platform, a few families linking immediately and their cries of joy lifting above the throng.

'Come on.' Danny pulls Jutta forward, weaving through the people and searching faces as they jostle, scanning for likeness in the eyes of those they once knew so intimately.

He stops short. Of course, he'll recognise Karin – her double is right beside him every day, in his bed every night. Her hair and dress are different, but the features identical. And the spirit within. He pulls on Jutta's hand, gently pushing her forward to where a woman and a man stand, arm in arm.

Karin is greyer, Jutta notes, but she carries it with her intrinsic style, the skill she had in nipping and tucking at her clothes to create something special. She has it still. Her face is lean but healthy, her hair short, and her eyes bright and alive. All Jutta's worries of her sister being trampled and ground by a system intent on equalising everyone are unfounded. It's Karin, uniquely, right there in front of her.

It takes seconds to claw away the disbelief before they walk forward and touch, fingers first, hands clasping and cheeks kissed and fondled, soon wet. Hugs so tight that for a second the two can barely breathe.

'Karin,' is all Jutta can think to whisper in her sister's ear.

'Ja-Ja. My Ja-Ja. Is it you at last?'

They draw away, look at each other fully, and it's then they both feel it: a twisting, a tightening in each core, a firm tug, fibres testing their strength again. Behind them, the two men are embracing for the first time as if they have been brothers all along. In that eddy of emotion, beyond the tears and the wounds that will need careful healing, Karin and Jutta are certain of one thing: their thread, made tenuous and frayed over the years, is intact. Stronger than wire, concrete or bullets, it has more endurance than any Wall.

And as the bricks tumble, the thread will weave and knit, and thrive again.

EPILOGUE

After – A United Germany

January 1993, Stasi Records Agency, Berlin

They sit side by side at a table in a large room, waiting for the files to be brought, fingers entwined under the wood. Since 1992, two years after the Stasi was formally disbanded, Germans from both sides of the divide have been able to access their secret files – notes on six million people, 125 miles of lives on paper, clandestine secrets and dull, day-to-day activities. The Stasi, as they so proudly pledged, wanted to know *everything*. And now, the former Voigt sisters want to know what they knew.

'Are you ready?' Jutta asks when a man approaches with several files. Brown, obviously.

'I think so,' Karin says. 'After all, it's my life.' She smiles. 'Though maybe they knew more about me than I did.'

Karin's file is inevitably larger, details kept since the Wall went up, and they open this one first. It dates from August 1961 and her time at the Charité, and includes a copy of every application for contact from her family – Jutta recognises her own writing on several, and the faded red stamp:

'REFUSED'. The reason is finally confirmed, scrawled in a margin alongside: 'Niece to Oskar Zelle. See file: Zelle. Caution. No access. Mail denied.'

The sisters look at each other; even now, they can't be angry at their uncle, for Gerda and Hugo's sake. It's just how it was. They finger the copious letters Karin wrote home over the years, each opened, a red line scored through the address: 'NO Delivery', and the same for those Jutta sent in vain to the Charité.

The entries in Karin's file become fewer as it's documented that she settled in to her job at the hospital, sponsored by Walter. A single line comments: 'Noted seen with ministry worker Otto Kruger. Intermittent observation', then later: 'No cause for concern. Block informer to observe.'

'Good old Frau Lupke,' Karin laughs. 'She must have been bursting out of her corsets with that responsibility. I wonder what she's doing now with no one to spy on?'

What's surprising – pleasantly so – is that the Stasi seemed to have no inkling of meetings between the two sisters after Jutta began to ghost through the divide. They suspected nothing, it seems, until the last days. The rest is a painstaking diary of Karin's time under interrogation, and she shies away from reading its contents; Jutta can tell it's still too raw, almost thirty years on.

The bulk of the file Karin already knows: a blow-by-blow account of her and Otto's life after they were freed, for several years under intense surveillance, the very least they expected after Otto's call on favours narrowly saved them from the worst fate of imprisonment. Their penance was to have every aspect of their marriage scrutinised, the births of Astrid and Sabine, and Karin's work as a seamstress and part-time designer, Otto's work in Leipzig constantly examined. The detail tailed off only as the years moved on and they proved their worth as good workers and non-traitors, with the files closing finally in 1979.

'That's when we started to breathe again,' Karin says. 'Not hearing the click on the end of the phone, or spying someone hovering outside the house. To live our lives in full.'

They switch then to Jutta's file, slimmer and created only a day or so before her arrest. Copies of her endless formal requests to visit Karin have been pinned in retrospect, notes linking her to Oskar's file. Her shadowing only began in earnest on that last day of meeting Karin; pictures of their meeting in the park, travelling to the Presse Café, shots inside of her talking to the boy Vopo, and then a grainy image of the van with his body partially seen on the pavement. Jutta's eyes spring with tears at the memory, made more vivid by his lifeless face. Alongside, in the narrative, it says: 'Erich Meixner, killed in the line of duty'. *Christ, they even told lies to themselves.*

Without access to his file, they might never discover if the Stasi knew of his yearning to flee the East. Jutta feels in her heart that Erich was only ever Otto's observer and never the GDR's informant, as there's no mention of his name in any of the surveillance on either sister. Likely, he was simply looking out for Karin, and Jutta by default. And in that final, fatal moment he was their guardian, though his incentive died with him on the pavement. She resolves to find his mother and contact her if she can, explain his protection and bravery at the last. That his loyalty to humanity was firm.

And then the thing Jutta really wants to know, what kept her awake and nearly drove her mad in the three long days she was kept in Berlin's Hohenschönhausen Stasi Prison, interrogated by the still anonymous Herr Brown: who betrayed her? Who knew when she was ghosting through on that day? At the time, her near insanity led her to believe it might have been one of the family: Hugo, Gerda or even her own mother. But it's here in black and white, faded but certain: not Axel, the most obvious suspect, but someone close to him. Bibi. Skinny, shadowy, peripheral Bibi, the girlfriend who hung onto Axel's every word, not through adoration, but a motivation that doubtless included Stasi money too.

On reading, it seems Axel did not bleed certain information in their pillow talk – the location of the Harzer Strasse portal isn't mentioned until after Jutta's escape with Danny – so Bibi must have known when Jutta planned to make that final trip, just not where. A secret rabbit hole to the very end. Jutta discovered soon after their getaway that the house and garage had been demolished within days, the void becoming part of the wide and ugly death strip that characterised the Wall in the 70s and 80s. But for a time it was their secret cavity – theirs alone.

Then, after the escape, a warning that makes Jutta relieved to have fled across an entire ocean with Danny: scribbled Stasi instructions to 'lift and detain' her at the earliest opportunity, payback for her and Danny's brazen exodus. Back then, she had been wracked with guilt at leaving Mama, but now it's proven to have been the most sensible, and safest, decision.

She and Karin spend several hours with the files, at times laughing, intermittently crying, and sometimes just mystified as to why one body of citizens would want to spy so intently on the very people they professed to value as their own.

'Why?' Karin says, again and again. 'Because in the end, we're proof, aren't we? This whole country is — that you can't control people's thoughts. What goes on in their heads. Or their hearts.'

Jutta nods and squeezes her sister's hand. They close the files and, with it, a chapter of history never to be forgotten, but one which no longer has the power to shape, contain or inhibit their lives or loves.

'Come on,' says Karin. 'Where shall we go for coffee?'

'Anywhere we like,' Jutta comes back. 'Anywhere we damn well please.'

Acknowledgements

Shaping this book and its time period would have been impossible without the 'third eye' of my brilliant editor, Molly Walker-Sharp, who keeps tabs on my indulgent ramblings and offers great alternatives, plus the crack teams at Avon books and HarperCollins, who champion me worldwide, book after book. So, too, my agent Broo Doherty at DHH Literary Agency, for her email chats and constant support in this unstable platform of pandemic writing. Also, to this book's copy editor, Rhian McKay, and proofreader, Anne Rieley – thank you and sorry for my appalling grammar.

On the end of Zoom, email and the phone are my writing pals Loraine Fergusson (LP Fergusson to her readers), and Lorna Cook; we *will* meet and drink wine in the same room soon, but in the meantime, thank you for your support.

I couldn't do any of this writing malarkey without the help of so many, especially in the very odd time that this book was researched and written. Writing is a singular occupation, but this author needs life, soul and conversation to function, alongside a good deal of coffee, of course. I am lucky to have a brilliant group of hardy walkers, coffee-slurpers and their associated dogs as my friends and sanity-aids: Gez, Micki, Hayley, Sarah, Kirsty, Jo, Marion, Annie and Heidi, and fellow scribes Sarah Steele and Mel Golding. Without them I would have lost my mind and be the size of an elephant. So too, the mutts: Erik, Hester, Ted, Indi, Diggory and Ziggy. And, of course, my own darling furry-boy, Basil.

Providing coffee are the ever-present brilliant baristas at Coffee #1 in Stroud, and Felt Café in the Brimscombe; I would have crumbled without regular visits for chat, cheer and caffeine.

Lastly, thanks go to Berlin and Berliners; I managed a swift research trip between lockdowns, and the amazing legacy you have created, in the Wall museums and monuments, helps outsiders like myself understand the oppression suffered and the sheer scale of its reach. I am in awe of the spirit of Berliners to overcome and emerge as a welcoming city.

Germany, 1944. Anke Hoff is assigned as midwife to one of Hitler's inner circle. If she refuses, her family will die.

"A powerful, haunting debut."—KATE QUINN, *New York Times* bestselling author of *The Alice Network*

The German Midwife

a novel

USA TODAY BESTSELLER
MANDY ROBOTHAM

A gritty tale of courage, betrayal and love in the most unlikely of places, for readers of *The Tattooist of Auschwitz* and *The Alice Network*.

The world is at war, and Stella Jilani is leading a double life.

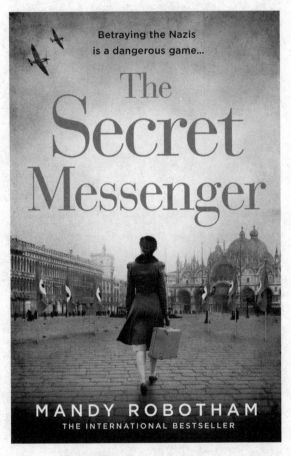

Betraying the Nazis
is a dangerous game...

The Secret Messenger

MANDY ROBOTHAM
THE INTERNATIONAL BESTSELLER

Set between German-occupied 1940s Venice
and modern-day London, this is a fascinating
tale of the bravery of everyday women in the
darkest corners of WWII.

Berlin, 1938
It's the height of summer, and Germany is on the brink of war.

A country on the brink of war.
A woman who will uncover its secrets.

The Berlin Girl

MANDY ROBOTHAM
THE INTERNATIONAL BESTSELLER

From the internationally bestselling author comes the heart-wrenching story of a world about to be forever changed.